**Praise for *New York Times* and *USA TODAY*
bestselling author Roxanne St. Claire**

"Consistent excellence is a mark of a St. Claire novel."
—*RT Book Reviews*

"It's safe to say I will try any novel with St. Claire's name
on it. Her writing is taut, funny, tense and
sparking-wire-on-wet-pavement sharp."
—*SmartBitchesTrashyBooks.com*

"On the fast track to making her name a household one."
—*Publishers Weekly*

"With Roxanne St. Claire, you are guaranteed
a powerful, sexy and provocative read."
—*New York Times* bestselling author Carly Phillips

**Praise for *New York Times* and *USA TODAY*
bestselling author Jill Shalvis**

"Shalvis thoroughly engages readers."
—*Publishers Weekly*

"Hot, sweet, fun, and romantic! Pure pleasure!"
—*New York Times* bestselling author Robyn Carr

"Witty, fun and sexy—the perfect romance!"
—*New York Times* bestselling author Lori Foster

"Shalvis' writing is a perfect trifecta of win:
hilarious dialogue, evocative and real characters, and settings
that are as much a part of the story as the hero and heroine.
I've never been disappointed by a Shalvis book."
—*SmartBitchesTrashyBooks.com*

Roxanne St. Claire
Jill Shalvis
Maureen Child

kiss me,
I'm Irish

HQN™

ISBN-13: 978-0-373-77654-2

KISS ME, I'M IRISH

Copyright © 2012 by Harlequin Books S.A.

The publisher acknowledges the copyright holders of the individual works as follows:

THE SINS OF HIS PAST
Copyright © 2006 by Roxanne St. Claire

TANGLING WITH TY
Copyright © 2003 by Jill Shalvis

WHATEVER REILLY WANTS...
Copyright © 2005 by Maureen Child

PLEASE RECYCLE
THIS PRODUCT IS RECYCLABLE

Recycling programs for this product may not exist in your area.

Contents

THE SINS OF HIS PAST   7

TANGLING WITH TY   189

WHATEVER REILLY WANTS...   355

THE SINS OF HIS PAST

Dear Reader,

The Sins of His Past is centered around Monroe's, an old-fashioned Irish pub undergoing a twenty-first-century transformation. When Deuce Monroe's professional baseball career comes to an untimely end, he returns to his hometown with the intention of taking over his father's bar. But nothing at Monroe's is what he expects. Vying for the ownership of the neighborhood watering hole is a sexy and daunting opponent, more threatening than any Deuce ever faced on the pitcher's mound.

When *The Sins of His Past* was originally released, my son was playing Little League and inspiring me to write baseball heroes. Now I'm celebrating the book's reissue in this anthology...just as that little ballplayer heads to college. Talk about twenty-first-century transformations! My writing has changed over the years, too. These days, my books usually include one villain and a few dead bodies, but in re-reading this novel, I remembered how much I enjoyed writing a sensual story with a conflict-rich romance driving every scene. Oh, and a baseball-playing hero.

Seamus "Deuce" Monroe is that endearing Irish mix of a wild card with a good heart and lost soul. He's hot, he's funny, he's vulnerable, and he's facing a few transformations of his own. So, I invite you to step into Monroe's, raise a glass (or cup of coffee, depending on which team you're rooting for) and enjoy this story about two people who have some sins in their past and love in their future.

Roxanne St. Claire

This book is dedicated to the gang
who gathers at our field of dreams every weekend.
From my side of the chain-link fence, I'm often reminded
that it's not whether you win or lose, but how incredibly
cute you look playing the game. Special love to the coach
I married, the shortstop who takes my breath away
and the littlest cheerleader by my side.

CHAPTER ONE

ONLY ONCE BEFORE could Deuce Monroe remember being speechless. When he'd met Yaz. He'd shaken the great man's hand and tried to utter a word, but he'd been rendered mute in the presence of his hero, Carl Yastrzemski.

But standing in the warm April sunshine on the main drag in Rockingham, Massachusetts, staring at a building that had once been as familiar to him as his home field pitcher's mound, he was damn near dumbstruck.

Where was Monroe's?

He peered at the sign over the door. Well, it *said* Monroe's. With no capital *M* and a sketch of a laptop computer and a coffee mug next to it. But the whole place just seemed like Monroe's on steroids. In addition to taking up way more space than he remembered, the clapboard had been replaced by a layer of exposed brick covered in ivy, and three bay windows now jutted into the sidewalk.

At least the old mahogany door hadn't changed. He gripped the familiar brass handle, yanked it toward him and stepped inside.

Where he froze and swallowed a curse. Instead of the familiar comfort of a neighborhood bar, there was a wide-open area full of sofas and sunlight and…*computers?*

Where the hell was Monroe's?

The real Monroe's—not this…this *cyber salon.*

He scanned the space, aching for something familiar,

some memory, some scent that would embrace him like his long-lost best friend.

But all he could smell was...*coffee.*

They didn't serve coffee at his parents' bar. Ice-cold Bud on tap, sure. Plenty of whiskey, rum and even tequila, but not coffee. Not here, where the locals gathered after the Rock High games to replay every one of Deuce's unpredictable but deadly knuckleballs. Not here, where all available wall space was filled with action shots from big games, framed team jerseys and newspaper clippings touting his accomplishments and talent. Not here, where—

"Can I help you, sir?"

Deuce blinked, still adjusting to the streaming sunlight where there shouldn't be any, and focused on a young woman standing in front of him.

"Would you like a computer station?" she asked.

What he'd like is a Stoli on the rocks. He glanced at the bar. At least that was still there. But the only person sitting at it was drinking something out of a cup. With a saucer.

"Is Seamus Monroe here?" Not that he expected his father to be anywhere near the bar on a Tuesday morning, but he'd already tried the house and it was empty. Deserted-looking, actually. A little wave of guilt threatened, but he shook it off.

"Mr. Monroe isn't here today," the young lady beamed at him. "Are you the new software vendor?"

As if.

He sneaked a glimpse at the wall where Mom had hung his first autographed Nevada Snake Eyes jersey at the end of his rookie season. Instead of the familiar red number two, a black and white photograph of a snow-covered mountain hung in a silver frame.

"Do you have a phone number where I can reach him?"

She shook her head. "I couldn't give you that, I'm sorry.

Our manager is in the back. Would you like me to get her?"

Her? Dad had hired a female manager?

Then a little of the tension he'd felt for the past few weeks subsided. This was the right thing to do. It took a career-ending injury caused by monumental stupidity, but coming home to take over the bar was definitely the right thing to do.

Obviously, someone had already exploited his father's loss of interest in the place and made one too many changes. Deuce would set it all straight in no time.

"Yeah, I'll talk to her," he agreed.

She indicated the near-empty bar with a sweep of her hand. "Feel free to have a cup of coffee while I get Ms. Locke."

Locke?

That was the first familiar sound since he'd arrived in Rockingham. He knew every Locke who had ever lived in this town.

In fact, Deuce had just had an email from Jackson Locke, his old high-school buddy. A typical what-a-jerk-you-are missive laced with just enough sympathy to know Jack felt Deuce's pain for ending a stellar baseball career at only thirty-three years old. Jack's parents had moved to Florida years ago…so that left Jack's sister, Kendra.

Deuce swallowed hard. The last time he'd seen Kendra was the week he'd come home for his mother's funeral, about nine years ago. Jack's baby sister had been…well, she'd been no *baby* then.

And Deuce had been a total chicken scumbag and never called her, not once, afterwards. Even though he'd wanted to. Really wanted to.

But it couldn't be Kendra, he decided as the hostess scooted away. Back then Kendra was weeks away from starting her junior year at Harvard. Surely the *Hahvahd* girl with a titanium-trap brain and a slightly smartass mouth hadn't ended up managing Monroe's. She'd been on fire with ambition.

And on fire with a few other things, too. His whole body tightened at the memory, oddly vivid for having taken place a long time and a lot of women ago.

This Locke must be a cousin, or a coincidence.

He leaned against the hostess stand—another unwelcome addition to Monroe's—and studied the semi-circle of computers residing precisely where the pool table used to be.

Someone had sure as hell messed with this place.

"Excuse me, I understand you need to speak with me?"

Turning, the first thing he saw was a pair of almond-shaped eyes exactly the color of his favorite Levi's, and just as inviting.

"Deuce?" The eyes flashed with shock and recognition.

He had to make an effort to keep from registering the same reaction.

Was it possible he'd slept with this gorgeous woman, kissed that sexy mouth that now opened into a perfect O and raked his fingers through that cornsilk-blond hair— and then *left* without ever calling her again?

Idiot took on a whole new meaning.

"Kendra." He had absolutely no willpower over his gaze, which took a long, slow trip over alabaster skin, straight down to the scoop neck of a tight white T-shirt and the rolling letters of *Monroe's* across her chest. All lower-case.

The letters, that was. The chest was definitely upper-case.

A rosy tone deepened her pale complexion. Her chin

tilted upward, and those blue eyes turned icy with distrust. "What are you doing here?"

"I came home," he said. The words must have sounded unbelievable to her, too, based on the slanted eyebrow of incredulity he got in response. He took another quick trip over the logo, and this time let his gaze continue down to a tiny waist and skin-tight jeans hugging some seriously sweet hips.

He gave her his most dazzling smile. Maybe she'd forgiven him for not calling. Maybe she'd stay on and work for him after he took over the bar. Maybe she'd…

But, first things first. "I'm looking for my dad."

She tucked a strand of sunny blond hair behind her ear. "Why don't you try Diana Lynn's house?"

Diana Lynn's house? What the hell was that? Had he gone to assisted living or something? "Is she taking care of Dad?"

That earned him a caustic laugh. "I'll say. Diana Lynn Turner is your father's fiancée."

"His what?" Men who'd had pacemakers put in a year ago didn't have fiancées. Widowed men with pacemakers, especially.

"His fiancée. It's French for bride-to-be, Deuce." She put a hand on her hip like a little punctuation mark to underscore her sarcasm. "Your dad spends most of his days—and all of his nights—at her house. But they're leaving tomorrow morning for a trip, so if you want to see him, you better hustle over there."

Deuce had been scarce for a lot of years, no doubt about it. But would his father really get engaged and not tell him?

Of course he would. He'd think Deuce would hate the idea of Seamus Monroe remarrying. And he'd be right.

"So, where does this Diana Lynn live?"

She waved her hand to the left. "At the old Swain mansion."

He frowned. "That run-down dump on the beach?"

"Not so run-down since Diana Lynn worked her magic." She reached into the hostess stand and pulled out some plastic menus, tapping them on the wood to line them up. "She has a way of livening everything up."

Oh, so that's what was going down; some kind of gold digger had got her teeth into the old man. Deuce hadn't gotten home a moment too soon.

"Don't tell me," he said with a quick glance toward the pit of computers to his right. "She's the mastermind behind the extreme makeover of the bar."

"The bar?" Kendra slid the menus back into their slot and looked in the opposite direction—toward the bar that lined one whole wall. "Well, we haven't been able to close long enough to rip the bar out yet."

He didn't know what word to seize. *We* or *rip* or *yet.*

"Why would you do that?"

She shrugged and appeared to study the bank of cherry-wood that had been in Deuce's life as long as he'd lived. He'd bet any amount of money that the notches that marked his height as a toddler were still carved into the wood under the keg station. "The bar's not really a money-maker for us."

Us, was it? "That's funny," he said, purposely giving her the stare he saved for scared rookies at the plate. "Most times the *bar* is the most profitable part of a *bar.*"

His intimidating glare didn't seem to work. In fact, he could have sworn he saw that spark of true grit he'd come to recognize right before some jerk slammed his curve ball into another county.

"I'm sure that's true in other business models," she said slowly, a bemused frown somehow just making her prettier. "But the fact is, the bar's not the most profitable part of an Internet café."

He choked a laugh of disbelief. "Since when is Monroe's an Internet café?"

"Since I bought it."

He could practically hear the ball zing straight over the left-field fence, followed by a way-too familiar sinking sensation in his gut.

"SINCE YOU *WHAT?*"

He didn't know. Kendra realized by the genuine shock in those espresso-colored eyes that Deuce had no idea that she and his father shared a two-year-old business arrangement. She'd never had the nerve to ask Seamus if he'd told his son. In fact, she and Seamus Senior had politely danced around the subject of Seamus Junior for a long, long time.

But it looked like the dance was about to end.

"I bought Monroe's a while ago. Well, half of it. And I run it, although your dad still owns fifty percent." All right, fifty-one. Did Deuce need to know that little detail?

"Really," he said, thoughtfully rubbing a cheek that hadn't seen a razor in, oh, maybe twenty-nine hours. Giving him the ideal amount of Hollywood stubble on his chiseled, handsome features. It even formed the most alluring little shadow in the cleft on his chin.

She'd dipped her tongue into that shadow. Once.

"Yes, really." She pulled the menus out again just to keep her hands busy. Otherwise, they might betray her and reach out for a quick feel of that nice Hollywood stubble.

"And you turned it into—" He sent a disdainful glare toward the main floor "—the Twilight Zone."

She couldn't help laughing. He'd always made her laugh. Even when she was eleven and he'd teased her. He'd made her giggle, and then she'd run upstairs and throw herself on her bed and cry for the sheer love of him. "We call it the twenty-first century, Deuce, and you're welcome to log on anytime."

"No, thanks." He took a step backward, sweeping her with one of those appraising looks that made her feel as if she'd just licked her finger and stuck it in the nearest electrical outlet.

When his gaze finally meandered back up to her face, she forced herself to look into his dark-brown eyes. They were still surrounded by long, black lashes and topped with those seriously brash eyebrows. The cynicism, the daring, the I-don't-give-a-rat's-ass-what-anyone-thinks look still burned in his eyes. It was that look, along with a well-known penchant for fun and games, and the occasional out-of-control pitch, that had earned him the most memorable yearbook caption in Rockingham High School history: Deuce Is Wild. And her brother was on the page to the left with his own epigram: Jacks Are Better.

Their gaze stayed locked a little too long and she felt a wave of heat singe her cheeks. How much did he remember? That she'd admitted a lifelong crush on her big brother's best friend and biggest rival?

Did he remember that she'd never once used the word *no* during their passionate night together? That she'd whispered "I love you" when her body had melted into his and a childhood of fantasizing about one boy finally came true?

Sophie hustled toward the hostess stand, holding out a manila envelope, and blessedly breaking the silence.

"The kid from Kinko's dropped this off," she said, giving Deuce a quick glance as though to apologize for the interruption. Or to steal another look.

Kendra took the envelope. "Are you sure they sent over everything, Soph?"

The young woman nodded. "And the disk is in there, too. For backup."

Kendra gripped the package a little tighter. This was it. Seamus and Diana Lynn were on their way to Boston, New York and San Francisco to nail down the financing that would allow her to finish the transformation of Monroe's into the premier Internet café and artists' space in all of Cape Cod. Two years of research and planning—and what seemed like a lifetime of agonizingly slow higher education—all came down to this presentation.

"Seamus just called," Sophie added. "He's anxious to see it today, so he has time to go over any fine points with you before they leave."

She glanced at Deuce, who managed to take up too much space and breathe too much air just by being there. He'd always be larger than life in her wretched, idolizing eyes, regardless of the fact that he was responsible for putting an end to all of her dreams.

Then a sickening thought seized her. Everyone knew that Deuce's baseball career was over. Was he back for good? If so, then he had the ability to wreck her plans once again. Not because she would fall into his bed like a lovesick schoolgirl—she'd never make *that* mistake again—but because he had the power to change his father's mind.

If he wanted Monroe's, Seamus would give it to him. If Deuce wanted the moon and stars and a couple of meteors for good measure, Seamus would surely book a seat on the next rocket launch to go get them.

The prodigal son had returned, and the surrogate daughter might just be left out in the cold.

Kendra squared her shoulders and studied the face she'd once loved so much it hurt her heart just to look at him.

Deuce Monroe could not waltz back into Rockingham and wreck her life…again.

But she'd never give him the satisfaction of knowing he had any power—then or now.

"You can follow me over there," she said with such believable indifference that she had to mentally pat herself on the back.

"You can ride with me," he replied.

"No thanks." How far could she push indifference? Didn't he remember what had happened the last time they'd been in a car together?

"You can trust me." He winked at her. "I've only been banned from race tracks, not the street."

Of course, he was referring to his well-publicized car crash, not their past.

"I just meant that I saw your father yesterday. You haven't seen him in years. No doubt you'll want to stay longer than I do."

"Depends on how I'm received." He turned toward the door, but shot her a cocky grin. "It's been a while."

"No kidding."

The grin widened as he added another one of those endless full-body eye exams that tested her ability to stand without sinking into the knees that had turned to water. "Is that your way of saying you missed me, Kendra?"

If any cells in her body had remained at rest, they woke up now and went to work making her flush and ache and tingle.

She managed to clear her throat. "I'm sure this is impossible for you to comprehend, Deuce, but somehow, some way, without formal therapy or controlled substances, every single resident in the town of Rockingham, Massachusetts, has managed to survive your long absence. Every. Single. One."

He just laughed softly and gave her a non-verbal touché with those delicious brown eyes. "Come on, Ken-doll. I'll drive. Do you have everything you need?"

No. She needed blinders to keep from staring at him, and a box of tissue to wipe the drool. Throw in some steel armor for her heart and a fail-safe chastity belt, and then she'd be good to go.

But he didn't need to know that. Any more than he needed to know why she'd dropped out of Harvard in the middle of her junior year.

"I have everything I need." She held the envelope in front of her chest and gave him her brightest smile. "This is all that matters."

She couldn't forget that.

"So what the hell happened to this place?" Deuce threw a glance to his right, ostensibly at the cutesy antique stores and art galleries that lined High Castle Boulevard, but he couldn't resist a quick glimpse at the passenger in his rented Mustang.

Because she looked a lot better than the changes in his hometown. Her jeans-clad legs were crossed and she leaned her elbow out the open window, her head casually tipped against her knuckles as the spring breeze lifted strands of her shoulder-length blond hair.

"What happened? Diana Lynn Turner happened," she answered.

The famous Diana Lynn again. "Don't tell me she erected the long pink walls and endless acres of housing developments I saw on the way into town. Everything's got a name. Rocky Shores. Point Place. Shoreline Estates. Since when did we have *estates* in Rockingham?"

"Since Diana Lynn arrived," she said, with a note of

impatience at the fact that he didn't quite get the Power Of Diana thing.

"What is she? A one-man construction company?"

Kendra laughed softly, a sound so damn *girly* that it caused an unexpected twist in his gut. "She didn't build the walls or houses, but she brought in the builders, convinced the Board of Selectmen to influence the Planning Commission, then started her own real estate company and marketed the daylights out of Rockingham, Mass."

"Why?"

"For a number of reasons." She held up her index finger. "One, because Cape Cod is booming as a Hamptons-type destination and we want Rockingham to get a piece of the action instead of just being a stop en route to more interesting places." She raised a second finger. "Two, because the town coffers were almost empty and the schools were using outdated books and the stoplights needed to be computerized and the one policeman in town was about to retire and we had no money to attract a new force." Before point number three, he closed his fist around her fingers and gently pushed her hand down.

"I get the idea. Progress." He reluctantly let go of her silky-smooth skin. "So Diana Lynn isn't a gold digger."

She let out a quick laugh. "She's a gold digger all right. She's dug the gold right out of Rockingham and put it back in those empty coffers."

He was silent for a minute as he turned onto Beachline Road and caught the reflection of April sunshine on the deep, blue waters of Nantucket Sound. Instead of the unbroken vista he remembered, the waterfront now featured an enclave of shops, which had to be brand-new even though they sported that salt-weathered look of New England. *Fake* salt-weathered, he realized. Like when they banged nicks into perfectly good furniture and called it "distressed."

He didn't like Diana Lynn Turner. Period. "So, just how far into him *are* her claws?"

"Her claws?" Kendra's voice rose in an amused question. "She doesn't have claws, Deuce. And if you'd bothered to come home once in a while to see your father in the past few years, you'd know that."

He tapped the brakes at a light he could have sworn was not on the road when he was learning to drive. "That didn't take long."

"What?"

"The guilt trip."

She blew out a little breath. "You'll get no guilt from me, Deuce."

Not even for not calling after a marathon of unforgettable sex? He didn't believe her. "No guilt? What would you call that last comment?"

As she shifted in her seat, he noticed her back had straightened and the body language of detachment she was trying so hard to project was rapidly disappearing. "Just a fact, Deuce. You haven't seen your dad for a long, long—"

"Correction. I haven't been *in Rockingham* for a long, long time. Dad came to every game the Snakes played in Boston. And he came out to Vegas a few times, too."

"And you barely had time to have dinner with him."

This time he exhaled, long and slow. He didn't expect her to understand. He didn't expect anyone to understand. Especially the man he was about to go see. Dinner with Dad was about all the motivational speaking he could stand. The endless coaching, the pushing, the drive. Deuce liked to do things his way. And that was rarely the way his father wanted them done.

Staying away was just easier.

"I talk to your brother Jack every once in a while," he said, as though that connection to Rockingham showed he wasn't quite the Missing Person she was making him out to be.

"Really?" She seemed surprised. "He never mentions that."

"He seems to like his job." It was the first thing he could think of to prove he really *did* talk to Jack.

She nodded. "He was born to be in advertising, that's for sure. He's married to that company, I swear."

How could he resist that opening? Besides, he was dying to know. "What about you?" He remembered the hostess calling her Ms. Locke. But these days, that didn't mean anything. "Got a husband, house and two-point-five kids yet, Ken-doll?"

Her silence was just a beat too long. Did she still hate the nickname he'd bestowed on her when she was a skinny little ten-year-old spying on the big boys in the basement?

"No, I don't, *Seamus.*"

He grinned at the comeback. "So why aren't you in New York or Boston? Don't tell me that *Hahvahd* education landed you right back in the old Rockeroo."

He saw her swallow. "Actually, I never graduated from Harvard."

He glanced at her, noticing the firm set of her jaw. "No kidding? You were halfway through last time…" He let his voice drift a little. "When my mother passed away."

A whisper of color darkened her cheeks as she was no doubt wondering what else he recalled about his last visit to Rockingham. Surprisingly, everything. Every little detail remained sharp in his memory.

"I got very involved in business here," she said curtly. Something in her voice said "don't go there" so he sucked in the salty air through the open windows of his rental car, immediately punched with memories.

"Smells like baseball," he said, almost to himself.

"Excuse me?"

"April in New England. It smells like spring, and spring means baseball." At least, it had for the past twenty-seven years of his life. Since he'd first picked up a bat and his father had started Rockingham's Little League just so Deuce could play T-ball, spring had meant "hit the field."

"You miss it?" she asked, her gentle tone actually more painful than the question.

"Nah," he said quickly. "I was about to retire anyway." A total lie. He was thirty-three and threw knuckleballs half the time. His elbow might be aching, but he could still pitch. But his taste for fast cars had lured him to a race track just for fun.

Fun that was most definitely not welcomed by the owners of the Nevada Snake Eyes, or the lawyers who wrote the fine print in his contract. He rubbed his right elbow, a move that he'd made so many times in his life, it was like breathing.

"You had a good year last year," she noted.

He couldn't help smiling, thinking of her little speech back at the bar. "You think anybody in Rockingham slowed down from all that *surviving* long enough to notice?"

Her return smile revealed a hint of dimples against creamy skin. "Yeah. We noticed."

The Swain mansion was around the corner. Instinctively, he slowed the car, unwilling to face his father, and wanting to extend the encounter with Kendra a little longer.

"I see my great season didn't stop someone from redecorating the walls of Monroe's." With mountains, instead of…memories.

Her smile grew wistful. "Things change, Deuce."

Evidently, they did. But if he had his way, he could change things right back again. Maybe not the pink houses and antique shops. But he sure as hell could make Monroe's a happening bar and recapture some of his celebrated youth in the meantime.

And while he was at it, maybe he could recapture some of those vivid memories of one night with Kendra. "Then I'll need someone to help me get reacquainted with the new Rockingham," he said, his voice rich with invitation.

She folded her hands on top of the envelope she'd been clinging to and stared straight ahead. "I'm sure you'll find someone."

His gaze drifted over her again. He'd *found* someone. "I'm sure I will."

CHAPTER TWO

DEUCE DID A CLASSIC double take as they rounded the last corner to where a rambling, dilapidated mansion built by the heir to a sausage-casing fortune once stood.

"Whoa." He blew out a surprised breath. "I bet old Elizabeth Swain would roll over in her grave."

Kendra tried to see the place through his eyes. Instead of the missing shingles, broken windows and overgrown foliage he must remember, there stood a rambling three-story New England cape home with gray shake siding and a black roof, trimmed with decks and columns and walls of glass that overlooked Nantucket Sound. The driveway was lined with stately maples sprouting spring-green leaves. The carpet of grass in the front looked ready for one of Diana's lively games of croquet.

"Dad lives *here?*" Before she could, he corrected himself. "I mean, his...his friend does?"

Kendra laughed softly. "He almost lives here. But he's old-fashioned, you know. He won't officially move in until they get married."

Deuce tore his gaze from the house to give her a look of horror. "Which will be...?"

As soon as the expansion of Monroe's was financed and finalized. "They're not in a hurry, really. They're both busy with their careers and—"

"Careers?" He sounded as though he didn't think owning Monroe's was a career. Well too bad for that misconception. It was *her* career. "Not that I think they should rush into anything," he added.

He pulled into the driveway that no longer kicked up gravel since Diana had repaved it in gray-and-white brick. As he stopped the car, he rubbed his elbow again and peered up at the impressive structure.

"I can't believe this is the old Swain place. We used to break in and have keg parties in there."

Oh, yes. She remembered hearing about those. At three years younger than Jack and his Rock High friends, Kendra had never participated in a "Swain Brain Drain," but she'd certainly heard the details the next day.

Her information had come courtesy of the heating duct between her bedroom and the basement in the Locke home. When the heat was off, Kendra could lie on her bedroom floor, her ear pressed against the metal grate, and listen to boy talk, punctuated by much laughter and the crack of billiard balls.

It was her special secret. She knew more about Deuce than all the girls who adored him at Rock High. Jackson Locke's little sister knew *everything.* At least, as long as the heat wasn't turned on.

"You won't recognize the inside of this house," she told him. "Diana's got a magical touch with decor. And she's an amazing photographer. All the art in Monroe's is her work. And look at this place. She's never met a fixer-upper she couldn't—"

He jerked the car door open. "Let's go."

She sat still for a moment, the rest of her sentence still in her mouth. What did he have against this woman he'd never even bothered to meet? It was almost ten years since his mother had died. Didn't he think Seamus deserved some happiness?

She hustled out of the car to catch up with him as he

walked toward the front door. "We can just go in through the kitchen," she told him.

He paused in mid step, then redirected himself to where she pointed. "You're a regular here, huh?"

A regular? She lived in the unattached guest house a hundred yards away on the beach. "I come over with the sales reports every day." She jiggled the handle of a sliding glass door and opened it. "Diana! Seamus? Anybody home?"

In the distance a dog barked.

"I have a surprise for you," she called. Did she ever.

"We're upstairs, Kennie!" A woman's voice called. "Get some coffee, hon. We'll be down as soon as we get dressed."

She felt Deuce stiffen next to her.

A smile tugged at the corners of her lips. "They're always…well, they're in love." She didn't have to look at him to get his reaction. She could feel the distaste rolling off him. As if he'd never spent the night at a woman's house.

"Have a seat." She touched one of the high-back chairs at the table under a bay window. "Want a cup of coffee?"

"No, thanks." He folded his long frame into a chair, his gaze moving around the large country kitchen, to the cozy Wedgewood-blue family room on the other side of a long granite counter, and the formal dining room across the hall. "You're right. I can't believe this is the same old wreck."

She decided not to sing Diana's praises again. Taking a seat across from him, she set a mug of steaming coffee on the table, and carefully placed the envelope in front of her.

With one long look at Deuce, she took a deep breath. Before Diana swooped in here and charmed him, before

Seamus barreled in and coached him, before the rest of Rockingham *discovered* him, she had to know. She just had to know for herself.

"Why did you come back?"

He leaned the chair on two legs and folded his arms across the breadth of his powerful chest, the sleeves of his polo shirt tightening over his muscular arms. She willed her gaze to stay on his face and not devour every heart-stopping ripple and cut.

"Well, I'm retired now, as you know."

The whole world knew he wasn't *retired*. His contract had been terminated after he blatantly disregarded the fine print and took to a race track—and wrecked a car—with a couple of famous NASCAR drivers. But, she let it go.

"Are you planning to…" Oh, God. *Ask it.* "…live here?" Please say no. *Please say no.* Could her heart and head take it if he said yes?

"Yes."

She sipped her coffee with remarkable nonchalance.

"I'm sick of living in Vegas," he added, coming down hard on the front two legs of the delicate chair.

"I thought you lived outside of Las Vegas."

He lifted one shoulder. "Same difference. I have no reason to stay there if I'm not playing ball for the Snake Eyes."

"What about coaching? Don't a lot of major leaguers do that after they…after they quit?"

He massaged his right arm again, a gesture she knew so well she could close her eyes and see it. But this time, his features tightened with a grimace.

"I don't know. We'll see. I'll need to find a good PT. You know any?"

A physical therapist who worked on professional athletes? On Cape Cod? "You'll have to go to Boston."

"That's over an hour from here."

Then go live *there.* "Two, now, with traffic." She sipped the coffee again and tried for the most noncommittal voice she could find. "So, what are you going to do here?"

Instead of answering, he snagged the envelope. She lunged for it, but he was too fast. "What is this?"

She wasn't ready to reveal her plans to Deuce. His dad would probably tell him all about their grandiose scheme, but she didn't want to. She'd shared her dreams with him a long time ago, and here she was, nine years later, and she still hadn't realized them. And he was the reason why.

"Just some paperwork on the café."

"It's a bar," he corrected, dropping the packet back on the table. "Not a café."

"Not anymore."

"Oh my God." Diana Lynn's gravelly tone seized their attention.

They both turned to where she stood in the kitchen doorway, a vision in white from head to toe, her precious Newman in her arms. "I recognize you from your pictures, Deuce." At the sight of a stranger, Newman yelped and squiggled for freedom.

Deuce stared at Diana for a moment, then stood. "That's what they call me," he said.

Diana breezed in, releasing the jittery little spaniel who leaped on Kendra's lap and barked at Deuce.

"I'm Diana Lynn Turner." She held out her hand to him. "And thank God for that pacemaker, because otherwise your father would have a heart attack when he comes downstairs."

Diana beamed at him as they shook hands, sweeping him up and down with the look of keen appraisal she was known to give a smart investment property. Her mouth widened into an appreciative smile that she directed to Kendra.

"No wonder you've had a crush on him your whole life. He is simply *delicious.*"

Diana was nothing if not blunt. Kendra willed her color not to rise as she conjured up a look of utter disinterest and a shrug. "Guess that depends on how you define delicious."

DEUCE FILED THE lifelong crush comment for later, and turned his attention back to the most unlikely maternal replacement he could imagine.

Her smile was as blinding as the sun in his eyes when he squinted for a pop fly. Jet-black hair pulled straight back offset wide, copper-brown eyes, and she had so few wrinkles she'd either been born with magnificent genes or had her own personal plastic surgeon. While she was certainly not his father's age of seventy-one, something about her bearing told him she'd passed through her fifties already. And enjoyed every minute of the journey.

He released her power grip. "You've done quite a number on this house."

She arched one shapely eyebrow and toyed with a strand of pearls that hung around her neck. "That's what I do. Numbers. What on earth made you decide to finally come home?"

No bush-beating for this one, he noted. "I retired."

She choked out a quick laugh. "Hardly. But your father will be over the moon to see you. How long are you staying?"

He casually scratched his face. He'd already admitted his plans. "A while."

"How long is a while?" Diana asked.

"For good."

"Good?" Her bronze eyes widened. "You're staying here in Rockingham for good?"

"Who is staying for good?" The booming voice of Seamus Monroe accompanied his heavy footsteps on a staircase. He came around the corner and stopped dead in his tracks.

"Good God in Heaven," he muttered, putting one of his mighty hands over his chest. For a moment Deuce's gut tightened, thinking he *had* given his father a heart attack. He barely had time to take in the fact that Dad's classic black-Irish dark hair had now fully transformed to a distinguished gray, but his eyebrows hadn't seemed to catch up yet. Then the older man lunged toward him with both arms open and squeezed until neither man could breathe.

Deuce thought his own chest would explode with relief as they embraced. Although his father had been the most demanding human who ever raised a son, he'd also loved that son to distraction. Deuce was counting on that. That and the fact that age might have mellowed the old man.

They slapped each other's backs and Dad pulled back and took Deuce's face in his hands, shaking it with only slightly more force than the hug. "What the hell were you thinking getting in that race car, son?"

Maybe *mellowed* would be pushing it.

Deuce laughed as he pulled away. "I was thinking I wouldn't get caught."

"You could have been killed!" his father said, his eyes glinting with a fury Deuce had seen a million times. And those words. How many times had Seamus Monroe uttered "you could have been killed" after Deuce had "gotten caught"?

There was only one answer. Deuce had used it a few times, too. "I wasn't killed, Dad."

"But your career was."

Deuce extended his right arm and shook it out. "Hey, I'm thirty-three. Time to let the young dudes take the mound."

Seamus made a harumphing noise that usually translated into "baloney" or something harder if ladies weren't present. Then he brightened and reached out for one of the ladies who was present. "And you've met the love of— Diana."

His life.

Mom couldn't be the love of his life forever, and the mature man in Deuce knew that. It was that temperamental little boy in him who wanted to punch a wall at the thought.

"Sure did. And I'm impressed with this house. Doesn't look anything like the old Swain place."

"Have you seen Monroe's?" Dad said, throwing a proud look at Kendra.

She still sat at the kitchen table, the brown-and-white dog sizing him up from her lap. The almost-blush that Diana had caused had faded, but Kendra's eyes were still unnaturally bright.

"Yep," Deuce said, his gaze still on her. "I saw the bar. Big changes there, too." He dug his hands into his pockets and leaned against one of the high-gloss countertops. "In fact this whole town looks completely different."

Dad squeezed Diana a little closer to his side. "This is the reason, Deuce. This lady right here has done it all. She's a one-woman growth curve." He slid his hand over her waist and patted her hip, then glanced back at Kendra. "And so's our little firestorm, Kennie."

"So what's going on down there, Dad? Kendra tells me you're sticking your toes into the Internet waters."

"We've been testing the waters for over a year and we haven't drowned yet." Dad laughed softly. "And if everything goes like we think it might, we're going in deeper. Right, Kennie?"

She leaned forward and slid her mysterious envelope across the table. "And here's the boat we're taking out."

"Oh!" Diana squealed and grabbed the envelope hungrily. "Let me see! How wonderful that Deuce is here for the final unveiling. Have some coffee, everyone. We'll go into the family room and have a look at Kennie's masterpiece."

Kennie's masterpiece? Not exactly *just some paperwork.* Deuce gave her another hard look, but she gathered up the dog and her mug and turned her back to him.

As the women moved to the other room, Deuce sidled up to his dad. "So, how you feeling? That, uh, thing working okay?"

The older man gave him a sly smile. "My thing works fine. I don't even take that little blue pill."

Deuce closed his eyes for a moment. "I meant the pacemaker."

Dad laughed. "I know what you meant. It's fine. I've never been healthier in my life." He looked to the family room at Diana, his classic Irish eyes softening to a clear blue. "And I haven't been happier in a long time, either."

Things had changed, all right. And some things weren't meant to change back.

"I can tell," Deuce responded. He purposely kept the note of resignation out of his voice.

He couldn't argue. Dad looked as vibrant as Deuce could remember him in the past nine years. Not that he'd seen him very often.

In the family room, Kendra had spread computer printouts of bar charts and graphs over a large coffee table. Alongside were architectural blueprints, and hand-drawn sketches of tables and computers. He took a deep breath and let his attention fall on an architect's drawing of some kind of stage and auditorium. What the hell was a stage doing in Monroe's?

He could try to deal with Dad's romance, but messing with the bar he grew up in might be too much.

"So what's this all about?" he asked.

"This, son, is the future of Monroe's." Dad squeezed into a loveseat next to Diana and curled his arm around her shoulder, beaming as he continued. "We've tested the concept, made it work profitably and now we're ready to expand it."

Deuce dropped onto the sofa across from them, close to where Kendra knelt on the floor organizing the papers. "It already looked pretty expanded to me," he said.

"Well, we did buy out the card shop next door and added some space," Diana said. "But Kennie's plans are much, much bigger than that."

"Is that so?" He looked at her and waited for an explanation. "How big?"

She met his gaze, and held it, a challenge in her wide blue eyes. "We're hoping to buy the rest of the block, so we can eventually add a small theater for performance art, a gallery for local artists and a full DVD rental business."

He worked to keep his jaw from hitting his chest.

"Tell him about the learning center," his father coaxed.

"Well," she said, shifting on her hips, "We're going to add an area just for people who are not technically savvy. They can make appointments with our employees for hands-on Internet training."

He just stared at her. All he wanted to do was run a sports bar with TVs playing ESPN and beer flowing freely. It sure as hell didn't take place on the *information highway* and karaoke night was as close to *performance art* as he wanted his customers to get.

But Deuce stayed quiet. He'd figure out a strategy. As soon as Dad found out that Deuce planned to buy the place, surely he'd change his mind. And Deuce would buy out Kendra's fifty percent if he had to. She could open her theater and gallery and learning center somewhere else in Rockingham.

He'd make his father understand that he had a plan for the future and it made sense. It didn't include baseball for the first time in his life, but that was okay.

His only option was coaching and with his track record for breaking rules, he doubted too many teams would be lined up to have him as a role model for younger players. He had no interest in television, or working an insurance company, or being the spokesperson for allergy medicine, like the rest of the has-been ballplayers of the world.

He just wanted to be home. Maybe he couldn't be the King of the Rock anymore, but this is where he grew up. And where he wanted to grow old.

But not in a flippin' Internet café.

That was one compromise he couldn't make.

It was impossible to concentrate with Deuce's long, hard, masculine body taking up half the sofa, his unspoken distaste for her plans hanging in the air. Not to mention the fact that his father now sought his opinion on everything.

Kendra hadn't counted on this kind of distraction.

"This chart emphasizes the growth of the Internet café business," she said, but for a moment, she lost her place.

The bar graphs and colored circles swam in front of her. And Deuce's long, khaki-clad legs were just inches away from her. Her gaze slid to the muscle of his thigh. Newman, the little brat, had actually taken up residence next to him and was staring at him like some kind of star-struck baseball fan. Even dogs were in awe of Deuce.

"You showed us that one, honey," Diana said quietly, leaning forward to pull another chart. "I think you wanted the research about how Internet cafés are the social centers of this century. How people don't want to be isolated while they are in cyber-space. Remember? The findings are here."

Oh, cripes. Of course she remembered. She'd written the analysis of the research. She'd used it to convince Seamus to launch the overhaul of Monroe's. She'd based her whole future on that trend.

And all she could think about was…thigh muscles.

"What do you think, Deuce?" Seamus asked for the twentieth time. "You see these cafés out in Vegas?"

"Never saw one in my life."

Kendra gave him an incredulous look, then remembered what his life was like. On the road, in hotels. "But surely you have a computer, a laptop or a PDA, and an email address."

He nodded. "I told you I got an email from Jack. And some of my friends' kids taught me a cool game called Backyard Baseball." He ignored her eye-roll and looked at his father. "Frankly, I don't know what's going on here in Cape Cod, but the rest of the world still expects to go into a bar and *drink*. They can't smoke, thank God, but I haven't been in a bar where keyboards replaced cocktails. At least not until today."

Seamus leaned back and regarded his son. "Well, our bar profits were sinking fast, son. Two years ago, we were as close to the red as I've been in many years. Big-name chains have come into this place in droves, squeezing our business with national advertising."

"Monroe's has been through tough times before, Dad," Deuce argued. "It always survives."

"The demographics of Rockingham have changed,"

Diana interjected. "This isn't the sleepy vacation town it used to be. Our population has skyrocketed, and the town is full of young, savvy, hip residents."

"And young, hip residents don't go to bars anymore?" Deuce asked. "They do in every other city I've ever been in."

An uncomfortable silence was his only answer.

Finally, Seamus asked, "What don't you like about this, Deuce?"

Deuce leaned forward, flexing the thigh muscle Kendra shouldn't have been watching. "I came home so I could take over Monroe's and run it as a first-rate sports bar."

Kendra closed her eyes and took the punch in her stomach. She *knew* it. She'd known this the minute he'd walked in the door.

Was Deuce Monroe put on this earth for the sole reason of ruining her life? He didn't know what he'd done last time—the result of their recklessness was her burden, and, ultimately, her loss. But this time, he could see what it meant to her.

And so could Seamus. She looked up at the man who'd been like a father to her ever since her own parents had distanced themselves physically and emotionally. But Seamus's gaze remained locked on his son, an expression of astonishment, joy and worry mixed in the lines on his face.

How could she let herself forget for one moment that Seamus loved Deuce above all and everything? No matter how many times Deuce had gone against his wishes, his love for his only child was constant.

"I had no idea, son."

Kendra just *knew* what was coming next. There was no way to avoid what was about to be said.

"Dad, the bar's been in the family for more than seventy years."

Bingo. There was the bomb she'd been waiting for him to drop. Monroe's belonged to *Monroes*. Always had... always will.

Diana leaned forward and snagged Deuce with one of those riveting stares that withered opponents at the negotiating table. "When, exactly, were you planning to tell your father that you intended to carry on that tradition?"

"Today," he replied without missing a beat. "I wanted to talk in person, not over the phone. My house in Vegas is on the market. I'm planning to move here as soon as we... settle things."

Seamus took a long, slow breath and pulled Diana back into his side with a gentle tug. "I wish you had told me sooner," he said to Deuce.

Why? Would that have changed things? Kendra had to bite her lip from shouting out her question. If Seamus had known Deuce wanted to take over the bar, would he have stopped her expansion plans from the beginning? Even when profits were so low they almost had to sell?

"I think Kendra has a say on all this," Diana finally commented. "She owns forty-nine percent of the business."

She felt Deuce's gaze and had no doubt he remembered she'd told him "fifty" percent. Lies. They always come back to bite you.

Kendra shifted again, wishing she weren't the only one sitting on the floor. "I'm sure you all know how I feel. The expansion is the business I've always dreamed of owning."

"But Monroe's," Seamus said quietly, "is my blood."

And so was Deuce.

Deuce, who hadn't come home from a road trip when his father had a pacemaker put in. Deuce, who'd refused to go to college on a baseball scholarship as his father had begged him, instead going straight into the minor leagues.

Deuce, who had never called her after they'd made love, so therefore had never even found out that she'd gotten pregnant…and lost that child.

"Are you serious about this?" Seamus asked his son. "Are you absolutely committed or are you just screwing around here until some better job offer comes along?"

"I'm dead serious, Dad."

Well. There went that dream.

"And you aren't serious very often," Seamus said with a soft laugh of understatement. "I guess this is something for me to consider."

"I came home to run the bar," Deuce said, his baritone voice oddly soft. "I can't play ball. I don't want to coach. I'm not interested in TV or business or anything else I can think of. I want to be home, Dad. I want to run Monroe's. I want to buy it outright, to free you from the day-to-day operations." He looked at Kendra. "Of course, I didn't know you'd already had such great help. I'm sure we can work something out. That is," he looked back at his father, his face sincere, "if you'll consider me."

Without a word, Kendra started to scoop up graphs and presentation pages. She'd have to take her idea elsewhere. It was still viable. She'd figure something out.

She'd spent every dime to buy out half of Seamus's business, but she'd been in worse places before. Worse financial, emotional and physical places. She would survive. She always did.

"What are you doing, Kennie?" Seamus's sharp tone stopped her cold.

"We don't need to go through this presentation. Not now, anyway," she said, wishing like mad that she'd driven her own car so she could escape.

She looked up to see a pained expression in the older man's eyes. They'd never discussed it, but in that moment, that look in his eyes confirmed what she'd always suspected. He knew who'd put an end to Harvard for her. He knew.

"Not so fast," Seamus said.

Could that mean he wasn't sure yet?

"Well, until you decide what to do…" She continued to gather papers, and Deuce reached forward to help, his arm brushing hers. She jerked away from him and cursed the reaction to the most casual touch.

Her mouth went bone-dry, and she realized with a sickening horror that a huge lump had formed in her throat. She would not give him the satisfaction of seeing her cry. Taking a deep breath, she forced herself to stand.

"I'm going to get something at home," she managed to say. "I'll be back in a few minutes."

"Where's home?" Deuce asked.

"Kendra lives in the guest house on the beach," Diana Lynn said. "Go ahead, dear. We'll be here."

Kendra shot her a grateful look. No doubt she'd picked up the near-tears vibe.

"Why don't you walk over there with her, Deuce?" Seamus asked. Clearly he had *not* picked up that same vibe. "I need a few minutes alone with Diana."

Kendra resisted the urge to spear Seamus with a dirty look. Couldn't she get a break today? But Deuce stood and gestured toward the door. "Show me the way," he said.

Kendra stole one more pleading look at Diana, who gave a nearly imperceptible nod. *Go,* her eyes said. *Let me talk to him.*

"All right," Kendra said. "We'll be back in a few minutes."

"Take your time," Seamus responded. "We have some serious thinking to do here."

But Kendra knew that, for Seamus, there was no *think-*

ing where Deuce was involved. The old Irishman ran on pure heart, and nothing filled his heart more than the love for his son. No matter how many errors—on the field or in judgment—Deuce made. He was Seamus's weakness.

And how could she blame him? He'd been her weakness, too.

Without another word, she headed toward the sliding door, with Deuce behind her, and Newman at his heels.

She'd barely stepped into the sunshine when Deuce leaned over and whispered into her ear, "Your whole life, huh? That's some wicked crush."

CHAPTER THREE

KENDRA NEVER MISSED a beat. At his comment, she reached down for the little brown-and-white dog, who leaped into her arms.

"Do you hear anything, Newman? I don't hear anything."

Newman barked and nuzzled into her neck. And licked her.

Lucky puppy.

"Oh, you're ignoring me?" Deuce asked with a laugh as he trotted down a set of wooden steps to catch up with her. "That's really mature."

"This from the poster boy of maturity." She set the dog down when they reached a stone path that paralleled the beach. "Or have you stopped setting firecrackers inside basketballs in the teachers' parking lot?"

He chuckled. "That was your brother's idea. Anyway, I've grown up."

"Oh, yes. I noticed in all the coverage about that racing stunt just how much you've grown up."

He considered a few comebacks, but there was nothing to combat the truth.

"Well, you certainly have," he said. At her confused look, he added, "Grown up, that is."

Her face softened momentarily, but then she squared her shoulders and she strode toward the house. He couldn't help smiling. Torturing Jack's little sister had always been fun. Even when she was ten and scrawny and folded into giggles, and tears. But it was even more fun now, when she was *not* ten and scrawny, but older and *curvy*.

"I live right here," she announced as they neared a gray shake-covered beach cottage at the end of the path. "You can come in, or, if you prefer, go down to the water and gaze at your reflection for a while."

He snorted at the comment. "I'll come in. Cute place. How long have you lived here?"

"About a year and a half. After Diana finished renovating the property, I was her first renter." She gave him a smug smile. "I introduced her to Seamus."

"I can't believe he's never even told me he was involved with someone."

"It's not like you actually *talked* to him a whole lot in the past year."

Past decade, is what she meant, and he knew it. "Not that I owe you an explanation, but I have been pretty busy playing ball."

"From October to March?"

"I played in Japan."

"The season you were out injured for four weeks?"

She knew that? "I was in physical therapy every day."

"During All Star breaks?" She moved ahead of him as they reached the back door, tugging a set of keys from her pocket. "Every single minute, you were busy?"

"I'm here now, aren't I? And you don't seem too happy about it."

She spun around to face him and pointed a key toward his chest. "Do you really expect me to jump for joy because you imploded your own career and now you want to come and horn in on mine?"

"I didn't know about this Internet café stuff. Dad never

mentioned it, he never mentioned a—a girlfriend, and he never mentioned you."

She stared at him for a minute, no doubt a thousand smart-aleck retorts spinning through her head. Instead she snapped her fingers to call the dog who'd meandered toward the beach, and pivoted back to the door.

Which gave him a really nice view of her hips and backside in worn jeans.

A flash of those taut legs wrapped around him on a blanket in the sand danced through his mind. She'd worn jeans that night, too. He remembered sliding down her zipper, dipping his hand into her soft, feminine flesh, then peeling the denim down her legs.

A rush of blood through his body didn't surprise him. In the years that had passed, he'd never remembered that night without a natural, instinctive and powerful response. For some reason, that sandy, sexy encounter had never felt like a one-night stand. Probably because it involved a girl who he should have been able to resist—his best friend's little sister.

"Look," he said, stabbing his hands in his pants pockets, which really just helped him resist the urge to reach out and touch her. "I had no idea things had changed this much, or that you and Dad had plans for something entirely different."

"Well, we do." She entered the house and held the door for him.

He followed her, but his mind was whirring. Was he expected to back off the bar entirely? His family name was still on the door, damn it. The only name that ever had been on that particular door, with or without capital letters.

"Maybe there's a compromise somewhere," he suggested. "Maybe we could keep a few computers in one corner of the bar—you know, for the people who aren't watching games? And you could find some nearby property for your gallery or whatever."

Instead of brightening, her scowl deepened. She opened her mouth to say something, then slammed it shut again.

"What?" he asked. "What were you going to say?"

"Nothing."

He dug his hands deeper. "You won't even consider a compromise?"

Inhaling unevenly, she closed her eyes. "I've already compromised enough where you're concerned."

"What the hell does that mean?"

She held up both hands as though to stop everything. "Never mind." She turned away, toward a small hallway behind her. "Excuse me for a minute."

She turned to stalk down the hallway, but he seized her elbow in one quick grab. "What are you talking about?"

"Nothing," she spat the word, shaking him off. "Forget I said that."

He let her go.

What had she *compromised* for him?

In the tiny living room, he dropped onto a sofa and stared at the serene water of the Sound through a sliding glass door, remembering again the incredible night they'd spent together.

He'd never forgotten that night. Maybe because he knew he shouldn't have seduced Jack's sister…but maybe because her response to him was so real and strong. So real, that he couldn't understand where "compromise" came into play. There were two very, *very* consenting adults during that beach-blanket bingo.

He'd come home after his mother had died of an aneurysm, too old at twenty-four to feel as though his mommy had left him, but brokenhearted anyway. Kendra had been about twenty, maybe twenty-one, and smack between her sophomore and junior years at Harvard. A business major, he recalled.

He remembered how impressed he'd been—she was smart, and quick-witted, and had grown up into a complete knock-out. Even in the chaos and sadness of his mother's passing, he'd noticed that Kendra Locke had spent every minute at the bar, calmly taking care of things he and his father were not even thinking about.

His last night in town, he'd gone to the bar and ended up staying until it closed, drinking soda and watching Kendra work. That's when he officially stopped thinking of her as Ken-doll.

The name just wasn't feminine enough for a woman that attractive. They'd talked and flirted. She made him laugh for the first time that week.

When her shift ended, they'd gone for a ride. He still could remember pulling her toward him in his dad's car and their first, heated kiss.

He leaned forward and raked his fingers through his hair. He'd felt guilty, and a little remorseful at seducing a girl he'd always considered a little sister. But she'd been willing.

No, no. That was an understatement. She'd been more than willing. Sweet, tender and innocent, he remembered with a cringe. Certainly a virgin. Was that the compromise she'd made?

Probably. And he'd been a world-class jerk for not calling afterwards. It wasn't as if he'd forgotten her. He just… couldn't. He looked down the hallway expectantly. No wonder she still hated him. Especially now that she had what he wanted.

He muttered a curse. Wasn't it *unspoken* that he'd always be back? Sure it had happened a little sooner than they all thought, but Dad always knew it. Didn't she realize that when she bought forty-nine percent—not *fifty*—of the bar that she was essentially buying into his inheritance?

He heard her footsteps in the hall and looked up to see her walking toward him, looking as calm as the waters beyond the glass doors. Game face *on*.

"How much time do you think we should give them?" she asked.

"Not too much. Evidently, they get easily distracted by each other."

She laughed a little and put both hands on the backrest of a bentwood chair, her casual indifference back in place. "We can go back. I got what I needed."

"What was that?"

"My wits." She deepened those dimples with a disarming grin.

Was she offering a truce? He was game. "I'm sure we'll work something out." He gave her a friendly wink. "You never know. I bet we work well together."

Her eyes narrowed. "I bet we don't."

"How can you say that?" He stood slowly, his gaze locked on her as he moved closer. "Don't tell me you forgot—"

"Newman!" She snapped her fingers in the air, a warning look flashing in those sky-blue eyes. The message was silent…but clear.

There would be no discussing that night.

The dog came tripping down the hallway with a bark, surprising Deuce by sidling up to his leg instead of that of the woman snapping for him.

Kendra rolled her eyes as Newman rubbed Deuce's pantleg.

"He likes me," Deuce noted.

"He's easily impressed. Let's go back to Diana's."

Laughing, he held the door for her. "I don't know. Think the jury's back already, Ken-doll?"

"We're about to find out, Seamus."

DIANA LOOKED HAPPIER than usual. Kendra noticed the diamond-like sparkle in her eyes, which usually meant she'd gotten what she wanted. Please God, let it be so. Diana would back Kendra and push Seamus to move on with their plans. She was always in favor of progress and change.

As Diana puttered in the kitchen, straightening an already neat counter, Seamus sat on the sofa, elbows resting on his knees and knuckles supporting his chin. He only moved his eyes, looking up as Kendra and Deuce entered the family room. Unlike his fiancée, Seamus looked anything but pleased with the turn of events.

All of the papers and sketches had been neatly piled on the coffee table. Would those documents be making the trip into banks and venture-capital firms this week...or going home with Kendra?

Kendra stood to one side, but Deuce took a seat across from his father. "So, Dad. Whad'ya think?"

For a long moment, Seamus said nothing, staring first at Deuce, then at the papers on the table. Kendra's throat tightened and she dared another look at Diana, who had paused in her counter-wiping and turned to watch the drama unfolding in her family room.

"I think I have quite a dilemma."

No one said a word in response. Kendra willed her heart to slow, certain that the thumping could be heard in the silence. Even Newman lifted his head from the floor, his classic King Charles spaniel face looking expectantly at the humans around him.

"Deuce, you need to understand something," Seamus began. "This Internet café and artist's gallery is something we've been working on for almost two years. I really like the idea of bringing Monroe's into the next century."

Deuce leaned forward and opened his mouth to speak, but Seamus silenced him with one look. Kendra wished she'd taken a seat when they walked in, because her legs felt shaky as she waited for Seamus's next words.

"And Kennie, you know that my father opened Monroe's in 1933, the year I was born. He ran it until he died, more than thirty years later, in 1965. Then I took over, at—" he looked at Deuce "—thirty-three years of age."

Kendra bit her lip as she listened. Did Seamus see this as poetic justice? As history repeating itself? As some etched-in-stone prediction from on high? *As the Monroe Man turneth thirty-three, so shall he inherit the bar.*

Sheez. Her gaze shifted to Deuce and she could have sworn his lip curled upward. Was he thinking the same thing? Or was he just so damn sure of himself that he could afford to be cocky?

Instead of a snide remark, though, Deuce leaned forward again. "Dad," he said, forcefully enough that he wouldn't be stopped by his father's glare. "Isn't there some way we can compromise? Some way to keep Monroe's in the family, as a bar, and find another property for this... other stuff."

"That's not feasible," Kendra argued before Seamus could respond. "These blueprints have been drawn up by an architect—an expensive one, by the way—expressly for that property and the other buildings on the block."

"So use one of the other buildings," Deuce countered.

"We are. As soon as we rip out the bar altogether and push that whole wall fifty feet in another direction for an art gallery."

"An art gallery? In that space?" Deuce looked as though she'd suggested turning it into a nursery school. "That's perfect for a pool hall and twenty TV screens, each tuned to a different football game on Sunday. They have these satellite dishes—"

"Sunday? That's one of our biggest days. We do so much Internet business—"

"Not from football fans."

"You two need to work this out," Seamus said.

"Precisely!" Diana slammed her hands hard on the kitchen counter. Kendra, like the men and the dog, turned to stare at her. "You need to work side by side, together."

"What?" Kendra and Deuce responded in unison.

"She's right," Seamus acknowledged. "I can't make a choice without hurting someone I care about. We'll go on our trip, and you two run the place together."

"What do you mean—together?" Deuce asked.

Diana came around the breakfast bar into the family room, her gaze on Seamus, a shared, secret arcing between them, but Kendra had no idea what it was. "Why doesn't Kendra run the Internet café in the day, and Deuce run the bar at night? Let the customers decide where and when they want to spend their money."

"Run a bar at night?" Kendra almost sputtered in shock. "And lose all my nighttime business?"

"That's been a tiny percentage of the profits," Seamus responded. "You've been shutting down by nine o'clock lately."

"But it's April now. The warm weather is starting, more tourists are coming." She worked to modulate her voice, refusing to whine. "Those are the people who need Internet access, who bring their laptops so they can work on vacation."

"People *drink* on vacation," Deuce corrected her. "At

least at night." He slapped his hands on his thighs and slid them over his khaki pants, a smug smile in place. "I think it's a great idea."

They all looked at her expectantly. Was she going to back down? Let Deuce appear more willing to take the challenge than she was?

No one came in that bar looking for a drink anymore. What remained of the liquor bottles had to be regularly dusted. She'd been running Monroe's as though it were a coffee shop and Internet café for a long time; her customers were loyal online users. The people looking for a neighborhood bar went to the bigger chains that had come into town.

"Okay. Fine. Whatever you want, Seamus."

"I want you both to have a chance." He stood slowly, his gaze moving between them. "I'd like to see the decision be made by you, not me."

"We'll let the people of Rockingham decide," Deuce said, looking at Diana as he echoed her thoughts. Sure, now they were allies.

But Deuce had no idea what he was up against, getting between a woman and her dream. Twice.

Her Internet café was significantly more profitable than a bar, and Diana and Seamus's trip was only two weeks long. There was no way Deuce could turn a profit in less than a month.

Seamus stepped toward Diana and slid his arm around her again. "Tomorrow, Diana and I are leaving for Boston, New York and San Francisco for meetings arranged with investors and banks." He paused and pulled Diana closer, sharing that secret smile again. "And we've decided to tack on an early honeymoon."

"What do you mean?" Kendra asked.

"We were going to tell you this morning, honey," Diana said, "but we were so surprised by Deuce's visit."

"Tell us what?" Deuce looked horrified. "Did you already get married?"

Diana laughed lightly. "No. But I found the most amazing timeshare in Hawaii. A gorgeous house in Kauai, on the water. We couldn't resist."

"How long will you be gone?" Kendra asked, a sinking sensation tugging at her stomach.

Seamus grinned. "A month in Hawaii, plus the two weeks of business trip."

"A month?" Kendra looked from one to the other. "You'll be gone for six weeks?"

"Great," Deuce said, standing up. "Diana, do you think you can find me a place to rent until I sell my house in Vegas?"

Kendra glared at him. "Why don't you wait to sell your place until we see who…what happens."

"You can stay here," Diana offered. "Newman seems to have taken a liking to you."

"I take care of Newman," Kendra said. Good Lord, she didn't want Deuce a hundred yards away from her for six weeks.

"You can handle him in the evenings," Deuce said, his gaze on her. "I'll be at the bar."

"There's no way you're going to be there, in charge and alone," she said quickly. "I'll do my paperwork at night."

"Then I'll do mine during the day."

Kendra hadn't noticed that Seamus and Diana had slipped into the kitchen, until she heard their soft laughter. They stood with their heads close to each other, slowly walking toward the hallway.

"I kind of hate to leave," Seamus whispered. "Just when it's getting interesting."

Deuce grinned at Kendra. She glared at him.

"This is *so* not interesting," she mumbled, turning to retrieve her papers and put them back in order.

"I disagree," he said, suddenly way too close to her back. "This could be very interesting. Remember the night we—"

She spun around and stuck her finger right in his face. "Don't go there, Deuce Monroe."

With a playful smile, he put both hands over his heart, feigning pain. "Was that night so horrible that you can't even think about it?"

If only he knew. If only. But he wouldn't, Kendra swore silently. He would never know.

She gave him a blank stare. "What night, Deuce? I have no idea what you're talking about."

"Is that right?" His voice was silky smooth, and the dark glimmer in his eyes sent firecrackers right down to her toes. "I bet I can make you remember."

"One bet's enough for me today," she said, seizing one of the sketches of the new Monroe's layout and holding it in front of her face. "And I bet I get *this*."

He slid the paper out of her hand, and leaned so close to her mouth she could just about feel that Hollywood stubble as it threatened to graze her.

"Let's play ball," he whispered.

CHAPTER FOUR

WITHOUT KNOCKING, Deuce leaned against the solid wood door that separated a back office from the storage areas piled high with empty computer hardware boxes. He'd done as much as he could for the past two days from Diana's home. He'd stopped into Monroe's a few times, perused the small kitchen and made a few changes around the bar. But he hadn't yet entered what he still thought of as Dad's office. Which was always occupied by Kendra Locke.

He eased the door open without any hesitation over the latch. Because there was no latch. There'd never been a working latch as long as he could remember. But, were the employees of Monroe's still as trustworthy today as in the past? He might have to get that old lock fixed after all.

Despite the unfamiliar high-tech logos and the aroma of a Colombian countryside surrounding him, the solid mass of wood under his shoulder felt very much like *home*. As the door creaked open, he half expected his father to look up from the scarred oak desk, his broad shoulders dropping, his eyes softening at the sight of his son—right before he launched into a speech about how Deuce could do something *better*.

Instead of his father's Irish eyes, he met a blue gaze as chilly as the glycol cooling block he'd just assembled on the long-dormant beer tap behind the bar.

"It's five-thirty," he announced to Kendra. "Time for

coffee drinking Internet surfers to pack up and go home. Monroe's is open for business."

She lowered the lid of her laptop an inch as she lifted her brows in surprise. "Today? Tonight? You've only been in town for two days. Don't you have to unpack, get settled and give me a week or two or three to prepare for these temporary changes in my business?"

"I'm ready for business. Tonight."

He stepped into the tiny space, noting that the old green walls were now...pinkish. The window that was really a two-way mirror over the bar was covered with wooden shutters that belonged on a Southern plantation. "And there's nothing temporary about..." He closed the door and peeked at the space behind it. Aw, *hell.* "What happened to the plaques commemorating Monroe's sponsorship of Rockingham's state champion Little League team?"

Her gaze followed his to yet another of those black-and-white nature still-life shots that he'd seen in about six places now. He could have sworn her lips fought a smile.

"Diana Lynn took that photograph," she said simply. "She was inside a sequoia in California. Pretty, huh?"

He didn't comment. He'd find the Little League plaques. Dad must have stored them somewhere. "There are two freaks left on the computers out there," he pointed over his shoulder with his thumb. "And they are both immersed not in the new millennium, but in the middle ages from what I can see."

"Runescape," she answered with a nod. "That's a very popular online medieval strategy game. And they are not freaks. That's Jerry and Larry Gibbons. Those brothers spend hours in here, every day."

"Do they drink beer?"

She shrugged. "It might impair their ability to trade jewels for farming equipment."

"They have to—"

"Stay," she interrupted, jerking her chin up to meet his gaze, even though he towered over her desk. "You can't kick out my customers at night. If they want to sit on those computers until 2:00 a.m., there's no reason for them not to."

"Suit yourself," he said affably. "But the TV monitors are about to be tuned into Sports Center, and the jukebox will be on all night. Loud."

She flipped the laptop open again and looked at the screen. "The jukebox hasn't worked for a year. My customers prefer quiet."

"It works now."

She gave him a sharp look. Did she have her head so deep in the books that she hadn't noticed him out there yesterday morning, installing a CD system in the box?

"No one is going to show up for a drink tonight," she said, turning her attention back to the computer.

"You don't know that." He resisted the urge to reach out and raise that sweet chin, just to see those mesmerizing eyes again. Regardless of how chilly they were. "With the front door open, anyone who passes by could stop in. Walk-in business is the heart of a bar." The fact that he'd worked the phone and called every familiar name in a fifty-mile radius wouldn't hurt either.

She shook her head slightly, her smile pure condescension. "Deuce, I hate to break it to you, but Monroe's pretty much shuts down around the dinner hour. We might have a few stragglers come in after seven or so, and Jerry and Larry usually stay until they realize they're hungry, but there's no business done here at night."

"And you just accept that? Don't you want to build nighttime revenue? I thought you were an entrepreneur.

A capitalist." He almost made a Harvard joke, but something stopped him.

"I'm a realist," she said. "People pop into an Internet café during the day, when they need access to cyber space or a break in their schedule. At night, at home, they have computers."

"So change that," he countered.

"I'm working on it." She leaned back in the chair—not Dad's old squeaker, either, this one was sleek, modern and ergonomic. Crossing her arms over the rolling letters spelling Monroe's on her chest, she peered at him. "Were you paying any attention the other day or were you so wrapped up in resentment that you didn't even see my presentation? Remember the plans? The theater? The artists' gallery? The DVD-rental business?"

He'd gotten stuck on one word. "Resentment? Of what?"

"Of the fact that your father has found…love."

His elbow throbbed, but he ignored it. "I don't begrudge my dad happiness. You're imagining things."

One blond eyebrow arched in disbelief.

"I don't," he insisted. "His…lady friend seems…" Perfect. Attractive. Successful. Attentive. Why wouldn't he want all that for his dad? "Nice."

"She is that, and more." She shifted her focus to the keyboard again, and she began typing briskly. "Now, go run your bar, Deuce. I have work to do."

You're dismissed.

"I can't find any wineglasses."

She gave him a blank look, then resumed typing. "I have no idea where they are anymore. I may have given them away."

She wanted to play hardball? With him? "Fine. I'll just serve chardonnay to the ladies in coffee mugs."

That jerked her chain enough to drop her jaw. But she closed it fast enough. "You do that." Type, type, type.

"And you don't mind if I use those coffee stirrers for the cocktails?"

She narrowed her eyes and studied the screen as though she were writing *War and Peace*. "Whatever."

"And until I have time to place some orders for garnishes, I'll be dipping into your supply of fresh fruit for some cherries and orange slices. Will that be a problem?"

Her fingers paused, but then blasted over the keys at lightning speed. Unless she was the world's fastest typist, she couldn't possibly be writing anything comprehensible. "I do a tight inventory on every item in stock," she said over the tapping sound. "Please have anything you use replaced by tomorrow."

"Will you give me the names of your suppliers?"

She hit the spacebar four times. Hard. "I'm sure you can find your own."

"Can I borrow your Rolodex?"

Now her fingers stilled—as though she needed all her brain power to come up with a suitably smartass answer. "There's a Yellow Pages in the storage room."

She launched into another supersonic attack on the keyboard, her body language as dismissive as she could make it.

Aw, honey. You don't want to do this. You'll lose when I start throwing curves.

She typed. He waited. She typed more. He wound up.

"Kendra?"

"Hmmm?" She didn't look up.

"That window right there. You know it's a two-way mirror into the bar?"

"I'm aware of that," she said, still typing. "I don't need to monitor my patrons' activities. I have staff for that, and no one is in there getting drunk or stupid. At least not on my watch."

Low and inside. Strike one.

"That's true, but…" Slowly, he crept around the side of the desk toward the fancy white shutters. "Aren't you just a little bit curious about what I'll be up to out there?"

"Not in the least. I expect it'll be you and the empty bar for most of the night. Pretty dull stuff."

A slider. Strike two.

He opened the shutters with one flick, giving a direct shot through the mirror that hung over his newly assembled beer taps. "I'd think a girl who'd spent so many hours with her face pressed to the heat register just to hear the boys in the basement would be naturally voyeuristic."

He heard the slight intake of breath just as he turned to see a screen full of jibberish. She opened her mouth to speak. Then closed it with the same force with which she snapped down the lid of the laptop. A soft pink rush of color darkened her pretty cheeks.

"Come to think of it, I'll work at home tonight."

Steee-rike three.

"That's not necessary." He grinned at her, but she was already sliding a handbag over her shoulder.

As she opened the door, she tossed him one last look. There was something in her eyes. Some shadow, some secret. Some hurt. As quickly as it appeared, it was gone.

"Good luck tonight," she said, then her pretty lips lifted into a sweet, if totally phony, smile. "Call me if you get hammered with the big nine-o'clock rush."

When the door closed behind her, the room seemed utterly empty, with only a faint lingering smell of something fresh and floral mixed with the aroma of coffee.

Taking a deep breath, he turned to the California

sequoia, ready to remove it for spite. But that would be childish.

Instead, he looked through the two-way mirror in time to see Kendra pause at the bar to check out the newly assembled beer taps. She touched one, yanked it forward, then flinched when it spurted.

She bent down, out of his view for a moment, then arose, a coffee mug in hand. Pulling on the tap again, she tilted the mug and let about six ounces of brew flow in, expertly letting the foam slide down the side.

She lifted the mug to the mirror, offering a silent, mock toast directly at him. Then she brought the rim to her mouth, closed her eyes, and took one long, slow chug. Her eyes closed. Her throat pulsed. Her chest rose and fell with each swallow.

And a couple of gallons of blood drained from his head and traveled to the lower half of his body.

When she finished the drink, she dabbed the foam at the corner of her mouth, looked right into the mirror and winked at him.

THE TASTE OF THE bitter brew still remained in Kendra's mouth several hours later. She'd walked Newman, made dinner, reviewed her inventory numbers, puttered around her bungalow, and even sunk into a long, hot bath.

But no distraction took her mind off Deuce Monroe. Her brain, normally chock-full of facts, figures and ideas, reeled with unanswered questions.

How could she get through six weeks of this? Where would she get the fortitude to keep up the cavalier, devil-may-care, I-don't-give-a-hoot acting job she was digging out of her depths? What could she do to make him go away? What if he discovered the truth about what happened nine years ago?

There were no answers, only more questions. The last one she asked out loud as she opened Diana's door for a third time to gather up Newman. "Why does that man still get to me after all these years?" The dog looked up, surprised.

"I'm lonely, Newman," she admitted. "Let's take another walk."

Newman never said no. He trotted over to the hook where Diana hung his leash.

Sighing, Kendra closed the slider and wrapped the strap around her wrist letting Newman scamper ahead while her gaze traveled over the wide beach. In the moonlight, the white froth sparkled against the sand, each rhythmic crest rising over the next in an unending tempo.

It had been a night much like this one, on a beach not three miles away, that Kendra Locke had given her love, loyalty and virginity to a boy she'd adored since first grade. And now, so many years later, that boy was at *her* café, driving away *her* customers, changing *her* plans and upsetting *her* peaceful existence.

"And he probably doesn't have a clue how to close the place," she told Newman, who barked in hearty agreement. "What if he screws up?" she asked, picking up her pace across the stone walkway to her beach house. "He doesn't know how to cash out or power down the computers."

Newman barked twice.

"I agree," she whispered, tugging his leash toward her beach house. "We better do what we can to save the place."

In ten minutes, she'd stripped off her sweats and slipped into khaki pants, an old T-shirt, sandals and, oh heck, just a dash of makeup. She rushed through the process, not wanting to change her mind, but definitely not wanting to arrive too late and find the café abandoned, the back door open, the computers still humming.

Kendra navigated the streets of Rockingham, mindful of the ever-growing population of tourists and locals. Something huge must be going on because even the tiny parking lot behind Monroe's was full. She finally nailed a parallel parking space a block away, and it was already ten-fifteen when she and Newman hustled down High Castle Boulevard toward Monroe's. He'd probably bailed by the time the Gibbons brothers left, around eight-thirty.

She expected the front door to be locked when she tugged at the brass handle. But the door whipped open from the other side, propelled by a laughing couple who almost mowed her down in their enthusiasm to get to their car. Kendra stood in the doorway, stunned as they brushed by her and mumbled excuses.

One step into Monroe's and she froze again. From speakers she didn't know she still had, Bruce Springsteen wailed. A stock-car race flashed on one TV monitor, a baseball game on another. Glasses and mugs clanged and loud voices of fifty or sixty people echoed with toasts and laughter, and somewhere, in the distance, she smelled… barbecued chicken.

Kendra ventured a few steps through the door. Had she fallen asleep in the bathtub and got stuck in a really vivid dream?

A total stranger tended the bar. A woman she'd never seen waltzed through a cluster of tables and chairs carrying an old brown drink tray laden with glasses. And, as though her eyes weren't playing enough tricks on her, Jerry and Larry Gibbons were over in the corner, flirting with some girls, sipping ice-cold brews from the brand-new tap.

Kendra tried to breathe, tried to think. How had he done this? How had he—

"Well look what the…" Deuce's chocolate gaze traveled over her, pausing at the floor. "…dog dragged in."

Newman skittered across the hardwood toward him, but Kendra tugged his leash. She opened her mouth, but before she could utter a sound, Deuce was next to her, sliding one solid, strong arm around her waist. His face dipped close enough for his lips to touch her hair.

"Don't tell me," he said, the musky scent of him mixed with beer and barbecue filling her head. "You were worried I couldn't handle the nine o'clock rush?"

The only rush she felt was a bolt of electricity charging from her head, down her body and leaving a thousand goose bumps in its wake. "I was worried you had no clue how to close up."

"We're not closing for hours, Ken-doll. And I hope you'll stay for the duration."

She looked up at him, her razor-sharp brain taking an unexpected vacation. Words, praise, criticism—anything intelligent—eluded her. Everything except the heart-stopping desire to kiss him. And that was not intelligent.

"How did you do this?" she managed to ask.

"Word spreads. It seems Rockingham is still a very small town," he said, his eyes glinting in a tease.

She glanced at the patrons, two deep at the bar. "And, apparently, a thirsty one."

She was enough of a professional to appreciate the revenue flow. And enough of a competitor to be more than a little bit jealous.

She sniffed. "What's that smell?"

"Profits," he whispered, that mighty arm squeezing her waist even tighter. "You smell revenue on the rise."

"I smell barbecue chicken."

"Oh that," he laughed, guiding her closer to the bar. "You know JC Myers owns The Wingman now?"

She assumed the ownership of Rockingham's favorite barbecue joint was a rhetorical question and didn't answer.

"He agreed to provide some emergency assistance."

"What emergency?"

"A munchie emergency. You can't serve gallons of alcohol and no food." He waved a hand toward the crowd. "We've got to keep these people happy."

"There's food in the back," she said defensively.

He rolled his eyes. "Granola bars and cupcakes."

"Muffins," she corrected.

"Not exactly sports-bar food."

Newman pattered around her and she scooped him up protectively, before she wandered farther into the fray. She saw some familiar faces from around town, and plenty of new ones. Who *were* all these people and why had they suddenly shown up?

"Who's tending bar?" she asked.

"You don't remember Dec Clifford? My old first baseman?"

As if she'd ever noticed anyone on any team he played on besides…the pitcher. "Vaguely. I didn't realize he was still in Rockingham."

"He's a lawyer in Boston now," Deuce told her, his hand firmly planted on the small of her back, making sure those goose bumps had no chance of disappearing. "And over there is Eric Fleming, outfielder. But now he's in commercial real estate in New Hampshire. That's Ginger Alouette serving drinks. She was a track star in high school, if you don't remember. She lives in Provincetown. Most of these people still live on Cape Cod—I just had to dig them up."

A lawyer from Boston, a developer from New Hampshire and Ginger from P-town. They'd all come to see him—to work for him.

"I'll get real staff soon," he promised. "I just wanted to get open as soon as possible and so I had a little help from my friends."

He was still the draw, not Monroe's Bar & Grill & Wannabe Cyber Café. Deuce was the main attraction and, suddenly, with sickening clarity, she faced the truth. He could make this work. He could make a raging success out of the bar…and she'd be doing Seamus a disservice by trying to fight it.

"I can't believe you brought a dog in here," he said, reaching for a quick pet of Newman, who nuzzled into Kendra.

She'd never dreamed the place would be packed, or Newman would have stayed home. As she would have. "I thought you'd…" *Be all alone.* "Need some—"

"Company?" he asked with a grin.

"No, just help." But that had been ridiculous. He had all the assistance he needed. She looked pointedly at the black screens of her computers. "How did you figure out how to get all the systems down?"

"I just installed a glycolic cooling unit, a CD player and a satellite dish, Kendra. It didn't take a Harvard degree to turn off a bunch of computers."

The comment jabbed her right in the stomach. She swallowed a hundred retorts and looked away. He had no idea what he'd said, and she could hardly zing him anymore for incompetence. He had it all going on, and more.

"Would you like a drink?" he asked, as they reached one empty barstool. "Dec, remember Jack's little sister? Get the lady whatever she likes. It's on the house."

Jack's little sister. That's what she'd always be to him. Not the owner of this establishment. Not the woman he'd deflowered a decade ago. Not…anything. Just Jack's little sister.

"On the house?" She allowed him to ease her onto a barstool. "I *am* the house."

He just laughed, leaning so close to her ear she thought he was about to plant a kiss on her neck.

"I believe you've already had a sample of our new draft selection, right, Ken-doll?"

She just looked at the bartender, vaguely remembering a younger version of his face that had no doubt spent hours with the baseball boys in the basement. She'd been so blinded to anyone but Deuce. "I'll just have a soda, please," she told him.

And then Deuce was gone. A whisper of "Excuse me," and the warmth of his body disappeared from behind her. She fought the urge to turn and watch him work the crowd. Instead, she cuddled Newman in her lap and gratefully accepted the cold drink for her dry throat.

"He's absolutely adorable."

Kendra turned to see the familiar, friendly face of Sophie Swenson, her hostess and right hand at the café. Sophie held a glass of white wine—in a stem glass—and her deep-blue eyes glinted with excitement.

"Yeah, he's adorable," Kendra assured her, with a disdainful glance back at Deuce. "But he knows it."

Sophie let out a soft giggle. "I meant the dog."

"Oh." Kendra couldn't help laughing as she pulled Newman higher on her lap. "Well, Newman knows he's adorable, too." She narrowed her eyes at Sophie, noticing the flush on her pretty cheeks, the way her gaze darted around the crowd. Would her most senior employee want to slide over to the Dark Side now? "You want to switch to a new evening schedule, Soph?"

Sophie shrugged and settled into the barstool. "If the action stays like this, I might. I mean is Monroe's going back to being a bar? What about the expansion plans?"

Kendra let out a long, slow sigh. "I have no idea," she admitted. "I just wish he'd go back to where he came from."

"He came from…here." Sophie's eyes were without humor. "I mean, his dad owns the bar."

Kendra's shoulders slumped slightly. "I own half of this bar."

Sophie raised a surprised eyebrow.

"Internet café," Kendra corrected, burying her fingers in Newman's soft fur and scratching him. "And I'm not going to walk away because the mighty Deuce has come home."

Sophie's gaze moved from Kendra to Deuce, then back to Kendra. "He's crazy about you."

Her heartbeat skidded up to triple time. "I doubt that."

"He hasn't taken his eyes off you since you walked in here."

Why did that fact send yet another shower of goose bumps over her? Kendra closed her eyes until it passed. "No, we're just in an oddly competitive situation right now."

Kendra stole one more glance over her shoulder. Ginger the track star-turned cocktail waitress gazed up at Deuce and giggled. Another athletic-looking man slapped him on the back.

But Deuce's gaze moved over everyone and locked on Kendra. There was that secret smile, that cocky tease in his eyes. And, as it had since before she knew how to write his name in cursive, the old zingy sensation washed over her.

Oh, Lord, not still. Not at thirty years old. That incapacitating girlhood crush had resulted in nothing but sleepless nights and pillows drenched in tears. A lost opportunity to graduate from the finest university in the country. And she wouldn't even think about the baby. She'd trained herself not to ever, ever do that.

Hadn't she paid enough for the honor of worshipping at Deuce's altar?

"Call it competition if you like," Sophie said, yanking Kendra back to the present. "But that man's got you front and center on his radar screen."

"Well then I'll just have to disappear."

"That's kind of difficult since you're both working in the same place," Sophie said.

"Not at all," Kendra said, gathering up Newman with determination. "I work days, he works nights. And never the twain shall meet."

Sophie tilted her head a centimeter to the right in a secret warning. "The twains are about to meet, honey. Hunky baseball player on your six."

Clutching Newman, Kendra slid off the stool and took a speed course through the crowd around the bar. The back door was closest, so she focused on it like a beacon for a lost ship. If she could just get into the kitchen before he got to her, she could slip into the back parking lot.

She breezed through the storage area, ignored the surprised looks from the borrowed employees of The Wingman who were plating up chicken in the little kitchen, and flung the back door open into the night.

"That wasn't so hard, was it?" she whispered to Newman, setting him gently on the concrete.

Newman sniffed at the corner of the Dumpster.

"No time for trash, Newman." She tugged on his leash and led him along a brick wall through the side alley and to the main road.

Where she walked smack into one six-foot-two-inch former baseball player wearing that triumphant grin that used to melt her in the stands of Rockingham Field.

"The party just started, Ken-doll," he said softly, placing those incredible hands on her shoulders and pulling her just an inch too close to that solid wall of chest. "You can't run away yet."

The definition of stupid, she thought desperately, is making the same mistake twice. And Kendra Locke, who'd scored a coveted scholarship to Harvard and masterminded the makeover of Rockingham's version of Silicon Valley was not *stupid*. Was she?

"I'm not running away," she insisted. "It's too crowded in there for a dog. And I—" she cleared her throat. "I have to go home."

"I'd like you to stay." He dipped his face close to hers. She didn't move. Couldn't breathe. Couldn't possibly think.

Deuce was going to kiss her. She opened her mouth to say something, something like "This is a bad idea," but before she could manage a word, he covered her mouth with his.

She stood stone-still as his fingers tightened his grip and his lips moved imperceptibly over hers. He closed a little bit of space between them, his chest touched hers, his legs touched hers, his tongue touched hers.

Was she really going to do this? She, the former Mensa candidate and Rockingham High valedictorian? Could she be that foolish and wild? Could she dare let history repeat itself?

Opening her mouth, she did the only thing she could possibly think to do.

She kissed him back.

CHAPTER FIVE

KENDRA SLID HER ARMS around Deuce's shoulders, which was all the body language he needed to completely close the space between them.

A soft moan rumbled in her throat as he tested the waters by grazing her teeth with his tongue. In that instant, it all came back. The magical kisses of an eager, sweet girl. The memory of that extraordinary night hit him as hard as the surf that they'd let pound them as they'd lain naked on the sand.

He touched the dip of her waist and skimmed his hands over the curve of her backside, hardening instantly against her stomach, moving automatically against her hips.

"Deuce." He could feel his name tumble from her lips as she reluctantly broke the kiss. "Newman."

Newman?

Then he realized the dog was parting them by pulling on his leash. He gave the leather strap a good tug. "Hey bud. Gimme a break."

That was enough to kill the moment. Even though her blue eyes were darkened by the same arousal that twisted through him, Kendra backed up.

"Listen to me," she said softly, but with a whispered vehemence that made him look hard at her. "I'm not the same girl I was back then."

"No, you're not," he agreed, pulling her just enough into him so there was no doubt of the effect she had on him. "Now you're a woman." He traced his thumb along her jaw. "Smart, willful and…beautiful."

She dipped away from his touch, the darkness in her eyes shifting from arousal to wariness.

"I'm smart all right," she insisted, and he sensed she was telling this to herself as much as to him. "Too smart to…" Her voice drifted as she managed to untangle herself from his arm. "I'm going home now."

He smiled at her. "I like you, Kendra."

She backed up farther and gave him a dubious look. "What are you up to, Deuce Monroe?"

"You don't trust me at all, do you?"

Her eyes suddenly widened. "Do you think seducing me is going to win you the bar? You think I'll just back down from this fight because you swept me off my feet and into bed?"

The words punched him. "No." Truthfully, the thought hadn't even occurred to him. "I just…like you."

Nothing on her face said she believed him.

"Why don't you stay until I close up?" he suggested. "We can talk about the business, about how we can… figure this out."

"You don't want to talk."

No, he didn't. But he would. "Come on, Kendra. Stay. I can take you home later."

Newman skittered toward the street, suddenly impatient with the conversation, and Kendra went with him as though she felt exactly the same. "Just lock all the doors when you leave. And put the cash in the green zipper case in the bottom drawer of the office."

"Oh, yeah, I'll put the cash in the office that doesn't lock."

"The desk does," she said, reaching into her pocket. "Here." She held up a key chain. "The little gold one locks the cash drawer. Leave it on Diana's kitchen table and I'll stop in and walk Newman in the morning."

Maybe he'd leave them on his dresser so she'd have to come in his bedroom to get them. Maybe, if he hadn't lost his touch, she'd be right there in the bed next to him in the morning.

He reached for her hand. "I'd really like if you'd stay."

She shook her head in warning. "My car's right there," she said. "Bye."

Before he could get a grip on her arm, she'd taken off with the dog in tow, hustling down the street. Guess he *had* lost his touch.

He let his arousal subside as he waited in the street to see her get into a car and drive away. Pocketing the keys, he watched until the taillights disappeared at the bend away from the beach.

He touched his mouth, the feel of her lips still fresh. He was not done with her. Not by a long shot.

The front door of the bar flung open and two of his old teammates came bounding out, their laughter loud, their guts showing that beer consumption had replaced batting practice as their favorite pastime.

"Man, Deuce, it's good to have you back." Charlie Lotane pounded Deuce's back. "This is going to be an awesome bar. You got the touch, man."

"Ya think, C-Lo?" The old nicknames came back easily. "I was just wondering if I'd lost it."

"Deuce, you are the man!" Charlie assured him over his shoulder. "We really needed a place like this in the Rock. Way to go, bro."

"Thank God you came back, Deuce."

Deuce watched them disappear down High Castle and suddenly wondered just what the hell he'd come back to prove. That he was still "the man" who could pack Monroe's? That he was still the main event in town? That he could still see adoration in Jack's little sister's eyes?

Was he that shallow and insecure?

The door burst open again and he welcomed the distraction.

NEWMAN CURLED INTO the corner of Kendra's living room, as at home in this beach bungalow as he was in Diana's mansion. He was sound asleep by the time Kendra realized exactly what she needed to do in order get her head back on straight.

She needed to read her notebook.

She'd never been one to buy a diary, with a pretty filigree lock, or an embroidered design on the cover. It seemed so planned and pathetic, as though a formal diary somehow legitimized her longings. Plus, she'd known at a very young age that such a girlish item would be too tempting to Jack…and the thought of him sharing her diary with the boys in the basement still sent a rush of heat to her cheeks.

So she'd kept a simple spiral notebook, college-ruled and ragged at the edges. It never drew anyone's attention; instead it blended in with her many schoolbooks, another tool of a brainiac child bound and determined to get to the Ivy League.

But this was no ordinary notebook. The dates of the entries were far apart, but over the course of about a dozen years, it was just about full. Written on both sides of every page, in a script that had started out awkward, moved to a girlish flourish, and ended up as scratchy as a doctor's prescription.

She hadn't looked at the book in at least four years. But tonight, her body still humming from the electrical charge of that kiss, she'd gone to the bottom of a box of rarely worn sweaters to find a piece of her heart that had never quite healed. Sliding her nail into one of the curled corners, she wet her lips, still warm from the taste of Deuce.

The man could kiss and that was a fact.

In truth, it had been right in the middle of that heart-tripping lip-lock that the notebook had flashed in her mind like a big red flag. Warning. *Warning.* Serious, severe discontentment and disappointment ahead.

She lifted the cover. "Perhaps we need a little history lesson," she whispered to herself.

She opened it randomly, to about the fifth or sixth page.

The words "Mrs. Deuce Monroe" decorated the margins. The *O*'s in Monroe were hearts. Kendra laughed softly. She had to. Otherwise, she'd cry. The penmanship was classic third-grade, early cursive.

Tomorrow, my family is driving all the way to Fall River for my brother's baseball tournament. And guess what???? Deuce is coming too!!! In our car!!! His parents said he could drive with Jack!!! I will be in the car with him for hours and hours!!! I'm excited and happy tonight.

Kendra smiled, shaking her head. She remembered the trip vividly. Jack and Deuce had traded baseball cards and listened to the Red Sox game the entire time and never once said a word to her. Except when they rolled in laughter because she had to stop and go to the bathroom so often. And they'd lost the tournament on one of Deuce's classic out-of-control pitches, so the trip home was real quiet.

She flipped to the middle. Her handwriting had matured, and the date told her the entry was made when she was fourteen years old.

I hate Anne Keppler. I just hate her and her black hair and her perfect cheerleader's body. He calls her "Annie"—I heard him. She's down there right now, playing pool and giggling like a hyena along with that completely *dumb* Dawn Hallet(osis) who runs after Jack like a puppy-dog. Oh, God. He likes her. Deuce likes Anne Keppler. I heard him tell Jack last night after everyone left their noisy party. He *kissed* her! I heard him tell Jack he got *tongue.* How gross is that?

Her limbs grew heavy at the memory of Deuce's tongue. Not gross at all, as a matter of fact.

A series of broken-heart sketches followed that entry, but many months passed before she wrote again. A few words about entering high school, taking difficult courses, then…

Oh, lovely little piece of paper…I'm holding my driver's license. Yes! The State of Massachusetts and some really obnoxious old lady with orange hair agreed that I could drive (they were mercifully understanding about the parallel parking problem—the parallel parking that Jack *swore* I wouldn't have to do). Mom said I could go to Star Market this afternoon for some groceries. Guess I'll have to take a quick spin past Rock Field…there's baseball practice tonight….

She'd taken that drive about a million times. And she'd made up another million excuses to wander over to the stands, to give something to Jack, to watch Deuce out in the field, throwing pitches, getting chewed out by Coach Delacorte. Rarely, if ever, did Deuce notice her. Still, she was certain that if she just waited, if she just grew up a little more, if she just got rid of the braces, if she just could fill a C-cup, he would realize that he'd loved her all along.

By the time she grew up and the braces came off and the bra size increased, Deuce had ditched Rockingham for the major leagues. She tried to forget him and, for the most part, with her focus on getting into Harvard, and staying there, she succeeded. It was even possible to work at Monroe's in the summers and not think too much about him.

Until Leah Monroe died, and Deuce came home, in need of comfort and love.

She didn't bother to look for a passage in the journal that described the night she lost her virginity on the beach. She'd never written about it, trusting her memory to keep every single detail crystal-clear in her memory.

But as time passed, she did turn to her red notebook to write about the pain. The first entry was made when it began to dawn on her that she'd never hear from him again.

Deuce has been gone for nine days. Like a fool, I check my messages every hour. I pick up the phone to see if it's working. I run to the mailbox for a card, a note, a letter.

The closest I can get to him is the box scores in the paper. He pitched last night. Lost. Does he think about me when he goes back to his hotel? Does he think it's too late to call? Or does he have a girl in Chicago, in Detroit, in Baltimore…wherever he is right now.

Oh, God, why doesn't he call? How could he have been so sweet, so loving, so tender? Was it all an act?

There was one more entry, but Kendra shut the note-book and tossed it on the table. The walk down memory lane was no pleasant stroll; the exercise had worked. She'd never meant any more to Deuce than Annie Keppler or any other girl in his past. Of course, since their paths were crossing again, being the professional player that he was, he hit on her tonight. One kiss in the dark. Another mean-ingless display of affection. He was just high on his packed house and she was the available female of the moment.

He had no idea how their one night of pleasure had ruined her entire life. Evidently, Jack had never told Deuce his sister got pregnant and had to drop out of Harvard. Even though her brother had stuck by her and was still close to her, Jack had been as embarrassed by her stupid-ity as her parents. And the father of her baby remained the closest-guarded secret in her life. She'd never told anyone. Not even Seamus, who had never, ever passed judgment on her. He'd just given her a job when she needed one.

Newman's sudden bark yanked her back to reality, fol-lowed by a soft knock on her door. "Kendra? Are you still up?"

Oh God. Deuce.

She grabbed the red notebook and stuffed it into the first available hiding place, the softsided bag she took to and from work.

"What's the matter?" She asked as she approached the door. Her voice sounded thick. How long had she been lying there, dreaming of Deuce?

"Nothing," he called. "I wanted to give you back your key."

Slowly, she opened the door a crack and reached her hand out, palm up.

He closed his fingers over hers, and pulled her hand to his mouth. The soft kiss made her knees weak.

"We made over a thousand dollars tonight," he whispered.

She jerked her hand away and let the door open wider. "Get outta town!"

He grinned in the moonlight, holding up her set of keys. "I did that already. And now I'm back." Stepping closer to the door, he whispered, "Can I come in and tell you about what a great night it was?"

How could he have been so sweet, so loving, so tender? Was it all an act?

She swiped the keys dangling from his hand. "No. Just leave these on Diana's kitchen table in the future. I'll be sure you can find them on my desk at the end of the day."

Then she dug deep for every ounce of willpower she'd ever had and closed the door in his face.

Something she should have done a long time ago.

DEUCE LACED HIS fingers through the chain-link fence that surrounded Rock Field and sucked in a chest full of his favorite smell. Freshly turned clay and recently mowed spring grass. A groundskeeper worked the dirt around the mound, raking it to the perfect height for a six-foot pitcher to slide some fire in the hole.

He didn't have to be at the bar for another hour or so for his second full night of operation. All day long he'd fought the urge to go to Monroe's and find Kendra to see what she really thought of his success the previous night. At the same time, he fought the urge to make a trip to his old stomping grounds.

Eventually, he lost one of the fights, and drove the short distance to Rockingham High, knowing that he'd probably arrive on a practice afternoon. In April, every afternoon was practice.

His elbow throbbed as he tightened his grip on the

metal, pushing his face into the fence as though he could walk right through it. Come to think of it, he *could* walk right through it. All he'd have to do is whistle to the groundskeeper, who'd amble over and ask what he needed, assuming he was a parent or even a scout. Deuce would introduce himself, and watch the man's face light up in recognition.

Deuce Monroe? Rockingham High's most famous graduate? *Well, get on the field, Deuce!*

He heard a burst of laughter and turned to see half a dozen lanky high-schoolers dressed in mismatched practice clothes, dragging bat bags. One balanced three helmets on his head, another circled his arm over his shoulder to warm it up.

Somebody swore and more laughter ensued; one boy spat as they started unloading their gear.

After a few minutes of stretching out, some of the players took off for windsprints and laps. A guy who looked to be about forty, wearing sweats and a whistle, jogged onto the field. He eyed Deuce for a minute, then started calling out to the players.

Rick Delacorte, the only coach who'd ever known how to handle him, had retired last year after twenty years at Rock High. Deuce had stayed in touch with Rick, knew he and his wife had headed out to Arizona to spend their golden years in a condo strategically located within driving distance of the Diamondbacks' stadium.

He couldn't remember the name of this new guy, somebody Rick said had moved up from Maryland or D.C. to take the job. Deuce watched him needle a few players, sending some more for laps. A couple of catchers started blocking drills, and the infielders lined up for hit-downs and cut-offs.

An easy sense of familiarity settled over Deuce as he

watched a few pitchers warm up for a long toss. In less than three throws, Deuce could see one of the kids limiting his range of motion. The new coach didn't notice, and Deuce bit back the urge to call out a correction. Instead, he sat down on the aluminum stands. Just for a minute. Just to see how they played.

He only realized what time it was when batting practice ended, and the coach called for the last run. He was seriously late for the bar, but hell, this had been too relaxing. As he stood, the groundskeeper emerged from the afternoon shadows behind the visitor's dugout.

"Excuse me?" the man called out.

Deuce acknowledged him with a nod.

"You lookin' for someone in particular, son?"

"Just watching the practice," he said, squinting into the sun that now sat just above the horizon.

The older man approached slowly, an odd smile tugging at his lips. "What do you think of the new coach, Deuce?"

Deuce started in surprise. "Do we know each other?"

The man laughed. "I know you, but you probably don't remember me. The name's Martin Hatcher and I used to be—"

"The Hatchet Man," Deuce finished for him, taking the hand that was offered to shake. "I'm sorry I didn't recognize you, sir."

The former principal of Rockingham High laughed easily. "Well, I'm not as imposing with a rake in my hand as I was waving your pink slips."

Deuce shook his head and chuckled. "What are you doing out here?" The juxtaposition of the feared and revered principal now in the position of field caretaker seemed preposterous.

"I'm retired, Deuce," he said, stuffing his hands in the pockets of his pants. "But I volunteer here just like a lot of ex-Rock High teachers and staff. I still love the school, so I do what needs to be done. Last week, I worked in the cafeteria for a few days. That's always a bit of an education in human behavior."

Deuce took in the network of wrinkles over the familiar face, and the shock of gray hair. He'd done his share to add to the whitening of that head, he was sure.

"Don't feel bad that you didn't recognize me, Deuce. I'm not sure I would have known you, either. But I heard rumors that your own retirement brought you back to town."

"Wasn't exactly retirement," he said with a grin. "More like lifelong detention."

That earned him another hearty laugh and a pat on the shoulder. "You always could charm your way out of anything, Mr. Monroe."

"I couldn't charm the contract lawyer for the Nevada Snake Eyes."

"Their loss, our gain. It's just too bad it didn't happen a season earlier."

"Why? I had my best year last year."

"Indeed you did. I thought you could have been a Cy Young contender."

Deuce snorted. "Not that good."

"But if you'd have pulled your little race-car exploit before Rock High hired him…" He jutted his chin toward the dugout where the new coach stood, surrounded by ballplayers, some of whom listened to his lectures, while others looked anxious to leave.

"What's his name?" Deuce asked.

"George Ellis. He's teaching science, too, which I think he's much better at than coaching."

Deuce's gaze moved to the field, then back to Martin.

"He's not bad. Lots of energy. Seems to know how to get them to hit."

"You'd have been better."

"Me?" Deuce coughed back a laugh. "No, thanks. I have no interest in going out there and motivating guys who think they know everything." Guys like *him*.

They fell into pace together toward the parking lot. "So you'd rather run a bar."

Deuce heard the skepticism in his tone. "It's called Monroe's, Mr. Hatcher. And, since I am called that, too, it feels like the right thing to do."

"I'm not your principal anymore, Deuce. You don't have to call me Mr. Hatcher, and you don't have to give me your load of BS."

Deuce slowed his step and peered at the man who once had spent hours threatening, cajoling and teasing Deuce. "That was no load of BS."

"Monroe's isn't even a bar anymore."

"We're working on that."

Martin chewed his lip for a moment, then lowered his voice. "Seems to me Kendra Locke has some pretty big plans for the place."

The Hatchet Man, Deuce remembered from numerous trips to his office, always had a subtle way of making his point.

"I have plans, too." But then, subtle had never worked that well on Deuce.

Martin paused at the edge of the parking lot, crossing his arms and nodding. "Kendra was a favorite student of mine. Of course, she was a few years behind you."

"Her brother Jack was my best friend."

"Oh, yes. I remember Jackson Locke. A rebel, but very artistic. And he liked those basketball bombs over in the teacher's lot." He chuckled again. "Let you take the heat for the big one that dented Rose Cavendish's old Dodge Dart, as I recall."

Deuce just smiled. "Ancient history."

"We got a lot of that around here," Martin mused, his gaze traveling toward the red brick two-story building of the Rockingham High that sat up on an impressive hill. "Kendra has quite a history, too."

Kendra? Where was he going with this? Deuce waited for him to continue, as he would have if he'd been sitting across Principal Hatcher's imposing desk, discussing his latest infraction.

"She went to Harvard, did you know that?" Martin asked.

"Yes."

"Didn't finish, though."

"That seems a shame," Deuce said. "She was real smart." And kissed like a goddess, too.

"I only had a few Harvard-bound seniors in my twenty-five years at Rock High. So I remember every one."

"Why didn't she finish?"

"You'll have to ask her," he said, unlocking the door of an older model SUV. "And by the way, she's *still* real smart."

"I know."

"And you still love baseball."

Deuce grinned. "I'm not going to coach."

The other man just laughed and climbed into the driver's seat. "You spent a lot of time watching practice."

That Hatchet Man. He was always an observant dude. "Nice to see you again, Mr…Martin."

"I'll stop in the bar sometime, Deuce. I heard you packed them in last night."

"News travels fast around Rockingham."

Martin nodded. "It sure does."

Deuce closed the driver's-side door and said goodbye, watching his old friend and nemesis drive away. Then he turned to the field and took one more deep breath of baseball.

But suddenly he really wanted to know why Kendra Locke had given up her dream, and why that one piece of news didn't seem to travel like everything else around Rockingham.

CHAPTER SIX

FLAT ON HIS BACK, the cold dampness of the tile floor seeping through an old Yomuri Giants sweatshirt, Deuce swore softly as the broken nozzle of the soda spritzer slipped from his fingers and bounced on his chest. He'd been under the bar for half an hour and still didn't have the damn thing working right.

Five days into his latest endeavor, and he was fixing his own equipment. At eight in the morning, no less. A decision he made the night before when the sprayer had malfunctioned. As much as he'd like to sleep after a late night running Monroe's, he wanted to get in before any of the Internet café customers showed up.

Yeah. *Right.* He shook off a dribble of club soda that trickled onto his cheek and clamped his teeth tighter over the flashlight that shone on the unit.

Who the hell was he kidding? Cybersurfers didn't care if the bar was being worked on while they shopped online and played medieval trading games.

He'd come in before the place opened because Kendra had made a science out of avoiding him. And Deuce didn't want to be avoided any more.

But when he'd slipped in the back that morning, he'd heard voices raised in confrontation from behind the partially closed door to the office. He picked up Sophie's complaints about an employee who was supposed to have done something regarding a software update, and Kendra's calmly spoken instructions that Sophie take care of the problem.

Instead of interrupting, he'd gone straight to the bar and slid underneath to inspect the faulty spritzer. As he worked, he heard the sounds of the café opening up, and the ubiquitous smell of coffee being brewed.

He just about had the nozzle reinstalled when the coffee aroma was superseded by something light and spicy and pretty. Turning his head, his penlight lit a pair of high-heeled sandals a few feet from his face. His gaze slid up, up, up a long set of bare legs to a short skirt with a flippy hemline.

Man, there was something to be said for a view from the floor.

One of the cream-colored shoes tapped.

"Come on, Deuce," Kendra whispered to herself. "Where did you hide the soda thingy?"

She shoved a few of the stainless-steel cocktail shakers to the side, and yanked at the hose that was connected to the nozzle in his hand. "What the heck's the matter with this?"

She pulled harder, hand over hand toward the end of the hose…where she gasped as they came face to face.

"Oh my God! You scared me. What are you doing down there?"

The flashlight beam made another slow journey up her legs, stopping on a particularly sweet mid-thigh muscle. It flexed under his scrutiny.

"Adjusting my equipment," he managed to say without unlocking his teeth. "And enjoying the show."

She backed out of the beam. "I should step on you."

That made him laugh and the flashlight fell out of his mouth. Slowly, he slid out from under the lower shelf and stood to his full height. She tried not to look at him, but failed.

He wiped at some grime on his jeans and held the sprayer toward her. "Soda, water or diet? They were getting all mixed into one messy flow last night."

"Certainly didn't affect the *cash* flow."

He grinned. "Oh, so you counted it already?"

Over the past week, they'd started an unspoken exchange. He locked the pouch in the drawer each night, and left the keys on Diana's kitchen table. She picked up the keys early the next morning when she walked Newman, while Deuce was still asleep. When her day was over—always a few minutes after he arrived—she took the pouch to the bank and left the keys on the desk for him. All the while, she managed to avoid spending any significant amount of time with him.

"As a matter of fact, I have a meeting with the architect in a few minutes," she told him. "I was planning to make a cash drop at the bank on my way."

"Oh, that's why you're dressed up?" He took another leisurely gaze over a silk blouse buttoned just high enough to make him want to…unbutton it. "I thought it was to impress me."

"I don't imagine a skirt and blouse are too impressive to you."

He shrugged. "You look nice. But I'm kind of partial to leather."

She rolled her eyes and opened her right palm to reveal two pills. "You're not helping my headache."

He retrieved a clean glass, filled it with water and handed it to her. As she put the pills in her mouth, he said, "Don't blame me. I heard you fighting with Sophie."

Her eyes popped open, but she managed to get the aspirin down. "I wasn't fighting with her," she denied hotly after she'd swallowed. "We were just working out some issues."

"Sounded like she wasn't happy."

She sighed softly and spilled the remaining water in the sink, her gaze moving across to the computer area where Sophie worked at a terminal. "She's not."

"What's the matter?"

"Just some coworker issues." She settled a sincere blue gaze on him. "Nothing I can't handle."

"Well, maybe I can help," he offered. "I know a little about teamwork."

She regarded him for a minute, an internal battle whether or not to confide in him waged over her expression. "She just has some problems with newer employees," she finally said. "Not everyone is quite as competent as she is and, well, she tends to let them know it."

"Like the veteran and the rookies."

She looked questioningly at him, then smiled. "Not all of life can be equated to baseball."

"Yes it can," he answered matter-of-factly. "Why don't you put her in charge of training?"

"Training?"

"Give her responsibility for their success. Coaches do that all the time in the spring when they're trying to build cohesion between the old, seasoned guys who know everything and the hotshots up from the minors who *think* they know everything."

She glanced at Sophie, then back at him. "What do they do, exactly?"

"If you give her the job of training them, and tie their success to hers, she might be more prone to want them to succeed."

"She does want them to succeed," she countered. "She also wants everyone to be as good as she is. With the computers, with the customers, with everything. And some of these kids are just out of college."

"Precisely." He glided the sprayer hose back into place and twisted a faucet to wash his hands. "But make her feel like their accomplishments reflect her skills. Trust me. It'll work."

She said nothing as he soaped and rinsed his hands, then gave him that gut-tightening smile. The real one. The one where she let down her guard. "Thanks for the advice. Now what are you doing here at this hour?"

"I wanted to talk to you."

"Oh?"

"I can't seem to get you alone for five minutes."

"I'm busy." She lifted a shoulder of indifference, but the cavalier act wasn't working. She was avoiding him and they both knew it. "I'm busy. You work nights. I work days. And, by the way, you're making my life complicated."

He managed not to smile. "I am?"

"All this money, Deuce. How can I make a compelling argument to your father that we shouldn't have a bar in here?"

"You can't. That's the idea. And look at this place." He gestured toward the computer stations, many that were taken with busy patrons. "You're not exactly losing money while I'm making it."

She nodded. "As a matter of fact, café and Internet access revenues are up, too."

"Good, then you won't mind investing in a pizza oven."

"A pizza oven?" She backed up to stare at him. "Now you want to turn this place into a pizzeria?"

He swept a hand toward the wall of booze behind him. "They drink, they have to eat. I did some research and pizza is a very high-profit item. Especially per slice."

She looked dubious. "I don't know."

"You might be able to serve it in the afternoon, too."

"With coffee?"

He winked. "It's best with beer."

"Deuce." Her shoulders sank. "I'm on my way to meet with the architect and you are changing my business plan by the minute."

"To the tune of a grand a night."

"I know. I can count." She put her fingertips to her temples and rubbed gently. His fingers itched to help alleviate the headache. "Let me think about the pizza oven and—"

"I'm just going to order it. I wanted to know if you have a particular supplier you use."

"I do. Buddy McCrosson, over in Fall River. But I have to deal with him because he's an old bag of wind and wouldn't give you the best price."

"Then you can come with me to pick it out."

"I can't, I have a new employee starting tomorrow—"

"Put Sophie in charge of your new employee." He gave her a victorious smile. "And we'll take a drive out to Fall River tomorrow."

She shook her head, a flash of terror in her eyes. Was she afraid of the spontaneous change to her plans...or of being alone with him?

"Kendra," he leaned lower. "We're partners here." He almost closed the space between her temple and his lips. Would a kiss on that aching spot make her feel better?

"We're not partners," she said stiffly, her eyes locked on his.

"But you can't avoid me for the next four weeks."

She closed her eyes as though his very proximity made her dizzy, sending a splash of satisfaction through him. He set his lips on the soft skin of her hairline and forehead and kissed. "I hope your headache goes away."

"You are my headache," she said softly. "You make my head *throb*."

He laughed softly. "Great. We can work down from there."

THERE WAS NO DOUBT Sophie loved the idea of creating a training manual and implementing it. She fairly danced out of Kendra's office the next morning, and even held the door for Deuce who had been waiting outside. For how long, Kendra had no idea.

"So that went well, huh?" he asked, his dark eyes glimmering.

She hated to admit it, but he'd been right, and one good turn probably deserved another. "Thank you for your advice," she told him. "I owe you one."

"Great. I figure we can be in Fall River by noon, pick out the pizza oven of our dreams and kiss off the rest of the afternoon with an intimate beachside lunch."

Intimate? Kiss? *Dreams?* She ignored the rush of anticipation that meandered from her heart through her stomach and settled way, way too low. "I owe you one, Deuce, not a day and lunch. Anyway, it won't take two hours to get there. We can be home and back to work by one o'clock."

"I need a pizza oven, sweetheart." He waved a dismissive hand toward the disarray of papers and files on her desk. "And you need a break."

That much was true. Seamus had called from San Francisco to tell her that a few of the meetings had gone so well that the investors needed some more data. She'd pulled that together, which was no mean feat considering she wasn't working evenings. Blowing off the day with Deuce seemed both insane and inspired.

He leaned one impressive shoulder against the doorjamb and her gaze flickered over the taut fit of his navy-blue polo shirt, tucked into the narrow hips of a pair of khaki pants. He'd dressed nicely for their day trip. She'd worn jeans and a sweater—not fully believing he'd follow up on his threats to take her to Fall River. But here he was…looking…

"You going to stare at me for an hour or are we leaving?"

Stare. She blinked. "You're imagining things. I'm just wondering what my restaurant supplier will think of you." She made a showing of hunting for her bag. "I guess if he likes baseball, we're in good shape."

"No," he said, his serious tone forcing her to look up. "Let's just leave my former career out of it."

She regarded him for a moment, the weight of her tote bag seeming as heavy as his voice. "Really?" She dropped the handle of the tote bag and just grabbed her purse. "That's not like you."

"I'm full of surprises," he said with a laugh, levity back in place. "I even have one in the parking lot."

In the kitchen she stopped to talk to Sophie and explain where they were going. Ignoring Sophie's subtle raised eyebrow implying "isn't this an interesting development?" she followed Deuce into the back lot, where his rented car had been replaced with a bright-red Mercedes two-seater… top down.

"Surprise," he said. "I decided to upgrade."

Her breath caught in her throat and all she could think about was the last time he took her out in a convertible. It was Seamus's car and she didn't remember the make, only that when he'd pushed the driver's seat all the way back, she'd fit perfectly between his body and the steering wheel.

Heat lightning flashed through her veins at the memory.

"I thought it would be nice since we'll take Highway 28 over to the south shore," Deuce said.

It took her a moment to erase the memory of his rock-hard body and soul-melting kisses to process what he'd just said. "The beach road? That'll take forever. Route 6 is much faster."

"What's your rush?" He opened the passenger door and indicated for her to climb in. "I thought it would be fun to see the beaches. I haven't been to some of those places in…years."

Oh, this was a bad idea. A joyride along the beach—*that* beach—in a convertible with Deuce. How did this happen? She had been so adept at avoiding him and now she was walking right into hell on four wheels.

Or was it heaven?

In the side-view mirror, she saw him study her backside as she slipped into the deep-red leather, already warmed from the sun. His gaze lingered just long enough for her to glance over her shoulder and burn him with a warning glare.

He made no attempt to look away. Instead, his scrutiny burned hotter than the leather against her body. "You always did do justice to a pair of jeans, Kendra."

Oh, hell. It *was* heaven.

DID DEUCE DELIBERATELY slow down as they passed the dunes of West Rock Beach? Did he even remember that this was the beach…their beach? Or was Kendra the only one who nurtured those memories?

In nine years, she'd never returned to West Rock Beach.

She battled the urge to look to her left, to look at the sandy backdrop and the few reeds of tall grass, and at the man who sat next to her.

"Tell me something, Ken-doll." The serious tone made

her stomach drop. "Do you think of me when you pass this spot?"

She leaned her head back and let the sun stream over her face. "Why would I do that?"

Laughing, he accelerated and pulled the gearshift into fourth, his knuckles just grazing the worn denim of her jeans. "You are bound and determined not to talk about it, aren't you?"

Oh, God. "Correct."

"You think if we just act like it never happened, then we can pretend it didn't, don't you?"

"Correct again."

She opened her eyes to find his gaze locked on her. "It did happen, Kendra. And I want to talk about it."

"Watch the road," she warned. "And I don't."

A truck rumbled by in the other direction, forcing blessed silence. Did he really want to do this? To what end?

"You're mad because I never called."

She snorted softly. "Ya think?"

His hand slid from the gearshift to her leg, his powerful palm and fingers covering half of her thigh and sending a wicked shot of excitement straight through her. She eased right out of his touch, earning a look from him.

"I'm sorry," he said softly.

She brushed her leg as though she could erase the impact of his fingertips. Yeah, right. "It's okay."

The wind off the waters of Nantucket Sound whipped her hair across her face, and she left it there, letting it hide the expressions that might give away her real feelings.

Wanting Deuce was so fundamental to her. It was like breathing.

Damn it all, nothing had changed. It was as if nearly a decade hadn't passed. As if he'd come home a month after they'd shared every intimacy, and picked up without missing a beat. And her stupid, foolish girl's heart was ready to just open up again.

"Are you sure it's okay?" he asked, breaking the quiet of her thoughts.

"You're forgiven for not calling," she said quietly. Maybe if she let him off the hook, he'd back away.

"You're not lying?"

She shook her head. "I would never lie." But she didn't exactly want the whole truth out there for discussion, either.

For what seemed like an eternity, he didn't speak. Eventually, she flipped the lock of hair off her face, using it as an excuse to glance his way. His jaw was locked tight, his eyes, behind his own sunglasses, were narrowed in deep thought.

"Then I'll tell you the truth," he said.

She waited while he collected his thoughts, and passed a pickup truck.

"I had to cut off everything that was Rockingham," he finally said, so softly she almost didn't hear him over the wind and the engine of the Ford F-150 he'd just blown around.

"Why?"

"Because…" he shook his head and ran his tongue over his lips. No act of nature could get her to look away as she studied his serious expression. Serious…and beautiful. It still hurt to look at him.

He barreled the car forward right up to the rear bumper of a minivan, then ripped into the other lane, floored it, and whizzed by the poor young woman in the driver's seat. He lowered his speed back to the limit and sucked in a breath.

"Without my mother to run interference…" He spoke slowly, candor softening his voice. "I couldn't handle my dad. Without my mother… I just missed her too much. I couldn't come back."

Seamus could be overbearing. Way beyond overbearing where Deuce was concerned. "I understand that." *But why the hell didn't you call to tell me?* Years of training herself not to reveal her true feelings to Deuce kept her from asking the question. Maybe that was foolish, maybe that was just chicken. But that was the only way she knew how to handle him.

The one time she had admitted her feelings…

"And if I couldn't come back…" he continued, "what was the use of calling you?"

She shrugged. "Oh, I don't know. Common decency? A lifelong acquaintance? Acknowledgement of…" *The baby I carried.* "…my feelings?"

"I'm really sorry, Kendra." He swallowed hard enough for his voice to crack. Her heart did the same. "It was a shitty thing to do."

This time she patted his leg. "Forget about it, Deuce. I forgot about it a long time ago." Liar, liar, liar.

"So why'd you leave Harvard?"

The question was so unexpected it practically took her breath away. "I lost my scholarship and couldn't afford to finish." That was the God's truth.

He shot her a look of pure disbelief. "You had almost a full ride. How'd you lose it?"

"My grades went in the toilet." Along with most breakfasts those few months.

Traffic forced his gaze back to the road. "What happened? You were an A student. A genius. I remember that."

Yeah, a genius who didn't use birth control. She repositioned herself in the bucket seat. "I screwed up, Deuce. It happens all the time. Or did you forget about the racing incident that landed you here?"

He gave her a wry smile. "Not that you'd let me."

She'd have to keep the conversation on him. Otherwise, he'd probe too deeply. "So, what was your thought right before you hit the wall in that car?"

"My dad's gonna kill me."

"He was furious," she acknowledged. "The language was colorful, I can tell you."

He glanced at her. "How did you screw up?"

"Let it go, Deuce." *Please.*

"Was there a guy involved?"

"Yes." The truth.

"Did you love him?"

"Yes." More truth.

"Do you still?"

Oh Lord. "Once in a while, I think about him," she managed to say, despite the real estate her heart was taking up in her throat.

"Did he…hurt you?"

She thought of the blood and the pain and the insane trip to the hospital. All the guilt and disappointment, and, the worst part, the relief. "They were dark days." She'd lost the baby, Harvard and Deuce. "But I survived."

She pulled the seatbelt away from her chest, sucked in a breath of sea-salted air and smiled at him, aware that for the whole conversation, his hand had stayed firmly planted on her leg. "So what kind of pizza oven did you want to get?"

He shot her another disbelieving look at her sudden segue.

"You know, the more I think about it," she added before he could answer, "the more I think pizza would be a big hit at the café. I did a little research and Baker's Pride, Blodgett and Lincoln seem to be the best options." They stopped at a light, but she let the words roll out and fill the air. "The best price would be Blodgett, which is truly commercial grade, and I think we might even be able to get a refurbished—"

His fingers squeezed her thigh. "We were talking about your love life."

She put her hand over his, instantly loving the power she felt in those fingers, the hint of masculine hair tickling her skin, the sinewy muscles that baseball had formed. "Now we're talking about pizza ovens. Isn't that why we're here?"

"One of the reasons," he said, turning his hand so they were palm to palm and threading his fingers through hers. "The other reason is because I've been trying to get you alone for a week and it's impossible."

"I'm busy." She congratulated herself on yet another half truth that could not technically be called a lie. Why didn't she extricate her hand from his?

Because she couldn't. Any more than she could look away as he leaned closer to her face. His mouth was a breath away. His eyes locked on hers and his lips parted as he closed the remaining space between them.

The kiss was hotter than the sun that burned leather seats, and sweeter than anything Kendra could remember. At least, since the last time he'd kissed her.

A horn honked and startled them apart.

He held up his hand in apology to the car behind them,

but didn't take his gaze from hers. "I'm not even close to done with talking about your love life." He shoved the gearshift into first. "Or kissing you."

CHAPTER SEVEN

DEUCE SAW THE LOOK of shock on Kendra's face when he'd introduced himself as Seamus Monroe to Buddy Mc-Crosson, owner of Fall River Restaurant Supplies. Either Buddy didn't put two and two together with the names, or he wasn't a baseball fan. Either way, Deuce and Kendra spent nearly two hours with the man and no one mentioned the Snake Eyes or their former pitcher.

Watching Kendra in action was definitely the best part of the meeting. Although she never lost that feminine, sexy aura that surrounded her, she pounded out a tough deal, negotiated for way more than he'd have even thought of, and managed to let poor Buddy think it was all his idea.

All the while, Deuce studied her long, capable fingers as she examined a refurbished oven and imagined them on him. He listened to her soft laugh and fantasized about hearing it as he slowly undressed her. And, of course, he took any excuse to brush her silky skin or touch her slender shoulder.

He hadn't been kidding when he told her he wasn't done kissing her. He wasn't.

While she'd gotten Buddy to knock off two percentage points of interest on a short-term loan and throw in an $800 fryer—surprising him completely with her willingness to add more unhealthy food to her café menu—Deuce had started planning where and how and when he'd get back to kissing her.

The minute they said goodbye to Buddy, he launched his plan into action.

"I'm starved," he told her as they climbed back into the 450 SL.

"Anything but pizza," she agreed, buckling her seatbelt. "There are tons of places between here and home."

"I know exactly where we're going." But he had no intention of telling her. "It'll be a little while before we eat, but I promise, it's worth the wait."

She gave him a curious look, but didn't argue. She slid the paperwork from their meeting into the side pocket of her door, then dropped her head back and closed her eyes, letting the sun light her face. As he turned to back out of the parking spot, his gaze lingered on her face, her long throat, her sweet lips.

He wanted to kiss her right then. Why wait? Because, as any good pitcher knew, timing was the key to success.

They listened to jazz and barely spoke as he drove toward Rockingham. When they finally stopped at a deli in West Dennis, she looked surprised.

"Barnstable Bagel?" She half laughed. "You in the mood for a Reuben?"

"Great deli sandwiches here, if I recall correctly." If he told her he was going for atmosphere instead of cuisine, she'd fight him. "Wait here. I'll be right back."

When he returned, she took the bag of food and drinks that he handed her and tucked it into the space behind their seats. "We're eating in the car?"

"I believe it's called a picnic."

She lowered her sunglasses enough to look hard at him. "A picnic?"

"Chill out, Ken-doll. You'll like it." He hoped.

When he pulled up to the dunes at West Rock Beach, he practically felt her whole body tense. He shut off the engine and turned for the bag in the back. "I've always liked this beach."

She backed away to avoid contact. "Is this your idea of a joke?"

"No," he said slowly, pulling up the deli bag. "This is my idea of a picnic."

"This is… We don't have a blanket," she said quickly.

"We can sit on the benches."

Barely disguising a long, slow sigh, she climbed out of the car and they walked toward a low rise of the dunes, then stopped to take in the panorama of the Atlantic Ocean. A cool, salty breeze lifted his hair and filled his nostrils.

"Why are you doing this, Deuce?" she asked quietly.

"This has always been my favorite beach."

Without responding, she reached down and slid out of her loafers, then bounded toward the weather-worn bench that faced the ocean. He followed her, lumps of sand sliding into his own shoes.

"And because I want to make up for not calling you," he said as he sat next to her.

"By coming here?" She crossed her arms and faced the water. "I told you, I've forgotten about it and I think you should, too."

"Turkey or roast beef?" He held out the two wrapped sandwiches and she took the one marked with the *T.*

"I'll take this one."

"You're lying, Kendra."

She looked up at him. "I like turkey."

"You haven't completely forgotten."

Wordlessly, she unwrapped the sandwich and made a little tray on her lap with the white deli paper. As he did the same, she nibbled at the crust of the whole grain bread, gazing at the blue-black waters of the Atlantic.

"Okay," she finally said, setting her sandwich in her lap, "I haven't forgotten. But I forgive. I mean, I forgive you for never calling. I don't see any reason to hold a grudge. Can we move on now?"

"But you remember everything else?"

She nodded, but didn't look at him.

"So do I," he admitted. Every kiss, every touch, even that long, shuddering sigh as he entered her.

He thought he saw her close her eyes behind her sunglasses, but then they ate in silence, only the rhythmic crashing of the waves and the occasional squawk of a gull breaking the mood. Two young mothers with three kids between them wandered by looking for shells, and a retired couple walked hand-in-hand by the water's edge. He stole a sideways glance to see which vignette held her attention.

Her focus was on the children. Funny, he'd thought she'd like the old people who still held hands. He regarded her as she took a bite of a potato chip, watching the children with rapt attention.

"You want kids, Kendra?"

Her jaw stopped moving and her whole being froze. Slowly, she wiped the corners of her mouth with a paper napkin and swallowed. "What brought that question on?"

He shrugged. "I don't know. You're about thirty, right?"

"As of last November."

"Well, don't most women your age want kids? Tick-tock and all that?"

She didn't answer, but that little vein jumped in her neck. She took a drink of water and he watched her throat rise and fall.

"I'm so involved with the café, I don't really think about it," she finally said.

He opened another water bottle for himself. "I want

kids," he announced, surprising himself with the sudden candor. By the look on her face, he'd surprised her, too. "I do," he continued. "Nine boys so I could have my own little team."

She leaned back and let out that pretty laugh that sounded like music. "I pity the poor woman who has to give you nine children."

"Adoption." He could have sworn she sucked in a tiny breath at the word. "Seriously. Adopt a couple of sets of twins and bam, you got an infield."

"You're nuts." She folded up the white paper carefully, her fingers quivering a little.

"Are you cold?" he asked, reaching over to touch her hands. "We can go back to the car."

She shook her head. "No, I'm fine."

God, he loved holding her hand, touching her skin. He squeezed her fingers.

"Listen to me," he said softly. "It wasn't as if that night didn't leave an impression," he said slowly. "Because it did."

She whipped her hand out from his grip. "What part of I don't want to talk about it anymore don't you understand, Deuce?"

"Why don't you want to talk about it?"

She blew out a disgusted breath. "Maybe because it embarrasses me."

"Why are you embarrassed? It was…" Incredible. Amazing. Mind-boggling. He got hard just thinking about it. "Great."

"I doubt you remember the details."

Oh but he did. "You're wrong."

She folded the deli paper into a tiny square and held a pickle to him. "Want this?"

"Don't change the subject again."

"I'm not changing the subject. I'm offering you a pickle."

"I'm offering you an apology."

"You did that already. Apology accepted. But you're going to owe me another one if you don't drop the subject."

He took the pickle and her deli wrap, stuffed them into the bag, and carried it all to a trash can about twenty feet away. She stayed on the bench, sipping her water.

When he returned, he held out his hand. "Let's take a walk."

She just looked up at him, a half smile tipping her lips, deepening her dimples. "Aren't you a little overdressed for a walk on the beach?"

He reached down and slid off his Docksiders and socks and tucked them under the bench next to her loafers. "Let's go."

For a moment, he thought she was about to refuse, but then she slipped her hand in his and stayed by his side as they walked down to the sand still packed solid by the morning tide.

"I wisely carried a blanket around in those days," he said. "Came in handy that night, didn't it?"

She playfully punched his arm with her free hand. "You won't let go, will you?" Before he could answer, she slowed her step, shaking her head. "Actually, as I recall, I grabbed the blanket from the bar before we left because it was chilly and you had your dad's car."

He frowned. "I thought I had a blanket in the trunk."

"See?" she said, her voice rich with both humor and accusation. "You don't remember a thing."

"Not true. I remember kissing you outside Monroe's, by that side wall." She'd tasted like oranges and cherries, as if she'd been sampling the bar garnishes.

"We were in the car the first time we kissed."

He closed his eyes for a minute. He could remember the taste of her, the need to pull her closer, but he didn't remember if they were standing or sitting. "Maybe. But I remember the kiss."

"Me too." She whispered the words into the wind, but he caught them.

Deuce let go of her hand and put his arm around her shoulders. "You were wearing a little pink top."

"Blue."

"Your hair was shorter."

"In a ponytail."

He tightened his grip and lowered his voice. "You had a snap-in-front bra."

"Finally, he gets something right."

"I bet I remember more details than you do," he insisted.

"You'd lose that bet."

"I would not."

"Cocky and arrogant as always." She dipped out of his touch and slowed her step. Deliberately, she pushed her sunglasses over her forehead and the look in her eyes hit him like a ninety-mile-an-hour fastball to the chest. "There is nothing, no detail, no minor, incidental facet of that night I have forgotten. Don't bet me, Deuce Monroe, because you'll lose."

He never lost. Didn't she know that? He took his own sunglasses off so she could see the seriousness in his eyes. "I'll bet you a reenactment."

She stopped dead in the sand. "Excuse me?"

"If I can remember more details about the night than you can, I get a reenactment. On the beach. Tonight. Maybe again the next night."

She shook her head, the only sound she could make was a disbelieving laugh. "And what if I win? What do I get?"

"A reenactment. That way we both win."

Just as her jaw dropped, he reached down and sealed the deal with that kiss he'd been wanting all day long.

BLOOD RUSHED THROUGH Kendra's head, deafening her and drowning out the sound of the waves. For stability, she reached up and grabbed Deuce's rock-hard shoulders just as he opened his mouth and deepened the kiss. Wide warm lips covered hers and the tip of his tongue slid against her teeth with unbelievable familiarity, a welcome invasion that made her whole body clutch.

He wrapped his arms around her and eased her against his body with a low, slow, nearly inaudible groan.

"For example, I remember that you like," he whispered huskily against her mouth as he broke the kiss, but not the body contact, "very deep, very long French kisses."

Arousal, quick and sharp, twisted inside her, forming a knot in her tummy and between her legs.

She dug deep for sanity and a clear head, but he ran his hands down to the small of her back and pressed her hips against his. Her throat felt as if she'd swallowed a mouthful of sand.

"And I remember," he said, making a tiny left-right motion with his hips, "that you can have an orgasm fully clothed and in the car."

Her hips responded with a mind of their own, driving against him with some uncontrollable need to prove him right. She couldn't argue with his memory. She couldn't argue with his body, kisses or silky voice either.

Lifting her face to his, she kissed him again for the sheer overwhelming joy of it, stalling the inevitable with one more dance of their tongues, one more minute of heaven.

With a long, deep breath she managed to ease him back and end the kiss.

"All lucky guesses," she told him. "You could be talking about any of the dozens of girls you seduced on this beach."

"No," he denied. "No one on this beach but you."

Wouldn't she like to believe that?

"I already told you two things you forgot," he teased. "And I bet you don't even remember what I wore that night."

She frowned and scoured her well-visited memory bank. Surely she knew every thread of clothing he had on that night. But all she could see was his face. His bare chest. His… Oh, of all the things to forget. What was he wearing that night? She had to blame the memory loss on the blood draining from her head to that achy spot between her legs. "Are you asking me if I remember what you wore?"

"You're stalling for time, Ken-doll. You heard me. What did I have on that night?" He raised a suggestive eyebrow. "That is until you undressed me."

Oh, yes, they'd undressed each other. She could still remember the feel of his flesh as she pushed his clothes away. As she closed her fingers around his shaft.

Another bolt of that heat lightning singed her at the thought.

She bit her lip and narrowed her eyes, infusing her tone with confidence. "A baseball shirt and jeans."

"Nice guess, but wrong."

"You don't remember what you were wearing," she countered. "You probably don't remember what you wore yesterday." But she did.

"Funny thing is, I do remember." He tunneled his fingers into the hair at the nape of her neck, his large hands engulfing the back of her head. Her stomach braced for another dizzying kiss. "I'd gone to the bar that night after having dinner with some relatives who were still in town for the funeral." He *did* remember that night. The realization that it was important to him made her almost as lightheaded as the way he was holding her. "So I had dress pants on, something like these. I wouldn't wear those with a baseball jersey." His smile was victorious.

"Okay, so you remember some things. But if we had a contest, I'd win." Why she'd admit that the night meant so much to her, she wasn't sure. Probably because the game was fun. His hands were fun. That last kiss was way more than fun.

"Care to exchange more memories, sweetheart? I'm really looking forward to the historic reenactment of..." He paused for a moment.

Bingo. She had him. "You don't remember the date."

"I do. Of course I do. It was June. Before the All-Star break." He dragged his hands up and down her spine, closing his eyes as though he was memorizing the feel of her, and for a moment she thought she might melt right into the sand. "June twelfth," he said. "A Friday night."

"I'm in trouble," she said with a laugh. "You're starting to scare me."

"I told you, I remember everything."

"The date and the style of my bra. Hardly everything."

He pulled her close again, putting his mouth up against her ear. "I remember what you said afterwards."

I love you, Deuce Monroe. I've always loved you and I always will.

Her heart really did stop, then it thundered in double-time against her chest. She waited for him to repeat her declaration and knew she couldn't deny it.

"You said…" His breath tickled her ear. "'I can't wait for the next time.'"

Yes, she'd said that, too. Maybe he didn't remember the whole I-love-you-forever-and-always part. She could hope.

"Guess what, Miss Locke?"

She backed away from his treacherous lips and looked at him. "What?"

"I think I out-remember you."

"Not a chance." Was there?

"What did I say to you when you left?"

She regarded him, looking for clues in those eyes. How could she forget? But she had? She had no memory of his last words to her. "You said, 'See ya later, Ken-doll.'"

He shook his head. "I win. I'll pick you up tonight after the bar closes. Say, midnight?"

"What did you say?" she asked, trying to ignore the voice in her head that was screaming *yes, I'll be ready at midnight!* "When we said goodbye, Deuce. What did you say to me?"

"I'll tell you tonight. Or better yet…" he grinned at her the way he did right after he left some poor kid at the plate not knowing what had hit him. "I'll tell you tomorrow morning when you wake up."

CHAPTER EIGHT

EVERY TIME THE FRONT door of Monroe's opened, Deuce glanced up from the almost empty bar, expecting to see Kendra. Not that he really thought she'd come down to the bar to speed up the closing process so they could get to the beach…but he hoped. His blood simmered at the thought. She wouldn't back out, would she?

After all, a bet was a bet.

At eleven o'clock, only two stragglers sipped beers and watched the end of a Celtics game at one end of the bar. The medieval game-playing twins had abandoned their jousting to work a couple of girls at a table, but they'd already closed their tab. A few other tables were ready to call it a night.

Very soon, he could close up and collect on his bet. At the sound of the great door creaking open, he turned to see Martin Hatcher pulling off a bright-green trucker cap as he entered.

His eyes lit up at the sight of Deuce. "There's my favorite knuckleball man," he said, ambling over to the bar.

"Kind of late for you, isn't it, sir?" Would the Hatchet Man settle in for a few hours? Not that Deuce wouldn't enjoy the conversation, but tonight he wanted to close as early as possible.

Martin slipped onto a barstool and crossed his arms. "I'm retired, son. So it's no longer a school night for me. How about a draft?"

"Coming right up." Deuce poured the golden liquid, tilting the glass to create the perfect head. "Here you go, sir."

Martin raised the glass in salute. "Lose the *sir,* Deuce."

Deuce laughed and leaned on the bar. "You'll always be the voice of authority to me, Martin."

The glass halted halfway to his mouth as his lips twitched. "I've never been the voice of authority to you, Deuce. You always marched to your own…authority."

Then he drank. One of the bar patrons held up a twenty and Deuce cashed them out and said good night. Two down, a few to go. He moved back down to where the ex-principal sat.

"Been to any more practices?" Martin asked.

Deuce shook his head, but Martin's look stopped him. He could never fudge the truth with the Hatchet Man. "All right. One. Well, two."

Martin released a soft, knowing chuckle. "How's the elbow doing?"

"Not bad, actually." He rubbed the tender spot, and blessed the workouts he'd been secretly doing every day. "I can actually throw a knuckleball again. But man cannot live by knuckleballs alone."

"Keep working out and you can play again."

"I can play now," Deuce said defensively. "It's the lawyers who blackballed me from baseball, not the doctors. I'd need more P.T., but…" his voice drifted away. "Anyway, I'm a barkeep now."

"You can't stay away from a ball field," Martin said with a wry smile. "I remember that was the only way I could really get to you. Detention, suspension, parental call-ins, nothing worked but keeping you off the field."

"That was where I wanted to be," Deuce agreed. "Although detention had its side benefits. That's where you find the cute bad girls."

Martin laughed at that and sipped some more draft, then glanced around. "But not your business partner," he mused. "She never did anything bad."

But she would. In an hour or two.

"Where is Kendra?" Martin asked.

Hopefully, slipping into something…easy to slip out of. "She only works days. I cover the nights."

"Interesting arrangement," Martin mused. "How's that going?"

"We're working on some changes." Deuce flipped on the water to wash the last of the glasses as a burst of laughter erupted from the Gibbons's table. Maybe they were getting ready to take the ladies home for a wild night of medieval sportsmanship.

"As I understand it, Kendra was already working on some changes for Monroe's. Did she tell you about them?"

Deuce looked up from the sink. "Of course. I've seen all the plans."

"What do you think?"

The truth was, he thought that her plans were great. But he also could make a sports bar profitable. Deep inside, he hoped for a compromise, but couldn't imagine her agreeing to it. "Jury's out."

Martin sipped. "She's been working on the whole cyber café and artists' space for a long time."

"Two years," Deuce noted. "That's how long she's been part-owner of this place."

"Oh, no, Deuce. She's really been at Monroe's for nearly ten or more." Martin's gray eyes looked particularly sharp. "Since she was first in college."

Why did Deuce get the idea he was being worked by

the principal? "I remember," he said, turning to stack the clean glasses.

"But then she dropped out."

Deuce froze at the odd tone in Martin's voice. Was he accusing him of something…or was that just residual fear of the principal teasing Deuce. He reached for more glasses, clearing his throat. "She said she had a bad break-up."

When Martin didn't respond, Deuce looked up. The man wore the oddest expression.

"You know women," Deuce said, the old awkwardness of sitting in the principal's office sluicing through him. "They get…weird."

Martin just nodded, then slid his glass to make room for his elbows as he leaned toward Deuce. "I'd hate to see her unhappy again."

What was he saying? "Do you think my being here is making her unhappy?"

Martin frowned. "Did I say that?"

"Well, what are you saying?" Deuce demanded.

"I'm saying that she has—or had—big plans for this place and I happen to know they don't include a sports bar."

Staring at the man, Deuce searched his mind for a reasonable explanation for Martin's strange message. Then the truth dawned on him. He started laughing, which made the old Hatchet Man's eyes spark like cinders.

"Martin, I'm not going to coach the high-school baseball team. You can't psyche me into it with guilt over Kendra's café plans, sir."

"You call me sir again and I'll write you up, son." He winked and pushed his empty glass forward. "What do I owe you?"

Deuce shook his head. "Truth is, I owe you, Martin. That one's on the house."

"Maybe I'll see you at practice this week. I'm working the grounds."

They both knew he would.

When the last glass was clean, the register was cashed out and the night's draw was tucked into the pouch, Deuce locked the drawer in Kendra's office and pocketed the keys. As he pushed the chair back from the desk, his foot bumped into something soft.

Bending over, he spied the nylon tote bag Kendra carried between work and home. She must have left it when they went to Fall River and forgotten to pick it up before she'd gone home.

Well, she had been distracted. He grinned at the thought, reaching for the bag. Did she really need it tonight? With one finger, he inched the zippered opening to see what it contained. A laptop, a calculator, some folders, a red spiral notebook.

Nothing earth-shattering.

Deuce took the bag with him to his car, sliding it behind the passenger seat and made a mental note to leave it with the keys on Diana's table for her to find when she came over to walk Newman.

Correction. Tomorrow morning, Kendra would wake up in his bed. Then he could give her the bag in person.

He gunned the Mercedes's engine and pulled onto High Castle with a sense of anticipation he hadn't felt since his last opening day.

FROM BEHIND THE TWO-FOOT protection of a sand dune, in the nearly moonless night, Kendra heard the rumble of the Mercedes's engine. Blue halogen headlights sliced into the night.

A trickle of guilt wound its way through her chest. Hiding out on the beach was a chicken thing to do, but if Deuce knocked on her door and melted her with that smile and annihilated her with that mouth…she'd be dead. She'd had all night to think about the "reenactment" he proposed, knowing full well he was basically asking her to sleep with him.

And, Lord have mercy, she wanted to say yes. Her skin practically ignited at the thought of giving in to the full-body ache he caused. She'd never say no if he had her out on West Rock Beach. Or in a bedroom. Or a car. Or the kitchen. Or…

The lights faded and she heard a car door. Kendra sank deeper into the sand.

She just had to keep avoiding him, and when Seamus and Diana returned, she'd tell them…*what?* She wasn't sure yet. The bar was profitable, no doubt. But the cyber café revenues were up as well. She was no closer to "working it out" with Deuce—as Seamus had instructed—than the day this all started.

She was, however, closer to giving in to that toe-curling attraction that had blinded and stupefied her for, oh, twenty-odd years now.

She imagined Deuce rounding the side of the house, peering at her darkened, quiet beach bungalow. Would he give up then, or would he knock?

He'd assume she was dead asleep…or out for the night. Then he'd surely go back to Diana's and slide the kitchen door open.

Newman would bark, so she'd know the coast was clear. After fifteen minutes, she'd sneak back into her house. Alone. Hungry. Achy.

Wrapping the blanket tighter around her shoulders, Kendra studied the C-shaped moon slice, surrounded by blackness and the smattering of stars that were always visible on Cape Cod.

Too bad she was a coward. They could have had one killer of a reenactment.

She closed her eyes and imagined his kiss, his hands, his breath in her mouth. A shudder quivered through her and she forced herself to listen for the noises to assure her he'd given up the idea and gone to bed. Alone. Hungry. Achy.

Why hadn't Newman barked yet? She wanted to rise up on her knees and peer over the sandbank, but with her luck that would be the very second Deuce chose to scope the beach.

Behind her, the grass rustled. She clamped her mouth closed to keep from even breathing, assessing how close the sound of that footfall really was.

She sensed him—felt his presence, sniffed his scent—before she actually saw him. Then he was there, not ten feet from where she sat, standing on the crest of the mound. Her eyes had long ago adjusted to the dark and she could make out every detail of him. His powerful chest rose and fell with a deep sigh. He stabbed his hair with one hand, leaving a lock loose on his brow, then he shoved both hands deep into the pockets of his jeans, his gaze out to the sea.

Surely the hammering staccato of her heart would give her away.

But he didn't seem to hear. He inhaled again, and closed his eyes as he let out the breath, shaking his head softly as though some thought amused or amazed him.

"Well this is just too damn sad," he said quietly. "I want her."

The admission drew a soft gasp from her throat, and he spun toward her, his surprise palpable even in the darkness. "Kendra?" In two long strides, he loomed above her. "What are you doing out here?" he asked.

She dropped part of the blanket on the sand and patted it for him to sit down. "Trying to avoid you."

He blew out a laugh and settled next to her, then reached over and brushed a strand of hair she hadn't realized fell on her cheek. His fingertips sent heat through her. "You're awfully damn good at that."

"Evidently I can run, but...well, you know."

He laughed again. "You don't have to hide, sweetheart. All you have to say is you'd rather not see me and I'll understand." He somehow managed to get closer, his body warmth far more effective than the blanket. "I won't hold you to the reenactment."

She nibbled on her lower lip, regarding him. "Anyway, we're at the wrong beach."

He smiled at her. "Let's not get hung up with the particulars."

She had no chance against this man. And, really, why fight it? The dark lock of hair still grazed his eyebrow, and under it, his eyes had the smoky, soulful darkness of arousal and desire. She could just smell the waves of his sexual appetite. Well, that might be a little of the Wing Man's chicken, but for some reason, that smelled sexy, too.

"I'm pathetic," she admitted, giving in to the urge to drop her head on his shoulder. "I even like the smell of barbecue on you."

He responded by pulling her into a hug. "Yeah? Bet it's nice mixed with the beer."

Oh, Lord, she had no chance.

He let out a small, low sound of masculine approval, sliding his hand under her hair to pull her closer. "We had a good night," he said softly. "About eight hundred dollars."

"We had a good day," she countered. "About six fifty."

"What a team," he chuckled. "Too bad we can't figure out a way to work the same hours."

She looked at him, knowing the kiss was inevitable. As he covered her mouth with his, she closed her eyes and let the sensations of warmth and want roll over her with the same force with which the ocean hit the sand.

"Oh, Deuce," she whispered into the kiss. "You're really messing with my plans."

"Forget your plans, sweetheart." His palm pressed the side of her breast and she ached for him to touch her.

"Is this the reenactment?"

"Mmmm." Slowly, easily, he leaned her back on the blanket. "Could be." He skimmed the rise of her breast, lingering on the pebbled nipple at the peak. "Remember that?"

A sharp, powerful bolt of desire stabbed through her, settling low between her hips and igniting the need to rock against him. "Yes, I do."

He eased on top of her, letting her feel the hardness of his erection as he spread his hand over her breast.

"Do you remember…" he kissed her hair, her eyelids, and slid his hand under the fabric of the cotton sweater she wore. "This?"

She gasped as the heat of his fingers seared her flesh, dropping her head back into the sand. She felt the grains crunch under her hair, and a sense of déjà vu flashed in her mind. "I do," she managed to say.

"And…" He grazed her stomach and found the clasp of her bra. "This?" He laughed softly as he unclipped it effortlessly. "I definitely remember this."

He kissed her again, parting her lips with his tongue, taking hers with authority. He tasted like mint, like soda, like…Deuce.

With his other hand, he pushed the sweater higher as their hips rolled against each other in perfect rhythm. Both hands on her, he spread the silken fabric of her bra and cupped her breasts, then lowered his head to suck her nipple.

Blood roared through her ears, deafening her to the sound of the sea. All she could hear was his ragged breathing, his whispered endearments, the sound of her own soft gasps with each flick of his tongue.

He traveled back up to her mouth, his whole body now covering hers.

She grasped the firm muscles of his backside, squeezing through the denim and pushing harder against him, vaguely aware of the sand that had somehow slipped between her fingertips.

Sand and Deuce. They belonged together.

With one hand, he unsnapped her jeans. She felt the fabric loosen, steeled herself in anticipation of his touch on her stomach. Still she quaked as his hand slid into her panties and a pleasure whipped through her.

"I remember this…" His tongue traced her mouth. "This sweet place." He put his lips against her ear and his breath fired through her. "I remember exactly what it felt like to be inside of you."

He parted her delicate skin and grazed his fingertip over her, mimicking the action of his finger with his tongue in her ear. A moan of delight caught in her throat. Very, very slowly he eased deeper into her.

"I want to make love to you again, Kendra." His voice was no more than hot, sweet air against her skin.

I'll call you.

The words suddenly reverberated in her head like a cannon shot into the night.

I'll call you.

"What?" Deuce lifted his head from her neck, his fingers suddenly still.

She didn't even realize she'd spoken. "You asked me what the last words you said were on...that night. You said 'I'll call you.' I just remembered."

He eased his hand away from her, and lifted himself just enough to look into her eyes. She half expected disgust, a look of "how can you hold me to that now?"

But that's not what she saw. Pain and remorse flashed in his eyes just before he closed them.

"I'm sorry I hurt you," he said gently. "It was a lousy thing to do."

Her heart twisted. "You had your reasons." Good heavens, was she rationalizing *for* him? She pushed him a little farther away. "But that doesn't make it right."

"No," he agreed. "It doesn't."

He removed his hand completely. Why had she remembered those words? Why had she said them out loud? Why couldn't he just be a normal, oversexed guy and keep going?

But he reached for one side of her bra, then the other. Disappointment spiraled through her and he covered her breasts, snapped the clasp and dropped a soft kiss on her cleavage.

"We're done," she said knowingly.

"Nowhere near." He tugged her sweater back over her chest and stomach. "I just also remember how uncomfortable the sand is." He eased her zipper up, his gaze on her face. "This time, we're going to be warm and snug in my bed." He tucked his hands under her shoulders and gently lifted her. "And tomorrow, I will most definitely call you. About six times. Before noon."

Before she could respond, he kissed her again and

pulled them both into a stand. The blanket fell off her shoulders, around her feet.

"Will you spend tonight with me, Kendra?" There was something so tender, so genuine about the question that her knees nearly buckled.

How could he have been so sweet, so loving, so tender? Was it all an act?

The words, in her own handwriting, danced before her eyes. She closed them to block out the mental image.

Could she be falling for him again?

This was it. Her moment to say no. Her senses had returned, she was on her feet and could use them to run right into her house and lock the door. Or straight into his bed and certain heartache. She took a deep breath, looked up at him and waited for "yes" or "no" to tumble out of her mouth.

"By the way," he whispered into her ear before she spoke, "You never heard the last words I said to you because you'd already closed the door."

She waited, her pulse jumping.

"I said that in my own way, I'd always loved you, too."

And then her decision was made.

EVEN IN THE MOONLIGHT, he could see the emotion spark in her silvery-blue eyes. A little fury, a lot of fear. Before he could decide what she was feeling, she jerked out of his grip, scooped up her blanket, and bolted up toward her house.

"Kendra," he called, taking long strides to easily catch up with her. "Where are you going?"

"Away from you."

He stopped for a moment, letting her get ahead, letting his blood settle and his brain work again. "Why?" It was the best he could manage, considering how far from his brain the blood actually was.

All he got was a dismissive wave of her hand over her shoulder as she continued her march toward the beach house.

He caught up with her as she reached the door. "What's the matter?"

As she spun around, he realized there was no fear, just fury in those eyes. "How dare you make fun of me...of that."

"Of what? I did say that, Kendra, and I meant it."

She speared him with a disbelieving look and crossed her arms. "Liar."

"I am not lying." He practically sputtered. "You were always—"

She put her hand over his mouth. "Don't. Don't make it worse. You didn't need to make that up to get me to go to bed with you, Deuce. It was pretty obvious which way I was going on that one."

Circling her narrow wrist with his fingers, he moved her hand from his mouth. "I wasn't saying that to get you to go to bed with me," he said softly. "I was trying to tell you that all those years when you were young, all those years you..." He didn't know what to call her feelings for him. He knew they were there. He'd seen it in her eyes. Hero worship?

"Crush," she supplied. "I'd call what I had a crush."

He smiled. "I like that. Anyway, I was always aware of you."

"Deuce. I was *ten*."

"I know," he agreed. "I was aware of you like a sister, then you..." He shook his head. This wasn't coming out right. Closing his eyes, he took a deep breath. "The way you looked at me—like I was the only guy on earth—

made me feel alive, Kendra. It made me feel great. I was just trying to say I loved you for it."

She searched his face, saying nothing. Wondering, no doubt, if he was even capable of the truth. He owed her the truth.

"That's why I never called," he finally said. "Because I kind of sensed I wasn't worthy of that level of…love."

She stared at him for a good thirty seconds before speaking. She shook her head, inched backwards. "You treated me like a baby for ten years, then a pariah for the next ten."

He couldn't argue with that. "Now I'd like to treat you like a woman." But that might be pushing it, and he knew it. He didn't wait for a response. "But that's probably not fair to you either."

She opened her mouth to speak, but he reached across the space between them and eased her jaw up.

"Shhh. You don't have to say anything." He kissed her forehead and ignored the hole in his gut. He had to turn around, walk away and let her be. He'd hurt her and he had no right to pick up where they'd left off as if…as if not calling her was acceptable.

It wasn't.

"Good night, Kendra." He turned and started across the stone path. He had his foot on the first of the wooden steps up to Diana's house when he felt her grip on his elbow.

"Wait a second."

He didn't move, giving her a chance to speak. When she didn't, he slowly turned around.

"It *is* fair." She took a deep breath and closed her eyes. "If you really see me as a grown woman, an equal, if you really can forget that little girl who worshipped you, and forget about the first time we…"

He grazed her cheek with his knuckle. "I'll never forget

the first time, but I sure would like another chance. With this woman." He let his thumb caress her lower lip and felt it quiver under his touch. "This grown, beautiful, smart, sexy woman."

"If that's true, then…"

"Then…what?"

She reached up and pulled him to her, seizing his mouth in a hot, demanding kiss.

"Is that a yes?" he asked softly.

"I just can't fight this anymore."

Neither could he.

CHAPTER NINE

DEUCE NEVER LET HER say another word. It was as though he thought if they talked any more, she'd change her mind. Even if he hadn't pulled her into his chest, even if he hadn't possessively turned the kiss into his own, even if he hadn't flattened his hands against her bottom and pressed her stomach against his surging hard-on, Kendra wouldn't have changed her mind.

Life was too short and this magic was too dizzying to let him walk away. Tonight, she wouldn't think about the past, about mistakes or bad choices. All she wanted to think about was the cliff-dropping thrill of making love to Deuce.

He started to pull her toward Diana's.

"No," she whispered, tilting her head in the direction of her bungalow. "My house. My bed."

He groaned softly and lifted her to her toes, letting her stomach ride the ridge of his erection. "Any house, any bed," he said huskily. "But only this woman."

Her heart plummeted with a roller-coaster dip.

They kissed across the walkway, pausing at her door for him to slide his hands over her breasts and down her waist, dipping his fingertips into the top of her jeans.

She rocked her hips into him, her body so hot and wet that if he'd pushed her pants down, she could have made love on the porch, standing.

He fumbled with the door that she hadn't even locked,

guided her inside, still kissing, still exploring, little desperate moans and surprised sighs escaping both of them.

The bungalow was pitch-black when the door closed behind them, and without turning on a light, Deuce yanked her sweater over her head and pushed her against the wall next to the door. His hands were everywhere, on her skin, under her bra, in her hair.

She ripped his shirttail out of his pants, silently cursing the buttons that she'd have to unfasten in the dark. Before she had the first one undone, he'd unsnapped her bra, easing the straps over her shoulders as he dipped his head to suckle her.

She almost screamed when his mouth closed over her breast.

Sliding his hands up the sides of her breasts, he caught her under her arms and pushed her up the wall, off her feet, never taking his mouth from the hardened nipple he sucked.

"Deuce," she half laughed, half moaned, still fighting one of his shirt buttons. "The bedroom?"

He licked the tip of her breast, his eyes closed with the pleasure. "I have to taste you."

The longing in his voice almost did her in. He wanted her as much as she wanted him and the thought nearly melted her.

Lowering her to her feet, he captured her mouth for another kiss, caressing the breasts he'd just tasted, giving her the opportunity to finish the damn buttons.

Finally she could push his shirt open and press herself against the coarse hairs of his chest.

As she did, he thrust his erection against her.

Her whole lower half coiled with want. She skimmed her hands over his granite shoulders, clasped them behind his neck and raised herself up, just for the sheer bliss of riding the hardness between his legs. Denim against denim and it was almost enough to give her one mind-boggling vertical orgasm.

With his hands on her backside, he easily lifted her higher and she wrapped her legs around his hips, letting her head fall back, her eyes closed.

"We aren't going to the bedroom, are we?" she managed to ask.

"All right." He was already carrying her there. "But it better be really close."

"At the end of the hall. One room. One bed. No turns."

"Good." He growled the word into a kiss, just as he crossed the threshold of her bedroom, and laid her on top of the comforter.

Like a magician, he slid her out of her jeans and ripped off his. More hot kisses trailed from her throat down her breasts, over her ribs and navel. He licked at the lacy edge of her underwear, his hair tickling her skin.

Her heart hammered inside her chest, her throat tightened with a scream of desire and her hips seem to rise and fall without any effort on her part.

She dug her fingers deeper against his scalp.

He trapped the flimsy material between his front teeth and began to pull them off her, as though taking the time to use his hands would be too much.

Neither one could slow the need to eliminate anything that came between them—clothes, time or space. He shimmied her underwear over her backside and down her legs.

Blood rushed through her head as he looked at her, the darkness stealing her chance to really study his face.

He said her name, once and again. Lowering his head, he stroked her with his tongue, slowly at first, crazy slow, then faster, shooting fire straight up her body. She grasped his head, spread her legs and surrendered to his mouth.

With wild, driving licks, he circled her sex, invaded her body and sucked the tender flesh until pleasure and pain knotted her. She bucked into his mouth. His fingers closed over her buttocks. Her flesh spasmed under his kisses, then, just before a climax rocked her, he feathered her stomach with kisses, drying his lips on her cleavage and stopping just long enough to suckle her hardened nipple.

His shaft found the heat between her legs. She was wet and warm and swollen with the need for him. Her throat too dry to speak, she tried to say his name, but her hips just rose and his erection inched into her.

"Kendra." His voice was as raw as her throat. In the dark, she could see the ache on his face, the need in his furrowed brow. "I don't have a…"

Condom.

Reality crashed down on her like a stinging shower of ice.

"Do you?" he asked hopefully.

She shook her head, as a million thoughts vied for space in her brain. Did she? Would she do without? Didn't he? And, oh, not again. Not *again.*

He let out a breath of pure frustration. "I have one. I have to go get it."

Diana's house might as well have been a million miles away.

"Not in your wallet?" She asked hopefully. Surely a guy like Deuce Monroe didn't leave the house unarmed.

He gave his head a vicious shake, and traced a line down her stomach. He slipped one finger into her moist flesh. "Just let me finish what I started."

For some reason, that struck her as terribly unselfish. Wasn't Deuce full of surprises today? She turned on her side, a move that eased his thick erection right into the space between her legs. "Not good enough, honey. I want you inside me."

He closed his eyes and slid along her, the velvet hardness of his erection torturing her flesh. "Right where I want to be." His breathing was still ragged and torn and under her hand she could feel his heart thudding as fast as hers.

"Go get one," she whispered. "Hurry. Don't stop to walk Newman."

He gave her a half smile. "Actually, it's in the car."

"They give you a box with every new Mercedes?"

He laughed. "I put it in the glove compartment this morning."

"You thought we'd have sex on the way to Fall River?"

"Hey," he chuckled, sliding in and out of the vortex of her legs. "A guy can hope."

He hoped? For her? She pressed her pelvis into him and sucked in a long, slow breath. "Go. No one is around. Grab those boxers, and get whatever you have in the car."

Reluctantly, he lifted himself from the bed.

"How many did you bring?" she asked.

"Just one..." He pulled on his boxers and grinned in the dark. "Box of twelve."

She giggled and watched him leave the room, an insane and wild and happy thrill dancing through her.

When she heard the front door open and close she scooted higher on the bed and slid between the cool sheets.

"I love him," she whispered and closed her eyes to let the joy of the realization rock her as thoroughly as his body just had. "I have always loved him and I always will." There was nothing, absolutely nothing, wrong with making love to someone you loved.

She glanced at the bedside clock. What was taking so long?

Dropping her head on the pillow, she ran her hands over her naked body, feeling her curves and flesh the way he did.

Maybe there could be a future. Maybe they could really and truly be together. Own Monroe's...together.

Was that so crazy?

The possibility sent wild sparks through her, curling her toes, making her heart tumble around as if it were no longer connected to her body.

Maybe Deuce could love her the way she loved him.

Finally, she heard the front door and she inched a little higher, purposely leaving the sheets low around her waist.

She heard his footsteps in the hall.

Suddenly the overhead light blinded her and she blinked, instinctively pulling up the sheet with one hand and shading her eyes with the other.

Deuce stood in the doorway, a look of horror and rage and confusion on his face.

"What's the matter?"

Something flew across the air and landed on the bed with a soft thump.

She blinked again.

All she could see was the tattered red cover.

"When the hell were you going to tell me there was a baby, Kendra?"

HE COULD BARELY speak, rage pounding through him, fighting for space in his veins against all that hot-blooded lust.

A *baby.*

Kendra's face was as white as the sheet that barely covered her, her eyes and mouth wide with shock. "You...you *stole* my journal?"

He snorted and took a step toward the bed, unable to tear his gaze from her, no matter how much he wanted to pick up that notebook and throw it as far as his injured arm could. "Hardly a time to think about ethics, Kendra." One more step, and she pulled the sheet higher. "Since you obviously have *none.*"

The fear on her face morphed instantly into something else. Her eyes narrowed to blue slivers as she leaned forward and pointed a finger at him, oblivious to the slip of the sheet when she let it go. "Don't you dare talk to me about ethics, Seamus Monroe. You had unprotected sex with the little sister of your best friend and never bothered to pick up the phone, ever, and say so much as thank you."

He opened his mouth to argue, then shut it again. There was no arguing with that. At least she didn't throw in the virgin part. Blowing out a pained breath he hadn't realized he'd been holding, he closed his eyes. "You should have called me."

"Maybe I should have." She slumped against the bed, but her gaze remained sharp. "But I kept waiting for you to do that."

Guilt punched him. "If I'd known…" His voice trailed off and his gaze landed on the worn notebook. He hadn't purposely read it, of course. "It fell out of your bag. I moved the bag to the front seat to remember to bring it in, and the whole thing spilled, then…I glanced down and saw the words on the page."

Lit by the inside car light. Damn. If he'd left the top down, he'd never have seen those unbelievable words.

Deuce's baby would have been a girl.

He'd frozen as the words slugged him. He'd read it twice. Felt the world slip sideways, then read on.

I wish I didn't know that, but the doctor told me.

The hospital put her little body to rest today.

He'd read more, but the first few sentences had singed his memory, where they would no doubt remain for the rest of his life.

Stunned, he'd sat outside in the car and tried to process what those few sentences told him. She'd been pregnant, lost the child and had been far enough along to have a body to bury.

And he'd never even known about it.

He'd stumbled back in the house with the notebook, without a condom, but with more anger and shame and betrayal than he'd ever known.

She pointed toward the hall. "I want to get dressed. Can you leave?"

"No," he said simply. "I want to talk about this."

"I just meant leave the room. We'll talk." She pulled the sheet up. "Fully clothed."

The fact that he'd just seen her naked, kissed her sense-less, and nearly shared the most intimate of personal re-lations with her seemed moot. He grabbed his jeans and shirt, then stepped out into the hall, dressing quickly in the bathroom. When he came out, her bedroom door was closed.

In the kitchen, he found coffee beans and a grinder. Questions, dozens of them, played in his head, as he went through the process of coffeemaking as he'd seen it done at Monroe's.

A baby.

The impact still kicked him in the head and heart.

And how had she handled that alone? How many people knew and didn't tell him? How far along had she been before… He sat at the table and stared at nothing while the coffee brewed.

God, why hadn't she told him?

He didn't actually focus until Kendra entered the room. She'd put on sweat pants and a T-shirt, and her little bit of makeup was smudged under her eyes as though she'd cried, or at least rubbed her eyes.

"I thought you hated coffee," she said, opening a cabinet and pulling out a mug.

"It seemed appropriate," he responded. "I think we're going to have a long night."

And not at all the kind of night he'd been envisioning an hour ago. The desire to climb *on* and *in* her still bubbled under the surface, pulling at him, making him feel guilty somehow. How could she have been willing to make love with that lie between them?

"How do you take it?" she asked, pouring a second mug.

"With whiskey." At her look, he offered up an apologetic gesture. "Hey, I'm Irish. But I'm also a wuss, so give me lots of milk and sugar."

Her movements were spare as she made both cups the same, her hands shaking just a tiny bit, her breath still a little uneven.

"You don't want to have this conversation any more than I do," he noted.

She turned from the counter, eyes blazing again. "Don't make this about you, Deuce."

"This is not about me," he countered. "This is about…" My *child.* Loss gripped him. "This is about what I did and didn't know."

As she settled into the chair across the table from him, she leaned her elbows on the table, and rested her chin on her knuckles. Her eyes looked sad, her complexion pale.

Not the fiery, sexy, hungry look he'd seen in the moonlight. Not the lover he'd had in bed. But a woman who'd experienced a great deal of pain.

He swore softly, fighting the urge to reach across the table and apologize for being the one to put her through that. Instead, he reached down for the anger he'd felt before. He needed answers. "Why didn't you tell me?"

She studied the coffee in her cup. "I just couldn't."

"Didn't you think I had a right to know?"

Her throat moved as she swallowed but didn't answer.

"Were you sure...I was...the..."

Slowly, she lifted her gaze and the expression "if looks could kill" reverberated in his head. "Don't you dare go there," she said, a cutting edge in her whisper.

Then where could he go? "How far along were you, Kendra? Why don't you tell me what happened?"

She inhaled and sighed. "I was just about seven months pregnant. Twenty-seven weeks, to be precise."

"And you had a miscarriage?"

"A stillbirth." She closed her eyes and took a deep swallow of coffee. When she looked at him, the pain in those blue eyes had turned to anguish. "I noticed that I hadn't felt...her...kicking or hiccupping."

When her voice cracked, he gave into the need to touch her. Rubbing his thumb over the soft skin of her hand, he urged her to continue.

"I went to the doctor and..." she tried to shrug, but her shoulder shuddered instead. "Evidently, she got tangled in the umbilical cord."

He felt the air and life whoosh out of him. "I'm so sorry."

She nodded and blinked, but a tear fell anyway.

"And I'm sorry I wasn't there...for you."

"I handled it," she said stiffly and he had no doubt she did.

"Your parents? Jack?"

She shook her head and took a swipe at that tear. "My parents moved to Florida. They were not happy with me. Jack was in New York."

"Then who took care of you?"

With a tight smile, she said, "Seamus."

For a moment, he thought she meant him. Then the truth dawned on him. His father. His father had been there instead of him.

"Does he know? That it was mine?"

"Damn you, Deuce Monroe." She shoved back from the table with a jerk so forceful and sudden, coffee splashed over their cup rims. "Have you ever, ever thought about anyone but yourself in your entire life?"

He stood as she did. "I didn't ask because I was thinking of me, Kendra. I just—"

"You just wanted to know where you fit in. How this latest piece of news revolves around *you*." She turned from the table and took her cup to the sink, spilling the coffee out with one hand and leaning on the counter for support with the other.

"No." He was behind her in a moment, both hands on her shoulders to turn her toward him. "No, you're wrong. I can't believe you had to go through that alone. I can't believe I was such a stupid, selfish idiot to let you go. I can't believe—"

She put her hand over his mouth. "I get the general idea. Believe it. Now, go."

"Go? You want me to go?"

She leaned back. "You want to pick up where we left off, Deuce? With the arrival of the much-delayed condom?"

The words sliced him. "I want to try and catch up."

"On ten years?"

He nodded, undeterred by her bitterness. She had a right to be bitter. He'd listen, he'd understand, he'd try to make up for the very, very wrong thing he did. "Please."

"Okay, here's the Reader's Digest version. I had to give up my scholarship, work for your dad—and, no, we've never discussed the father of the child, but he's a very smart man—and, at a snail's pace, I got my degree in business and finally decided what I could do with my life and put together a brilliant plan for doing it. And then guess what happened?"

He just stared at her, the lingering acidic taste of coffee in his mouth. "I showed up."

"Bingo."

"To screw up your life again."

Her laugh was without any heart. "I'm lucky that way."

The impact of his arrival, of his cavalier expectations that Monroe's would be his, settled over his heart like the loss of the biggest game of his life.

How dare he? Who did he think he was?

He stepped away from her. Away from her warmth, her gaze, her sadness, all that femininity that he wanted to explore and have. "I'd better go."

"Back to Vegas?" she asked, a mix of hope and dread on her face.

"I was, uh, just thinking of next door."

"Okay," she whispered.

But he couldn't leave until he knew one thing. Why had she kept it from him? "Why didn't you pick up the phone and call me, and tell me. Why didn't you want support or advice or…demand something?" *Like marriage.*

"I guess you didn't read that whole journal."

He'd read enough. "Why?"

She looked up at him, the exquisite sweetness on her face squishing what was left of his heart. "Because I loved you. And I knew you'd do the right thing. And I didn't want to ruin your life or your career."

That kind of love, he suddenly realized, was a far cry from hero-worship. That was unselfish, noble and real.

That kind of love wouldn't have ruined his life at all. Hell, it might have saved his life. But it was too late to find out. All he could do now was somehow make it up to her.

He had to leave—he had to leave Rockingham. He had to let her have her dream, without the constant presence of the man who'd caused her nightmare.

Without another word, he pressed his lips to the top of her head, closed his eyes and inhaled that fresh, sweet scent of Kendra.

"See you later, Ken-doll."

CHAPTER TEN

KENDRA SOMEHOW MADE it through the motions of work the next day, regardless of the fact that her mind felt blank and her heart raw. Oddly enough, she had slept well, collapsing into deep, dreamless sleep after Deuce had left. When she woke, she decided that her sound sleep was a result of a clear conscience.

He finally knew the truth.

She could move on, the secret was out. She could finally let go of the one thing that forever tied her to Deuce. Except that she'd fallen back in love with him.

Oh, get real, Kendra Locke. She'd never fallen out of love with him.

When her office phone rang and she saw Diana Lynn's cell phone number on the caller ID, Kendra pulled together some focus. She opened her laptop so she could give Seamus some figures if he needed them, and hit the speaker phone.

"Kennie, we've made some progress," Seamus's voice filled the little office. "How about you and Deuce? Have you?"

Oh, yeah. Great progress last night. "We're working things out," she assured him. "The bar business has been...pretty good."

"I knew it," the older man said. "That boy has a golden touch."

Absently, she ran her hand down the front of her Monroe's T-shirt. *He sure did.* "How did it go in San Francisco, Seamus?"

"Well, I do have some news."

She held her breath and waited.

"There's one firm out here very interested in funding the project. Very."

There was something not entirely positive about his tone. "What's the 'but'?" she asked. There had to be one.

"They want to see better Internet café revenue numbers. Want to see that we're able to really pick those up by thirty percent for at least a month."

"They have improved," she said, clicking at the program of spreadsheets she'd been using that week. "But…" she peered at the screen. "Not quite thirty percent."

"All we need to do is close this month with a thirty percent increase, Kennie. Any chance we can do that?"

"He's not interested in the bar revenue?" That was up about eighty percent.

"Not if they're going to put the money in the cyber stuff. Think about it, Kennie. You might be able to come up with something."

"Maybe. How's Diana?" Kendra longed for the woman to return. She needed a friend. She needed to confide in another female who might understand the power of Deuce.

"She's great."

"You're leaving tomorrow for Hawaii, right?"

Seamus cleared his throat. "She's in charge of the schedule. We'll be in touch."

Kendra clicked out of the spreadsheet and stared at the blank screen. "I hope so."

"How are you and Deuce getting along?"

Hadn't he asked that already? "Fine."

"Just fine?"

Oh, well, there was this little incident last night. Almost

sex that turned into a total freaking confession. "Yep. He's doing really well with the bar."

"Is he playing ball?"

Kendra frowned. "I think he wanders over to the Rock High field on occasion, but, Seamus, he's *retired*."

She heard him blow out a breath. "Yeah, I know."

Guess Seamus didn't let go of his dreams so easily, either.

"Have a blast in Hawaii."

"Get those numbers up by thirty percent."

Fat chance. "Really, don't give those investment people the idea that I can do that," she said. "Not without the actual funds we need. It's a Catch-22."

"It's worse than that," he said somberly. "There's really no one else but this firm. All the others are just not interested in investing in this competitive and soft market."

Kendra closed her eyes and let the disappointment spiral through her.

"So, if we meet these numbers, we can do the whole project with this firm," Seamus continued. "But if we don't, then Monroe's is going to stay just like it is."

She had to swallow the lump in her throat before she answered. "Then I guess we'll have to try and make that magical number."

"That's my girl," Seamus said with a laugh. "Now I better go find my other one."

"Give her a kiss for me."

"And you give Deuce…my best."

As she held down the speaker phone button to disconnect, she closed her eyes at the catch in his voice. They always had that in common, she and Seamus. They loved that boy.

"You look like he asked you for the witch's broomstick."

She started at the sound of Deuce's voice. "How long have you been out there?"

He strode into the office, all power and dark good looks, and Kendra cursed the way her body hummed at the sight and scent of him.

"Long enough," he said, dropping into the guest chair in front of the desk, "to remember my dad harbors the secret hope that I'm here playing baseball."

She smiled. "Some dreams die hard."

"They sure do," he said, more to himself than to her. "How'd you know I've been to Rock Field, by the way?"

She was done lying to Deuce. "Because I know you better than you know yourself."

He nodded, his eyes rich with warmth. "You know, Ken-doll, it occurred to me this morning that we have quite a history."

She felt heat rise from her heart. "Yes, we do."

"We've known each other almost all our lives, and you spent a good bit of it listening to me grow up in your basement."

The heat blossomed into a full blush. "I did learn a lot through that heat register."

"And we've shared some, well, intimate moments." His gaze darkened and her body tensed. "And some losses."

She waited.

"You were there after my mother. And, well…" They both knew the other loss. It was an old scar for her, but a fresh wound for him.

"We do have a history," she agreed. And, oddly enough, a friendship. It was her problem that she still loved him. And not his fault.

For a long moment, he just looked at her. Then he shook his head a tiny bit, in amazement or confusion or something she couldn't name.

"I don't know, but—" he glanced at the calendar on the wall "—you have a little time before the month ends. And all you need to do is increase your Internet café business by thirty percent."

She almost wept at the change of subject. He'd almost said something…meaningful. Intimate. But the moment had passed. "A thirty-percent increase in profits, yes." She pulled herself back to the business problem at hand. "That would be the witch's broomstick you saw me pining for on the way in."

"Or you have to give up your dream."

Some dreams die hard. The echo of her words filled the room, but she didn't say them out loud again. "I'll find another," she said.

He glanced around her desk, his gaze on her Rolodex. "You have Jack's number at work in there?"

Jack? Why did he want to talk to her brother? A new worry trickled through her. Would he tell Jack the truth about the baby she'd lost? Jack never knew his unborn niece was fathered by Deuce Monroe, and Kendra wanted to keep it that way.

"Don't worry," he said gently, obviously seeing the horror on her face. "I just want to talk to him about something. About an idea I had."

"What is it?"

"I'm not telling." He grinned. "But you can press your face to the nearest heater and listen, if you like."

That made her laugh. "How do you know I did that anyway?"

"'Cause I know you almost as well as you know me."

DESPITE THE HELLACIOUS traffic on the way to Logan Airport, Deuce was waiting at passenger arrival ten minutes before the flight he'd come to greet. As he glanced around the terminal and tracked the progress of the plane's arrival, his mind skimmed through all he'd done in the past week or so.

He'd made incredible progress and was only hours from making Kendra's dream come true, that's what he'd done.

And when he wasn't making arrangements, calling old acquaintances, emailing others and meeting on the sly with Principal Hatcher—he still couldn't think of him as Martin—he was hanging around Kendra to get the most of his last few days and weeks with her.

It took every ounce of willpower he could muster, but he hadn't so much as held her hand. He hadn't kissed her, or snuggled in for a good whiff of her sweet feminine perfume, he hadn't put his arm around her slender waist, or taken any number of opportunities at the bar to slide up behind her and let her know what she did to him.

He should have called after they'd made love; that was a stone-cold fact. He should have been there to help her through the pregnancy, and then…the tragedy. Hell, he could have easily paid for her to continue her education after she'd lost the baby.

And she'd never asked for help or pity. Not once. Now was the time to pay her back and that's what he'd spent the past week doing.

Then he'd have to go back to Vegas. Even though he liked being home, liked being at the bar, liked the idea that he might enjoy a mature and equal relationship with his father. But he'd be a constant reminder to Kendra of the past, and Seamus would want him around a lot. However, before he left, he had to help her get what she wanted.

And that's where Jack Locke came in.

When Jack sauntered across the wide-open terminal and flashed that audacious grin, Deuce knew he had the only man for the job. Kendra's brother was six-foot-two inches of irreverence and trouble who now, at thirty-three, held the position of one of the top art directors on Madison Avenue and was rewarded richly for his talent.

Except you'd never know it by the look of him, in a shirt that might have cost a fortune, but had been worn for a long time, and a pair of jeans that looked as old as their friendship. Burnished brown hair fell to his shoulders, a few locks almost covering that where's-the-party glint in his green eyes.

Jack had been a good-looking teenager, able to charm the panties off half the cheerleaders in Rock High, but as a man he'd grown into someone who looked completely comfortable in his own skin. And still charming those panties off, no doubt.

"Hey, man," Jack dropped his duffel bag and they did a guy's bear hug. "Great to see you, Deuce."

"I thought you came from some big meeting in New York," Deuce said, indicating Jack's well-worn shirt and jeans.

"I'm the art director. Creatives don't dress up." Jack grinned again. "And I half expected to see you in a Snake Eyes uniform."

Deuce laughed as they started toward the parking lot. "Maybe someday," he said. At Jack's look of surprise, he held up a hand. "A *coach's* uniform. I've got my agent looking around for the right gig."

Saying it out loud made it more palatable. The thought of being around major league baseball and not being a player still felt like lead in the pit of his stomach, but it was the only thing he could do.

"That's a pretty big change in plans, isn't it?" Jack asked. "Who put your head in that direction?"

"You know, you won't believe it when I tell you."

"Shoot."

"Martin Hatcher."

"The Hatchet Man?" Jack hooted with a quick laugh. "Where'd you see him? Stop by the detention hall for old time's sake?"

"Actually, I've spent a bit of time with him down at the field, and he comes in the bar once in a while. He's convinced me to give coaching a shot." Even though he had high-school coaching in mind, the seed had taken hold and given Deuce a direction he needed. "Plus, he's been almost as helpful as you on the project."

Jack slowed his step as they reached the elevator. "We're on for tonight?"

"You bet."

"Does Kendra know yet?"

"I told her we're having a little class reunion, but didn't mention you."

Jack laughed softly. "Little, huh?"

Deuce shook his head. "You know, she's so focused on trying to get this magic number for the investment people, that she's sort of distracted and oblivious."

As the elevator doors whooshed shut in the parking garage, Jack looked hard at Deuce. "This is a pretty major effort on your part, all for her, you know?"

Deuce shrugged, pressing the button for the fourth floor even though it was already lit. "She deserves it. She's worked really hard. And…" *And I owe her big.* "It'll be good for the bar in the long run. I mean, the whole artists' community and Internet café thing."

Jack's look was dubious at best.

"Seriously," Deuce continued as they reached the parking lot and he indicated the direction to the car. "She's just got her heart in this cyber café and artists' space, she's worked so hard for it, and her ideas, really, are pretty ingenious, but you know how smart she is…"

Jack stood still and stared. Then he turned toward the terminal and squinted, holding his hand over his eyes and looking hard into the distance.

"What is it?" Deuce asked.

"I'm just seeing if there are any airborne farm animals out there."

"What? Why?"

"'Cause don't you think that if you could fall in love, then pigs could fly?"

Grinning, he gave Jack a friendly push on the back. "Are you kidding? Deuce is wild, man."

"Jacks are better." The response was ingrained.

They laughed as Deuce reached the Mercedes and unlocked the trunk with the click of the keychain. He let Jack give him a hard time about the expensive convertible and steered the conversation to cars and work and old times.

He never answered Jack's question.

KENDRA HADN'T PAID too much attention to Deuce's quiet planning of some kind of high-school reunion, expecting that the gathering of old Rock High friends would generate plenty of bar business, but would do nothing to help her get the elusive thirty-percent increase in the Internet café business.

But she remembered him saying that he'd be gone all day to get someone at Logan Airport, and that left her to worry about Newman. The dog wasn't used to total abandonment, so during a quiet hour in the early afternoon, she slipped out of Monroe's to take him for a walk.

The little guy had been delighted with the company, and not thrilled when it came time to say goodbye. He was particularly playful, but it wasn't funny when he snagged her key ring from the chair and bounded up the stairs of

Diana's house. Kendra hustled after him, taking the steps two at a time.

"Don't you dare, Newman," she called. "I need those keys."

She heard him scramble down the hallway as she turned the corner, but stopped her chase at the sight of an unmade double bed in the guest room.

Deuce's room. Deuce's bed.

Utterly unable to resist the temptation, she entered the room, immediately picking up his distinct masculine scent, and some kind of sixth sexual sense sent a shiver down her spine. She stared at the impression his head had left on the down pillow, drawn to the bunched-up sheets and comforter, mesmerized by the casually dropped T-shirt and a pair of well-worn sleep pants on the floor next to the bed.

Deuce slept *there.*

Newman barked outside the door, and she heard the keys fall on the floor as he scampered downstairs, evidently done with his silly games.

But she couldn't stop *her* silly games…pulled by some powerful force that compelled her to sit at the edge of Deuce's bed, run her hand over his sheets, maybe take a quick sniff of that pillow.

She didn't know whether to laugh or cry at the dismal depths she'd reached. Mooning over his pillow aroma, for God's sake. Why not just whip out her trusty notebook and inscribe "Mrs. Deuce Monroe" in the margin?

Newman's yelp suddenly turned furious and loud, and Kendra stood to call him. But just as she opened her mouth, the sound of men laughing drifted up the stairs. She froze, and listened. Newman was silent, then she heard the oddest thing.

Her brother.

She closed her eyes, rushing back through time, practically feeling the grates of the heat register pressed to her ear, her heart hammering as she waited for Deuce's voice.

Was her imagination playing some kind of trick on her?

But there it was, the low timbre of a voice she'd know anywhere, anytime. Deuce was having a conversation with his best friend, Jack…in earshot of Kendra.

The years slipped away as she listened.

"I wondered when you'd get back to those flying pigs," Deuce said.

Flying pigs? Surely she misunderstood him. She took a few steps to the door, as rapt by his conversation as she had been with his bed.

"It's written all over your face, dude." That was definitely Jack. What was he doing here?

Oh, of course. The *reunion.* He must want to surprise her. Well, the surprise was going to be on him when she skipped into the kitchen and announced—

"You're a goner over her," Jack added, just loud enough for her to hear over her slamming heartbeat. "I can't believe it. Deuce Monroe is in love."

That heartbeat skipped, then stopped. Kendra closed her eyes and gripped the doorjamb. *Deuce is in love?*

"Don't get your pants in a bunch, Jackson," he replied. "She may be your sister, but she's a grown woman."

His…*sister?*

A wave of euphoria and sheer disbelief threatened to unbalance her. Deuce was in love *with her?* Was she hearing this right?

Or was this some really unfair and heartless trick of her imagination and memory? The confession she'd dreamed of hearing through that heating duct for all those years… was it possible? Was she dreaming?

She missed what Jack said because Newman let out a joyful yelp. Someone must have given him a treat.

They laughed at something, and she waited for more. To hear him confirm what she thought she'd heard...that Deuce was in love with her.

"So what are you gonna do about it?" Jack prompted and she made a mental note to kiss him for that later.

Her grip tightened on the wooden frame, her throat so dry she thought she'd choke. What *was* he going to do about it?

I'm going to...love her. Marry her. Give her nine children.

"You don't understand." Deuce's voice was low, but clear enough for her to hear. "This situation is a lot more complicated than you realize."

"Because of the bar?"

"Because..."

Kendra held her breath and waited for the explanation.

"Because I have a habit of getting in the way of your sister's happiness."

Aw, Deuce. You are my happiness.

She heard the pantry door close and Newman barked, drowning out Jack's response. Damn if this wasn't exactly like when the heat blasted on and she couldn't hear what they were saying.

"Yeah, that's true," Deuce agreed.

What was true?

"But there's more to it, isn't there?" Jack asked.

Even up the stairs, she could hear Deuce sigh. She imagined him running a hand through his thick hair, his dark eyes clouded over with trouble. "I'm a...reminder of something I think she'd rather forget."

Her stomach clutched as she waited for them to continue. Hadn't he promised her he wouldn't tell Jack the truth?

"No matter what you think you remind her of, Deuce,

she's been through worse. Believe me. She's one tough cookie."

They had no idea they were talking about the same thing. About her baby, her loss.

"She deserves to have her dreams, Jack. She wants this big cyber gig and artists' space, and I'm afraid I'll just stand in her way."

Did he really believe that?

"Are you sure you're not just copping out of something real?" Jack asked.

"Nope, I'm sure. I'm just trying to recapture my glory days, and Kendra's trying to build something spectacular. I don't belong in Rockingham anymore. I shouldn't have even come back."

She wanted to call out. *No, no, Deuce. You're wrong.*

"I think you're terrified that something or someone might tame wild Deuce," Jack said.

She heard Deuce laugh softly. "If anyone could ever tame wild Deuce, it's Kendra Locke."

The world tipped sideways and Kendra leaned her face against the cool wood of the doorjamb.

It's Kendra Locke.

How many years, how many hours of eavesdropping, how many innings of baseball had she endured just to hear him say that? A distinct rush of exhilaration ricocheted through her.

"But I can't stay here and keep my hands off her. I can't stop thinking about her. I can't stop wanting her."

A lifetime of waiting and listening had come to this.

"So I gotta leave. My agent has some bites from a couple of minor league teams looking for pitching coaches."

The words reverberated as the sliding-glass door opened and closed, Newman's bark now coming from outside.

Peering out the window, she saw Deuce and Jack walking toward the beach, tossing a football back and forth with Newman bounding between them.

"I let you walk away once before, Deuce Monroe," she whispered against the glass. "But not again. Not this time."

Scooping the keys from the floor where Newman had left them, she tiptoed down the stairs and out the front door.

She wasn't going back to work today. She had a reunion to go to tonight and she intended to show up in grand style.

If information was power, she had enough to change his plans. It was time to play the game Deuce's way…wild.

CHAPTER ELEVEN

EVERY SINGLE COMPUTER in Monroe's hummed and flashed and zipped through cyberspace, connecting Rock High graduates around the world. Only about forty or fifty attended the reunion in person, but that had never been the genius behind Deuce's idea. What he wanted—and what he got—was a successful cyber reunion.

From his barstool perch, Deuce surveyed the crowd who drank and laughed with gusto, but more than anything, they emailed and IM'd and reunited with old friends in two dimensions.

This night alone would yield Kendra her thirty percent increase for the month, then he could leave with a free conscience for what he'd done to her all those years ago.

"Did you hear that?" Jack's easy laugh pulled Deuce back to the present. "Martin knew it was me who painted that mural in the girls' locker room."

Martin's gray eyes twinkled as he tipped his draft to his lips. "I don't think Deuce is listening."

"Sure I am. As a matter of fact, I was just thinking about my own sins of the past."

Jack grinned at the older man. "That was a beautiful mural. But I didn't know you realized the extent of my talent, sir."

"Drop the sir," Deuce warned, forcing his focus on the two men. "He'll nail you."

But while Martin explained that he'd overlooked Jack's

locker-room artwork because the baseball team was in the state finals, Deuce's gaze slid once again to the front door. When two young men entered Monroe's, he cursed the disappointment that thudded in his stomach.

Why would he think Kendra would show up tonight? She didn't answer her door or her phone. She was totally missing in action and his fantasies about her "stopping in" to the bar only to realize it was a cyber-reunion set up to benefit her half of the business were just that…fantasies. Like every other thought he'd had about Kendra Locke for the past few weeks.

"I can't believe that, Deuce," Jack said. "Can you?"

"Sorry. What did you say?"

Jack gave him a knowing smirk. "Get your head in the game, dude."

"My head's in the game," he insisted.

"Then listen to the Hatchet Man," Jack said with a sly glance at Martin. "'Cause he's saying something important."

Deuce looked at Martin. "What's that?"

"George Ellis quit the team."

For a moment, Deuce couldn't imagine what that meant. Who was George Ellis and what team did he quit? Then it hit him, more from the expectant look on Martin's face than anything. The Rock High coach and the school baseball team.

"Will he finish the season?" Deuce asked.

"His wife just found out she's pregnant and wants to go home to her family," Martin told him. "George said he'd stay until we have a replacement, but he obviously doesn't want to be away from her that long."

A flash of desire sparked in him. And images of pure bliss followed…coaching Rock High baseball, running the bar at night, married to Kendra and raising some babies of their own.

And then he saw the two men look at each other, as though he'd spoken out loud. Had he?

"My agent's looking for coaching positions with some top teams," he told them, certain the insane thought had been kept to himself. "Sorry."

Martin shrugged. "It was just an idea. I thought there might be something to keep you here."

"There is something to keep him here." Jack looked hard at him. "What the hell's the matter with you, man?"

"I told you, Jack, it's…" The front door open and Deuce looked without thinking. Someone whistled. A loud voice went silent. And Deuce could practically feel his jaw hit his chest with a clunk. "…complicated."

Jack held a beer bottle frozen in midair on its way to his mouth as he stared. "No way," he muttered. "There's no way that's my sister."

Martin beamed. "No reunion is complete without the valedictorian."

Deuce's brain powered down as fast as the computers at night. He tried to think, to comprehend what he saw, but he couldn't do anything but…look.

Black. Leather. Curves. He managed to interpret that much. A sweater cut low and deep. Leather pants, skintight and painted over a round backside and long, tight thighs. Black shoes, with mile-high heels and a dozen sexy straps begging to be unfastened. With his teeth.

Swinging her pale blond hair as she looked from the bar to the dozens of computers and over the crowd, Kendra's piercing blue gaze finally landed on him.

Wordlessly, she strutted over, and he could just imagine the tap of those edible high heels on the hardwood. But the music was too loud to hear. Or was that the blood rushing out of his head and down through his suddenly very alert body?

Jack swooped in and saved him by closing his sister in a bear hug. "I thought I'd shock you," he said with a laugh, pulling back to look at her. "But the shock is on me."

She pulled away and gave him a pat on both cheeks, and then another kiss. "Hey Jack, wonderful to see you." She shot a more serious look at Deuce. "It appears I over-dressed for the reunion."

He slowly shook his head and didn't even bother to hide his full-body inspection. "Not at all." A grin pulled at his mouth. "You look—" there just wasn't a word to do her justice "—perfect."

Color rose in her cheeks, making her even prettier as she brushed the leather with a casual hand. "You like?"

Oh yeah. "I like."

"Why didn't you tell me it was an online event?" she asked, a friendly accusation in her voice.

"I wanted to surprise you."

She laughed lightly, the sound tugging at his heart. Her lips hitched in a sweet, but inviting, smile. "Looks like I'm going to make the extra thirty percent after all."

He nodded, taking in the happiness glimmering in her eyes. "Yep."

Pulling away from her brother she stepped close to Deuce, a muskier, heavier scent than she normally wore drifting up to him. She rose on her toes, put her mouth against his ear and whispered, "Remind me to thank you properly later on."

Every hair on the back of his head stood straight up. And that wasn't the only thing.

He turned to nearly brush her lips with his. "You're going to have a hard time in the sand with those shoes, Ken-doll."

She curled one long leg around his calf, her heel playfully scraping the denim of his jeans. "I'll take them off."

He closed his eyes and fought the temptation to kiss her. Right there in front of Jack, the Hatchet Man and a few aging classmates. He resisted, but, man, he wanted to.

And then there was that foolish fantasy flash again. Coaching Rock High baseball, keeping an eye on the bar at night, married to Kendra and making love every night until she couldn't walk in those shoes.

He had a really good reason for calling his agent and starting the search for a coaching job. He had a really good reason for letting Kendra realize her dream without him intruding and turning it into his monument to sports. He had a really good reason for keeping his hands off her for the past week and arranging this event so that she made her magic number for the investor.

He knew he did, but for the life of him, good reason had evaporated and was replaced by the need to taste her skin, feel her body and love her every imaginable way and then some.

And if the look in her eyes was any indication, she was feeling the same overpowering need.

KENDRA TOOK THE ice-cold bottle of beer that Dec Clifford offered and slipped out the back door for fresh air. Scooting up on the hip-high brick wall that lined the parking lot, she inhaled the cool evening air and took a deep drink.

She'd danced until she worked up a sweat, laughed until her face ached, and even shared a warm and funny instant message exchange with none other than Annie Keppler, who'd French-kissed Deuce all those years ago. Annie was married and living in Buffalo.

And Deuce?

He hadn't taken his eyes off Kendra for the entire night.

No matter when she caught his gaze, it was returned. All night long, his look had shifted from amused to aroused and everything in between.

The back door creaked as it opened and Deuce appeared in the moonlight.

"Hey lady in leather." He crossed the narrow parking lot to where she sat. "What are you doing out here all alone?"

"Getting air." She held up the beer. "And breaking the rules by bringing a bottle outside."

He walked right in front of her, so his stomach touched her knees.

"Oh yeah?" He put his hands on the leather above her knees, sending fire up her thighs. "I like to break rules."

"That's why they say Deuce is wild."

As easily as he did everything, he gently parted her thighs and slid right into the opening so they were chest to chest. "You look pretty wild yourself tonight, Ken-doll."

She took another drink, then held the bottle to him. "Want some?"

His hands still firmly on her legs, he put his mouth over the top of the bottle, tipped his head and let her give him a slow sip, never breaking eye contact.

Her whole lower half knotted at the sexy move and, without thinking, she wrapped her legs around his waist.

"Why d'ya do it, Deuce?"

He raised his eyebrows. "'Cause I was thirsty?"

"I mean the cyber reunion. The thirty percent. You know if I get that investment money…your dad'll be hard-pressed to keep Monroe's as a sports bar."

"Yeah, I know." He lifted one shoulder. "I give up. It's yours."

"Not like you to be a quitter," she said, carefully setting the beer bottle on the bricks next to her. "Or are you just dying to coach so bad that you're ready to give up on that lifelong dream of owning Monroe's?"

He lifted both eyebrows in surprise. "How'd you know about my coaching?"

"The modern version of a heat register."

He looked warily at her. "Are you serious?"

"Were you?"

His eyes turned smoky dark. "I don't know how much you heard, but, I'm serious, yeah. The bar is yours. I mean, the café. And I'm stepping aside."

Not so long ago, that would have filled her with joy. Tonight, it hurt. "You know, owning Monroe's is not my lifelong dream."

"What is?"

She was holding her lifelong dream, he was wrapped in her leather legs at the moment. "You first."

A little smile snagged the corner of his mouth. "Well, not so long ago, my lifelong dream was playing in the major leagues. I can't do that, so, I guess my dream has to change."

"That's never easy."

His smile turned tight. "No, it isn't. Okay. Your turn. If owning the Kendra Locke-inspired premier cyber café and artists' performance space isn't your lifelong dream, then what is?"

"You."

She felt the air escape from his chest. "Excuse me?"

"Yep." She nodded, a sudden lightness lifting her heart. "All I've ever wanted to do in my whole life is be with you."

His jaw slackened. "Me?"

She locked her hands around his neck and pulled him closer. "You really didn't read the rest of that journal, did you?"

He shook his head. "I felt bad enough about what I did read."

"Shhh." She put a finger over his lips. "We can't change history. But we can change the future." Leaning forward, she dipped to his mouth and as gently as she could, she kissed him. He eased her closer and she tightened her legs, and let their tongues collide and tangle.

He pulled back enough to look in her eyes, an expression of pure hope and sin. "Let's start right now."

She trailed one finger over his cheek, loving the slightly roughened feel of his beard. "I want to make love to you, Deuce Monroe. And nothing, nothing at all, is going to stop me this time."

Just then the back door opened again and she felt Deuce let out a sigh of frustration.

"Hey Deuce," Jack called. "Someone named Coulter is on the phone for you. Says he's been trying to reach you all day."

Deuce closed his eyes for a second, then turned to Jack. "That's my agent. It can wait till tomorrow." He reached into his pocket and pulled out keys. "Do me a favor, Jackson." He pitched the keys across the parking lot and Jack caught them with an easy snap that came from years of playing baseball together. "Lock up for me when this shindig is over. I have something I have to do."

Jack peered into the shadows where they sat.

"Is Kennie with you?"

"I'll take care of her," Deuce promised. "You can drive my car home. Just handle the bar, okay?"

Kendra leaned forward and whispered, "It's a cyber café."

He slid his hand all the way up her thigh and gave her rear end a mischievous squeeze. Then, his hands still firmly on her backside, he lifted her from the wall and set her on the ground. "Tell me you don't need anything in there," he said huskily. "'Cause I really don't want you to change your mind."

She patted the flat pocket of her pants. "I have a car key and a house key right here. No purse."

He started to tug her toward the street, then froze mid-step. "You're sure, right? I mean, you're sure you want to…repeat history?"

If anyone could ever tame wild Deuce, it's Kendra Locke.

She could still hear the honesty and wistfulness in his confession. Sliding her arms around his shoulders, she pulled herself into his chest. His return embrace was automatic and just as powerful.

"I have never been more positive of anything in my life."

Deuce pulled her into him for a lusty kiss before he'd even turned the ignition off. They'd never make it inside, to either house. He was so hard and achy for her, it was a miracle they'd made it home at all. Especially considering that he'd kissed her at every light and was nearly blinded when she reached over and slid her hand up his thigh.

Somehow, they managed to get out of the car and into Diana's house. Newman barked and Kendra grabbed a treat from the pantry to bribe him into silence.

Deuce took her hand and pulled her toward the stairs, pausing only to kiss her again, and skate his hands over her leather-clad backside again. She arched into him with a soft moan.

"Upstairs," he managed to say.

They kissed and caressed and whispered and laughed their way up the steps, and Kendra pushed him into the first bedroom.

Oh, so that's where she'd been when she'd overheard his conversation with Jack. He started to tease her, but she was already pulling off her sweater and all he could manage was to kick the door closed and guide her to the bed while he devoured the black lace bra with his eyes and then his hands and, finally, blissfully, his mouth as she fell backwards onto his bed.

He freed her breasts from the lace, immediately bearing down to taste her flesh, loving how her whole body shuddered when he sucked her nipple deep, deep into his mouth.

He murmured her name and licked the tip into a hardened pebble, and she rewarded him with a writhing, helpless sigh.

Pulling up her leg, he took one sexy shoe in his hand and grinned. "Nice cleats." He slowly unbuckled the strap of one, then the other.

He trailed kisses down her stomach and unzipped the outrageous leather pants. Sliding them over her hips, he discovered nothing but a tiny bit of black satin barely covering her.

"Aw, Kendra, you're killin' me, honey."

With a soft laugh of victory, she tugged at his polo shirt and pulled it over his head. As soon as his chest was bare, he covered her to feel her silky warm skin against his muscles. As he captured her mouth again, she dragged her hands over his stomach and slipped into the waistband of his jeans.

Her fingers closed around him and white lightning shot through his body as she stroked him.

They struggled together to get his pants off, laughing softly at their desperation. Finally, he was down to his boxers. He pushed them off and eased her onto her back.

Taking his erection in her hand, she stroked the length of him. "I love that I can do this to you," she said huskily.

"Every day, all the time," he whispered. "All you have to do is walk into a room and I'm hard."

He gently straddled her and caressed the concave of her stomach, the rise of her breasts, the dip in her throat, the angle of her jaw. He wanted to dive into her, to pound into the heat and warmth of her, but he forced himself to slow down. To look at her.

He'd known this woman since she was a child, he'd basked in the glow of her admiration for years and years, and he'd loved her body once before.

But this was different.

He traced a line from between her breasts, over her stomach, down to the edge of the black triangle of satin that covered her.

This time, this night, something was completely different.

She closed her eyes. He slipped his finger under the fabric, over the soft tuft of hair and onto the wet, swollen nub.

She sucked in a breath as he touched her. He tenderly rubbed her, and sweet torture darkened her face as she sighed and turned her head from side to side. Her breasts rose and fell with each breath.

"Do you like that?" he asked.

She nodded, far away and lost in pleasure.

He leaned over her and eased the little silk patch to one side, revealing the glistening blond hair. She was moist and ready. "And I love what I do to you," he whispered.

She arched in response and he dipped his head to kiss her. He stroked her once with his tongue. Just once. Easy, slow and deliberate. She tunneled her fingers into his hair, rocked her hips up and asked for more.

Blood pulsed through his head, heating his veins and surging into a potent, aching hard-on.

Her legs were smooth against his face, and warm, as he kissed and suckled her, then he slipped the little thong over her hips so she was as naked as he.

Straddling her again, he pulled open the nightstand drawer and lifted out one foil packet. She watched, taking quick, frayed breaths as he sheathed himself, then lowered himself on top of her.

Once again, she arched upwards and his erection slid between her legs, against her opening.

"Deuce," she whispered as his tip found entry. "I love you."

Her words jolted more blood through him and he entered her almost the moment she spoke.

That's what was different.

"I love you," she repeated, kissing his mouth, his neck, his shoulder as he pulled back and plunged in again.

Everything intensified: the hot, wet walls that enveloped him, the silky curves of her breasts, her sweet confessions, her hungry kisses.

She rose to meet every thrust, and he ground out her name as sweat rolled down his temples and stung his eyes.

Each time, he was deeper into her, lost in the heat, the ecstasy, the pure bliss of her unguarded response. Each time, his body sparked like a flint, his senses overloaded by the womanly smell of her, his head threatening to explode as thoroughly as his body. Each time, pleasure rocked him and stole his breath and brain and heart.

Each time, he was more in love with her. Oh, yeah. That's what was different tonight. He loved her.

And as he realized that, he lost the control he'd barely ever had, finally giving in to the release, spilling into her as she unraveled with a climax as staggering as his.

He collapsed on her, kissing the moisture of her perspiration, letting the heat of their bodies melt together, attempting to get his breath back.

He managed to lift himself from her and look into her eyes.

"I do love you," she whispered, the only other sound the deafening thump of their heartbeats. "I always have and I always will."

Nothing in his life—a life full of glorious moments of victories and success—nothing had ever felt anything quite as complete as hearing those words.

And suddenly he realized that he hadn't come home to find hero-worship at all. He hadn't come home to find glory or admiration or memories of better days. He'd come home to find love and security.

And he had. He held it right here in his arms and he could hold it there forever.

"I love you, Kendra."

She closed her eyes and exhaled as though he'd given her the most precious gift in the world. And yet, he was the one who felt lucky.

Deuce tightened his grip on Kendra as though he thought she'd leap out of bed and run. He should know her better than that by now.

Instead, she slid her leg over his hip and let him pull her so tightly into his chest that she had no idea where she ended and he began. She nuzzled into the dusting of black hair on his chest, inhaling and pressing her cheek to the granite-hard muscle.

He loved her.

"You know what I just realized?" he asked her.

"That you love me?"

He smiled down at her. "Besides that. I realized I

came back to Rockingham for all the wrong reasons." He squeezed her again. "It wasn't about running the bar."

She punched him playfully. "You could have fooled me."

"What I wanted," he said slowly, as though the realization was just forming in his mind, "was to figure out who I really was. Without the crowds, without the fame."

"Did you figure it out?"

He smiled and pulled her closer. "I'm in the process."

Somehow, she managed to breathe. Managed to swallow and smile. But then a digital phone beeped "Take Me Out to the Ball Game" and he fell back on his pillow.

"That's my agent's ring," he said, not moving.

"Why don't you put him out of his misery and answer?"

"Because he's going to tell me I got a job coaching in Greenville or Gainesville or somewhere I don't want to go."

The second ring started. "So tell him you're staying here."

He pushed himself up from the pillow and surveyed the floor for his cell phone. "I think I will," he said with finality.

Kendra's toes curled with happiness. She pulled the sheet higher and watched the muscles of Deuce's back tighten as he reached down to pluck the phone out of his jeans pocket.

"Coulter, it's midnight on the east coast and I'm real busy right now. This better be good."

Suddenly, all the air came out of him in one long whoosh. "Are you serious?" he asked, sitting up straighter. "They do?"

He shook his right elbow, then rubbed it. "Well, it's a lot better." He laughed softly. "Maybe by All Star break."

She bit her lip as Deuce listened, then hooted. "They'd actually reinstate my contract? I can be there in May."

She took a deep breath, uncurled her toes and gave in to the way-too-familiar physical pain of heartbreak.

CHAPTER TWELVE

DEUCE TRIED TO CONCENTRATE on the instructions Coulter was barking at him about training and timing, but all he could process was the fact that Kendra had scooped up her clothes and disappeared into the bathroom.

Was she leaving?

She couldn't leave. He'd just realized he loved her. He needed to tell her again—to show her again.

"Coulter, can't this wait until tomorrow?" he growled into the phone. "I'm seriously in the middle of something here." Like changing his life.

"Call me first thing in the morning, Deuce," the agent ordered. "We have to go over the fine print of this contract. It's not exactly the cakewalk you had last year."

"I bet it's not." He stared at the bedroom door.

"Some things have changed."

Deuce's gut tightened. "They sure have."

When he hung up, he went straight to the bathroom. "You okay in there, Ken-doll?"

The door swung open.

She was the lady in black leather again, all of that sexy sweetness replaced by the sharp-eyed Mensa candidate who'd fight him for her cyber café.

"I have to work in the morning," she said simply, slipping by him, her gaze never even fluttering over his undressed body.

He managed to grab her elbow. "What's the matter with you?"

Her eyes widened. "I can't spend the night here."

"Can't or won't?" he asked, scrambling to pick up and pull on his boxers. "You don't even know what I talked to him about."

"I don't have to know the details of your contract." She opened the bedroom door. "I've been here before, Deuce. I know the drill."

"Look, I know I have a lousy record, but honestly you don't—"

Newman barked from the kitchen as the sliding glass door opened.

"That's Jack," he said. "You can stay here. He doesn't—"

"Did you miss me, Newman?" A woman's voice traveled up the stairs, and Kendra froze in place.

Not Jack.

"That's Diana." Kendra's face registered the shock he felt.

"Anybody home?" Dad's call was louder, but completely familiar.

Kendra tapped his bare chest. "Get some clothes on. I'll deal with them."

She headed down the steps without looking back. "What are you guys doing home already?"

In thirty seconds, he was dressed and following in her footsteps. The three of them were still hugging and fawning over the dog by the time he got in there.

"Deuce!" Dad seized him in a bear hug immediately.

"What are you doing back so soon?" Deuce asked, returning the hug and gave Diana a quick embrace. "I thought you were in Hawaii."

They looked guiltily at each other. "We never made it."

"No?" Kendra asked. "Why not? You called and said you were on your way."

"We went to Vegas instead," Dad said, a boy's grin breaking across his face. "Show them, Di."

Diana held up her left hand and Deuce blinked at the rock.

"He didn't want to do the honeymoon before the wedding," Diana said. "Who knew your father was such a traditionalist?"

"Oh." Deuce made the sound, knowing he should do better than "oh" but unable. He looked at Kendra. Surely she'd squeal or jump with joy.

But her expression was a blend of torture and surprise. Finally, she reached out for Diana. "Congratulations." Then she threw an arm around Seamus and pulled him into a three-way hug. "I really wanted to dance at your wedding, though."

"We'll have a big party at Monroe's," Diana promised, pulling back to beam at Deuce. "We have so much to celebrate."

"We have even more to celebrate," Deuce said, his gaze sliding to Kendra.

Diana sucked in a little breath. "What is it?"

"I can only think of one thing that could make me any happier." Dad said with conviction. What did he think they were going to announce? "Go ahead, make my day."

"Kendra made her thirty percent."

"Deuce is going back into the majors."

Their simultaneous announcements earned stunned looks from Seamus and Diana.

"Excuse me?" Diana asked.

"Did I hear what I think I heard?"

"He just got the call." Kendra's eyes were bright, and her smile was forced. "They're reinstating his contract."

"Deuce!" Diana exclaimed. "Isn't that wonderful?"

"I don't know," he said, his gaze sliding to Kendra. "Is it?"

He saw her swallow. "I'll let you guys catch up," she said, far too quickly. "And you have Deuce to thank for the thirty-percent windfall. He's…" she paused and looked at him, her blue eyes full of something he'd never seen before. Something so much deeper than hero-worship and adoration. Something that filled him with that same sense of completion he'd felt upstairs when they made love.

He could live for that look.

"He's incredible," she finally said. "There's never been anyone else like him."

"I've always known that." At the sound of his dad's voice, Deuce turned, expecting the old beam of pride. But instead, the Irish eyes were full of sadness and disappointment.

Why wasn't Seamus happy about the majors?

Why wasn't *he?*

Seamus crouched at home plate, a worn catcher's mitt barely hiding the frown he'd worn since they arrived at Rock High field for some practice.

"Why are you separating so late?" he demanded as he threw the ball back to Deuce on the mound.

Deuce shook his right arm, visualized perfect release timing and threw again.

His dad had to dive to catch the far outside pitch. "Why are you striding to the left?"

Deuce rubbed his elbow and caught the toss. Taking a deep breath, he held his glove in front of his face, stared into the strike zone and started his wind-up.

"Why are you curling your arm like that?"

Deuce paused, kicked the rubber and let out a frustrated

sigh. Then he looked hard at the man who'd caught more pitches for him than anyone in the major leagues. "Why are you so ticked off at me?"

The return look from Seamus was harsh, but that might have been the weary bones aching as the older man pushed himself into a stand. Most likely it was a dirty look; his dad would never let the pain show.

"I'm not ticked off."

Coming off the mound, Deuce flipped his hat, wiped his brow with his forearm, and resisted the urge to spit. "You've been irritated with me since you got home last night," Deuce said. "You're married, the money's coming in for the café and I'm going back to the majors. Just what does it take to make you happy, Dad?"

That earned him a wry smile. "Same thing it's always taken, son. I want you to be happy. When you're happy, I'm happy."

"Happy is relative," Deuce mused.

Dad just nodded and tossed the extra ball he held, his gaze on the far fence. "Damn nice of you and Jack Locke to arrange that cyber reunion for Kennie," he said slowly. "Guess you really didn't want the bar after all."

So this is where it was going. The bar. "I wanted to help her," he said. "It didn't have anything to do with me not wanting to run Monroe's. I would have been perfectly happy to…" To what? Marry Kendra and have those nine kids and a lifetime of what they'd had the night before?

Yep.

"I'd have been perfectly happy to run the bar, Dad." Deuce finished the thought by putting his arm on his father's shoulder. "I'm sorry if I disappointed you."

"Not me," he said. "Diana."

"Diana?" Deuce pulled back and peered from under his cap. "How'd I disappoint her?"

"She imagined herself a matchmaker." Dad smiled as they walked to the water pitchers in the dugout. "It was her idea to let you two work it out alone together. In fact, she wanted to make a contest out of it. But I just wanted to let nature take its course."

"Nature took its course," Deuce said quietly.

Dad froze mid-step. "It did?"

"If its course was to make me fall stupidly in love with her, then, yeah. Nature's right on course." It felt good to admit it, he realized, guiding his father to the shade of the dugout.

"But you're going back to Vegas tonight," Dad said, as though he didn't understand. "And that was some lousy goodbye for a woman you love. She waved at you and scooted out the door."

Deuce could still see the look on Kendra's face when she'd said goodbye. All breezy and light. For a moment, he'd thought maybe she was glad he was leaving. As though her admissions of love and lifelong dreams hadn't been real.

If he hadn't seen how she'd looked when he made love to her…if he hadn't heard the truth in her voice when she said she'd loved him, he might not have believed it. But he'd seen and he'd heard and he believed.

"It wouldn't have worked anyway, Dad." He had to try and believe *that* instead. "We…have some history. Stuff you don't know about."

Dad spun the red lid of a thermos. "I know about the baby, Deuce."

Deuce stared at him. "You do?"

"I got eyes and ears, son. I saw her expression every time she passed that jersey on the wall. That's why I took it down."

"*You* took it down? I thought Diana did."

Dad took a sip of water and swallowed hard. "You're gonna have to stop blaming Diana for everything you don't like around here. She's my wife now."

Deuce sighed. "I didn't know about the baby. She didn't tell me. I had no way of knowing."

"You could have called her."

"You could have called me," Deuce countered.

Dad rolled his eyes. "You just do the opposite of everything I say anyway."

"That's not true. Not always. Okay, most of the time."

"More often than not," Dad said. "And in that case, I felt I needed to butt out."

Deuce dropped on to the bench with a thud. Looking at his dad, he decided it was time to ask the one question he'd never dreamed he'd ask his father. "I'm supposed to get on a plane tonight for Vegas. Tonight." The thought stabbed at him. Not another night with Kendra until…until when? Why should she wait for him? She might think it could be another ten years till he showed up again. Even though he knew with his age, elbow and history, he'd be lucky to get one more year as a reliever.

Then, he'd come home again. And would he destroy her life a third time? "What should I do, Dad?"

He waited for the advice, the sage quote from Mickey Mantle, the guidance he so desperately needed. He waited, he realized, for someone to tell him it was okay to follow his heart and not his head.

Come on, Dad. Tell me something.

Play to win. Hit it out of the park. Throw a curve when they expect a fastball…some straightforward baseball analogy to make him understand how he could justify walking away from his last shot at glory…or ignoring the happiness that Kendra offered.

But his father just ran a hand through his mane of white

hair and smiled. "Only you know what's important in your life, son. Only you know the answer."

The answer was as loud and clear as an umpire's call.

"IF YOU DON'T let me in this house this minute I'm going to break the door down." The threat was accompanied by three loud raps at Kendra's door.

Kendra sighed heavily, knowing it was a complete waste to ignore him. She stuffed her new blue notebook under the sofa cushion and padded barefoot to the front door to open it with no small amount of disgust.

"Cut the drama, Jack."

Jack grinned and put his arms on his sister's shoulders. "Why are you ignoring me?"

"Why aren't you sleeping late? You must have been at Monroe's until two or three last night."

"The last email exchange was at two-thirty and I couldn't sleep this morning. Deuce and his dad left to go play baseball, and Diana blew out a few minutes later dressed to beat the world. That left me with a dog who doesn't know how to make coffee." He looked at her little galley kitchen. "Don't make me go to some cyber café for my fix, Ken."

She smiled and tilted her head toward the kitchen. "Come on, I'll make you a cup. What time are you going to the airport?"

"My flight leaves Boston at one, so I should get the heck out of here soon. Will you take me?"

"Isn't Deuce taking you?"

Jack's eyes darkened to a deep sage as he regarded her. "It's a little inconvenient for him to go all the way to Logan Airport twice in one day."

Twice. In one day.

"So, he's leaving today?" She congratulated herself on not allowing a crack in her voice.

"He got on an American flight at six-twenty tonight. His agent wants him in Vegas by tomorrow morning."

"Oh." Kendra managed to scoop the grounds into the coffee filter without spilling a single grain. "Well, sure. I'll take you to the airport."

If she played the timing right, she might never have to see Deuce again. She could take hours returning from the airport in Boston, and by the time she got home, he'd be gone.

"He's in love with you."

Jack's statement jerked her back to reality.

"He's in love with the fact that I'm in love with him," she said. At least, that's how she'd just written it in her brand-new diary, which she was far too old to keep, but much too sad not to. "He's addicted to hero-worship and I give it to him in spades."

"True."

"At least I know who I am and what my weaknesses are," she said, more to herself than her brother. "You know, I was horrified when he showed up here a few weeks ago. So certain he had the power to ruin my life and wreck my world."

"And you showed up in leather pants and wrecked his." Jack laughed softly. "But he was gone long before you put on the battle gear, Ken."

"I don't think so, but you're sweet to try and make me feel better."

Jack plopped his elbows on the counter and looked hard at her. "I'm not trying to make you feel better. I think the guy's nuts if he walks away from you again—"

"Again?" This time her voice did crack.

"He told me about the baby."

Her arms suddenly felt very heavy. "He did?"

"Well, truth be told, I started to tell him about your... history. And then he told me it was his."

"You were very busy this morning," she said, trying for a light tone. Then she closed her eyes for a moment. This was Jack. She didn't have to pretend. "I'm sorry, Jack. I never wanted you to know."

He shrugged. "I managed not to punch his face off, but only because he looked good and truly miserable about it."

She took a step closer to the counter and put her hand over his. "So how do you feel now that you know who the father of that baby was?"

"I feel sad because you and Deuce would make some awesome babies together."

She felt the color rise to her cheeks.

"And you know what else I think, Kendra? I think that if I ever find a woman who loves me as unconditionally as you love him, I would grab hold of her and never, ever let her go."

He flipped his hand and squeezed hers.

"I hope you do, Jack."

"And while I'm doling out brotherly wisdom, here's something else for you to ponder."

Jack was a rebel, but he'd never steered her wrong. Whatever he told her would be true and right. "What is it?"

"We made up all that stuff in the basement because we knew you were listening."

For the first time in hours, she laughed. "I knew that." But not what she heard yesterday. Deuce loved her. He'd admitted it.

"You did not," he countered, sounding very much like the teasing big brother he was. "But it's nice to see you smile."

The fact was, she had her business, her friends, her brother and her integrity. She didn't have Deuce, but she had a lot to smile about.

SINCE SHE'D BEEN so creative in avoiding Deuce all day, Kendra's decision to hang around Logan Airport all afternoon and into the evening made no sense at all.

Before Deuce had gotten back to Diana's, she'd packed Jack into her car and they'd taken off for the airport.

Then Jack's flight had been delayed, so she stayed and spent a few more hours with him. Then she dawdled in an airport bookstore, and pretty soon she was hungry, so she had some pizza and then she looked at her watch. It was just past five.

She tried to tell herself she'd just killed some time to avoid the traffic back to the Cape, but who was she kidding?

She'd stayed long enough to say goodbye to Deuce. She had to kiss him one last time, and whisper once more that she loved him.

With a little smile and a pounding heart, she headed toward the main check-in for American. Anyone on Flight 204 to Las Vegas should be in line there right about now.

She understood his decision to play his game, to renew his contract. Jack said he'd only be a reliever, and this would probably be his last season, but it didn't matter.

For the first time in her life, she felt free. Not of loving Deuce—she always would—but of that desperate feeling that somehow her life was incomplete without him. It wasn't. It was full. So she could certainly be strong enough to wish him well and say goodbye.

She scanned the line for a tall, handsome, powerful man with bedroom eyes and a sexy smile. Her knees weakened as blood rushed to her nerve endings, but she continued walking past the long line of people checking in.

No Deuce.

She slipped outside and studied the people checking in at curbside.

No Deuce.

Back in the terminal, she followed the path from baggage check-in to the entrance to the gates, as far as she could go without a ticket. She watched dozens of passengers walk through security, dozens of men—some tall, some dark, some not bad looking…but no Deuce.

The monitor told her his flight was on time. But she must have missed him. He must have arrived early. Of course, he was anxious to get back to his real field of dreams.

Baseball was still his true love. If he didn't know who he was without the crowds and the competition, then he'd find out next year or the year after. Deuce would never choose a boring life in Rockingham over the major leagues. Even if that boring life included her.

She waited about ten more minutes, then swallowed hard and headed toward the parking lot.

The biggest victory, she decided on the drive home, was the fact that there were no tears this time.

It was time to face one last demon, and it was time to celebrate her life.

DEUCE STOOD AT the crest of the sand dune and peered into the darkness. At the far end of West Rock Beach, he saw a faint light, someone holding a flashlight and sitting on a blanket.

Finally, he'd found Kendra.

Why hadn't he thought of coming here first? Instead he'd been all over Rockingham, back and forth to Monroe's and her house with no luck. Her cell phone didn't answer, and Jack's flight had been delayed, but had taken off. He'd checked all that while trying to find her, anxious to tell her of the decision he'd made.

He called her as he approached, not wanting to scare her.

He heard her gasp of surprise in response. "Deuce? Is that you?"

"You sure like to hang out on beaches in the dark, don't you?" he said as he got closer.

She flipped the flashlight off, but he could still see her in the moonlight.

"I'm…what are you doing here? Your flight left hours ago."

"I didn't make it." He reached the blanket and looked down at her. Under the flashlight was a dark-blue notebook with a pen clipped to the cover. He dropped to his knees and looked at her face in the dim light. "You come here often?"

She shook her head, her gaze locked on him. "Except for a picnic the other day, I haven't been here for ten years."

He sat next to her, not too close, but still on the blanket. "What are you doing?"

"I'm celebrating."

Celebrating? Well, that was the last answer he expected. "The cyber café and artists' space?"

"No."

"The fact that Seamus and Diana got married?"

"No."

"My reinstatement to the Nevada Snake Eyes?" Please say no.

"Sort of."

He let out a half laugh, half sigh. "You're celebrating with a notebook and pen? No champagne?"

"I'm writing." She picked up the flashlight, and flipped it on, the yellow beam directed at the notebook. "Want to hear?"

Did he? "Go ahead. Hit me."

Very slowly, she picked up the notebook and opened it. She flipped open to the first page.

She cleared her throat and looked at the words.

The year I learned to read, to tie my shoes and to add one-digit numbers, I fell in love with Deuce Monroe.

A completely unexpected and foreign tightness squeezed his throat at the words.

The year I learned the real meaning of life, I lost his child.

He tried to swallow, but it was impossible.

And this year, the year I realized a professional dream, I am finally able to let him go. Really go. Not pretend that he's coming back. Because even if he does,

She stopped and looked at him.

I won't be waiting for him. And it doesn't even make me cry.

He blinked, and felt the moisture on his lids. "Well, then. You must be the only one," he said with a self-conscious laugh.

Eyes wide, she reached over and wiped the tear from his eye. "Now you tell me why you're not on that plane to Las Vegas."

He captured her finger and wrapped his hand around it. "Because I'm not leaving. I'm not taking the job. I'm not letting you go."

Her jaw dropped as she stared at him. "What?"

He tapped the page. "If I go, you won't wait for me and I don't want to live my life without you."

She breathed slowly, evenly, studying his face, taking in his pronouncement. "Deuce, you can't live without baseball."

"I won't. I'm taking the job as the Rock High coach."

"You are?"

He nodded. "And I'm probably going to have to help you at Monroe's."

"You will?"

"'Cause I want nine kids and that'll keep you real busy."

She laughed, but even in the moonlight he could see her tears.

"That's okay, isn't it?"

"You're crazy," she said, shaking her head. "Absolutely nuts."

"About you." He slipped his hand around the nape of her neck and pulled her closer to him. "I love you, Kendra. I love your strength and your intelligence and your ability to stand up to me. And I love that you've loved me your whole life. If you ever stopped, I couldn't stand it."

"I'll never stop, Deuce. I just was willing to let you go if I had to. Willing to be independent and alone, even if I still loved you."

"You can be independent, but not alone. Please not

alone. Will you marry me, Kendra Locke? Can I make you Mrs. Monroe?"

She reached down and picked up the pen she'd been writing with. "You know, I've been practicing that signature my whole life. It's about time I get to use it."

Easing her back on the blanket, he tucked her body under his.

"Is that a yes?" he asked, his whole being suspended until he heard what he wanted.

"Well," she said with a sly smile. "It's true that Monroe's has always been run by Monroes."

"Say yes, Kendra." He kissed her eyelids.

"And Seamus does like me better than you."

"Say yes, Kendra." He kissed her cheeks.

"And Martin Hatcher really wants you to coach."

"Say yes, Kendra." He kissed her mouth.

"Yes, Deuce."

Happiness and contentment curled through him as he pulled her body into his. "About those nine kids," he said huskily, his chest tight with a heart that might burst. "We'd better start. Now."

He took her mouth in one long, leisurely kiss, tasting the sweetness of her, filling himself up with it.

"We've had pretty good luck on this beach before." She laughed into his kiss and slid one leg around his. "But I don't want nine kids, Deuce."

"What do you want, Ken-doll?"

"I want you, Seamus."

He pulled her into him and rocked against her, unable to believe that this loving, brilliant, wonderful woman would be his partner for the rest of his life.

"You got me. For life."

"And maybe one little girl."

He put his mouth against her ear and whispered, "As long as she has a good arm, I can work with that."

* * * * *

TANGLING WITH TY

Dear Reader,

It's been a heck of a long time since 2003, when I wrote this story! I had almost forgotten I'd written a sexy Irish hero. Mmm, I can hear Ty speaking in that brogue right now....

I digress.

We all have our ideas of what our perfect hero would be like, and luckily for me, I get to create them for a living. Ty was one of my all-time favorites. I hope he finds a place in your heart, as well!

Happy reading,

Jill Shalvis

Visit Jill at her website, www.jillshalvis.com, or on Facebook, www.facebook/jillshalvis.com or Twitter, www.twitter/jillshalvis.com.

To Megan Nicole, my warrior princess

CHAPTER ONE

A NAKED MAN WOULD have changed everything, but there wasn't one in sight. So, as always, Nicole Mann got up with the alarm. As always, she showered, dressed and nuked a breakfast burrito in less than eight minutes.

And as always, she was out the door of her apartment at top speed to get to the hospital for what was likely to be a double shift due to a late-spring flu outbreak.

Yes, her life was completely dictated by her work. So what? Being a doctor was a dream-come-true, and if she'd worked at that dream-come-true nearly every waking moment, forsaking just about everything else—including naked men—she could live with that. Being a doctor was what she'd wanted since she'd graduated high school fifteen years ago at the perfectly extraordinary age of twelve.

"Psst."

For a woman who prided herself on nerves of steel, Nicole nearly leapt out of her skin at the unexpected whisper coming out of the darkened hallway of her apartment building.

But it wasn't the boogey man or any other menacing threat. It was just the owner of the building and her friend, Taylor Wellington, peeking out her door. Taylor was nice and beautiful—reason enough to hate her—but she also happened to be in possession of that disarming ability to talk until Nicole's eyes crossed. It completely wore down her defenses.

That they'd—polar opposites—become friends still baffled Nicole.

"Psst!"

"I see you," Nicole said. "Did I wake you?" Not that the perfectly-put-together Taylor looked anything other than...well, perfectly put together, but it did happen to be the crack of dawn. A time she considered sacrilegious.

"Oh, no, the living dead couldn't wake me," Taylor assured her. "I set my alarm so I'd catch you." Her beautifully made-up eyes toured Nicole. "Honey, I thought we talked about the camouflage gear."

Nicole looked down at her camouflage cargo pants and green tank top, fitting snug to her lean form. Her wardrobe had been formed back in the expensive days of medical school when she'd been forced to shop in thrift stores, but sue her, she'd developed a fondness for the comfortable garb. That Taylor cared what she wore at all was still a surprise.

Nicole had only lived in this South Village building a few weeks, having moved from another larger building where no one ever even looked at one another. She'd only moved because that place had been sold and the new owners had plans for it to go coop. She'd come here for its convenience to the hospital, and because it was small. Fewer people to deal with. That this building was also falling off its axis was neither here nor there, as Nicole didn't care what it looked like, as long as her bed was in it. "Why did you want to catch me?"

"I knew if I didn't, you'd forget. We're planning Suzanne's engagement party tonight."

Ah, hell. Suzanne Carter lived in the apartment next to Taylor's. The three of them, the only ones in the building, had shared many laughs and much ice cream, but Nicole still didn't want to plan a party where she'd have to dress up and smile and make nice. She hated making nice.

"You'd forgotten," Taylor said.

"No, I…" Okay, she'd forgotten. She couldn't help it, she was singleminded. Always had been, just ask the family she never managed to see. This year alone, she'd forgotten one sister's homecoming from college, her mother's annual April Fool's Day bash and her own birthday. But her family understood something Taylor didn't.

Nicole was a firm loner. Connections to people tended to give her hives. Ditto planning engagement parties. "I'm sorry. I…might be late."

Taylor gave her a long look. "Don't tell me. You have something new to pierce."

Nicole rolled her eyes. Taylor had been teasing her about the silver hoops she had lining one ear, but Taylor had no way of knowing that each was a trophy of sort, and a badge of honor worn proudly. "Not a new piercing, no."

With the patience of a saint, Taylor just lifted a brow.

Nicole racked her brain for her elusive people skills, but as she didn't have any, they failed her. "We're short-staffed at the hospital, and—"

"Save it, Super Girl." Taylor lifted a hand against the upcoming stream of excuses. "Let's just cut to the chase, shall we? Weddings, and all the trappings, give both of us gas." She looked right into Nicole's eyes and gave her a take-your-medicine look. "But this is for Suzanne."

Suzanne had been the only other person besides Taylor to instantly, genuinely accept Nicole, no matter how abrupt, aloof and self-absorbed she was.

The three of them had only met recently after Taylor had inherited this building with no funds to go with it. She'd rented out space to Suzanne first, then Nicole had come along. They had little in common really. Suzanne, a caterer, kept them in to-die-for food and Suzanne's personal favorite, ice cream. Taylor, with her dry wit, kept them all amused and, though she'd kill Nicole if she heard her say it, mothered them to death. And Nicole…she had no clue what she added to the mix, so them caring about her still mystified.

But they all shared one common trait—a vow of singlehood. They'd talked about it, often toasted to it and had jointly coveted it… Until Suzanne had done the unthinkable and fallen in love.

Nicole sighed. "I'll find a way to be here."

"Don't worry, they say you can't catch wedding fever."

"Hey, don't worry about me. My work is my life. I'm too into it, too selfish to be anything but single."

"Right. Our singlehood is firmly intact."

"Firmly."

But they stared at each other, a little unnerved. That Suzanne, one so steadfastly single, was now getting married cast a shadow on their vow. Surely neither of them could possibly make the fall into love. Not when they kept their eyes open and their hearts closed.

Yep, heart firmly closed. They were safe that way, totally and completely safe.

TWENTY-FOUR EXHAUSTING hours later, again just before dawn, Nicole dragged her sorry, aching body back up the three flights of stairs to her loft apartment.

It was dark again, or still. It seemed she lived in the dark.

Work had been especially brutal. An unexpected heavy fog had created a pileup on Highway 5 South. As a result of the forty-two car accident, she'd been in emergency surgery all day, without a break to so much as sneeze. She'd removed two spleens, pinned four legs, reset more shattered ribs than she could remember, and had delivered twins in an emergency caesarian.

Then she'd been asked to stay another shift, and after a quick nap when she'd dreamed of being chased by a white wedding dress and cake—where had *that* come from?— she'd willingly taken on whatever had come her way. And plenty had.

Now all she wanted was food, a shower and a bed, and not necessarily in that order. She had her Taco Bell bag clutched to her chest, her mouth watering in anticipation of the four regular tacos and extra-large soda. Not the usual breakfast of champions, but food was food and she'd been craving spicy since her second surgery.

And then after the food…oblivion. At least until she had to be back at the hospital again, which happened to be that afternoon for a staff meeting, and then to cover someone else's shift that night. She already had four surgeries lined up, ready to go.

Had she remembered to grab the hot sauce? She hoped so, she was pretty certain her kitchen—if you could call the hole in the wall that—didn't have any food in it except for something that had gone green a week ago, and—

"You little buggering piece of sh—" A rustling sound, followed by the squeal of metal on metal, blocked out the rest of that shocking statement made in a deep, Irish brogue. "I'm going to…damn me again, you worked at the last job, so bloody hell if you won't work here…"

This was spoken so calmly, so confidently in that accent, it took a moment to decipher that the man was making some sort of threat.

Fine. Nicole was in the mood to kick some ass, as long as her Taco Bell didn't get crushed. Once in a while, having an IQ higher than her weight had some benefits. During med school she'd needed an outlet for all the technical work so she'd taken karate. Like everything she set her mind to, she'd excelled.

Bring it on. She took a defensive stance, then dropped it to set her food down on the top step. No need to risk breakfast. She moved up the last step. There was nothing on this level but her loft and the attic. Nothing but the narrow hallway, which at the moment had a man lying full-length in it. His arms were outstretched, and he held some sort of measuring tool along the scarred wooden planks, swearing the air blue in the most interesting of Irish lilts.

Nicole had to laugh. Or she would have, if she could have taken her eyes off that long, lean, hard male body stretched out so enticingly on the floor in front of her. He had legs from here to Timbuktu, covered in Levi's that most effectively accented the muscles in his thighs and calves.

And then there was his butt, which was very lovingly cupped in that worn denim. His shirt had ridden up, showing a good amount of tanned, damp skin stretched taut over the rippling sinew of his lower back. The rest of it wasn't bad either, smooth and sleek in the plain light-blue T-shirt that invited her to Bite Me in bold black letters.

In spite of the scare he'd given her, she grinned. Bite Me was her official motto. "Um...excuse me."

His arms, stretched over his head, didn't drop the strange gadget in his hands, which was sending out red lighted bleeps. In fact he didn't do anything but sigh. "Be a luv," he said in a voice deep and husky as sin but suddenly utterly devoid of the accent. "And hand me my notes?"

Nicole, still in her defensive stance, craned her neck and saw a small notepad at his hip. It looked as if it had been roughly stuffed in and out of a pocket on a regular basis.

Apparently she hesitated a hair too long, because he

pushed up to his elbows and turned his head, giving her a glimpse of jet-black hair cut so short it stuck up in spikes, hitting her with the lightest, most crystal-clear blue eyes she'd ever seen.

He took one look at her with her fists still up, her legs slightly bent and let out another sigh, rubbing his jaw. "We going to duke it out over a notepad then?"

She dropped her fists to her sides, and, keeping her eyes on the most gorgeous stranger she'd ever seen, she bent for her Taco Bell bag. "Who are you and why were you swearing in my hallway?"

"Heard that, did you?" He flashed a grin. "I don't suppose you'd not repeat any of it to the owner? She specifically said no swearing in her hallways."

Hmm. Nicole was surprised Taylor hadn't put this man under lock and key in her bedroom, given her fondness for horizontal gymnastics, and the fact that sexuality rolled off this man in waves.

With one smooth motion, he came to his feet, startling her anew because, granted, she was on the shrimpy side of average height, but he and his hardasgranite body had to top six feet by several inches.

Which meant her head, if she lifted her nose to nose-bleed height, maybe came to his broad shoulder. Between their height discrepancy and her sudden, startling attraction to him, she felt defensive. She hated feeling defensive. It tended to put her on the offensive. Taking one step back, she balanced her weight on the balls of her feet, once again ready for anything.

"Wouldn't have used that language if I'd have heard you coming." A bit chagrined now, he cocked his head and scratched his jaw, which, judging by the dark shadow there, he hadn't shaved in a few days. "Went and startled you, I see."

She narrowed her eyes. Yep, his accent was gone, but there was something stilted about how he sounded now, as if he were hiding something.

She knew well enough about hiding secrets, but didn't like it when others did the same. "Answer my questions, please."

As she'd raised an accusatory finger directed toward his very fine chest, he lifted his hands in surrender. "No need to shoot, I'm just the architect. Ty Patrick O'Grady at your service."

"You're the...architect."

"For the building here. It's going to be renovated." As if to prove he was harmless—harmless, ha!—he propped up the wall with his shoulder and gave her a disarming little half smile that sent sparks of awareness shivering down her spine. "Needs an architect before anything else, you know," he said. "Turns out this place is a historical monument, and is in desperate need of some serious structural repair."

As the place was smack dab in the middle of elegant, sophisticated South Village, where the rich came to play, and everyone else came to pretend to be rich, Nicole decided she could buy that. Especially since this particular building was the current eyesore of the entire block.

Taylor had been having one expert or another through here for weeks in anticipation of a major renovation. "So you're working up a bid for the owner? Suzanne?" she asked, watching him carefully.

Now he smiled, slow and sure. "No, not Suzanne. *Taylor,* but good try. It'd take more than a peewee to trip me up, darlin'."

A peewee? He'd just called her a peewee? She'd give him peewee.

He lifted one jetblack brow at the narrowing of her

eyes, and dared to smile at her obvious temper. "Want to see my ID or are you just going to clobber me with that lovely smelling Taco Bell bag?"

"What happened to your accent?"

His face went curiously blank. "What accent?"

"You had an Irish accent. Are you an immigrant?"

"Yep, just got off the boat from Australia, mate." He grinned. "Or maybe that was…" His accent went from Aussie to Austrian in a heartbeat. "From another continent entirely."

A smartass. "It's awfully late to be working on a bid."

"You mean early, don't you?"

That might be; she had no idea whether she was coming or going. "Whichever. Why are you here now?"

"I'm what you'd call a busy man…now, darlin', you've got me so flustered, I've gone and missed your name."

Nicole crossed her arms. "It's not darlin', I'll tell you that."

He let out another smile, which she had to admit could melt bones at fifty paces. "Do I have to guess then?"

"Dr. Mann," she grudgingly gave him. "Now, if you don't mind, I've got tacos to eat." And a date with a bed.

Alone.

Where that thought came from, she had no earthly clue. She always slept alone.

Always.

She stared at him still staring at her with a little, knowing smile that made her want to grind her teeth for some reason. "What? You going to make a crack about me being far too young to be a doctor? I get a lot of littlegirl jokes. Go ahead, give me your best shot."

He took a good, long look down her body, then slowly, slowly back up again, stopping at the points that seemed to be connected to her loins, since they all came alive with a little flutter that annoyed her even more. "You look all woman to me."

Oh, definitely, she was too tired for this. She brushed past him and stopped at her door, slapping her myriad of pockets, looking for the keys she could never quite remember where she'd left.

"Problem?"

Scowling, she ignored him and switched her Taco Bell bag to the other arm to check her back pocket. No go. Damn, that was the trouble with cargo pants. Comfortable, yes. Practical, with their twelve million pockets to lose things in, no.

"Dr. Mann—"

"Please," she said to that quiet, outrageously sexy voice as she closed her eyes. "Just…go away." If she didn't gobble the food and hit the bed, she'd fall asleep right here on her feet.

She could do it, too. She'd slept on her feet before, during med school, during the long nights of residency….

A sharp click had her blinking rapidly at her…opened door? Ty Patrick O'Grady, architect, sometimes owner of a sexy Irish lilt, man of a thousand curses and one incredible smile, held up a credit card. "Handy, these things, aren't they now?"

"You…broke in?"

"Easily."

"Are you a criminal?"

He laughed, low and sexily, damn him. "Let's just say I've been around. You need a better lock."

"You can't just—"

"Did you find your keys?"

"No, but—"

"Just get inside, darlin'." He gave her a gentle shove as he took the Taco Bell bag from her fingers just before the thing would have dropped to the ground. "Before you fall down."

She stepped over the threshold, reaching back to slam the door. Unfortunately he was on the wrong side of that door and ended up inside her very small place, which seemed that much smaller with his huge presence in it. "And I'm not your darling," she said, turning away.

"Nope, you're Dr. Mann."

She sighed and faced him again. "Okay, so I'm stuffy when I'm tired. Sue me."

"I'd rather call you by your first name."

"Nicole," she snapped, then grabbed her Taco Bell from his fingers and headed into the kitchen, which happened to be only about four steps in. "Feel free to let yourself out."

Naturally, and because she suspected he was as ornery and contrary as he was magnificent looking, he followed her instead.

"What are you doing?" she demanded.

"Making sure you don't fall down on your feet."

"We've already established I'm a grownup."

"You're right about that. Um…" He watched her shove aside a pile of medical journals and rip into the bag with a wince. "How about some real breakfast?"

"This *is* real." And her mouth was watering. "Goodbye, Mr. Architect."

"You know, you're very welcome," he said when she grabbed a taco, leaned against the counter and took a huge bite. "Glad I could help."

"Yeah. Thank you for breaking and entering." She nearly moaned when the food hit her tongue, but managed to hold it back, sucking down a good part of her soda before practically inhaling the rest of her first taco.

When she reached into the bag for the next one, he sighed.

She eyed him. "You forget where the front door is? Wouldn't want it to hit you on your way out."

"You should really make yourself some healthier food—"

"There's meat, cheese, lettuce and shell here…I've got all the food groups represented."

"Yes, but—" He watched her lick a drop of sauce off her thumb. "I'm assuming you just got off some brutal shift at the hospital?"

"Yeah…" She paused for a long, amazingly refreshing gulp of soda. "Don't take this personally, okay? But could you go away? I've got a date with my bed, and it doesn't include anyone else but me and my pillow."

"Now that's a crying shame." He added a slow grin that upped her pulse.

"Don't get any ideas. I don't play doctor with strangers."

"Who'd want to play with *that* attitude?" He grinned when she growled at him. "And I wasn't propositioning you, Dr. Nicole Mann. I just think you should eat something that has more nutrients than…say a paper bag. Why don't you let me cook—"

He broke off when she burst into laughter. Feeling less like she was going to die on the spot now that she had something in her belly, she set down her taco and headed for the front door. While she was certain he could "cook" up something all right, she wasn't interested. Yes, she enjoyed looking at a great specimen of a man such as himself, but she didn't feel the need to do more than look. "Goodnight," she said, holding the door open.

"Let me guess…" He sauntered up to her with that loosehipped stride of his, all long, lean grace. His eyes, those amazing blue, blue eyes, seemed to see straight through her. "You have a thing against real food?"

"No, I have a thing against strangers offering to cook for me. Let's face it, Mr. Architect." She offered him a nasty smile she reserved for the lowest forms of life—men on the prowl. "You weren't offering to cook me *food*."

"I wasn't?" He lifted a black brow so far it nearly vanished. "And what did you think I *was* offering to cook?"

"Let's just say I'm not interested, whatever it was."

With a slow shake of his head, his mouth curved. He wasn't insulted. Wasn't mad or irate. But he *was* amused at her expense.

"Let's just say," he said, mocking her.

"Goodnight," she repeated, wondering what it was about him that made her both annoyed and yet so…aware.

"Goodnight. Even though it's morning." He lifted a finger, stroking it once over her jaw before turning and walking out the door.

When he was gone, she put her finger to her tingling jaw. It wasn't until a moment later she realized his last few words, "even though it's morning," had been uttered in that same Irish accent he'd claimed not to have.

THAT DAY TY PULLED his own long shift. He had three jobs going in downtown Los Angeles, two in Burbank, four in Glendale and, he hoped, the new one right here in South Village.

It was odd, how fond he'd become of the place. Maybe because the city, just outside of Los Angeles, was a genuinely historical stretch of streets from the great old Western days. Thanks to an innovative—and wealthy—town council, most of the buildings had been rescued, preserved and restored, leaving the streets a popular fun spot filled with restaurants, theaters, unique boutiques and plenty of celebrities to spy on.

Ty had little interest in the swell of young urban singles

that crowded the streets on nights and weekends, but he did love the atmosphere.

He especially loved all the work, for there were plenty of buildings still in the prerenovation stage, needing architects.

Being a relatively new architect in town without the usual partners and office staff meant more work for him. It meant a lot of running around. It also meant lots of time holed up with his drawing table.

He didn't mind the extra hours or the hard work. In fact, that was how he liked it. If something came easy or was handed to him, he was suspicious of it.

That came from his early years, when nothing had been either easy or handed to him, before or after he'd quite literally crawled, scratched and fought his way out of the gutter.

Old times, he thought, and tossing his pencil down, he leaned back in his chair. He put his feet up on the drawing table and looked out the window at the San Gabriel Mountains. No doubt, California was beautiful. Not beautiful like say…Rio. Or Tokyo. Or any of the many places he'd been through on his quest to get as far away from where he'd started as possible, but beautiful in the way that he felt…at ease.

Not that the feeling would last, it never did. Sooner rather than later the need to move on would overcome him…he thought New York might interest him. But for now, California, land of hot blondes, health food and sandy beaches, was good.

It was also a great place for anonymity, and that, really, was the draw. Here, he could be whoever or whatever he wanted. It didn't matter to anyone.

And here, surrounded by the success he'd so carefully built, he was exactly that.

Someone.

Someone with a full bank account, thank you very much. And an office that spelled success, inside a huge, sprawling house with every luxury at his fingertips.

Never again would he have an empty belly or the bonegnawing fear of the unknown, both of which he'd lived with during his beyondhumble beginnings in the seediest of areas in Dublin, Ireland.

He rarely thought of it now, there was no need. He'd put it all behind him, years and years ago. He'd moved on.

Now nothing could hurt him as he continued on his merry way to fill the bank account even more, to do the work that so pleased him. And if he managed to get lucky in between those two things with a California babe here and there, so much the better.

He thought of this morning, and one Dr. Nicole Mann. Not the typical California babe, that was certain. But with her fatigues and tough takeitonthechin attitude, she was easily the sexiest little number he'd ever seen. And he did mean little, for she'd barely come to his shoulder. Still her body had been honed to a curvy, mouthwatering perfection by what he suspected was sheer will on her part— it certainly wasn't a result of her diet if her "breakfast" was anything to go on. Definitely, the one thing the good doctor had in spades was will. She could kill with just her eyes, these longlashed, huge eyes, the gray of a wicked winter storm. Her hair, shiny, dark and cut short to her stubborn chin, made him think of silk.

He would have laughed at the impression she'd made on him, if there was anything funny about it. She was different, and because of it she'd grabbed him on a level he didn't want to be grabbed at. So he wouldn't think about her or her perfect, meantforhotwildsex mouth.

Straightening, he put his feet firmly on the ground. He

liked his feet on the ground. To do that, he had to keep a certain distance from others, and that included sexy Dr. Mann. Spinning in his chair, he propelled himself the few feet to his computer and booted it up. To clear his head of stormy gray eyes and that kissable frown, he'd work.

His email account opened, showing twentyeight unread messages. Skimming through, he deleted each as he took care of various work issues.

And it was all work. Except the last one. He didn't recognize the sender's address, but didn't think anything of it until he opened the mail.

Are you Ty Patrick O'Grady of Dublin?

Surging to his feet, he stared at the email. The words were still there. Stuffing his fingers in his hair he turned a slow circle. No one knew where he was from. No one.

But when he bent to look at the screen again, the words hadn't changed.

Are you Ty Patrick O'Grady of Dublin?

Hell, yes, he was. But who wanted to know? And why? There was nothing good about his past. In fact, there was so much bad, his stomach cramped just thinking about it.

He reached toward the keyboard to delete the message, but his finger hovered just over the key.

Who was asking?

No. It didn't matter. None of his past mattered, and with another low oath and yet another slow spin around the room he came back to his computer. Stared at the message some more.

Then slowly reached out and punched Delete.

CHAPTER TWO

AFTER TWO STRAIGHT days of hell at work, Nicole drove home. She could tell it wasn't her usual time to be doing so—the usual time being very, very late or very, very early—because there wasn't a single parking space to be found in all of South Village, much less on the busy street where she lived.

Shops, galleries and restaurants were all hopping with activity, reminding her that everyone else but herself had a life outside of work. But then, she'd decided long ago that medicine *was* her life. All she needed now was a place to park her car. Finally, after circling the block—twice—swearing in a very satisfying manner and even getting flipped off in the process, she got a spot down the street. The walk to the apartment felt good. So did the bag of fresh croissants she purchased at a corner deli. They'd go splendidly with the takeout hamburgers in a bag in her other hand.

Finally, she came to her building. It really was the wince spot of the area, though the turrets, mock balconies and many windows gave the hundred-year-old place its own charm and personality. Albeit a neglected, falling-down kind of charm.

The two storefronts on the ground floor were empty, though Suzanne planned to open a catering shop in one of them. Taylor was doing her best, working on the renovation day and night, gathering bids and selling off some of her antique collection to do it.

There were plants hanging from window boxes in front of the two apartments on the second floor. Taylor's boxes were effortlessly green and flowery, Suzanne's looked a little wilted since she spent most of her time at Ryan's now.

Nicole could have bought her own place. Her mother often hounded her about it. After all, doctors made tons of dough, right?

Ha! She was twenty-seven. Maybe by the time she was forty she'd have half her college loans paid off. Then again, given that she tended to spend her extra time working at clinics for free to ensure that the less fortunate got medical care, maybe not. Didn't matter. Work was who she was, what she did and there wasn't time left over to tend to so much as a single little plant, much less a house of her own.

She liked things that way.

Exhausted, she staggered up the stairs to her loft. It was still light outside, which confused her. She squinted at her living room. How different it looked with sunlight streaming through the big window. On the street below throngs of people were heading toward chic restaurants and cafés. A glance at her watch told her why. It was five in the afternoon. People were meeting for after-work drinks or early dinners. The thought of socializing like that startled her somewhat. When she wasn't pouring herself into work, she truly preferred to spend her time alone.

She wolfed down the fast food first, while reading one of three medical journals on the table in front of her. The hamburger and super-size fries were the perfect accompaniment to the article on a new and innovative artery replacement. Then, with the sun still shining in all the windows, she headed into her bathroom, still reading, nibbling on a croissant as she stripped for a mindnumbingly hot shower.

No one could ever say she couldn't multitask.

After her steaming shower, she padded naked back into her bedroom, heading directly for the bed, until she glanced at her answering machine, which was blinking.

Damn it, why did she have one of those things again?

Because the hospital administration, tired of not being able to get her when they needed, had insisted. With a sigh, she hit the message button. If it was work, she'd just roll over and die right now.

"Nicole, baby, it's me. Mom," her mother clarified in her cheerful, laughing voice, as if Nicole wouldn't recognize the woman who'd been nagging her all her life. "Are you working too hard? Are you getting any rest? Are you eating right? Are you ever going to call me and put my mind to rest that my baby isn't working herself into an early grave?"

Nicole sank to her bed and ran the towel over her short mop of hair—her idea of styling. Since she'd just called her mother last week, in fact, called every week, she refused to feel guilty.

"Once a week just isn't enough, Nicole," her mother said with her perfectly startling ability to read her daughter's mind. "I want to *hear* you."

Nicole rolled her eyes but a smile escaped anyway.

"Honey, listen. I'm making pot roast on Sunday. Your father called your sisters and everyone is coming—the husbands, the kids, everyone."

Oh, good God. Nicole had three sisters, each of whom had a husband, the requisite minivan, the house in the burbs and at least two kids. The thought of that entire noisy, happy bunch all in one place made Nicole suddenly need another hamburger.

"So, honey, you have to come. We'll expect you by four, and let me warn you, if you don't show, I'll…well, I'll call you every single day for a week."

As Nicole's mother was quite possibly the bossiest, nosiest, most meddling, warm, loving person on the planet, Nicole believed her.

But everyone under one roof? Laughing, talking, happily arguing sisters, sticky toddlers, drooling babies, stinky diapers… She felt a headache coming on already. She loved her family, she did, but sometimes she felt as if she was an alien, plopped down in the middle of a planet where she didn't belong. They were all so…normal. Something she'd never been. Despite her genius IQ, she couldn't deal with people outside of medicine. It was so difficult for her to get out of her own head, she rarely knew what to say to people and some of the basic niceties escaped her. That her family loved her anyway, even though she was intensely introverted, was a strange and odd miracle she tried not to think about too often.

"So, we'll see you Sunday," her mom said as if it'd been decided. "It'll be fun to be all together."

Fun wasn't quite the word Nicole would have come up with. Maybe she'd have work. Yeah, that was it, she could add a shift and—

"Love you, baby."

Ah, hell. Sunday it was.

Still naked, she plopped on the bed. It only took two pillows over her head and approximately twenty seconds for sleep to conquer her the same way she'd conquered her world.

She dreamed. She would have thought she'd be haunted by the blood of her second surgery that day. A patient had burst an artery and by the time she'd gotten everything under control she'd been standing in a sea of red.

But blessedly she'd left that behind at the hospital. Instead, in dreamland, she was two years old again, and memorizing the book of presidents her parents had kept on the coffee table. For fun, she'd recite them backwards to her hotshot, know-it-all sisters Annie and Emma.

It had been their first inkling that Nicole was going to be different.

The dream shifted and she was six, helping Emma with her seventh-grade algebra.

At twelve, she'd helped Annie with her PSAT testing. *A genius,* were the whispers around her. *Off-the-scale IQ,* they said. *A prodigy.*

At twelve, Nicole should have been into lip gloss, pop bands and boys. Instead she'd been fascinated by science. She operated on frogs. She dissected bugs.

Yet kids her own age remained a mystery to her, a complete mystery.

And now that she was grown up, she was still different. She should have learned to deal with others by now. Learned to be a social creature, well rounded and defined.

But the reality was that she'd rarely dated and had no idea how to do anything but heal. It was what she was. Who she was. A doctor.

Nothing else.

So why did the next dream involve one tall, dark and sexy Irish architect with a killer smile and eyes that made her yearn for something completely out of her reach?

Turning over, she sank back into an exhausted and dreamless slumber.

"Wake up, Nicole, you're scaring me."

Nicole snuggled more deeply beneath her covers. "Go away, Mom, I don't have school today."

"I had better not look anything like a woman old enough to be your mother."

Nicole jerked her eyes open, heart pounding. Okay, good, she was home. The sun was shining again, how annoying.

And Taylor sat on her bed, looking as stunningly beautiful and elegant as ever.

With a groan, Nicole shut her eyes again. "I didn't help you with the engagement party plans, right?"

"No, but I forgive you because you're going to reschedule. I brought you breakfast."

Nicole smelled something delicious. She cracked open an eye and saw a tray filled with mouthwatering food.

"I should tell you—as if you couldn't guess—I didn't cook this. Suzanne's catering a big brunch this morning and made this up for us. You frightened the hell out of me, not answering your door. You never even heard me calling for you like a banshee, and we all know I don't like to sound like a banshee. Who sleeps like that?"

Nicole blinked. "Well…"

"You've overworked yourself again, haven't you? Nicole, honey, that's just plain bad for you."

Nicole closed her eyes, rendered stupid by this display of concern. Maybe if she was really still, Taylor would vanish. A figment of her imagination.

"Not much of a morning person," came an amused male voice from the other side of the room.

If Nicole had thought her heart had raced at the sight of Taylor in her bedroom, it went off the scale now. Even after their very brief encounter, she recognized that slightly Irish voice, she recognized it immediately. And if it brought a series of shivers down her spine that she couldn't attribute to a morning chill, she could shove the reaction aside in favor of temper. "What the hell—"

"Now before you get all pissy at me…" Taylor put a hand over Nicole's chest, pushing her back. "Let me explain."

Nicole could take Taylor down any day of the week. Her workouts, when she could fit them in, guaranteed that.

The only exercise Taylor ever did was lifting and setting down her hairbrush. Oh, and her lipstick.

No, what held Nicole back from wrapping her fingers around Taylor's neck was one tiny little detail.

She slept in the nude.

Which meant that in order to kick Taylor's ass, she'd have to get out of bed.

Naked.

"Why is he in here?" she settled for asking between her teeth while clutching the sheet to her chest.

From his perch holding up her wall, Ty's gaze zoomed in on her—a very blue gaze that was lit with amusement, curiosity and plenty more—and for just a flash in time, she lost her train of thought.

Taylor craned her neck and looked up at the tall, dark, ridiculously gorgeous man. "You've met?"

"You could say that," Nicole said.

"Oh, good, because I'm thinking of hiring him to fix up the building, which apparently is about to fall off its axis. Not," she added quickly, "that you need to worry about it, I'm getting it all fixed pronto."

"Taylor." Nicole rubbed her temples. "The point. Get to the point. *Why is he here?* Specifically, in my bedroom."

"Well, I was standing there in the hallway yelling for you, and beginning to freak out when you didn't answer, when he offered to break in since I didn't have my keys on me. He's not only an excellent architect, he's quite the handyman."

"Let me guess," Nicole said dryly, watching Ty smile

at her from behind Taylor's back. "He got in with a credit card?"

"Why, yes. A handy little trick, don't you think?"

"Hmm." Nicole narrowed her eyes at the ease he displayed standing there in her bedroom. As if he belonged.

But no one, especially a man, belonged in her bedroom, no matter how good he looked in a light-blue chambray shirt shoved up past his forearms, and a pair of jeans that made her hormones stand up and quiver. "Is the credit card trick something you picked up in Ireland?" she asked.

"Why ever would you think that?" he asked innocently.

As if he'd ever been innocent. "Because I hear it in your voice."

"That's the English, luv," he said, pushing lazily away from the wall, coming close enough to peruse the tray from Suzanne. Then, picking up a piece of toast, his gaze tracked over Nicole from head to toe, and back again, making every single atom in her body leap to attention. Sinking his teeth into the bread, he chewed a moment, then licked the butter off his finger with a sucking sound that caused an answering tug in Nicole's nipples for some annoying reason. "Went there for a while," he said.

"Thought it was Scotland."

Leaning in, he put the toast to her lips, pressing until she had no choice but to open and take a bite. "There, too," he said lightly, making her take yet another bite, his thumb stroking across her bottom lip at a dab of misplaced butter. "And also Australia, if you're interested in keeping track."

She felt the touch all the way to her toes and back up, and at all sorts of other interesting spots along the way. It didn't help that her eyes were level with a most erotic spot on his body—the juncture between his thighs—and the intriguing bulge there.

"I had to make sure you were okay," Taylor said, picking up a piece of peach from the tray. "I'm sorry for the invasion, but you've done nothing but work since you moved in here, and you sleep like the dead."

Ty let out another innocent smile. "And you talk to yourself while doing it."

Nicole opened her mouth, but Taylor stuffed the peach into it. At the explosion of sweet nectar in her mouth, she sputtered.

"That was a piece of fruit," Taylor said. "I realize you might not recognize it, given that it's actually one of the important food groups and not purchased from a drive-through."

"Taylor—"

"You're going to kill yourself this way," Taylor said softly, her eyes showing their worry. "It's not right. Promise me you'll eat all of this mountain of food. The eggs, the sausage, the toast, the fruit, everything."

Nicole sighed. "I never had a landlord care what I put inside my body before."

Taylor went still, then brushed the crumbs off her hands. "Is that all I am?"

Nicole looked into Taylor's eyes, saw the hurt added to the worry, and flopped back to stare up at the ceiling. "*This* is why I don't socialize."

Taylor stood a little stiffly, when the elegant Taylor was never stiff. "I'm sorry. I'll go. Just make sure Suzanne gets her tray back—"

Nicole reached out and grabbed her wrist. "Look...I'm the sorry one."

"No need."

Nicole sighed at the cool hurt lingering in Taylor's face and tugged on her wrist until she sat back at her side. "I'm an idiot, all right? An idiot who doesn't know how to... have friends."

"So we *are* friends?"

"You know we are. Unless you shove any more fruit down my throat."

"In that case…" Taylor spread her silk skirt carefully and made herself comfortable on the bed before reaching for a piece of toast. "There's enough here to feed an army. Ty, some sausage? Don't be shy, hon, Suzanne is so nervous about her upcoming nuptials that she's overcooking to compensate."

"Taylor," Nicole said in a warning voice that turned into a squeak when Ty suddenly joined them.

On the bed.

His long denim-covered legs brushed hers. There were the covers between them, but given the electric zap she felt at the brush of his warm, hard body, and given the way the current continued to run through her, there weren't enough covers in all of South Village to keep between them.

And then there was how her heart gave a little leap when he turned his head and pierced her with those amazing eyes of his.

Instant lust. She'd heard about it but had never experienced the phenomenon firsthand.

She didn't like it.

Gripping the sheet to her chest for all it was worth, Nicole watched as her two uninvited houseguests helped themselves to the tray of food balancing on her knees.

It was an unreal feeling having Ty's long fingers hover over the plate only inches from her very naked body as he decided on a slice of apple.

It crunched between his white teeth as he looked at her.

Unreal, she decided, and definitely…arousing, if the way her body tingled was any indication. "I…need to get up."

Taylor used the fork to bite into the homemade hash

browns, then moaned. "Oh, these. *These* are to die for. Ty?"

Leaning in, he opened his mouth to the forkful Taylor was offering him.

"Fabulous, right?" Taylor said as he chewed.

He licked his lips, and for an instant, as he looked at Nicole, something hot and dangerous flashed in his eyes. "Oh yeah."

"More?" Taylor asked. "A man your size, who works as hard as you do, needs to keep up his strength."

Still gripping the sheet, Nicole grated her teeth. "I really need to— *Hey!*" she said around the bite of warm hash browns Ty shoved into her mouth. And not too gently either. She had to open quickly and use her tongue to keep from spilling them down her front.

His electric-blue eyes never left hers. She would have opened her mouth and blistered him if she hadn't had it so full of the food. And oh man, the food. Heaven.

Not that she was going to admit it. "I don't eat breakfast," she said, trying not to moan in pleasure as the food started to hit her stomach. "Just—"

"Coffee," Ty finished for her, bending so close his lips almost brushed hers. "We've heard. It's here." She could feel his body heat, the warm breath that caused goose bumps to skitter down her side. "You're going to give yourself ulcers the way you eat." He tsked. "And you claim to be a doctor."

"Oh, I definitely like you," Taylor said to Ty, who grinned at her. "We can tagteam her. I know you like to move around a lot, but I don't suppose after this job you'd stay on and reprogram my friend here?"

"I *really* have to get up," Nicole said, jaw clenched. "So if you could…" She gestured to the door.

"Go ahead." Ty's eyes were lit with the dare. "Get up."

Nicole thought about how very naked she was under her sheet and gripped it tighter to her chest. She'd never been shy, had never felt anything but comfortable in her own skin. This came from years of no privacy in a tiny house with too many family members, then college dorms, and more recently, the locker area at work, which wasn't much bigger or more private than her bedroom happened to be at the moment. But in front of this man, she suddenly felt... inadequate. He was red-blooded, through and through. She figured she knew his type; big boobs and breeding hips, with lots of hair to drape over his chest, that's what he'd want.

Her virtual opposite.

Not that she cared. She just didn't plan to flaunt her small boobs and small hips anywhere near him.

Then, from across the small bedroom, under a mountain of clothes and more medical journals on a chair, came the unmistakable sound of her beeper going off.

Taylor held out her hand to keep Nicole in bed. "It's your day off."

"I can't just ignore it." But it was a shame she hadn't piled more clothes on top of the beeper before last night. A few more days' worth and no one could have possibly heard the thing go off. "Okay, fun's over. You guys did good, you fed me. Now get lost."

"Nicole," Taylor said sternly, still sitting on the bed. "Do not get that pager."

Nicole turned to Ty, whose daring, smiling gaze had never left hers. "I have to."

"Sure you do, darlin'." He lifted an inviting hand. "Go right ahead, if it's meaning that much to you."

"You have to move first."

Generous to a fault, he scooted down on the bed a tad,

giving her enough room to leave the bed if she so desired. "Go on now."

With as much dignity as she could muster, which wasn't much, she grabbed the sheet and held on to it for dear life as she slid from the bed. Standing was a bit tricky, but she wrapped the sheet around her so fast her head nearly spun. Surely no one had gotten a glimpse of anything. Still, she didn't quite dare to look back and catch a peek at Ty's face as she headed, chin thrust high, toward the chair.

She had to shove the medical journals and clothes to the floor to verify, but yep, it was work.

"Don't tell me." Taylor stood up. "You're going in. You're hopeless, you know that?" With a dramatic sigh, she headed toward the door. "But we'll be there, Nicole, if you fall."

"We?"

"Suzanne and I, of course. Ornery as you are, you'll need us to stick by you. So go. Go work yourself to exhaustion again. Enjoy."

"I will, thanks." Half amused at the genuine compassion and worry that she'd seen on Taylor's face, she turned back to face Ty. "Don't let the door get you on the ass on your way out. I'm taking a shower."

"Maybe you'd better take your caffeine with you." He held out a mug of coffee.

"Thanks." Grateful but not about to admit it, Nicole held on to the sheet for dear life and hobbled into the bathroom. She shut the door harder than she should have, and clicked the lock into place with what sounded like a gunshot.

She might have had to wake up with an audience, then eat with one, but hell if she'd shower in front of one, no matter how pretty he was.

Still, the hot steam worked wonders, and she stayed

there for a good long time, until the hot water turned warm, then tepid. Finally, she stepped out and sighed.

Damn, she'd been looking forward to a day off.

There was one dry towel left on the rack, which meant she needed to seriously consider the pile of things behind her bedroom door as well as the pile now on her floor, both of which she so lovingly referred to as Laundry Mountain Range. Tucking the towel beneath her armpits, she studied herself impassively in the mirror.

Not bad, she'd give herself that. And though she'd prefer to be taller than so damn short, her bones weren't bad either. Thanks to her workouts, she was a lean, mean, fighting machine.

But breasts would have been nice.

Laughing at herself, she turned away. What would she have done with cleavage? It wasn't as if she had dates lining up.

Still smiling, she opened the door and marched into her bedroom, dropping her towel as she went.

Because she had excellent eyesight, she therefore had a front-and-center view of Ty sitting on her bed, holding a glass of orange juice.

He had a front-and-center view, too. Of her.

The glass slipped from his fingers and fell to the floor in tune with her shriek as she bent down for her towel. *"What are you doing?"*

"I…"

Straightening, she studiously avoided looking into his face as she refastened the towel. "I thought you left!"

"Yeah, I…"

"You said that already!"

Ty knew that, but he was still flummoxed by the sight of her tight, lean body all dewy and damp from her shower.

Standing now, he wasn't reassured by the fact his knees wobbled.

What was wrong with him? She wasn't his usual type, meaning stacked and blond and soft. There was nothing soft about Nicole, not her tough, angular body, not her voice, and most definitely not her eyes.

So why couldn't he stop thinking dirty little thoughts? Or take his eyes off her? "Sorry. I just wanted to be sure you at least drank some juice."

"Can't do that now, can I?" With jerky movements, she tightened the towel even further over her breasts.

Breasts that he now knew were a perfect handful, tipped with tight rose-colored nipples. Somehow he managed to walk to her, lift her chin and look into her furious and... damn it, very embarrassed, eyes. "I'm sorry," he repeated softly.

"Yeah."

He gazed at her grim mouth, and unbidden, his thoughts turned to kissing her until she was soft and pliant, until she sighed and gave herself over to him and the pleasure he could give her. He, Ty Patrick O'Grady, no-good bastard, blackheart. "You should know I'm attracted to you in a way I can't quite seem to get over."

"And yet you've seen me naked. Imagine that."

She didn't believe him. He sucked in a breath and inhaled the scent of her shampoo and ridiculously, his body reacted.

Perfect.

Now all his thinking had taken him to a place he had no business going, not with this woman. She wasn't the type to put up with a man afflicted with a serious sense of wanderlust, a man who never knew when he was going to decide to up and relocate.

Hell, he'd never found *any* woman, on this continent or otherwise, who'd put up with that.

Not that he wanted one to.

"You're beautiful, Nicole," he heard himself say as he stroked a finger over her cheek, her jaw. "So damn beautiful."

It wasn't until he got down the stairs and into his car that he let out the breath he'd been holding and stared off at nothing.

He'd meant what he'd said. He was attracted to her in a way he couldn't get past. And she *was* beautiful, with or without that mouthwatering body and all that creamy, creamy skin exposed. So damned beautiful he ached.

Not a good thing, not a good thing at all.

CHAPTER THREE

NICOLE WORKED SO MANY hours over the next two days she managed to forget Ty had seen her very naked. At the end of a particularly long, atrocious shift, she stood in front of her locker in the doctor's lounge and realized she actually had the next day off.

Sleep, here she came.

"That was an interesting sigh," said a male voice from behind her. A voice that made her wish she'd gotten out of here five minutes ago.

Dr. Lincoln Watts. Head of Surgery. And ruler of his domain.

Not that she didn't appreciate his skill, because he was truly gifted. But that gift didn't extend to his people skills.

In short, out of the operating room, he was a jerk. The nurses hated him, the aides feared him. The other doctors merely tolerated him, mostly because he ruled over all of them, but also because it was too much trouble to cross him.

Oh, and he had the memory of an elephant.

As the youngest doctor on staff, Nicole had learned to keep a low profile. She did her job; she did it well. It was all she'd ever wanted.

Even with Dr. Watts staring at her ass. "Can I help you?" she asked politely, turning to look at him so he had to raise his gaze.

He took his time about doing so, and for the first time

she was glad she had small, unimpressive breasts. She wanted to give him as little pleasure as possible.

"Can you help me," he repeated with a little smile as he finally met her gaze. "Why yes, I believe you can."

Damn.

"Come with me to the benefit tomorrow night."

The benefit he referred to was an annual event designed to extricate money from rich patrons and deposit it directly to the hospital's coffers. It put critical funds at the hospital's disposal, as well as provided write-offs for the hospital's patrons. Everyone was happy.

However, it required an evening of stiff smiles for Nicole, who hated dressing up, hated being "on" and hated the forced mingling. This year she'd arranged to be on shift so as to avoid the entire messy affair. "Sorry, I'm working."

"I can rearrange that for you."

At a considerable cost, one she figured would involve him and his bed. "No, thank you. I don't mind missing it."

"I want you to come with me."

And what Dr. Watts wanted, Dr. Watts got. "I'm sorry, Dr. Watts, but that wouldn't be fair to the others."

"Linc."

"Excuse me?"

He traced a finger over her shoulder and she just barely restrained her shudder. "Call me Linc," he said softly. "And I'd consider it a personal favor if you went with me."

Nicole might have mastered calculus by the age of eight but she'd never mastered basic political correctness 101. "I said no."

His eyes darkened, and without another word, he strode off.

Uneasy, Nicole watched him go and wondered if she'd just screwed herself by not screwing the boss.

SHE WENT HOME. On the front steps of the building sat a brass lion, its mouth open wide in a silent roar. Shaking her head, she walked past it. Just inside were a vintage-looking gramophone, an ornately decorated headboard leaning against the wall and a marble clock.

Taylor, the poor little rich girl. She'd inherited this building without any of the money she'd become accustomed to in her spoiled youth, with the exception of the antiques she'd been collecting all her life. She'd been selling off the beloved pieces to cover the costs of bringing the building back to its former glory. *Resourcefulness.* It was one of the things Nicole appreciated most about Taylor, as Nicole had been forced to be resourceful all her life.

A three-foot-high wooden carved bear holding a fish and wearing a grin sat on the first flight of stairs. Along the second flight were stacks of prints. Nicole was staring at one of a bowl of fruit, thinking she was just starving enough to actually eat fruit, when Taylor stuck her head out of her apartment.

Damn. More party plans. "I'm really tired," Nicole said pathetically, figuring Taylor would take pity on her.

Instead Taylor reached out, snagged her wrist and yanked her into her apartment. "We need to talk."

"But—"

"You're tired, yeah, yeah. I know. I figured that much and planned the party without you."

Gratitude filled Nicole, and she felt a little bad about her peevishness. "Thank—"

"Don't thank me yet, Super Girl. You're going to need a dress."

"Oh, no—"

"Oh yes. And know it up front, we're going fancy on this one."

"But—"

"That'll teach you to leave me alone to plan things."

"Well, unplan them."

"No." Taylor leveled her stubborn gaze on Nicole. "Suzanne deserves this."

"Yes, but—"

"*Fancy,*" Taylor said firmly. "As in silk and lace and high heels and makeup and hairdos and everything."

Nicole had faced two life-threatening surgeries that day. She'd faced Dr. Watts. And she'd rather face a fire-breathing dragon on top of all of it than get "fancy." "You're kidding me."

"Honey, I never kid about fashion."

Nicole paled. "Fashion?"

"You and me. At the mall. Your next day off."

Nicole let out a string of curses that had Taylor laughing. "Oh, and since you owe me on planning the party without you, you can pay up right now. I need a little favor."

Nicole thought of her bed and sighed. "Taylor—"

"Don't worry, it's not difficult. I just need you to run to Ty's office and give him these." She dumped a large set of plans into Nicole's arms. "And this." She added a file. "Did you like him?"

"What?"

"Did you like Ty?" Taylor laughed at her expression. "What's not to like, right? He's sexy as hell, and in possession of a body I could just gobble up." She sighed dramatically. "It's too bad we're too much alike. We'd kill each other."

Nicole shook her head. "I'm not going to ask."

"But I'm going to tell. Ty and I, we're fellow wanderlust spirits."

"You've got wanderlust?"

"Through and through, until I came here and found

home. But Ty hasn't found his home yet. Fighting our own prospective and warring needs would be like living in a battlefield. Nope, much as I'd like a good, naughty affair—and I'm quite certain Ty can do good and naughty—he's not for me."

Nicole put her hands over her ears—or at least she tried to around all the stuff in her arms—and Taylor laughed again. "Just go. Tell him I'm giving him the job. The address of his office is on the label, and it's only three minutes from here."

Before Nicole could blink, she'd been turned around and shoved out the door. She whirled, but only to hear Taylor's lock click into place. "I'm not doing this," she said through the wood.

"Then come back in and help me pick out napkins and plates and menus for the party."

Nicole stared down at Ty's name and address and felt a peculiar flutter in her belly. Why was it that every time she thought of him her skin went all hot and itchy and her nipples got happy? "This is a bad idea, Taylor."

"Since when are you afraid of anyone, much less a man?" Taylor asked through the door.

Since that man could simply look at her and make her feel things she didn't understand. "I…can't."

"Just drop the plans off, Nicole. You don't have to marry him."

Yeah, Nicole. You don't have to marry him. Somehow that didn't make her feel any better. With a sigh, she headed down the stairs instead of up, and got back into her car.

TY HAD A HEADACHE and another email. This was not what he needed after a long day at work. He stood staring at it. He shut his eyes, swore, and stared at it again.

I think you're Ty Patrick O'Grady of Dublin.
I think you were born to Anne Mary Mulligan of Dublin.
Please confirm.
Margaret Mary

Why a Margaret Mary would be looking for him was anyone's guess, only none of them were good.

Who was this formal-sounding woman, and why did she care who he was? What did she know of the boy he'd been? And he *had* been a boy when he'd left Dublin, a young boy who'd never looked back. Why should he? He had nothing to look back for, no roots, nothing. His father had taken himself to an early grave in a drunken brawl when Ty had been a year old. His mother had run a tavern with rooms above it she'd used as an inn when they'd needed the money. Which had been all the time. Ty had been nothing more than a mistake she didn't like to be reminded of.

That had often worked in his favor, as he'd had the freedom to do as he pleased. And since his mother rarely remembered to feed him, much less clothe him, and only begrudgingly gave him a mat to sleep on, the freedom pleased him plenty. He "borrowed" clothes, stole food and ran with a crowd that made the L.A. gang-bangers look friendly.

When he'd turned ten he'd witnessed his first murder. Over a pair of boots. When he'd turned eleven, his mother had sold the inn and moved on.

Without him.

By the time he'd turned sixteen, he'd been beyond redemption. Or so he'd thought. That's when he'd made the mistake of trying to pick the pocket of a vacationing Australian. The man, Seely McGraw, had been a cop, of all things, and instead of dragging Ty off to jail, he'd dragged him home with him. To Australia. Ireland had been happy to see him go.

In Australia, Seely had seen him through the rest of his school years. Civilized. Humanized. And yet the vagabond within him had survived.

When Seely had died, Ty had given in to his wanderlust, going wherever he wanted, when he wanted. Europe, Asia, Africa. Even South America. Then he'd come here, to the States, and had landed in California.

For the first time in his life, he'd fallen in love with a place. Created a home for himself.

He wondered how long that would last before the wanderlust yearning overcame him again. Given his past, he didn't figure it would be long. But for now he enjoyed himself, occasionally marveling over how far he'd come.

Life was good right here, right now. He had a job he loved, and money with which to do as he pleased when he pleased.

But now someone wanted him to think about his past, where he'd been a son-of-a-bitch Irish runaway.

Rare temper stirring, he hit Reply and typed:

Who wants to know?

No, that would only encourage this, when he wanted nothing more than to forget all about it. But before he could delete it, he heard a knock at the front door, which he'd left open for the pizza he'd ordered. He needed that pizza. "Back here!"

Hopefully they hadn't forgotten the beer this time, he seemed to be in a mood for it. Standing up, he stared down at the computer one more time, stared at his response, finger still poised to delete...

"Ty?"

Not pizza, but Nicole. Her wide gray eyes stared into his, and in a flash, pure lust sped through his blood.

And between his thighs.

Whether it was the monster headache he had, or the unwanted hunger for this woman, it was a weakness, and he hated weaknesses. He wanted the taste of her mouth, the feel of her body beneath his hands, and given her expression, every bit of his wanting showed on his face.

Her mouth opened, then carefully closed. On instinct, he looked down at himself and realized he hadn't put on a shirt after his shower or fastened his jeans.

Doing that now brought her gaze from the tattoo on his arm right down to an area of his body that seemed to have this hyperawareness of her. "I thought you were the pizza," he said, the metal-on-metal glide of his zipper seeming extraordinarily loud, echoing between them.

"Uh…" Nicole jerked her head up and stared into his eyes with a blank expression, as if she couldn't remember what she was doing there.

Christ, that was arousing.

And confusing as hell, because this woman, and this woman alone, seemed to be able to mess with his head.

She thrust out a set of plans. "From Taylor." She slapped a file against his chest as well. "You've got the job, Mr. Architect." And she turned away.

"Nicole."

She was careful not to turn back to look at him. "Yes?"

What had he been going to say? Something. Anything. "I…got the job?"

"I just said so, didn't I?"

Ah, his sweet, sweet Nicole. "Well, then. We need to celebrate."

She pivoted back to face him. "Celebrate?"

"Mmmhmm." Oh yes, he was enjoying that spark of

temper and heat in her eyes immensely, as it happened to match his.

"You know that Irish accent you pretend not to have?" She put a hand on her hip. "It was there when you first called out, before you knew it was me. And you know what else? You didn't look in the mood to celebrate. You looked mad." She peered around him at the computer. "At that?"

"Nope." Setting down the plans and file, he reached down to sleep his screen, but hit Enter by mistake, sending the reply to the mystery emailer.

Furious at himself, he stared at the screen and uttered one concise oath.

"What?"

"Nothing." And it would be nothing, he'd see to it. Turning away from the computer, he forced a deep breath before leaning back against the wall to properly soak up the sight of Nicole. She wore hip-hugging black jeans and a plain black tank top that didn't quite meet the jeans. The peek-a-boo hints of bare, smooth skin decorated by a diamond twinkling from her belly button made his mouth water. She hadn't done much to her hair other than plow her fingers through it, and the only makeup she wore was a glittery lip-gloss. She was attitude personified, and yet he suddenly, viciously, wanted to devour her. *Needed* to devour her. "What does it matter what mood I was in then? I'm in the mood to celebrate now."

"Well, I'm not."

Indeed. She seemed tempered and unguarded, and very undoctorlike. Something he'd have realized from the very first if lust hadn't slapped him in the face. He could see the strain in her eyes now, the unhappiness in the set of her mouth. "What's the matter with you?"

Lifting a shoulder, she looked away.

"Nicole?" Shocking how much he wanted to pull her

close and cuddle. He, a man who'd never cuddled, or been cuddled, a day in his life. "Bad day at work?"

Another negligent shrug.

She was going to make him drag it out of her. Fine. He suddenly wanted to know badly enough to do so. "Did you...lose a patient?"

A sigh much too weighted for such a little thing escaped her. "Not today. Thankfully."

"Someone threaten to sue you?"

Her mouth curved. "Not today. Thankfully."

Hmm. A sense of humor under all that armor. He liked that. "Did you get an email giving you a very unwelcome blast from your past?"

She studied him for a long moment, while he kicked himself for letting her slip past his guard enough that his mouth had run away with his good sense.

"Is that what happened to you?" she finally asked.

"We were talking about you."

"I don't want to talk about me." To prove it, she crossed her arms.

"Ah. You're a hoarder."

"A *what?*"

"You hoard your emotions. I appreciate that in a woman, as I do the same."

"That's not exactly something to be proud of."

"No kidding. If I had a dime for every time a woman tried to get me to open up and cry all over her..." His mouth curved. "Well, let's just say I'd be one wealthy man. So..." He cocked his head. "We're both in a mood, full of temper and restless energy. Might as well pool our resources, darlin'."

Her brows came together. The earrings up her ear glittered as she cocked her head. "Let me guess. We could pool resources in the way of, say…having wild animal sex, maybe up against that wall?"

God, she was something all riled up. Not to mention what image her words had just put in his head. "Well…"

"You're thinking about it, aren't you?"

"Oh, yeah, I am."

Cynicism hit her gaze now, and he had to be quick to reach out and grab her wrist when she would have whirled away. "I'm thinking about it, Nicole, because *you* said it. I'm a guy, we're visual creatures, and you just gave me one amazing visual."

"There it is again," she accused. "Your accent. It comes out with temper or…"

"Or…?"

"When you're…"

"When I'm what? Turned on?"

She crossed her arms over her chest. "You should know, I agreed to bring you the plans so I could tell you I'm not going to act on my attraction to you."

He felt heat spear him. "You're admitting to an attraction?"

The look on her face was priceless. "Oh, just forget it." She upped the ante by putting her hands on his chest. Staring down at her own fingers, she spread them wide, as if she wanted to touch as much of him as he could.

"What are you doing?" he asked a bit hoarsely.

"Pushing you away."

But she wasn't pushing.

Because he needed a grip and she wasn't providing one, he put his hands over hers, entwined their fingers.

She let out a slow breath, and he did the same. Then their gazes met.

"We should have just talked about our day," she said shakily.

"Mine sucked," he offered.

"Mine too."

"I got that blast from my past and I didn't like it."

"I got hit on by my boss."

"What blast—" she said, at the same time that he said, "*What?* What do you mean hit on by your boss?"

"Never mind—" They both started, then halted, stared at each other and let out a breath.

Then, inexplicably, Nicole's lips twitched.

His did too, and beneath his fingers, hers relaxed. Her smile, which came slow and surprisingly sweet, warmed him in a way he hadn't expected.

"How about we don't talk at all," she whispered, and leaned forward a very tiny fraction of an inch so that their mouths were lined up.

Lined up but not quite touching.

Ty ached to remedy that, but there was the matter of what had happened to her at work, something he found he couldn't let go. "Nicole, about your boss—"

"No talking," she said firmly.

"But—"

She put her fingers to his lips, which brought him back to the animalsex thing.

With a little sigh, she leaned into his throat. "Damn it, you smell good. Who'd have thought you could smell good?"

She smelled good, too, so good he nearly took a bite out of her. "Why wouldn't you have thought so?"

"Because I really don't want to like you." Her eyes clouded. "You have no idea how much I don't want to like you."

"But you do."

She said nothing, and he smiled, pulling back far enough to look down at her. Sunlight sliced across half her face, illuminating her expressive eyes. "Listen up, darlin', because my accent is about to make a return."

With that he bent his head, slid his jaw to hers, then put his mouth at the sensitive spot beneath her ear. "I don't want to like you either. So damn much, I don't." Having said that, he let out a slow breath to steady himself, and she shivered against him. "But it's too late. I already do." His fingers untangled from hers, so they could move up her back. "So let's use that to our advantage. Let's forget today." He plowed his fingers through her short, silky hair, holding her head in his palms.

Her eyes, hard and cynical only a few moments before, were wide as saucers as he tipped up her face. Lowering his, he repeated, "Forget today. Forget the stress."

She licked her lips. Swallowed hard.

And shot a hot ball of lust into his belly. "Hell," he said grimly. "Let's go for broke and forget our own names, what do you say?"

She sucked in her breath. "I never forget my name."

"That's because you're too logical." He was loving the way his touch seemed to interfere with her breathing. Through her tank top he could feel the outline of her nipples, tight and straining against the material of her shirt, dying for some attention. He was dying to give that attention. "Sometimes, Nicole, you just have to go with the flow."

"Going with the flow is not a strong suit of mine," she said a bit shakily.

"I'm beginning to see that."

She fisted her hand on his chest. "I don't like complications in my personal life, Ty."

"Complications can be a good thing. Temporary complications, of course." His voice lowered a fraction. "Are you ready?"

Looking a little wild, a little panicky, she chewed on her lower lip.

Stared at his mouth.

Arched her body just a little, just enough to drive him nearly right out of his living mind.

"Nicole? Are you ready?"

"Just do it."

"Do what?" he asked huskily, teasingly.

"Kiss me!"

She looked so frustrated he nearly laughed. Nearly. Because there was nothing funny about how turned on he was, about how much he wanted her. "As you wish."

Brushing his mouth over hers, he slid the tip of his tongue along the seam of her lips in tune to their twin moans.

And kept his promise as he made them both forget their names.

CHAPTER FOUR

NICOLE'S HEART POUNDED in her chest as pleasure swept through her. She didn't know how she could be attracted to this man in this way, when he was the last person she figured she should want to feel such aching desire for.

They were polar opposites, for God's sake. She was tense, an overachiever, dedicated to her work over and beyond all else.

He was laidback. Easygoing. Not exactly forthcoming with his real self.

Okay, so maybe they shared that last trait.

But what was it Taylor had said about him…he was willing to let life take him where it would. Here. There. Anywhere. Not her, she knew exactly where she wanted life to take her. She'd always known.

And where she wanted life to take her had nothing to do with a man. With sex. With *feeling*.

She wanted life to take her right along the same path she'd been going. She wanted to be a great doctor. She wanted to try new and innovative surgeries, and be successful at them. She wanted to save people's lives.

And not think about her own.

Yet there was no denying, he did something to her, something to her insides. He made her yearn and burn for human contact. Physical contact.

And that was something she rarely allowed herself because it made her open. Vulnerable.

She didn't like to be open and vulnerable.

But that's exactly what he did, without even laying a finger on her. He could have done it with just his eyes, but he had his hands on her now. She wanted to hate him for that, even as she wound her arms around his neck, even as she tilted her head for better access and kissed him back with everything she had.

Her body's immediate reaction surprised her. Consumed her. She certainly hadn't planned on feeling this aching desire, and for a man she hadn't yet decided to trust. Her fingers ran over the sexy tattoo on his arm, then up his slightly rough jaw. He ran his down her back. She slid her fingers into his short hair and gripped hard. He rocked their bodies together.

"This is insane," she decided.

"Yeah." With a sexy growl deep in his throat, he slipped his hands beneath the edging of her top so that his fingers played at the base of her spine, stroking over bare skin, while his mouth danced over hers again, making her do just what he'd said he could do. Making her forget today, forget the stress.

Forget her name.

She wanted to pull away, wanted never to have goaded him into this embrace. Hard to do, since she'd practically climbed up his halfnude body in a desperate attempt to get even closer.

End it, she told herself.

Instead, she continued to kiss him back with everything she had. Her tongue encouraged his, her hands claimed his sleek, muscled chest, while her insides melted at the hard, hot feel of him beneath her fingertips. She clung crazily to him as the only solid object in her frenzied world. And his lips…Lord, his lips! They were warm, firm and deliciously demanding. She could have said the same thing about his hands, which were at her waist now, his thumbs lightly caressing the quivering flesh just beneath her belly button. A knot deep inside her tightened. Her legs wobbled. And her nipples had long ago hardened to needy points, as if he'd already touched her there.

But he hadn't, and that she wanted him to more than she wanted her next breath no longer shocked her. She wanted this man.

Then, from somewhere behind them came the ping of a computer snapping her back to reality. For those glorious few moments he'd actually made her forget that she stood in his house, mewling all over him, practically begging him for something she was not prepared to give.

"Your computer is calling you," she said far more unevenly than she would have liked.

Still leaning over her, his mouth wet from hers, he slowly blinked, giving her a heavylidded look that made her want once again to melt all over him. "What?"

Pulling all the way free of his hands so she could get her brain functioning again, she stepped away, disturbed by how devastating one simple kiss had been.

Bottom line, when he laid on his easygoing charm, he was dangerous to her mental health, and this power seemed such an innate part of him she just needed to stay the hell away, period. "Your computer," she repeated, licking her lips and tasting him on her. "It's calling you."

It took him a while because first he watched her tongue dart out to lick her lips, but finally he turned his head and looked at his computer screen.

His breathing wasn't even either, Nicole noticed, just as she'd noticed every little detail about him. Like his bare chest, lightly tanned and hard with lean muscle. Or his faded, soft jeans, and the not-so-soft bulge behind the zipper.

She turned him on. The unexpected knowledge, along with the overwhelming and equally unexpected power of that, blew her away.

She turned him on. She, the original geek, turned on the sexiest, most erotic, most sensuous, passionate man she'd ever met. And that shouldn't have been so...thrilling. "You have mail." Her voice sounded breathless again. Not good. If she wasn't careful, he'd notice and take it as an invitation. "Aren't you going to look?"

"Yeah." Blocking the screen with his big body, he read the email, then put the computer on sleep mode. And though his face was carefully creased in one of his trademark easy, slow smiles, tension came off him in waves. "Where were we?" he asked in a light lilt that could have melted Iceland as he reached for her.

"Oh, no," she said, backing up, right into a wall. "Not so fast." She slapped a hand to his chest, his *bare* chest, which radiated heat. Her fingers started to curl into him, wanting more, so she wrenched it back. "I'm out of here."

"You going to let a little kiss bother you then?"

She lifted a finger and pointed it at him. "You are *not* going to goad me into another one."

"Because that would be...mind-blowing?"

"Because that would be...stupid." She ducked beneath his arms and moved to the center of his office. "I came here to give you the plans and tell you I'm not attracted to you."

"Which we've proved is a lie."

"Okay, so I don't *want* to be attracted to you," she amended. "And now I'm gone."

He waited until she got to the door. "Would it be so bad, Nicole, if we gave in to it?"

Not turning to him, not daring to, because at one look

from him, she'd cave. Instead she tipped back her head and studied the ceiling. "Yes."

"Because…?"

"Because. Just because."

"We'd heat it up good, darlin', you know that."

Since her body was *still* heated up good, she had no doubt of that. Then his computer beeped again, accompanied by a surprisingly low and vicious oath from Ty. Turning back, she caught his unguarded expression as he reached for the keyboard.

Fury, plain and simple.

Wondering what was wrong, she sidled up behind him almost without realizing it, so that when he whipped around hiding the screen, she would have fallen backwards if he hadn't grabbed her around the waist.

Fingers gripping her tightly, he lifted a brow. "See anything interesting?"

"No."

His voice had lost all of its warmth. "You were right to run, Nicole. You *should* run. Now." He let go of her, and she stumbled back. By the time she regained her balance, he had turned away, hands fisted on the windowsill as he stared outside.

She stared at his stiff back. "I didn't see anything."

"You'll have to be quicker next time, huh?"

His temper stirred hers. Whirling, she stalked through the door, then down the hallway, and was reaching for the front door when he wrapped his long fingers around her elbow and spun her around. He had both his hands on her arms now, holding her still. He towered over her, her dark-haired, blue-eyed mystery man with the low, gruff voice and the sexy mouth that she was attracted to only every breathing moment she looked at him.

She struggled to free herself, but he wasn't having it. "I

can bring you to your knees with one well-placed kick," she warned him.

"A moment ago I might have been in the mood for an all-out, dragdown, dirty fight, but not now." His hands gentled, and he used one to cup her face. "I snapped at you and I'm sorry."

"Fine."

He sighed at her unbending, rigid stance. "Look, I was feeling nasty, all right? And I tend to take it out on anyone around me." He sighed again. "Which is why I don't often have anyone around me."

She wanted to stay mad. Mad gave her energy to leave. But with him looking at her in that disarming way, with his hands still on her…it all dissolved.

"I'm sorry," he repeated softly.

"I said fine."

"Forgiven?"

She had to shake her head. "I'm usually so nasty when I'm not working, no one wants anything to do with me. My own family would rather I just— Damn it. *Damn it.*" She slapped her forehead. "I forgot to go to the family dinner my mom planned. There'll be hell to pay for that."

"Why?"

"You don't have a family like mine, I take it," she said wryly. "Big, bossy, noisy and more demanding than any work schedule I ever face."

"No, I don't have a family like that." His eyes were curiously flat again. "I don't have one at all."

No. No, that wouldn't tug at her either.

"I really am sorry," he said very quietly, cupping her face, letting his long fingers stroke her skin. "Don't let me and my foul mood chase you off."

"I…need to go."

"You know, I never would have pegged you for a chicken," he taunted softly, and stopped her in her tracks.

She put her finger to his chest. "Take that back." No one called her a chicken, and— And his chest…damn! His chest was captivating her all over again.

His smile reached his eyes again, when instead of continuing to poke him she ended up dragging her finger in slow circles from one pec to the other. "I am not going to sleep with you," she said, but mmm, he had the best body. When her fingernail scraped over his nipple, he made a little hiss through his teeth. The sound shot straight to her good spots. "I'm not."

"There you go, your mind in the gutter again." His voice was a little rough around the edges now, even rougher when her finger ran over his nipple again.

"You weren't thinking it? Not even a little?" she whispered.

"Well, I know you were."

"I can lust after you and still keep my distance."

"Can you?"

"Watch me." She whirled to the door, put her hand on the handle, and…hesitated. "Are you…going to be okay?"

"Okay?"

"After that email." She glanced at him, but he'd perfectly shuttered his expression.

"Don't you worry about me, darlin'."

She had the feeling no one did. He had no one, which was almost beyond her comprehension. Her own family was a regular pain in her ass. But they were also always there for her, no matter what, and always had been. She couldn't imagine being totally alone.

"I can see those wheels turn, doctor."

"I was just wondering how it was you came to be all alone. What happened to your family?"

"Personal questions? From you?" His smile seemed a little off. "Tell you what. I get a question for every one of yours. Let's start with this one. How is it you're so beautiful and sexy, and yet the fact that we turn each other on makes you nervous as hell?"

Beautiful? Sexy? Those weren't adjectives she attributed to herself. Brainy, yes. Technically minded, yes.

But sexy? The man needed glasses. Only there didn't seem to be a thing wrong with those amazing eyes of his. She opened the door to his soft laugh.

"Let me guess…you have work?"

"Right," she said. "Work."

All the way home it wasn't that mocking laugh of his that Nicole thought about, but the flash of a shocking emotion she'd never imagined from Ty Patrick O'Grady.

Vulnerability.

TY WORKED THE NEXT few days as if he had a demon on his heels, and he did.

Her name was Dr. Nicole Mann.

But he was a man used to ignoring his emotions, and he could continue to do so through this job.

So why he made more trips to Taylor's building than was strictly required, he had no idea. Today was no exception. It was late afternoon, three days after The Kiss.

And damn, it had been some kiss. Truth was, he wanted another taste. He wanted her gripping him tightly, wanted her weak for him. He wanted her to care.

Odd, when *he* didn't want to care. God, how he needed not to care.

TAYLOR CAUGHT NICOLE sneaking up the stairs to her loft apartment after a long day of work. "Hey, come in for a sec."

"Um…well…" As always, she thought longingly of her bed, and of her plans to be in it within ten minutes. Of the new medical reports in her arms that she was dying to dig into.

"Oh, save the puppydog eyes, I'm immune. You can't just work, read about work and sleep." Taylor crooked her finger, a gesture she expected to make people come running. "Come on and take your medicine like a woman, Dr. Mann. I've got Suzanne inside and she's so excited it's almost making me think there's something to this love crap after all."

"Then why don't *you* go get married?"

"Not in this lifetime. I told you, you and me, single forever. Now get in here. It's time to try on the dresses I got us for the engagement party."

Nicole wished she'd taken a double shift. "You didn't have to do that."

"Yes, I did. You'd have never gone to the store with me to try them on, and I know damn well you don't have a single dress worth a damn in your closet."

"Nicole, is that you?" Suzanne stuck her head out Taylor's door and grinned, her red hair piled on top of her head, her gorgeous lush body zipped into some shimmery black cocktail dress that made her look like a sex goddess. "What do you think?" She spread out her arms and turned in a slow circle. "Is Ryan going to like this?"

Having rarely seen Suzanne in anything other than her usual catering uniform of black bottoms and a white blouse, or her gauzy sundresses, Nicole shook her head in amazement. "Are you kidding? He's going to attack you on the spot. *I'm* attracted to you wearing that."

Suzanne laughed and pulled Nicole inside. "This is so much fun. Now for you…"

Rule number one, never let them take you inside.

"This is going to be good." Taylor rubbed her hands together and looked Nicole up and down. "Strip."

Nicole merely laughed at the command, but Taylor just crossed her arms and waited expectantly. Nicole's smile dissolved. "No. No way."

"Yes, way."

"Hey, stop that." Nicole held on to her shirt as Taylor tugged at it. "Get your paws off me."

"I got the perfect dress. Don't worry, it was on terrific sale at a discount outlet, since I know how cheap you are."

"How do you know that?"

"You live here, don't you? The dress is emerald green, sparkly and designed to drive men wild." She held up a shimmery piece of material that was far too small to possibly be a dress. "It'll show off your great body, though you're going to need a hell of a pushup bra."

"Gee, thanks." Nicole pulled off her shirt.

"You ought to think about buying a set of boobs," Taylor said, making Suzanne choke on her soda.

Nicole glared at Suzanne, who pressed her lips together and wisely refrained from so much as smiling.

"Hey," Taylor said, lifting her hands. "Just thinking out loud here."

"Why in the world would I want to do such a stupid thing as buy a set of breasts?" Nicole asked. "To catch a man? I don't want a man."

Taylor lifted a brow. "If you tell me you're interested in women—"

"I'm not a lesbian, you idiot." Nicole stepped out of her pants. "I'm just happy being alone, that's all."

"Yeah." For a moment Taylor looked inexplicably... sad. Because that was so unusual, Nicole almost asked her about it, but Taylor held out the green material. "Luckily, as I've always said, you don't have to be celibate to be single."

"Who said I was?" Nicole looked at the dress in her hands, and realized she had no idea how to get into it.

"So you're telling me you're getting some?" Taylor snatched back the dress, straightened it out and slipped it over Nicole's head. "You're too uptight and grumpy to be getting any. Unless you're giving him his and not getting yours."

Nicole pulled her face free. "*What?*"

Suzanne cleared her throat. "I think she means maybe you're giving him orgasms but he's not giving them to you in return."

Nicole divided a glance between the two woman, each watching her with such pity in their eyes, she had to laugh. "You're both nuts." She yanked the dress down her hips and quickly ran out of material.

"I see Ty looking at you," Taylor said casually, tapping a wellmanicured nail on her perfectly painted lips.

Nicole pretended not to hear that.

"Ty?" Suzanne fussed with the straps of the dress at Nicole's shoulder. "Who's Ty?"

"My architect," Taylor said. "Remember? I told you about him. But since you were kissing Ryan at the time, you might have missed it." Taylor never took her eyes off Nicole. "He's tall, dark and sexy as hell. Not to mention his delicious, eatmealive accent."

"An accent can't be delicious," Nicole said, and both women laughed at her. "What? It can't."

"She's gaga over him," Taylor decided with delight.

"We'll have to invite him to the engagement party," Suzanne agreed.

"What?" Nicole got a bad, bad feeling as she smoothed down the dress. "Now why would you go and do that?"

Both women were staring at her. "What now?" Self-conscious, she crossed her arms. "What are you staring at?"

"My God." Taylor shook her head. "I can't believe it."

"Wow." Suzanne sighed dreamily. "Just wow. You're beautiful, Nicole."

Nicole just stared at them, then laughed.

"You are," Taylor said softly.

Nicole shot them a last fulminating look, then stalked over to look into the antique standalone mirror Taylor had in one corner. What she saw made her jaw drop.

It wasn't often she slowed down enough even to look in a mirror. She dressed for comfort, wore little makeup and had her hair cut short for convenience. If she had to think about her looks, she saw herself in a white coat. Sexless, really.

She didn't look sexless now. The emerald color made her skin glow and brought out her eyes. Even her hair, usually worthless in the way of obeying or looking good, seemed…well, decent. Maybe more than decent. And her body…she actually had one.

"You have to wear it." Taylor said of the dress that clung to every inch of Nicole's form. The spaghetti straps held the snug bodice up in front, crisscrossed over her slim spine in back, where the dress dipped sinfully low. The hem came high on her thighs, and slipped higher with her every movement.

"You almost look like you've got boobs and hips," Taylor noted.

"You look gorgeous," Suzanne said, with a long look at Taylor. "You have such a beautiful body, Nicole."

"A little skinny." Taylor sniffed, but then smiled. "But some men go ape for a toned body like that."

Someone knocked at the front door, and while Taylor

went to answer it, Suzanne said quietly, "You really do look amazing. This is going to be so much fun."

How to tell her she'd rather have a root canal? "I'm not wearing stockings or heels."

"Okay."

"I mean it. I—"

"You'll never guess who I found," Taylor said, coming back into the room. "A man. And just when we wanted a man's opinion, too. He just wanted to drop off some papers, but…" Smiling the smile of a cat with the canary's tail still hanging out of her mouth, Taylor moved aside.

Ty stood there, looking sweetly baffled. Until he saw Nicole, then all that sweet bafflement turned to heat as his eyes slowly took in the crazy dress she wore.

"What do you think?" Taylor asked Ty innocently. "Good enough for an engagement party?"

"Good enough to eat," Ty said, the Irish heavy in his voice.

CHAPTER FIVE

THE LAST TIME TY HAD seen Nicole she'd been walking away from him, and the taste of her had still been on his lips. He'd watched her go and decided not to do that to himself again.

No more watching.

Well, he was looking plenty now, wasn't he? Looking so hard he could see her every little breath, which seemed too quick and shallow for her to be half as calm as she was pretending, standing over there in that killer dress.

But hot as that bod was, it hadn't been the dress that nearly brought him to his knees. No, the look in her eyes had done that. The look that said "back off" and "want me," all in the same flash of those gray, gray eyes.

Suzanne and Taylor were grinning at him proudly, as if they'd personally created the vision standing before him.

"She does look good enough to eat, doesn't she?" Taylor said, clapping her hands. "Just wait until we get on the thigh-high stockings and dome heels."

"Okay, I'm done." Nicole pointed a finger at Ty. "You. Stop staring. And you." She whirled on Taylor. "No stockings. No high heels that say do me or otherwise."

Ty did his best to stop staring as she turned her back on him to chew out Taylor, but as he caught a good sight of the rear view, he nearly swallowed his tongue. Now he could see why the stockings would have to be thigh high, the dress dipped so low he caught a peek-a-boo glimpse of her peach, silkylooking panties.

Nicole, rough-and-tumble ready, tomboy, warrior of her world...and she wore peach silky panties. If that didn't completely destroy him, he didn't know what did.

"I have got to get to work," she grumbled, bending for her discarded clothes and showing more peach silk.

Not that he was looking. Nope. Not looking—

She caught him looking. With a furious glance that singed the hair right off his arms, she stalked by, giving him a quick scent of shampoo and clean, very angry woman.

"Hey, I thought you decided to cut back your hours," Taylor called out to her. "So you don't kill yourself before you hit the big threeoh."

"No, *you* decided I should cut back my hours. I decided to stop trying to convince you I'm just fine."

"You're not fine." Taylor stood beside a nodding Suzanne for unity. "You live and breathe that job, without time for anything or anyone else. It's not right, Nicole. You're hiding out from life. Tell her, Ty."

Nicole dared him to say a word with stormy eyes.

He lifted his hands. "I don't—"

"Oh, please." Taylor pointed to Nicole's face. "See those dark circles under her eyes? Lack of sleep."

Ty hadn't slept well either, mostly from the memories of Nicole's mouth on his, from the feel of her body beneath his hands, from the little needy sounds that had escaped her throat before they'd broken apart for air.

Under the circumstances, with his own dark circles beneath his eyes, he didn't really feel he had the right to say anything.

"If I want a mother, I'll call mine," Nicole said.

"Which reminds me, yours came by." Taylor lifted a

brow. "Checked me out. I must have passed muster, as she told me to make sure you get your sleep, eat your veggies and don't take extra shifts at the hospital."

Ty lifted his own brow at Nicole's impressive and colorful opinion of that. Then watched her very fine ass sashay to the door.

"Don't ruin that dress yanking it off," Taylor told her. "And use a hanger!"

The door slammed, and Taylor snickered.

Suzanne sighed. "You shouldn't have baited her that way."

"Are you kidding? If I didn't, she'd never have put the dress on, much less agreed to wear it. And she really does need to eat more veggies, you said so yourself."

"She didn't agree to wear the dress," Suzanne said.

"Oh, she'll wear it." Taylor tossed them both a positive smile. "She'll wear it with bells on."

Ty was just thankful he wouldn't have to see it. In fact, he was still thanking his lucky stars when Suzanne turned to him and said, "You'll be invited to the engagement party, of course."

"Me?" Panic was a taste he hadn't eaten in a good long time.

"Yeah. I think you're going to be around a while." Suzanne gave him a little smile.

Oh, boy. There were matchmaking plans in those eyes. Unintentionally, he backed up, making both women laugh.

"Don't tell me a man who wears clothes as well as you do has an aversion to dressing up like Nicole's?" Taylor said.

"No, but I do have an aversion to being set up."

"Set up?" Taylor cocked her head to the side. "Most men would be drooling to go out with a woman who looked the way Nicole just did."

"Not me. I get my own women, thank you. Didn't you want to show me your contractor bids? You wanted my opinion, right?" He could hear the desperation in his voice. "Can we get back to that?".

"We're not talking marriage here, Ty." When he didn't relax, Taylor just sighed. "Fine. I'll let you in on a little secret I think will help the situation here, all right? Nicole and I? We plan on remaining single. *Forever*. No white dress, no white cake and no diamonds on our ring fingers. If there's any hooking-up going on, it's of the one-night variety only. Follow?"

"But telling him that only gives him an unfair advantage over Nicole!" Suzanne protested.

Taylor kept her amused gaze on Ty. "I have a feeling he's the one who needs the handicap. Hurt her though," she said casually. "And we'll hurt you."

"Oh, definitely," Suzanne agreed.

They weren't serious, Ty thought. They couldn't be serious. He laughed to prove it.

They didn't laugh back.

"Actually," Taylor said seriously, "if you hurt her, we'll hunt you down and cut off your balls. So…" She clapped her hands and smiled. "Ready to get to work?"

American women were insane, he thought. Completely insane.

TWENTY MINUTES LATER, Nicole ran back out of her loft. She needed to lose herself in something, and the first thing to come to mind had been the hospital. Her mind was now firmly on work.

Okay, not true. Her mind was still wrapped around the way Ty had looked at her in that dress. Oh, man, how he'd looked at her in that dress. Her knees still were a little weak. Who'd have thought a man could have such heat in his eyes? She'd nearly imploded on the spot from the intensity.

But she was absolutely *not* going to waste time thinking about that, or analyzing her reaction to it. She was going to concentrate on work—

She came to an abrupt halt in front of her car. The streets were filled with shoppers and diners, with people who had nothing to do all day other than wander.

But Nicole had plenty to do. And she'd get to it, if sitting on the hood of her car hadn't been Taylor and…and the man she'd just promised herself she wouldn't think about.

Heads together, they were poring over an opened manila file and laughing. Until they saw her.

Well, Taylor kept laughing. But Ty's smile slowly faded. "You changed," he said.

"Yeah, it's hard to operate in a cocktail dress."

Taylor, who had her feet propped up on the bumper of Ty's car, which was parked right in front of Nicole's, waved her closer. "Ty is trying to help me decide on a contractor. These two right here?" She held up two different bids. "They're young and cute. And expensive. But very good at what they do, apparently." She looked at Ty for approval, who nodded. "And these two…" She switched papers around and held up two more bids. "They're a tad bit older, more experienced, slightly cheaper…but I guaranasstee you, they'll have beer bellies and plumber cracks hanging out the backs of their low-riding jeans, and it won't be pretty."

Ty rolled his eyes. "Tell me you're not hiring a contractor based on his ass."

"Okay, I won't tell you." Grinning, she popped up, hugged Nicole, and started toward the building.

"Well, gee, I guess we're done," Ty said to her back, standing up himself.

FREE Merchandise is 'in the Cards' for you!

Dear Reader,

We're giving away FREE MERCHANDISE!

Seriously, we'd like to reward you for reading this novel by giving you **FREE MERCHANDISE** worth over **$25**. And no purchase is necessary!

You see the Jack of Hearts sticker above? Paste that sticker in the box on the Free Merchandise Voucher inside. Return the Voucher promptly...and we'll send you valuable Free Merchandise!

Thanks again for reading one of our novels—and enjoy your Free Merchandise with our compliments!

Pam Powers

Pam Powers

P.S. Look inside to see what Free Merchandise is **"in the cards"** for you!

FM-ROM-12

We'd like to send you two free books to introduce you to the Romance Collection. These books are worth over $15, but they are yours to keep absolutely FREE! We'll even send you 2 wonderful surprise gifts. You can't lose!

REMEMBER: Your Free Merchandise, consisting of **2 Free Books** and **2 Free Gifts**, is worth over $25.00! No purchase is necessary, so please send for your Free Merchandise today.

The Reader Service - Here's how it works:

Accepting your 2 free books and 2 free mystery gifts (gifts valued at approximately $10.00) places you under no obligation to buy anything. You may keep the books and gifts and return the shipping statement marked "cancel." If you do not cancel, about a month later we'll send you 4 additional books and bill you just $5.99 each in the U.S. or $6.49 each in Canada. That's a savings of at least 25% off the cover price. It's quite a bargain! Shipping and handling is just 50¢ per book in the U.S. and 75¢ per book in Canada.* You may cancel at any time, but if you choose to continue, every month we'll send you 4 more books, which you may either purchase at the discount price or return to us and cancel your subscription.

*Terms and prices subject to change without notice. Prices do not include applicable taxes. Sales tax applicable in N.Y. Canadian residents will be charged applicable taxes. Offer not valid in Quebec. All orders subject to credit approval. Books received may not be as shown. Credit or debit balances in a customer's account(s) may be offset by any other outstanding balance owed by or to the customer. Please allow 4 to 6 weeks for delivery. Offer available while quantities last.

▼ If offer card is missing write to: The Reader Service, P.O. Box 1867, Buffalo, NY 14240-1867 or visit www.ReaderService.com ▼

BUSINESS REPLY MAIL

FIRST-CLASS MAIL   PERMIT NO. 717   BUFFALO, NY

POSTAGE WILL BE PAID BY ADDRESSEE

THE READER SERVICE
PO BOX 1341
BUFFALO NY 14240-8571

NO POSTAGE
NECESSARY
IF MAILED
IN THE
UNITED STATES

Turning around, Taylor smiled. "I just figured, since Nicole didn't *really* have to be at work, and since I'd bet the bank she hasn't eaten, that the two of you could go out."

"No," Nicole said quickly. Too quickly, but damn it, she couldn't help it. Eat with Ty? No. No way.

But Taylor danced her bossy butt into the building and vanished.

Ty reached for Nicole's hand, tugging her close enough that he could look into her face. "Hey," he said softly.

"Hey."

"Sorry about upstairs."

"You mean about staring at me in that dress?"

His mouth quirked. "Not for staring, no. Sorry you were so uncomfortable in it. You looked…amazing."

"Yeah. Funny what a low-cut, tight number like that does for a man. Did you lose a lot of brain cells?"

He let out one of those slow, dangerous smiles. Dangerous, because she couldn't take her eyes off it. That, combined with his warm hand in hers, and suddenly she stood there on the sidewalk, completely forgetting she didn't want to stand there with him. Staring at him.

"Darlin'," he said, "I lose brain cells every time I look at you."

His voice melted her all the more. Unfair, very unfair. "Well, if this does it for you…" She gestured down to her militarygreen cargo pants and plain white T-shirt. "Then you have even bigger problems than I thought."

His seeall blue eyes never left hers. "It has nothing to do with what you're wearing. Or how you look."

Oh, God. Why did he say such things? No one had ever said such things to her, and she had no idea how to handle it. If she'd been hands deep in an emergency surgery, or up to her eyeballs in X-rays…*those* she could handle.

But this wasn't work, this was far more personal than work had ever been, and she was at an utter loss. She inhaled a breath and held it.

"Yeah," he said. "Scary shit, huh? Let's go eat, Nicole."

"Because Taylor said to?"

"Because I can't get you out of my head. We might as well spend some time together and see where it goes."

"It's going nowhere."

He smiled again. "Let's go see."

"No." She fumbled for her car door, slid in. "I've really got to go." She turned the key.

And the engine simply coughed.

She turned it again, with more force, but she got that ridiculous wheezing noise that told her the battery was dead. Again. "Damn it."

"Sounds like battery trouble." Easy as he pleased, he opened her door, tugged her out. "Lucky for you, my car runs like a sweetie. I'll drop you off at the hospital, then charge your battery while you're at work."

"I don't want—"

"It's no trouble."

Naturally he didn't take her right to work, but stopped at a cute little sidewalk café a few blocks away. "For sustenance," he explained as he got out and came around for her.

Came around for her. Nicole stared at him as he led them to a table, while she tried to remember the last guy who'd opened a door for her.

Or put his hand lightly on the base of her spine, touching her as they walked.

Her skin still tickled. That it wasn't an entirely unpleasant experience had her head spinning. "Who are you?" she said over the table, bewildered, which wasn't a common problem for her.

He lowered his menu and smiled. "What you see is what you get."

"Why do I sincerely doubt that?"

"I don't know. What about you? Is what you see what you get?"

She glanced down at her plain clothes, ran a finger over the silver hoops in her ear and lifted a shoulder. "I think so."

"Tell me about the earrings. What do they mean?"

"How do you know they mean something?"

"A hunch," he said, which she didn't like, because it was true.

How did he seem to know her so well? "There's one small hoop for every year of medical school," she admitted. Her own personal badges of honor, during a difficult time when she'd been struggling to survive in a fastpaced, adult world while still in her late teens.

With a slow smile that bound her to him in a way she didn't understand any more than the ease with which he seemed to know her, he lifted the sleeve on his own shirt, revealing the tattoo she'd seen before. It was a narrow band around his tanned, sinewy bicep in a design that was incredibly sexy. Just like the rest of him.

"I got a part of it for every year I made it through college," he said. "Finished it when I graduated and started my internship in Sydney."

"Badge of honor," she whispered, and at this unexpected common ground of a deep, soul-felt connection, she felt herself warm to him in a new, different way.

The waitress came, and when Nicole tried to order just coffee, Ty took over and ordered enough food for an entire third-world country.

"I'm a growing boy," he said with a shrug and a big,

unrepentant grin. "And besides, I promised Taylor I'd feed you."

"Is that why we're here? Because you promised Taylor?"

His smiled faded, but before he could speak, the waitress came back with bread and butter. When she was gone, he grabbed a piece of bread and said, "We're here because I wanted to spend time with you." He slathered butter on the hot bread. "And I think, behind all that coolasice stubborn orneriness, you want to spend time with me as well." He handed her the bread.

"This is *not* headed to the bedroom." She took his offering because the butter was melting all over, making her stomach growl. "Not yours *or* mine."

"Of course not." He sank his teeth into his own piece of bread. "You have to go to work."

She took in his innocent gaze. "I mean ever. This isn't going to the bedroom, yours or mine, *ever.*"

"Well, now, that's just a crying shame, given how combustive we are just sitting here, much less kissing."

Hearing him say it, in the Irish accent he didn't acknowledge, made her pulse quicken. "We need to forget that kiss."

Now he laughed, the sound rich and easy.

"We do," she protested.

"Much as I'd like to oblige you, darlin', I'm going to be around. A lot. We're going to run into each other. Nobody's going to be forgetting anything."

"You've thought about this."

"Hell yeah, I've thought about this." His eyes were crystal-clear, and very intent on hers. "Last night I decided never to so much as look at you again."

"What happened?"

"What happened?" He shook his head, and as the waitress come back with their order he dug in with a gusto that forced her to do the same. "*You* happened."

Since she didn't intend to touch that statement with a ten-foot pole, they ate in silence. Nicole had to admit, it felt good to fill her belly. How she managed to forget to eat so often was beyond her, but she liked this feeling of... satisfaction. Since she intended to deny herself any other kind of satisfaction—say sex with Ty, with which she was quite certain he would have no trouble satisfying her— food would have to do.

"So." After inhaling enough food for an army—where did he put it all in that long, hard body?—he leaned back in his chair. "What's up for today, doc?"

"Surgeries. Meetings. More surgeries."

"Are you good?"

"The best."

He smiled. "I bet you are. Did you always know this is what you wanted?"

"From day one." She wondered the same about him. "Were you always going to be an architect?"

Some of his good humor faded, just a little. So little, in fact, she thought maybe she'd imagined it. "Not always," he said lightly.

When she just looked at him, he sighed. "Let's just say I didn't have the most auspicious of beginnings."

She felt a smile tugging at her lips. "A troublemaker, were you?"

"Of the highest ranking."

"I'm shocked. Were you—"

"Oh, no. This is about you." He lifted a brow. "Your mom is something."

Nicole stared at him. "You met her, too?"

"Darlin', the way she stormed the building, everyone met her. What a dynamo." He smiled. "You're like her."

"I am not."

His smile went to a full-fledged grin. "Are too."

She set down her fork. "She has a bazillion kids, a husband, two bazillion grandchildren and runs her world like Attila the Hun."

"Yeah, you share that last part. So what was it like, growing up with such a large family?"

He wasn't just idly asking, he'd leaned forward, his entire attention on her face. He really wanted to know. "Well…" She thought about it. "I never had my own bed. And I had to wait hours for the bathroom. Oh, and I wore a lot of hand-me-downs." She hesitated, then admitted, "But there was always someone around when I needed them." Always. And, she also had to admit, she hadn't thanked any of them enough for it. "What about you?"

He suddenly didn't look so open. "I already told you, I don't have a family."

"What happened?" she asked quietly.

"Well, I never knew my father, and let's just say my mother is better off forgotten." Expression closed, he reached for his iced tea. "Need a refill?"

"No, thank you." Behind his nonchalance, she saw his regret, and a sadness she couldn't reach. But more than that, pain. "Ty—"

"Don't," he said softly. "Please, don't."

Before she could respond, he tossed some money on the table and stood. "Let's get you to work."

"And after that?"

His light-blue eyes gave nothing of himself away now. "What do you want to happen after that?"

"If I said nothing?"

"I'm not sure I'd believe it."

"Ty—"

"Look, Nicole…do we have to figure it out right now?"

He touched her cheek, let out a smile that was short of his usual levity. "Do we really have to decide right this very minute?"

With a shake of her head, she took his offered hand, and shocking herself, tipped her face up when he leaned in for a sweet kiss. Or what *should* have been a sweet kiss, but was instead only an appetizer.

He pulled back, and she opened her eyes. There was a question in his, but she shook her head. "Work," she said.

"Work, then." And he took her outside.

Work would be good. At work she could bury her thoughts and concentrate on what mattered. Her job.

Not the man who had unexpected depths and a touch she couldn't seem to forget.

AND SHE DID MANAGE to bury herself in work. The emergency department was overloaded due to a strange and violent outbreak of a flu, which had severely dehydrated an older woman to the point that her kidneys failed. After that, they'd taken out an appendix from a hockey player, and then sewn a finger back on a carpenter who'd managed to cut it off with his table saw.

By the end of the shift she'd nearly managed to forget all about Ty. As she stood in front of a vending machine in the reception area of the hospital on her way out the door, her cell phone rang.

"Honey, I dropped off some food for you. Your nice landlady let me in, so I stuck it in your fridge."

"Mom." Nicole had to laugh. "I have food."

"No, you had a rotting head of lettuce and two sodas. Now you have food. Taylor is very beautiful, isn't she? Is she married? I didn't see a ring, but—"

"Mom—"

"Just say thank you, Nicole."

"Thank you, Nicole."

"Funny. Don't forget to come to dinner this Sunday."

"I'll try."

"Try harder than last Sunday. I'll even shamelessly bribe you. I'll make you brownies. Your favorite."

"Mom—"

"*Double* fudge brownies."

Nicole had to laugh. No matter how long and bloody her day had been, her mother never failed to bully a smile out of her. With her mom, she always felt warm and loved, even when she wasn't warm and lovable at all.

And some people never had this in their life. Some people, like Ty. "I love you, Mom."

"Well." Her mother's voice got thick, and she sniffed. "I love you, too, baby. See you soon."

"See you soon," she promised, then sighed. She would have to make sure she did before her mother showed up at her place with more food she wouldn't eat.

Her eye on the chocolate caramel bar in the vending machine, she put a dollar in.

It ate the money and didn't spit out the candy.

"Why you—" She kicked it. This had always worked in the past, but now the machine mocked her with silence.

"You have to have the right touch." Dr. Lincoln Watts glided his body directly up behind hers, so close that she nearly choked on his expensive aftershave. His arms surrounded her as he reached past her to punch in the buttons on the machine.

The candy bar dropped.

Nicole stepped forward until she was practically kissing the machine before she turned in his arms. "Thank you." He had until the count of three before she used her fists.

"Now you owe me." There was a little smile on his lips

that she was certain he considered sexy, but it creeped her out. No wonder all the nurses hated him.

She'd already changed back into her own clothes, and his eyes were eating her up. "Do you have any interesting tattoos to go with all those earrings of yours?" he asked a little huskily.

She stared at him. "Is that an official question?"

"Go out with me tonight."

"Dr. Watts—"

"Linc," he corrected gently, with a not-so-gentle look in his eye as he stroked her cheek.

She pushed his hand away, met his gaze to make sure he saw her anger, and spoke carefully so as to not confuse the idiot. "I don't go out with people from work. I don't mix work and my personal life. Ever."

"I'm not 'people.' I'm a doctor."

"I don't care if you clean bedpans, my answer is the same."

His jaw tightened. His eyes became distinctly not so friendly. "You're turning me down again?"

What was it with too-smart, too-good-looking men? "Yes. I'm turning you down. Again."

"That's a bad plan, Nicole."

"Dr. Mann."

He looked her over for a long moment, then stepped back, his eyes ice. "I can make your life hell here. You know that."

"No, I can make *your* life hell." God, she hoped that was true.

She was the youngest doctor on board, the newest, and she wasn't naive enough to forget there were hidden politics in force, or that Dr. Lincoln Watts had all the strings to pull and she had none.

Still, she kept her head up high as she walked past him

and out the doors of the hospital. That she had just now remembered she didn't have her car made a perfectly bad ending to a perfectly bad day. Spoiling for a fight, with no one to go nose-to-nose with, she stalked over to a pay phone to look for the number of a cab company.

CHAPTER SIX

DRAWING AND DESIGNING were what Ty had been born to do. Envision and create, and then move on.

He was good at it, especially the moving on part. He could do it right now, just pack up and go. Hell, he didn't have anything he couldn't buy again. In fact, he had moving down to a science. He could pack up and get out of anywhere within a half hour if he had to.

But Taylor's building, while appearing to be a dump, had huge potential, and the job stirred his creative juices enough that he didn't feel like thinking about moving on, not yet.

At the moment he stood on the roof, staring down at the third-floor living-room window—Nicole's window to be exact—trying to figure out a way to pop it out a little to fit the early1900s traditional facade of the place. The challenge excited him, and he retrieved his notepad from his pocket and hunkered down, yanking the cap off his pen with his teeth so that he could write. He was a page into it when he heard the screech of tires.

Nicole slammed out of a cab, which reminded him he'd fixed her car for her. He took one look at the strut in her walk, at the fury pouring off her in waves, and wondered what had happened to make her look as though she was spoiling for a fight.

Though he still had measurements to take in the rafters, he told himself he could come back later, and shimmied down from the roof to the mock balcony in front of her living-room window. He'd just landed on his feet when he saw her clearly through the glass, stalking in her front door. Slamming it. She saw him immediately, he could tell by the slight narrowing of her eyes—ah, how lovely to be so welcomed.

With a kick-ass attitude he couldn't miss, she headed toward him, opening the window so fast he thought for a moment she meant to push him down three stories to his death.

"What are you doing here?" she demanded.

"Just thought I'd drop in."

"Funny," she said without a smile. "You hang outside windows often?"

"Just yours." He cocked his head at the unmistakable unhappiness in her gaze. "You going to invite me in?"

"Nope."

"What if I say please real nice?"

"Oh, fine." She turned away. "Suit yourself, you're going to anyway."

Yes, he was. And her stress drew him like a magnet. He threw a leg over the sill, climbed through and straightened, studying her stiff spine. Coming up behind her, he put his hands on her shoulders.

"Shh," he said when she flinched, and gently began to knead at the knots she had in her neck. There was a virtual rock quarry there, not to mention the heat of the rage she was so carefully controlling. Given how much of the world she took on her shoulders on a daily basis, her stress level had to be off the charts. He ached for her.

But in spite of his genuine need to soothe and comfort, there was more. Beneath her white shirt he could see a hint of yellow lace bra, and he wondered if her panties matched. "How did you get so tense today, doc?"

"I tend to get that way when some asshole puts his hands on me uninvited."

He went still.

"Not you," she said.

Still, Ty suddenly felt very tense himself. "Who put his hands on you uninvited?"

She lifted a slim shoulder. "Just some jerk at work."

"Your boss again?"

Another lift of her shoulder.

"Goddammit." Now he was trying to control *his* temper, but he had to do it. She didn't want his anger, and she sure as hell didn't want compassion, so what was he supposed to do with all this unexpected violence? Keeping his voice light took about all he had. "Do I need to go caveman for you and kick some serious butt?"

That startled a laugh out of her, a genuine one, and he relaxed slightly, keeping his hands working on her neck. If she'd been hurt, she wouldn't be laughing.

"I handled it," she assured him.

"Yeah, well, I hope you kicked his balls into next week."

"Nah, just his ego."

She said this very proudly, and that made him smile. "Good girl." He dug for more taut muscles, thinking she was so petite beneath his fingers, so…perfect. "Sure I can't go reinforce it?"

"No way." She was quiet a moment, biting her lip as he started on a kink at the base of her shoulder blade.

He didn't want her to bite her lip, he wanted her to let out the helpless moan, wanted her to give him a sign that he was making her feel good, that he was helping her let go of all the fury, but apparently he couldn't have everything he wanted.

"Ty?" she said softly after a moment.

"Hmm?"

"Thanks." Turning to face him, her lips curved. "You know, for having caveman tendencies and wanting to go bash in a head and all."

The way she was looking at him made him want to beat his chest with his fists and howl at the moon. He'd meant to stay away from her. Why the hell hadn't he stayed away? "Nicole?"

While most of her anger had faded, she still had a good amount of wariness in those jaded eyes. "Yeah?"

"I'm going to put my hands on you."

"You already have."

"More hands."

"Why are you announcing this?"

"So you don't kick *my* balls or ego into next week, warrior princess." Cupping her face, he tilted it up. Slowly. Giving her plenty of time to settle in.

Or back away.

She didn't back away, but neither did she settle in. Instead, she stiffened, just a little, just enough to break his heart. "No, don't get all tight again." His lips whispered against hers. "I'm going to kiss you now. Say yes."

"Ty—"

"Yes or no, Nicole. I don't want you to mistake me for any other asshole doing this without permission."

"I—I know who you are."

"Yes or no."

"Yes. Okay? Yes! Put your hands on me." Her arms snaked up around his neck. Fisted in his hair. "Kiss it all away, Ty. Can you do that?"

"Oh yeah." His hands slid from her face to her hips and he pulled her close. "I can do that."

She went up on her tiptoes to meet him halfway as he covered her mouth with his, cutting off anything else hanging between them, of which there was plenty. With a rough, appreciative groan, he invaded her mouth with one sure glide of his tongue, figuring she'd either kiss him back or belt him one.

She kissed him back. In fact, she mewled and arched her body to his like a cat in heat. His arms banded around her more tightly, lifting her off the ground as his mouth slashed across hers in a fiery kiss that only left him needing more, more, more. And when they finally broke apart, she staggered back, placed a hand over her heart and licked her wet lips. "What the hell was that?"

"Not sure." He hauled her back against him. "Let's try it again and see if we can figure it out."

"Hmm." Then they were kissing again, tongues caressing and plundering, hands touching anywhere they could land as they ate each other up.

Ty had never felt anything as fast and as hot and as combustive as this. Her hands pushed up his shirt. He shoved up her light shirt. She kicked off her shoes, went up on her tiptoes and hooked a leg around his hip, straining against the biggest erection he'd ever sported.

Never letting go of her mouth, he had his hands up her shirt and she had hers on his zipper when the *beep, beep, beep* of her pager nearly jerked his heart right out of his chest. "Don't listen," he said against her lips, gripping her at the waist to hold her still.

With a soft little moan, she opened her eyes. "I have to."

"Nicole—"

"I have to." Stepping back, she licked her lips again, as if she needed that very last taste of him, and pulled down her shirt with fingers that trembled. She avoided his gaze as she went looking for the offending beeper. "I'm sorry. I shouldn't have let it go that far."

"There were two of us inhaling each other."

"Still, I should have—" She looked down at the pager.

"Let me guess. You have to go."

"Yeah."

"Yeah." He backed away, shoving his hands in his pockets to keep them off her. "Goodbye, Nicole."

"I'm sorry."

"Me, too." And he left before she could count off each and every reason why they should never have let anything like this happen.

He already knew every single one of them.

He just couldn't remember why they mattered.

SOMETIME IN THE MIDDLE of the night Ty gave up staring at the ceiling and went into his office. Not one to waste precious hours, he sat at his desk and decided he'd work off the restlessness.

Okay, horniness.

He should have kept his hands and mouth to himself. Should have, would have, could have.

Regrets? Is that what he felt, when he'd promised himself to never have them? Never to look back? *Live life to its fullest,* he'd always told himself. *Get everything you want, and smile all the way to the bank as you do it.*

It turned out it was no easier to work with a hard-on than it had been to sleep with one. So he turned on his computer, where he found another email from his friendly stranger.

Dear Ty Patrick O'Grady of Dublin,
You asked who I am. Of course you want to know! I'm Margaret Mary Mulligan of Dublin. I'm twenty-four years of age, and I'm also the daughter of Anne Mary Mulligan. Which makes me your half sister.

Actually, I'm not sure about the half part because I don't know who my father is. Our mother, as you probably know, is dead.
You're my only family. I want to know you. Please write back.
Margaret Mary

Ty stared at the email for so long the words leaped and jumped in front of him. A sister? He had a sister?

Was it even possible?

He thought of his mother, professional troubleseeker, professional manscrewer, and knew it was entirely possible. With a sigh, he hit Reply.

Dear Margaret Mary...

Ty sat there, fingers poised over the keys, and couldn't figure out what he wanted to say. *How are you?* Too formal.

How about *What do you want from me?* Nah, too defensive.

Dear Margaret Mary. Of Dublin.

He stopped to laugh. So formal, this mystery half sister. But then his smile faded. This could only bring trouble and rotten memories, neither of which he wanted. Thinking that, he typed:

Why now? Why me?
Besides, there could be a dozen of us for all I know.
Maybe you should try one of them.
Ty Patrick O'Grady

He hit Send, then sat there staring at nothing for who knew how long, until his computer beeped, indicating an incoming email.

"So you can't sleep either," he murmured and leaned forward.

Dear Ty,
I'm so glad you wrote. You have questions, questions are good.
But there is no one else. She told me herself before she died. Not that her word ever meant anything, but on this, I want to believe her.
It's just you and me.
Aren't you even curious?
Margaret Mary

Curious? Hell, no. He'd rather not think about his past at all. He'd rather look around him and see where he was right this moment. How far he'd come. And he'd come pretty damn far.

It's just you and me.

Damn her for that, for putting it into words so simply. So strongly. Clearly she didn't relish being alone, as he did.

She was young, very young, and probably had idealistic hopes about a family around her, hopes he'd never entertained for himself.

Ah, hell. He hit Reply.

Margaret Mary,
If you're looking for family to be a comfort, forget it. I didn't get the comfort gene. If you're looking for a hand-

out, you'd have better luck with our mum herself, dead or otherwise.

Best leave it alone.

Ty Patrick O'Grady

He hit Send. It was the right thing to do, he'd been on his own so long he didn't have any business opening his life to another person.

He *was* a loner, through and through. No family, no long-term lover. And if he gave a fleeting thought to what it might be like to be different, to let Margaret Mary in, to let Nicole in, he let it go.

Not his thing. Besides, he didn't know how to let anyone in.

Since he couldn't seem to sleep or entertain himself, he figured he might as well start his day. That meant pulling out the plans he was working up for Taylor's building.

It was the attic that was concerning him today, as Taylor had fond hopes of a place to store all the antiques she couldn't seem to stop collecting. The last time he'd been there, he'd gotten distracted by Nicole.

Seeing as Nicole was no doubt killing herself at work, he decided the crack of dawn was a perfectly fine time to crawl around in the attic to his heart's content without disturbing a soul.

And he did just that, getting filthy in the process as he crawled through spiderwebs the size of his car. Straddling a beam, he pulled out his pad, and was happily making notes when he heard a door open. The sound came so close, he looked around, baffled, until he realized it was the apartment door directly beneath him.

Nicole's.

Because of the way the building was built—on a slight incline—the roof was really on two different tiers. On the higher level was the attic. Right next to that, but a full level below, was the loft apartment. There were two ways into the attic, the way he'd come in, through the third-floor hallway, or through a trap door at the far corner of Nicole's living room.

Due to a vicious storm only a few months ago, when a tree had fallen through the bedroom area of the loft, much of that part of the roof had been redone. But not the attic portion, which was still incredibly rickety. Reaching down, he opened the trap door.

It made a loud creaking sound, but Nicole, standing just inside her front door, never looked up. Ty realized this was because she had on a set of headphones, which, given the volume of her singing—so off-key he had to smile—meant she couldn't hear anything.

Before he could attract her attention, she'd kicked off her shoes, then crossed her arms in front of her and whipped off her top.

She wore a tiger-striped bra—did she have any idea how sexy her secret lingerie fetish was?—and then put her hands to the button on her pants. Oh, boy. "Nicole!" He was barely braced on the studs now, but he leaned over way farther than he should, knowing he had to make her see him or she'd be good and pissed by the time she was naked, and generally he liked his women soft and smiling and mewling with lust when they were naked.

Still singing, she shucked her pants, kicking them across the room with an abandon that normally would have made him grin.

Her panties did not match her bra. They were purple, lacy and very, very tiny. Turning in circles in a little shimmy of a dance, she headed toward her bedroom, giving him a good, long look at her backside as she wriggled and shook.

"Oh man," he whispered to himself, and leaned out as far as he dared. "Nicole—"

He crashed right through the ceiling. The air whipped his face; the floor rushed up to greet him, but all he saw was a tiger-striped bra and purple lace panties.

NOT MUCH SCARED NICOLE. But Ty falling through her ceiling shook her to the core. By the time she reached him, which took longer than it should have since she wasted five seconds just staring at the huge mass of him on her floor, he hadn't budged.

"Oh my God, Ty. *Ty.*"

He was on his side, face gray through all the drywall dust. Dropping to her knees at his hip, she leaned over him. "Ty, can you hear me?"

Nothing. But she could see his chest rising and falling, and she nearly sobbed in relief. "Okay. You're going to be okay. You are."

Surging up, she grabbed her portable phone, dialed for an ambulance; calm, cool, in control. As she always was in an emergency.

Then she looked down at the big, handsome, far-too-still man on her floor and wanted to fall apart. Her hands shook as she gently put them on him. What to do? God, what to do? Every ounce of medical training she'd ever had flew right out the window. "Damn it, get it together, Nicole." She ran her hands down his limbs, frowning at his right ankle. Not broken, she didn't think, but already swollen. Then she got to his right side, and the possibly cracked ribs, and had to take a deep, calming breath. "You're going to be okay," she whispered, having no idea which of them she was talking to.

There was a huge knot forming on his head, and he hadn't regained consciousness. "Ty." She cupped his face, his beautiful, too-still face, with the long dark lashes and strong, sharp jaw. "Come on, Ty. Come back to me. Wake up." She checked his pupils. Uneven. Concussion, if he was lucky. "Please, Ty. Please wake up. For me, do it for me, okay? Wake up and I'll—"

He groaned. Coughed. Rolled from his side to his back and groaned again, eyes still closed. "Shh, darlin'," he said in a rough whisper. "It's too early to be yelling."

"Ty." Her eyes burned with the relief. "You're back."

"You…didn't finish your sentence. What will…you do…if I wake up?"

That he could joke, even now, horrified her. Then he tried to sit up, his face in a grimace of agony as he held his head.

"Don't move," she said in a rush, helping him lie back. He'd turned green. "You might have broken something, at the very least your big fat head. *Don't*," she repeated when he kept trying. "Just hang on a damn second."

"Shh," he begged, eyes still closed. "No noise."

"Are you nauseous?"

He cracked one eye open, ran it over her, then closed it again. "I am, yes. Though I refuse to puke on the very lovely underwear you're wearing. You're so pretty, Nicole." He sighed, then went utterly still and silent, terrifying her.

"Ty!"

"Yeah, here." He didn't open his eyes. "Did you know that when you say my name in that soft, sexy voice of yours, I almost wish we were going to go for it. You and me."

"Ty—" But a sudden pounding at her front door had her leaping up, reaching for her clothes. "Hold on!" she called, hopping back into her pants.

"Nicole?" Taylor knocked louder. "Honey, what was that crash?"

Nicole pulled on her shirt and hauled open the door. "Ty fell through my ceiling. The ambulance is coming. Oh, God, Taylor, look at him. He hit his head, he's concussed, and I can't remember what to do!"

Taylor grabbed her hand and ran toward Ty. "Oh, you poor, big, sexy baby. You're not going to be sick all over my floor, are you?"

Ty choked out a laugh that ended on a groan and some fairly inventive bad words.

"Don't make him talk," Nicole begged, ridiculously panicked. It was just a bump on the noggin. Lord knew, his head was hard enough to handle it.

Taylor grabbed Nicole's shoulders and gave her a little shake. "I'll go wait for the ambulance. Stay with him." She hugged her hard. "It'll be okay, honey."

"That's my line," Nicole whispered as Taylor ran out, leaving her with the big, bad, broken Ty lying at her feet.

CHAPTER SEVEN

NICOLE WENT IN the ambulance with Ty. Took him into ER herself and spewed out orders.

Hovered and tried not to wring her hands. Tried to focus on what she was doing. They took care of his bruised ribs, his sprained ankle. Noted his concussion, which worried her the most.

Yes, his head was big and hard. But damn, he'd hit it hard.

She dealt with the staff and their curious expressions, knowing she'd shown her hand when she'd yelled out directions in a wobbly voice.

She'd never yelled while on duty.

Well, the staff would get over it. The question was, would she?

She filled out Ty's paperwork, which was more time-consuming than she'd ever realized, being on the other side of the fence for the first time.

Taylor was in the waiting room, looking unusually scattered and stressed. Suzanne was there too, leaning on the tall, dark, gorgeous Ryan, who had his arms around her in a way that made Nicole take a moment. Had she ever leaned on a man like that? Ever had a man who wanted her to? Ever been offered true affection from a man?

Nope. But then again, she'd never wanted such things. She didn't want them now. Not when she was strong enough to stand on her own two feet.

When she could convince them to go, she sent Taylor, Suzanne and Ryan home, promising them Ty—and his hard head—was in good hands and going to be fine.

And he would be. She would see to it, all by herself.

TWO HOURS LATER, Nicole sank to the cot at Ty's hip and stared at the sleeping, still far too pale man.

With the proper care and rest, he was going to be fine.

But when was *she* going to be fine?

He'd gotten under her skin. There was no other excuse for her ridiculous panic at the apartment. None.

Outside the cubicle, machines bleeped, footsteps squeaked, voices carried, some raised, some hushed. There were smells too: antiseptics, medicine and the scent of fear and pain. Normal ER sounds and smells.

But inside the cubicle, life seemed suspended. It was just the two of them, one unconscious, the other wondering what had happened to her life. Lightly, she reached out and touched the bandage on Ty's head. "You scared the hell out of me, Ty Patrick O'Grady," she whispered.

"Of Dublin," he said in a heavy Irish brogue without opening his eyes.

Had he really spoken, or was she hallucinating on top of everything else? "Ty?"

"You scare me, too." His voice sounded raspy, and more than a little goofy from the drugs they'd given him for the pain. "You and my sister both. I have a sister, did I tell you?"

"No." She covered her mouth to keep her hysterical, relieved laugh in. "You haven't told me much about yourself at all."

"She found me on the Internet. Wants to know me. Everyone wants to know me." His words were slurred, but the Irish lilt was unmistakable. So was his sudden crooked grin, though he still didn't open his eyes. "You want me, too, don't you, doc? You want me as much as I want you. Say it for me."

Her heart leapt in a new sort of panic. "Keep your mouth zipped, you big idiot, you're drugged."

"Is that why my body is floating away from my head? Your head is floating, too, doc. You're so pretty. Makes me wish I could stay in one place for once, you know that?"

"Please…please, shut up or you're going to say something you'll regret." She wanted to run, and she wanted him to keep talking.

"You do want me. I know you do."

How the rough-and-tough man could lie there looking so adorable in his cockiness was beyond her. "Ty."

He let out a long sigh. "Maybe that's just me with all the wanting then." He sighed again. "You're screwing with my head, all three of you."

Three? He was worse off than she'd thought. That, or he'd had too many drugs. Leaning in close, she checked his pupils, making him grin. "I'm okay, darlin'. Sweet of you to worry though."

She sat back. "This sister…you talked to her?"

"She wants a family, but who the hell needs family? I don't need anyone. I haven't since I was fifteen and on my own."

She went very still on the outside while her heart did a slow roll. "That still only makes two, Ty. Your sister and me."

"But then there's *her*."

"Her who?" If he said he had a wife she'd have to kill him.

"My mother. She didn't want me. I probably never told you that."

Nicole sighed and put her hand on his chest. Her own ached like hell. "No."

"I'm a bad seed. Probably should have warned you before now, but I didn't want to scare you off. The truth is, you name it, and I did it. Stole clothes, stole food— Am I upsetting you?" he asked, opening his eyes to see hers welling up.

"Ty. *Rest*," she begged, wanting to wrap herself around him.

"Can't. There's someone jack-hammering in my head. I didn't even know I had a sister."

"I know," she said in response to his baffled voice, stroking him with her hands, trying to quiet him because she didn't want to hear this, didn't want to know about him because, damn it, how was she supposed to keep her distance if she knew about him? "Please, Ty, I want you to—"

"I don't want to like her." After that statement, he was quiet for so long she thought he'd fallen asleep, and she just sat there, soaking him up. She'd imagined he'd had a rough childhood, but she hadn't imagined it as bad as it must have been. Because she couldn't help herself, she touched him, ran a hand over his arm, his jaw, wishing she could take his pain as her own.

"You feeling sorry for me, doc? Cuz if you are, I'm going to tackle you down right here, right now, and kiss us both stupid."

"You're in no position for tackling, much less kissing."

"Try me," he warned, and reached for her, missing by a mile. "Damn."

"Ty." She touched his pale, pale face. "Lie still."

"Yeah." Sweat broke out on his forehead. "Lying still now."

"Good, because you've got to save your energy for healing. You need to—"

"Nicole? Darlin'?" He closed his eyes tight. "I'd love to hear the lecture, really. But if you don't mind, I'm going to puke now."

THE NEXT TIME Ty opened his eyes, he was still in a damn hospital bed. Still in a fartoosmall hospital gown with no back. Still feeling green and shaky and in too much damn pain to believe that the shot some mean nurse had given him a short time ago had worked.

He hated hospitals with an unreasonable vengeance, and had ever since he'd been twelve and was beaten within an inch of life. His own fault. He'd broken into a restaurant, only to get caught by the owner as he'd been stuffing his face with food from the fridge. Didn't matter that he'd been starving, or was a skinny little runt, the guy had gone berserk. The beating had landed Ty in the emergency room, where he'd been treated like little more than the wild animal he was. Once there, he'd barely outwitted the juvenile authorities. All he remembered, when he let himself think about it, was a vicious, snarling, vivid, Technicolor pain and the bitter stench of his own fear.

Now, being in another hospital brought it all back, quite unpleasantly.

Nicole's face floated into view above his own: her wide, expressive gray eyes, the short-cropped hair that so suited her arresting face, and the silver hoops up one ear. Then there was that mouth, with the full lips he so enjoyed nibbling on.

Another hallucination? He'd had some doozies since he'd been here, all of them involving her tiger-striped bra and purple panties.

"Hey," she said, sounding very doctor-like. She wore a

white coat and had a stethoscope looped around her neck. How official. "How are you feeling?" she asked. "Still nauseous?"

In all the other hallucinations, she hadn't talked, she'd just smiled all sultry-like and had bent over his body, giving him pleasure such as he'd never known. "I like the other outfit better," he said, closing his eyes.

"What?" She put her hand on his forehead.

She thought he was still out of it. "Never mind. Let's blow this Popsicle stand."

"No can do."

He stopped in the act of tossing his blankets aside. "Doc?"

She clutched a clipboard to her chest, looking very in control in her own environment. Bully for her, but he wanted control in *his* own environment, thank you very much, and lying flat on his back in a scanty gown wasn't doing it for him.

"You need to stay overnight for observation, Ty."

"I don't think so." He sent her a tight smile. "Hand me my clothes."

"I mean it."

"So do I. Hand me my clothes or get an eyeful, and believe me, the gown hides nothing." Carefully, trying not to let out the pathetic moan he wanted to, he got himself in a sitting position. His ribs were on fire, so was his ankle, and his head…well, the pain in his head didn't bear thinking about because if he did, he was going to toss his cookies again. Since the good doctor, sexy as hell in all her disapproval, was glaring at him instead of handing him his things, he put his feet to the floor.

"Ty, don't be stupid."

"More stupid than falling through your ceiling, you mean?"

"You're still drugged. You can't get yourself dressed much less get yourself home."

"I don't feel drugged."

"Really? How many fingers am I holding up?"

He squinted at her hand. She had no fingers. And now that he took a good look, her head was separated from her body. A shame, really, because it was such a beautiful head. Bossy and stubborn, but beautiful.

"Ty? How many?"

"I'm not sure. But I can tell you you're wearing a tiger-striped bra and purple silky panties."

She didn't look amused.

Ty returned to his efforts of getting up. He looked at his ankle. Just touching it to the floor hurt enough that he had to suck in a breath. "Sure this thing isn't broken?"

"Just badly bruised."

Okay, then. Moving on. Next move—getting upright. With that feat in mind, he leaned his weight forward.

Dr. Sexy crossed her arms and frowned.

With a grunt of effort, he went for it, and surged to his feet. Or foot, as he held his screaming ankle off the ground. Ribs burning, head feeling like it had blown right off, he thrust out his arms for balance. The back of his gown flapped cool air on his bare ass.

As he waved wildly, Nicole tossed down her clipboard and leapt toward him. "Damn it." She shoved her shoulder beneath his arm, taking his weight, which, given how little she was, had to be considerable. "What the hell is wrong with you, you stubborn—"

"Shh." He wrapped his arm around her, gasping for breath as everything in his vision faded to a spotted gray. For a cold, clammy, sweaty moment he thought he was going to pass out, but the litany coming from the woman supporting him kept him conscious.

"Of all the idiotic, moronic…"

The ringing in his ears drowned out the rest of her monologue as she sat him back down, but he got the gist. He also got the pain. Holy shit, he hadn't imagined he could feel anything so much, but every muscle in his body had started a mutiny. Unable to hold back a low groan, he rolled to his side and panted for air.

"I'm going to call the nurse and get you another pain-killer."

"Don't. She's mean."

"Baby."

He laughed, then nearly cried at the fire in his ribs.

"I wouldn't laugh," she advised, but there was something in her voice now, something… He managed to crane his neck and peer over his shoulder. Yep, that was his ass hanging right out for the world to see. He closed his eyes. "You getting a good view?"

She tossed his blanket over him. "I'm a doctor. I've seen it all."

"Yeah, well, this isn't quite how I imagined you seeing me. Nicole, I'm not staying here overnight."

"But—"

"I'm not," he said, and looked up at her. "I…can't."

"Why not?"

"I hate hospitals."

"Everyone says that."

"But I mean it."

She stared at him for a long moment, then sighed and sat next to him. "Okay, so you have a hospital phobia—"

"I'm not staying."

"You can't go home alone, you'll need someone to watch over you, help you."

Much as that went against the grain, he had to agree

with her, if only for the simple fact that he couldn't even see straight. "For how long?"

"At least tonight and all day tomorrow. Maybe even a second night. After your hard head improves, then you can hobble around on your own if you're careful."

"Fine."

"Who's going to help you?"

"I'll figure it out."

She crossed her arms. "I know you don't have any family you'll call."

That cleared some of the haze from his vision. "Really? How do you know that?"

"You...told me."

Given the look of compassion in her gaze, he'd told her plenty. Terrific. "You listened to the ramblings of a drugged man?"

"You were happy enough to let your mouth run."

What had he said? "Did I mention anything about your interesting lingerie fetish? Because I have to tell you, Nicole, I find it fascinating that you're so tough and impenetrable on the outside, and so..." A smile curved his lips. "So incredibly soft on the inside."

"You're changing the subject."

"I'm trying."

She blew out a breath. "You didn't say anything embarrassing, if that's what you're worried about. You just said...you had a sister you didn't know about and that she was emailing you."

"And...?"

"Just that...your mother didn't want you."

Hell. He'd spilled his guts all over her. Her voice had softened, and that was definitely pity on her face. He didn't want her pity, he didn't want anyone's pity. He wanted out of this bed and he wanted that now. "Well. This has been fun."

She held him down with a hand to his shoulder. "I'm sorry, Ty."

For what? he wondered. Falling through her ceiling or for being so pathetic as to have his own mother cast him aside? "This isn't your problem."

She nodded, agreeing, and turned away. Made it to the door, which she studied for a long minute, as if fascinated by the wood. Then she turned around. "I know you're alone. That you're too proud to ask any friends for help. As a doctor, I can't release you knowing that."

"I'm leaving, Nicole, come hell or high water."

"I know." She closed her eyes. Opened them again and leveled them right on him. "Which is why you're coming home with me."

SHE WAS CRAZY. Or so Nicole told herself the entire drive home with Ty dozing next to her. She let Suzanne and Taylor fuss over getting him up the stairs. She gave him another pain pill, which he bitched about like a two-year-old but finally took when she threatened to pull out a needle instead.

Then she settled him in her bed and stepped back, wondering why just his pale face made her want to fuss. She'd never fussed a day in her life.

Ty looked around at the no-frills bedroom with the bare walls, at the bed with its navy-blue comforter and two pillows, and not a thing out of place except on the chair in the corner, which held some clothes and a perilous stack of medical journals. "Not even a romance novel to read?"

"I have those." She gestured to the journals and he shook his head.

"I guess I'm not surprised," he said. "God forbid you

actually take time off when you're off. So. You're really giving up the bed for me?"

"You didn't like the hospital, remember?"

"Hmm."

Nicole glared at him. "What does that mean? What's wrong with the bed?"

He blinked sexy eyes at her. Waggled his eyebrows suggestively. "You're not in it."

Wasn't he something. "I'm taking the couch, big guy."

"You don't have a couch, you have an ancient, scary-looking futon masquerading as a couch. The only other thing you have out there is a nice-size hole in your ceiling and a mess on your floor."

"Nothing that can't be fixed." She did have the futon, ancient or otherwise, and put together with a blanket, she'd be fine. "Goodnight, Ty."

He leaned back against her pillows and looked at the ceiling, his faced lined with pain. "Aren't you going to read me a bedtime story?"

"Sure. Once upon a time there was this idiot who fell through a ceiling and landed on his head."

He closed his eyes. "Ha ha."

"So why are you afraid of hospitals?"

"I just don't like them, all right?"

"All right." He didn't look at her, didn't move a muscle, and yet she *knew* in that moment his pain was more in memory than physical. "Look, don't get too comfy. I'll be waking you every few hours."

He cracked open an eye. "Is that a promise?"

"To check on your hard head, Ace."

"I got something else you could check on."

"Uh-huh, and with all the drugs in you, it'd work really well, too."

A ghost of a cocky smile played around his mouth. "Try me."

"Goodnight, Ty."

"'Night. Nicole?"

At the door already, she turned.

"Why did you take me home with you?"

She lifted a shoulder. "Because you were hurt."

"Truth."

She sighed. "I don't know why."

He nodded, and closed his eyes again. Almost immediately, his breathing evened out as the drugs finally claimed him.

For a long moment Nicole stood there, just staring at him. She had a man in her bed, when she'd never put one there before, much less *yearned* for one. There'd always been too much to do, too many people to save.

Now he lay in her bed, and she was yearning. Yearning and hurting at the same time, because he'd never get serious. Oh, she believed he was serious about getting into her purple panties.

But for him, this was simple lust.

That scared her. It scared her because she thought maybe, just maybe, she could feel more than that in return.

NICOLE DIDN'T GO to sleep, but kept herself busy, mostly continuing to watch her patient. She swept up some of the mess in her living room. She cleaned out whatever was growing in her fridge, and she reassured Taylor and Suzanne that Ty was fine. Twice. After an hour and a half, she sat at his hip, munching on a bag of pretzels. "Ty?"

He didn't budge.

"Ty?"

"I knew you'd be back, begging me to take you."

"I'm here to check on you."

"Then check on me." His voice was groggy but there was nothing groggy in those eyes when they opened and watched her with an intensity that made her squirm.

"How are you feeling?"

"I'd feel better if you stopped sucking on that pretzel. It's making my blood drain southward."

"You're fine," she decided, swallowing the pretzel and leaving him to go back to sleep, which he did instantly.

She went to the living room and proceeded to watch the clock tick. After another hour, she went into the bedroom again. Moonlight streamed over the bed, highlighting the long, lean form lying there. He'd kicked off the covers. He was sprawled on his back, one arm over his eyes; his big chest rose and fell evenly. She knew this because he wore only a pair of boxer briefs, ribbed cotton, charcoal-gray.

They fit him snugly just below his navel. He was bruised and cut over a good portion of his torso. He also had scars that had nothing to do with his fall. A long, nasty-looking one low on his flat belly that looked like a knife wound. A puckered one near his collarbone that looked like an old burn, and another on his arm. There was a long scar down one muscled calf, and another on his thigh. And then there was the tattoo he'd shown her—an intricate design winding around his left bicep.

And he called *her* a warrior.

She had bits and pieces of him now, and had put together a picture of how he'd grown up and become the man he was. There were still quite a few pieces of the puzzle missing, but he wouldn't welcome her curiosity. She shouldn't feel that curiosity at all, but did. He'd raised himself, a fact she couldn't deny made him all the more fascinating.

How could his mother, any mother, turn her back on a

child? What kind of mother did that, let her own son think she didn't want him?

That it hurt her, hurt her for him, was another concern. She shouldn't feel this way, this possessive, protective way. He certainly wouldn't want it, nor, for that matter, would he want her compassion. He was far too proud for that.

And yet she couldn't tear her eyes off his beautiful form. So she sank to the bed at his side and wondered what the hell she was going to do with him.

"You going to watch me sleep all night?"

She jumped back up, pressed nervous hands to her stomach. "You're awake."

"Want to see how awake?"

Since he was talking with his eyes closed, very carefully not moving a muscle, she smiled. "Do you know where you are?"

"In your bed. Without you." His voice was low, husky. Unbearably sexy. "Want to check anything else? My temperature maybe? I'm hot, darlin'. Really hot."

"You're hurt."

"Not that hurt."

She eyed him. He still hadn't moved a single muscle. And suddenly, the doctor inside her vanished, replaced by a mischievous woman who knew she was safe. "You don't think so? You really think you could...?"

"I know it."

"Yeah? Then prove it. Come get me, big guy."

He pried a bleary eye open, closed it again when she sent him a cocky smile.

"Come on, come get it," she dared, making him groan.

"Can't you help a man out a little and come down here?"

"Nope."

"Ah, now see, that's just plain old mean."

"Goodnight, Ty."

"We already said that."

"We're going to say it several more times yet tonight. You can thank your concussion for that."

He swore colorfully, making her smile again. A man who could put together those descriptive words was going to be okay.

The next time she checked on him, he was in such obvious discomfort and pain she ended up sleeping in a chair at his side to watch over him more closely. In the deep of the night, he shifted, then groaned, and she was there, reaching out to touch, to soothe. Though he didn't say a word, she knew he was awake, and terribly uncomfortable. "I'm sorry," she whispered.

"Me, too. I'm sorry I fell through your ceiling. I'm *really* sorry I did that."

"Need another pain pill?"

"Yeah. I've decided I like those."

"And the doctor? How about her?" She had no idea why she asked, and held her breath, wishing she could take it back.

But a weak smile touched his mouth. "Maybe I decided I like the doctor more than a little."

"That's only because I'm holding the goods."

His eyes opened at that. "You have the goods all right."

She blushed. *Blushed.*

"And I'm not talking about your tight little hot bod either, Dr. Nicole Mann."

She had no answer for that, but as he drifted off, none seemed to be required.

BY MORNING NICOLE was the hoarse, groggy one. Since when had one single patient taken so much out of her?

Since she cared. Too much.

But she had an even more pressing problem at the moment. She wasn't convinced Ty could handle the day by himself. He hadn't yet managed to get out of the bed without her support, and though he did keep up a healthy stream of come-ons, she knew damn well he was all talk and no go.

So she did it. For the first time in her entire professional life, she picked up the phone and took the day off.

And wondered if she'd gone completely off the deep end.

CHAPTER EIGHT

AFTER SHE'D CALLED in to the hospital, Nicole stood in the middle of her living room, idle. *Idle.*

What was she going to do with herself with only one patient to take care of?

The entire day loomed large in front of her, when she'd never allowed herself a leisurely moment in her life. With a shrug, she pulled up a stack of medical journals and other related work reports she could read.

But for the first time since she could remember, they didn't appeal. So she sat in front of the TV she'd turned on only a few times since she'd purchased it several years ago.

And in no time flat, discovered the utter, addictive joy of daytime television. With the remote in hand, she clicked back and forth between *Bewitched, I Love Lucy* and *Court TV.*

Then the phone rang, annoying her. So did her caller.

"Hello." The lazily cultured voice was Dr. Lincoln Watts. "Slacking off today?"

Nicole's finger tightened on the phone. "I'm entitled to call in."

"Did you stay up too late?" His voice lowered. "Or did your lover keep you in bed this morning?"

"I won't be in today, Dr. Watts. That's all that concerns you. *Period,*" she said with shocking calm, and because the commercial was over and *I Love Lucy* was starting again, she hung up the phone. She stared at her hand on the remote and realized she was shaking with fury.

Not even two seconds later came the knock on her door. Damn it. She got up, and gaze still locked on the TV, opened the door.

"Morning." Suzanne held a covered tray that smelled so delicious Nicole promptly forgot about the TV.

"Not for you." Suzanne slapped Nicole's hand when she went to lift the cover. "For Ty. Tell him I hope he's feeling better."

"You brought Ty food and not me?"

"Yes, and don't cheat him by eating any of it. He needs his strength to heal." She whistled slowly at the hole in the ceiling of the living room. "That poor, poor baby."

"He's not a baby." Nope, as Nicole had now seen just about every inch of his long, hard, perfectly formed body, she could say that for certain. "And food doesn't heal." She lifted her chin. "My skills as a doctor are going to do that."

Suzanne shot her a look of pity. "Oh, honey, have you got a lot to learn about men. There's only one way to reach them, and it's not, contrary to popular belief, through their penises. It's through their stomachs. Now give him this tray with a nice morning smile and you'll see what I mean. You *can* smile this early, can't you?"

Nicole glared at her.

Suzanne laughed. "Well, honestly, I don't see you smile that often. Actually, I don't see you do anything but work."

"Not today. I called in."

"You…*called in?*" Suzanne slapped a hand to her mouth in disbelief. *"You?"*

Nicole rolled her eyes. "It's not that big a deal."

"To you it is. You, the workaholic, took a day off to care for Ty. That's huge."

"He *did* fall through my ceiling."

"You took a day off." Suzanne marveled at that for a moment. "Wait until Taylor hears you're falling for him. She's going to be the last one of us holding on to that vow of singlehood."

"Oh no." Nicole laughed. Fall for Ty? *Ha!* "I don't know what you think is going on here, but you can just wash it right out of your hair. I'm staying single forever, just like Taylor."

"Uh-huh."

"I am." She meant it. Ty would finish his job here and sooner or later he'd be gone. Long gone. He wouldn't so much as look back, as looking back wasn't in his genes.

She wouldn't look back either, she'd—

She'd miss him. Damn it. She'd really miss him.

But she'd carved out a good life for herself. She had her career, a family that was only slightly dysfunctional, and friends, even if they were nosy as hell. She had all she needed.

"I used to be in denial, too," Suzanne said with a knowing smile.

"It's not denial."

"Right. Hey, I'll come back later for the tray and any details you want to share."

"There won't be details."

But Suzanne had already walked away. "Damn it," Nicole muttered when Suzanne's laughter floated back up the stairs. Shrugging it off, she went back to her shows.

And wondered if Ty was dreaming of her.

TY CAME AWAKE in slow degrees. When he was fully conscious, he carefully opened his eyes.

The sun rudely pierced into the room, stabbing him with the brightness until he closed his eyes again. He took mental stock and decided his entire body felt as if he'd been thrown under a steamroller.

Except for his head. His head felt as if he'd put it into a giant vise and cinched it down.

With no little amount of struggle, he managed to get to a sitting position. From there he eyed the bathroom door, only a few feet away.

It might as well have been a hundred miles. Determined, he staggered up, and for his efforts, nearly passed out. Gripping the back of a chair, he took a handful of deep, careful breaths. Daggers shot upward from his ankle. His ribs screamed. He had no doubt his head was going to fall right off. But he made it to the bathroom, shut the door and leaned back against it.

"Ty!" From the other side of the door came Nicole's worried voice. "What are you doing!"

"Considering getting sick."

"Are you okay? Are you hurting? Do you need any help?"

"No, yes and no."

"Ty—"

When he was done, he opened the door, about two seconds away from passing out.

Nicole was right there, wrapping herself around him, taking his weight. "Of all the fool things to do, getting up by yourself, trying to walk, moving around as if you didn't drop yourself on your head just yesterday…"

"Not back to bed," he said when she turned him that way. "Not unless you're coming, too."

Her arms were around his bare middle, carefully avoiding his hurt ribs. He liked the feel of her hands on him. Too much. She took him to the living room where he could see the blanket strewn over the futon. An episode of *I*

Dream Of Jeanie was on TV. Next to the futon was a half-eaten bowl of cereal.

"Are those Frosted Flakes?" His mouth started to water. "And I love that show."

"It's a Jeanie marathon. This is the one where she gets stuck in her bottle." She looked at the TV. "I think I'd like to be able to toss my ponytail and have my every wish come true. You've just missed *I Love Lucy.* She was working on a candy assembly line. Honest to God, I've never laughed so hard...what?" she asked self-consciously as he stared at her.

It was just that her eyes were laughing. Her cheeks were flushed. And her hands were still on him. Irresistible combo. He found his insides stirring, and not just the part of him that usually stirred while staring at a beautiful woman, but something in his chest. She looked...*happy.* It wasn't a look he'd seen on her before, making him realize he hadn't often seen her outside of work mode.

He liked this side of her, he liked it a lot. "You haven't seen these shows a hundred times?"

"Are you kidding?" She laughed, a sweet, simple sound. "We weren't allowed to watch anything but public television growing up. I never even had a TV until a couple of years ago, but I rarely turn it on. I can't believe what I've been missing. And *The Brady Bunch!* What a crackup—" She narrowed her eyes when he grinned. "Stop that."

"You're pretty damn adorable, Dr. Dweeb."

Her mouth opened, then shut. "I never know how to take you," she finally said.

"Take me any way you want, darlin', just take me."

She stepped back, which left him holding up his own body. He braced his legs, shooting an arrow of pain from his ankle directly to his ribs. Clutching them made his vision waver again and he gritted his teeth.

"You fool," she said softly, reaching for him again, easing him down. "Sit. Lucky for you Suzanne took pity and brought you a tray of food."

"You mean you aren't going to slave over a hot stove for me?"

"I don't slave over a hot stove for anyone."

"Hence the Frosted Flakes."

"Hence the Frosted Flakes," she agreed. "Pouring milk into a bowl, now *that* I can do." Shrugging, she set a heavenly smelling tray on his lap. "I think I missed the girlie gene. I don't cook, I don't sew, and..." She lifted a napkin Suzanne had folded into a flower. "I sure as hell don't fold napkins into shapes."

It took an effort to smile when his head was pounding, but she looked so unexpectedly vulnerable, he tried. "I like you anyway."

She didn't smile back, but she didn't slug him either. "You do?"

"Yeah, I do." She hadn't turned out to be anything as he'd imagined. She wasn't aloof or spoiled, or insensitive, but was warm and giving and incredibly compassionate. In fact, he had to resist the urge to pull her close and bury his face in her hair. Not only would it hurt like hell to do so, but the urge was wrong. He had no business feeling this way, none at all. "I think you're a pretty incredible woman, Nicole. And sexy as hell to boot."

She let out a deprecatory smile. "I've never been accused of being sexy before."

"Then you're not listening, because I've been thinking you're the sexiest woman I know from the first time I set eyes on you."

"Well." Brushing her hands on her jeans, she backed away, looking around her as if searching for some way to keep her hands busy. "I've got to..."

When she just turned in a slow circle, at a complete loss, he wanted to laugh. "Work?" he finished for her.

"No. No work today. I, uh…" She avoided his gaze, lifted the lids off the food Suzanne had left him. "Here. You need food before you get more pain meds."

Obediently he picked up a fork, groaning at an ache in his shoulder. Definitely he was getting too old to be falling through ceilings. "Why no work today?" He saw the truth in her eyes and gaped at her. "You called in? For me?"

"Well, what were you going to do? Make your own breakfast?"

"You didn't make breakfast," he pointed out, moaning again, this time at the taste of Suzanne's homefried potatoes melting in his mouth.

"You complaining?"

"Nope, not at all." He took another bite, studied her. "You took a day off for me. I think you're crazy about me."

"Shut up and eat."

"Yeah. Okay." He shoveled in more food. "Thanks," he said into her inscrutable gaze. "For taking care of me."

"Yeah, well, don't get excited. I would have done the same for a stray puppy."

Oh, yeah. She was crazy about him.

NICOLE HAD NEVER known the guilty pleasure of a day off. She'd heard her coworkers talk about how they occasionally stayed home simply to brain-rest, doing nothing more than eating junk food and watching soap operas all day long, and she'd always felt a sort of superior smugness about not feeling the need to do the same.

Soap operas. *Please.*

But—and she couldn't quite believe it—they were wonderful. She sat on the floor, crosslegged, in a ratty old pair of sweats and a comfy tank top, cradling a bowl of popcorn in one hand and the remote in the other. On the futon above her, crashed out cold, slept Ty.

It was odd, the feeling of contentment. Odd and terrifying.

When someone—two nosy someones—knocked at her door, she rolled her eyes. "You know, this is getting insulting," she whispered as she opened the door and faced Suzanne and Taylor. "I can take care of him."

Suzanne passed her a tray, probably loaded with lunch, because heaven forbid "poor baby Ty" starve to death with Nicole's inability to so much as toast bread. "Frosted Flakes three times a day is not nutritious."

Taylor grinned. "And…don't take this wrong…but we're not quite sure you know how to take care of a *man*."

"He's not a man, he's my patient."

"I think he'd say differently." Taylor held out a laptop computer to her. "Tell him I locked up his car, but this was in it and I thought maybe he'd want it."

"He's not going to work, I won't let him." Nicole knelt to put the tray of food on the floor beside the door before rising to take the computer.

"Really." Taylor lifted that superior blond brow and gave her a knowing, far-too-self-righteous smile. "Know what I think?"

"If I say yes, will you go away?" Nicole asked.

"I think Suzanne's right," Taylor said. "I think I'm in danger of being the last one holding out for permanent singlehood."

Suzanne nodded while Nicole sputtered. She kept her voice low with great effort. "Just because I don't think he should work doesn't mean—"

"Honey." Suzanne put her hand on Nicole's arm and sent her a sweet smile. "It's okay you're after him."

"I'm *not* after him," Nicole said through her teeth.

She jabbed a finger toward Taylor. "And I'm still firmly single."

"Okay, but just remember, you can stay single and still have wild monkey sex—"

Nicole slapped a hand over Taylor's mouth, glancing over her shoulder to make sure Ty was still asleep. "Okay, you guys have to go now."

"Why?" Taylor tried to peer past Nicole. "You get him naked yet?"

"Goodbye." Nicole tried to push them out of the way of the door so she could close it.

But Taylor kept her nose in the way. "Just one peek—"

"Goodbye," Nicole said firmly and put her hand on Taylor's face to hold her out as she finally closed the door.

Her relief was short-lived.

Ty had turned his head toward her. His eyes were open. Clear.

Curious.

"Hey." She came forward, wondering how much he'd overheard. "How's the head? You doing okay?"

"You could have told them you had me *nearly* naked but don't know what to do with me."

He'd heard it all. Perfect. "Oh, I know what to do with you," she assured him. "I just…" She stopped the teasing words because his eyes had gone so hot it caused a mirroring flame inside her.

For just a moment she wondered what it would be like to let him kiss her again, this time allowing him to peel off her clothes and make love to her. Eager for exactly that, her body actually leaned toward him in a show of willingness, but she had to remember, he was destined to walk away.

At least she was smart enough to know that wouldn't work for her, walking away. "I just…"

"Come here, Nicole."

He was sprawled on the futon. A light blanket covered his long legs and lap, but had fallen away from the rest of him, leaving his chest and arms bare. Bare and roped with muscles.

And bruises. "Are you feeling better, Ty?"

"Are you coming here?"

She pressed back against the door. "No, that's not such a good idea right now."

His eyes were still hot but he just lifted a shoulder, the fact he was too weary to move working in her favor. "I'll take the laptop."

She held it to her chest. "I don't think you should work."

"I don't think you should worry about it."

If she'd fallen on her head she'd probably be feeling nasty, too, so she gave in. Sort of. "Come get it," she said, holding it out.

"Come and get it?" he repeated incredulously.

"That's right."

"You're into S and M, right?" He struggled to his feet, and the blanket fell away from him. His shorts were low on his hips, and for some reason, her gaze attached itself to that area of his body and couldn't be torn away.

Then she caught him trying to hide his grimace of pain, and she had to lock her hands on the computer in order not to rush over there and do something stupid, like touch him.

"When I get over there," he warned her grimly, trying to straighten. "I'm going to—"

"Fine." Damn him, he looked so pale. "Here." She moved toward him before he took a single step and gently pushed him back down, putting the computer on his lap. "Work. I don't care."

"Fine."

"Fine." She turned away. "I'll just…" What? Suzanne had just provided lunch. What else was there to do?

You could stare at him all day.

"I don't suppose you'd do me a favor," he said a little gruffly.

She turned back. "I am *not* helping you take a shower."

He stared at her for a flash before letting out a laugh that ended in a quick grab to his ribs and a groan. "Measurements," he grounded out. "I need you to go downstairs and measure a few things for me so I can get something done while I'm wasting your day." He hadn't bothered to cover himself back up. The sight of a nearly nude male body shouldn't have stirred her, not when she saw such things all the time.

But she had to admit, it wasn't every patient that had a body like his.

"Can you do that?" he asked.

"I suppose." He shouldn't work, but who the hell was she to mother the stubborn man? They didn't have a relationship or a commitment. He'd never get serious enough to have a commitment. And it wasn't as if they cared about each other.

Okay, *she* cared. Knowing that, and because she needed to get away from the sight of him for a few minutes, she snatched the paper he offered her out of his hands and headed toward the door.

"You'll need a measuring tape," he called out. "And be careful when you—"

"I think I can manage a few measurements." Taylor would have a measuring tape. And Suzanne would have ice cream. Because damn if she didn't need something good and fattening to take her mind off the other craving she had.

For one Ty Patrick O'Grady.

BECAUSE NICOLE WAS hoping Ty had gone back to sleep, and because she had to make sure she was entirely under control before she saw him again, she took her time about getting the measurements he needed.

And if she stopped at Suzanne's apartment and mooched three brownies and a scoop of ice cream off her first, who was going to care?

Except her jeans.

When she finally walked back into her apartment, the living room was empty. So was the kitchen.

She found him on her bed. His laptop was open and hooked up to her phone line. He had his email program open but his eyes were not.

"Ty?"

He didn't budge. He was sprawled on his back, his head turned slightly away, his chest rose and fell evenly with his deep breathing. Bruises bloomed on one side, and because he once again hadn't bothered with covers, she could quite clearly see his swollen ankle. He needed to ice that, and probably take more meds, she thought, moving closer. She'd just check his vitals first, and—

And the email caught her eye.

Dear Ty,

I'm not looking for comfort or a handout. And leaving it alone was never an option.

We're family, linked by blood. Can you really say you're not interested? You have such a full life that you don't need this, the only other living relative you have?

I have a lot to offer, and I want to meet you. I want to know you. I want to be family.

I'm staying at the local youth hostel if you are interested.

Please, *please* be interested.
Margaret Mary.

Nicole stared at the letter, her heart in her throat at Margaret Mary's raw need. And if *she'd* felt it, what had Ty felt?

"Did you see enough?"

Nicole nearly leapt out of her skin. Looking groggy, sleepy, unrested and irritable, Ty struggled to get up.

"No," she said, reaching for him. "Just stay—"

He slapped the computer closed. "Yeah, I'll stay. I'll stay the hell out of your way. If you'll stay out of mine."

CHAPTER NINE

NICOLE STARED AT TY as he got to his feet and very carefully straightened.

"Where did that come from?" she asked.

"Forget it." He looked around. "Where are my clothes?"

"Right there," she said, pointing to the folded stack on her nightstand. "But—"

"I have stuff I have to take care of." He grabbed his pants, then looked at them with a pained expression, as if he knew getting them on was going to hurt like hell. Jaw tight, he shook them out, then bent slightly at the waist. Sweat broke out on his brow and he wavered for a second.

"Oh, Ty. Get back in bed."

"Since I doubt that's an invitation," he said, his voice more than a little strained, "I'll pass, thanks."

"I don't get it. Your options were staying in the hospital for observation or coming home with me. You agreed, so what's changed?"

"I told you. I have things to do."

"Like go to the youth hostel?"

His head whipped toward her.

"I, um…" She clasped her hands together and rocked back on her heels. "I saw more of the email than I meant to."

"You see more of everything than you're meant to."

"What does that mean?"

"Nothing." He waved away her efforts to help him,

though he had to sit back down to work his pants up. By the time he stood again, his chest had a fine sheen of sweat on it and he was breathing like a mistreated racehorse. Getting his shirt on took another long, painful moment, during which time Nicole watch the tattooed design on his bicep bunch as he struggled. She bit her lip and clenched her fists to keep from helping.

And then he was heading toward the door.

"Ty—" When he looked at her impatiently, she sighed. "You can't drive on those painkillers I gave you."

"I didn't take the last two."

"You didn't—" She shook her head, understanding now why he was hurting so badly. "You really are a fool."

"No shit, doc." He had his computer tucked against his good side, and was half out the door, but he hesitated. "Thanks."

"For what? Pissing you off?"

Now he sighed. "For being there."

"Okay."

Crystal-blue haunted eyes watched warily as she walked up to him. When she got close enough, he closed his eyes, sighed again, then looked at her as he reached out and stroked her jaw. "I have to go," he whispered, running a finger up the hoops in her ear.

She barely resisted the urge to turn her face into his hand and kiss his palm. "Tell me why."

"Because I'm not fit for company." He stepped back and dropped his hand.

"Sometimes, Ty, you *have* to let people in."

"You're speaking from experience, of course."

She ignored the sarcasm. "I let my family in. And Suzanne and Taylor." *And you,* she wanted to say. Horrifying, how much she wanted to say it, how much she wanted *him* to want it as well.

"Goodbye, Nicole."

"Wait…. You're not going to even write her back?"

"Do you really care?"

"You know I do."

"Actually, I know no such thing."

"How can you say that after last night?"

"We're different, you've said so enough times."

"Maybe those differences are more surface than I thought," she admitted.

"Meaning?"

"Meaning…we're both loners. We're both workaholics. Maybe we connect on a more fundamental level than I imagined possible."

"You're a doctor. Your own words, remember? I was hurt and you're sworn to heal. You would have done the same for a puppy."

She swallowed hard at her own words thrown back in her face and looked right at him, the hardest thing she'd ever done. "I care about you."

"Yeah, well, you shouldn't. Goodbye, Nicole."

And then he was gone, and she was staring at the closed door thinking that his goodbye had sounded a lot more final than just see-you-later.

It sounded like…well, goodbye.

And really, that was perfectly fine with her. More than fine.

Which didn't explain the tear on her cheek.

ONCE HE GOT HOME, Ty slept for two days straight. Then he lay around for a third and fourth in a funk that was very unlike him.

It was too quiet. That had to be why he thought of Nicole only every living second. To combat that, he cranked up the music. Watched TV. Worked.

But still, he thought of her. How could he not? She was smart and sexy and beautiful, and he wanted her. Yet he'd wanted plenty of women before, so why he felt so down about how he'd left her, he had no idea. They didn't have anything going, she didn't want to have anything going.

Neither did he. Yeah, he would have loved to sleep with her, hold her, sink into her body and lose himself, sating this inexplicable desire for her. But he hadn't, and it was over. He'd never been one to wonder about might-have-beens.

And yet he wondered now. Ironic that in his life, he'd had no patience for people who hesitated. Fate and destiny were out there to be taken advantage of, not to sit around and accept. He'd taken charge of his destiny, and because of it he had a great life. And if once in a while it was too… quiet, then he took care of it. It had never been difficult to find a woman interested in a good time, short-term of course. Maybe that's what he needed now. A bout of mutually satisfying, hot, sweaty sex.

Too bad he could hardly move.

Five days after falling through the ceiling, he drove by the youth hostel. Just out of curiosity, he told himself, not because of a strange sense that he was missing something, something important. He got out of his car and asked the young tattooed kid at the desk for Margaret Mary. He waited for what seemed like forever, his heart pounding uncomfortably against the ribs that still hurt, only to be told she wasn't around.

Good. Fine. It had been stupid to try to see her anyway. He didn't need to add trouble to his life, and family would be trouble.

Since he was out, he went by some of his jobs, ignoring his aching ribs, burying himself in the stuff he'd neglected over the past few days. By the time he got home, he was suitably exhausted. Dizzy with it, in fact. Maybe now, finally, he could sleep.

But at midnight he was still staring at the ceiling of his bedroom. He probably should have given in and taken some painkillers, but he hated the loss of control so he gritted his teeth and told himself he'd feel better tomorrow. Deciding to work, he flipped on a light, but the lines on the plans blurred and jumped around, making him feel nauseous.

Time for oblivion, he thought, and reached for the bottle of pills. But a knock at the door stopped him. Since he couldn't think of a single reason for someone to be knocking at his door at midnight, he ignored it.

It came again.

Struggling into a pair of sweat pants, he figured that since he didn't feel like crying as he moved, he must be improving. Still, by the time he hobbled to the door, he was ready to sit down. And when he opened it, he nearly *did* sit down, right there on the floor. "Nicole!"

She stood there, arms braced on the jamb on either side of her, head down. When he said her name, she lifted her face. Her short, dark hair was up in spikes, as if she'd shoved her fingers through it repeatedly. She wore a spaghetti-strapped tank top under overalls. One strap had slid down her shoulder. Her smooth, sleek arms were taut, her tight little body quivering with tension.

But it was her eyes that held him now, as they were filled with so many things it hurt to look at her.

"I woke you," she said. "I'm sorry, I'll just—"

He wrapped his fingers around her arm to stop her from backing away. Skin to skin. The jolt nearly brought him to his knees. Now was a hell of a time to realize that with her standing right here in front of him everything suddenly felt good. Right.

He hated that. She was nothing but a damn string on the heart he didn't want to feel.

"I shouldn't have come," she whispered.

No, no she shouldn't have. Because now he didn't know how to let her go.

"I just…I saw your light." She lifted a shoulder, gave him a little smile.

The smile lifted him in a way it shouldn't, and just like that, the funk was gone.

He'd have to dwell on that later because right now he wanted the feel of her. Needed the feel of her in a terrifyingly bad way.

"It's just that Taylor said she hadn't seen or heard from you," she said. "And you didn't make your checkup appointment the hospital gave you, and—"

With a little tug, he had her inside.

"So I just drove by, just to see…and well." She smiled again, stopping his heart. "Like I said, I saw the light—"

He shut the door behind her. She took one step back, away from him, right up against the wood.

Perfect.

"So." Her smile shook a bit now. "I just wanted to see for myself that you were doing okay—" She stopped when he planted an arm on either side of her head. "Are you going to say something?" she whispered, licking her bottom lip.

Oh yeah, he liked that little nervous gesture.

"Ty?"

"You want to give me a checkup?"

"I…uh…"

He found his own smile. "You're nervous, doc. I know it sounds sick, but I like that. I like that a lot."

She pressed her fingers to her eyes, which gave him better room to crowd her body.

So he did.

"You know what?" she murmured, still covering her eyes. "I'm going now." Then she dropped her hands and shoved at his chest, which shot a white-hot arrow of pain right through his ribs. Doubling over, he groaned, vaguely aware of her horrified gasp.

"Oh, Ty—" Her hands came around his bare middle. "Damn it—"

"I know, I know, I'm so sorry."

He sucked in a careful breath and looked at her when she said it again. Her hands on his skin moved lightly, not a doctor's hands, but a woman's, as she murmured her apologies over and over, as she tried to soothe. And little by little his vision cleared so that he could straighten slightly.

"Are you okay?" she whispered.

"I'll let you know when the stars clear from my head."

"God. I'm so sorry."

"I know."

"I...wouldn't hurt you on purpose."

"I know."

But she already had. Nicole could feel it. She just didn't understand. *He* was the one who didn't want a relationship. *He* was the one who'd kept her at arm's length with his light, easygoing, teasing attitude. He was the one...

Wasn't he?

"Nicole." That was it, that was the only word to escape his lips, but his gaze seemed to say so much more. Eyes hot, he lowered his head so that their lips were only a breath apart. "Why did you come?"

She licked her lips again. "I told you, I—"

"*Why,* Nicole?"

She closed her eyes, trying to hide the truth from him. She'd come to be in his arms. She'd come to give him what she'd held back all this time. She'd come to see if she was going crazy, or if this…this thing went both ways.

"Nicole?"

"Y-yes?"

"I should tell you, watching you struggle at this social stuff is an incredible turnon. Knowing you're usually buried in work, that you never look up from that work for anyone, and you are now…because of me…"

She stared down at his hand as it entwined with hers and tugged. Then she was staring at his strong, sleekly muscled back while he led her through the house.

"I'm taking you to my bedroom now," he said over his shoulder. "Stop me."

She kept following him.

He tugged her into a room lit only by the moonlight dancing through the wall of windows. Then he flipped on the light and she was blinking at him like an owl.

"I want to see this." He stepped so close she could see nothing but him. Around her, she had an impression of a large room, an equally large bed with tossed blankets and sheets.

Then he backed her to that bed, his eyes glowing with intent and emotion. "I think you came for this, which just so happens to be what I'm looking for as well."

"You— But you're hurt." Since when did she stutter? The mattress bumped her high on the back of her thighs. Her heart was drumming so fast and so loud it was a wonder he hadn't asked her if she was having a heart attack.

"Say I'm wrong." He lifted a finger and nudged off the other strap of her overalls. The bib fell to her waist, leaving just her thin tank top, which hid nothing from him, including the fact she was aroused. Very aroused.

His head dipped, and for a long moment he just looked,

making her nipples tighten and pucker against the thin material all the more. "Nicole." His voice was husky. "You're not saying no."

"I—"

"No starts with N." He used both hands now, gliding his fingers up and down her arms. He met her gaze. Waited.

She licked her lips, which wrestled a low groan from him. And then he leaned in even closer. "Say it. Say no."

"I don't want to say it." Almost before she'd finished, his mouth closed over hers. She opened to him and he groaned again. Then he was inside, tasting her as if he was a starving man and she was a ten course meal. Which worked for her because suddenly, or maybe not so suddenly, she was starving too, starving for this.

Breaking only for air, he raised his head and stared at her from slumberous eyes before he came at her again, changing the angle of the kiss, settling his mouth more firmly over hers. Her lips clung to his as her fingers fisted in his hair, holding him to the plundering, caressing kiss because she didn't want him pulling back again. She wanted this mindlessness, craved this hot, sensual heat, and needed even more.

They broke apart for air again, and stared at each other. His hands lifted to untangle her arms from around his neck. He danced his fingers back up, wrapping them around her spaghetti straps. Still holding her gaze in his, he gave a hard tug, peeling the material down to her waist, exposing her bare breasts.

Dropping his gaze, his chest rose and fell with his uneven breathing as he looked at the breasts she knew damn well were too small. Thinking it, she lifted her hands but he caught them, held them at her sides.

"Are you saying no?" he asked thickly.

"Ty—"

"Are you?"

His eyes were fathomless, his body tense. Against her belly she could feel him, hard and pulsing. He wanted her. He wanted her in a way she hadn't been wanted in too long. "I'm not saying no," she said softly.

The tension left him in a long sigh. "Thank God," he murmured, and let go of her wrists to cup her breasts. "You're beautiful."

And in that moment, she felt it.

"And these..." His thumbs rasped over her nipples, making her let out a horrifyingly needy sound. "Oh yeah, these..." Bending his head, he swirled his tongue over one, then blew a soft, warm breath over it, forcing that sound from her again. "Mmm. A perfect mouthful." Proving the point, he sucked her into his mouth, laving her with his tongue over and over until she'd refisted her hands in his hair and tossed back her head, panting for air.

It wasn't enough. Kicking off her shoes made her even shorter but she didn't care. Rising up on the balls of her feet, she hooked a leg over his hips and strained against the swollen ridge of his erection.

That ripped a deep, deep groan of pleasure from his chest and he pulled back to look at her with eyes heavy with desire. "Last chance."

She tugged at the tie of his sweats, making him let out a laughing moan. "Okay, so you don't want a last chance." With a notsogentle shove, he pushed her backwards, tumbling her to the mattress. He put a knee on the bed and grabbed the hem of her overalls. Looked at her. Pulled. Tossing them over his shoulder, he did the same with her tank top, leaving her in just a lightblue silky thong.

"Now." His other knee hit the bed. Towering over her, he looked down and let out a smile that made her swallow hard. "Let's discuss this lingerie thing you have going."

With one finger he traced the silk down her hip, over her mound, stopping just shy of the spot that would make her a complete wanton.

"I— It's—"

"And this stuttering thing. That's new." His smile was tight and just a bit intimidating as he hooked a finger in the panties and whipped them off.

"You're overdressed," she managed to say when he just looked down at her, his eyes shining like crystal and very intense.

"Yeah. About that." On his knees leaning over her, he'd gone utterly still. "I should tell you, I can't move."

"Oh, Ty!" Scampering up to her knees, she faced him, putting her hands on his bare, hot, deliciously hard chest. "I'm sorry, I—"

He put a finger to her lips. "Don't even think about being sorry or turning back into a doctor." Very slowly, very carefully, he lay down on his back. Then let out a slow breath.

"Okay?" she asked, leaning over him now, their positions reversed.

Lifting his hands, he cupped the breasts that were in his face. "Very okay." Raising his head, he replaced his fingers with his tongue, leaving his hands free to skim down her spine, down the backs of her thighs, which he urged open. Grabbing one leg, he pulled, so that she fell over his chest, straddling him.

She was careful to brace herself high, on his pecs, rather than press on his ribs. "Still okay?"

His hands glided up her legs, her hips, her waist, cupping and squeezing her breasts before sliding down the quivering muscles of her stomach. "So damn okay." His hands met over her belly button, and his thumbs danced down, down, until they slid into the curls at the apex of her thighs.

"Ty—"

"Oh yeah. Love it when you say my name like that. Like you're hot and shaky and on the edge. On the edge for me."

She was. Hot and shaky and on the edge. For him. She ached with it, ached with the desire and emptiness and the need for him to fill her up.

"I've wanted you since that first moment I saw you," he said, sinking his thumbs lower, making her gasp. "Say you want me back."

She cried out when he gave one long, slow, sure stroke of his thumb right where she needed it. "I want you."

"Then take me. Take us both the hell away." His voice was rough, and when she lifted up, yanked down his sweats and came right back on him, gliding hot, damp skin to hot, damp skin, he groaned.

"Nicole—" He tried to surge up, hurt himself, and let out a pained, frustrated growl.

"Shh." She pressed him back. "Let me—"

"Yes."

"Don't move."

"I won't if you will," he swore, and their next kiss was an avaricious feeding frenzy of mouth and teeth and tongues and wordless murmurs and demands, while their hands tore at each other. She stroked his chest, then ran her fingers down his belly to wrap a fist around the hot, velvety steel of him, while he did something magical with his fingers, leaving her a gasping, panting mass of nerve endings. The tension inside her built and pulled and made her crazy, more so when he rubbed his straining erection back and forth over her exposed, swollen flesh.

"Condom," he said through gritted teeth. "Nightstand."

"Got it." She tore it open, straddled him again. Took him in her hands and protected them both. Then he took over, guiding her over him so that he brushed against her slick opening. Gripping her hips, pulling her down as he thrust up, he slid home, stretching her, filling her to the hilt.

The sensation of having him inside her was so powerful, so…complete, she sobbed out his name and fell over him to meet his mouth with hers. His grip on her hips tightened, and he lifted her almost entirely off him before plunging her downward again, harder.

"Oh, my— *Ty*."

"I know." His head fell back and his powerful body quivered beneath hers. "I know."

Her legs tightened at his hips as she lifted herself back up, slowly moving him in and out of her body in a delicious, sensual ride, going faster, then faster still as the pressure built. Her pulse beat in her throat, her breath soughed in and out of her lungs as they hammered each other, over and over. Nothing had ever felt like this, no one had ever made her feel like this, as if she was home right there in his arms. Each thrust, each flex of his hips brought her closer, and then he tugged her down and put his mouth to a breast.

She exploded, and like the entire frenzied mating, there was nothing easy or slow about it. Shudder upon shudder shook her body, rippling across her flesh, until she was nothing but an exposed nerve ending, weightless and helpless as what felt like a train wreck occurred in her head, her heart, her soul.

Vaguely, from far, far away, she heard Ty cry out, too, felt him go rigid beneath her as he found his own release. His fingers dug into her hips as he pumped into her body, hard, one last time.

Seeing him, hearing him while he sought his pleasure, unbelievably triggered yet another tremor within her, and her body arched mindlessly into his as she lost herself again.

The next thing she felt were his strong, warm arms pulling her down, turning them both, so they lay face-to-face, limbs entangled. His heart hammered against her cheek while she continued to try to catch her breath. She couldn't. She felt battered, bruised and yet so wildly euphoric she was surprised she wasn't floating high in the air.

Oh yeah, she was at home here in his arms, and given how relaxed Ty felt next to her, he felt at home, too. And just like that, for the first time in Nicole's entire adult life, she felt good at something other than work.

CHAPTER TEN

WARM AND SATED, Nicole opened her eyes and found Ty watching her through his own halfopened baby blues.

He was so beautiful. It wasn't often she needed a physical release, which meant it wasn't often she'd had recreational sex. But this…this had been nothing like her previous sexual encounters.

First of all, she'd had an orgasm. Easily. Almost from just looking at him. Second, she'd nearly wept at the intensity of it.

And third, she wanted to do it again.

But Ty didn't utter a single word. He didn't have to, as with each passing second, his gaze grew more pained, more exhausted.

And more guarded.

"Go to sleep," she whispered, a weariness replacing her pathetic, and it seemed, premature, joy.

His lids fell shut. Without a word.

And when he was out like a light, she left.

Without a word.

TY WASN'T SURPRISED when he awoke alone, but damn, he had to admit to feeling disappointment. If he was smart, he'd attribute that to the morning hardon that wouldn't quit even after a gutsucking cold shower. But even he knew enough to admit his problem wasn't physical.

Before he could give too much thought to the matter,

he called Nicole at home. What he planned on saying, he hadn't a clue. *Hey. Good orgasm, huh?* Or, *Why did you leave? I wanted to get laid again.*

Maybe he should stick with the truth. *I woke up reaching for you and when I found you gone I was lonely as hell.*

But in the end, he said nothing because he got her answering machine and hung up. She'd left without a word, and he should have the grace to accept that. Last night had been nothing more complicated than two adults taking care of their needs.

He just hoped he got to take care of her needs again soon.

He went about his day, somewhat heartened that he didn't feel like throwing up every time he moved. And then there was the fact his entire body hummed with the remembered vibrations of spectacular sex.

And it *had* been spectacular. Fireworks, earthquake, the entire enchilada.

Not that he hadn't had really spectacular sex before, but…ah, hell. He'd never had really spectacular sex before. Not like that anyway, where he'd really, truly lost control, giving everything he had over to a woman, keeping his eyes open when he came so that he could see into hers, and feel her heart and soul while she did the same.

Scary stuff.

Work helped a little, as he was swamped. And when he went by Taylor's building to discuss the plans with her, he told himself he would just peek in on Nicole.

Just to say hey.

Naturally, she was at work. Most likely not even thinking about him.

Taylor and Suzanne plied him with food and laughter. It felt good, which was strange. Normally such a thing would smother him. After all, he hadn't even slept with either of

them and they wanted to spoil him and talk to him and…
be friends.

It wasn't often he'd been friends with a woman, much
less two of them, but resisting either Taylor or Suzanne
was pretty much impossible.

Plus, he liked them, at least until he was reminded that
the engagement party was that night and as their friend,
he was expected to attend.

Two more strings on his heart.

And seeing as he had those strings, he figured he might
as well go all the way. Once again, he drove to the youth
hostel and asked for Margaret Mary.

And once again was told sorry. Only this time, he was
sorry, too. She'd moved out, moved on, he was told.

Ty gripped the front desk and wondered at the drop in
his stomach. "Moved on to where?"

The young kid shrugged. "I think she said she was interested in seeing Seattle."

Seattle. One thousand miles away. Did she have a car?
Did she have money? Or was she out there, all alone, no
means and no friends, and too young to know danger when
she looked it in the face?

Ty had no idea what his sudden rush was, but he raced
home for his email.

Nothing. No long, windy messages from her, no short
appealing messages from her, nothing.

What did that mean? Had she given up on him? It
wouldn't surprise him, as he deserved exactly that.

For the first time, *he* initiated contact.

Margaret Mary of Dublin,
I am Irish and I am stubborn and I am sorry. I know this
is nothing but a lousy excuse, but please try to under-

stand. Family has never given me anything but pain and
suffering.

But I have the feeling you would have been different. I
don't know what changed my mind, whether it was the
fall on my head (long story) or the fact that I woke up
alone this morning and knew I'd done that to myself (another long story).

So Margaret Mary of Dublin, am I too late?

Ty Patrick O'Grady, your brother.'

Leaning back in his chair, Ty looked out of his great
big picture window at the San Gabriel Mountains. What
a glorious view this huge house gave him.

This huge, *empty* house.

When had that happened? When had the house become
too big, too quiet? There had been a time when that's all
he'd wanted, his own space and quiet.

But now, he needed…more. What, exactly, he wasn't
certain.

But definitely, things were missing. And, if he was admitting such things, people.

He was missing people.

NICOLE MANAGED, with a good amount of swearing and
disgust, to get herself ready for the engagement party that
night. She also managed to avoid Taylor and her bag of
makeup and hair stuff by staying late at work, because
nylons, a fancy dress, mascara and a dab of gloss was as
good as she was going to give.

The party was taking place at Ryan's house, which Suzanne was moving in to. The moment Nicole walked in,

she was assaulted by the scent of delicious food—thank God—and music and laughter.

And hugs. Everyone wanted to hug her. Suzanne. Taylor. Ryan. She pushed away Suzanne and Taylor because they were hooting and hollering at her in the dress, and let Ryan in for a good long hug.

"Hey, that's my almost-husband," Suzanne protested when Ryan, tall, dark and gorgeous, hugged Nicole back.

"Just being sisterly," Nicole said, and gave Ryan a smacking kiss on the lips, enjoying Suzanne's hiss and Taylor's laugh.

Then another man walked up to them. He was tall, dark and gorgeous too, more so, if that was even possible, with sharp blue eyes, a sometime-Irish accent and attitude to match hers.

"Hey," she said, a little defiantly, but damn it, she suddenly felt…conspicuous.

That Ty's gaze nearly gobbled her up from head to toe and all the spots in between didn't help. "Hey, yourself," he said.

Suzanne pulled Taylor and Ryan away with a completely obvious and annoying wink.

Leaving her alone with Ty. Unable to stand still, she shifted on the stupid heels, nibbled off her gloss. Before she could stop herself, she tugged at the hem of her dress. Damn, she felt stupid. Exposed.

Ty stepped closer, and she shifted again, feeling the need to smack him. Kiss him. If only she was dressed in jeans.

Then Ty put a hand on her waist and squeezed gently. "You steal my heart."

Ah, hell. When he said shit like that, her heart just tipped right on its side. "Stop it."

"It's true. You're amazing."

"A pair of heels and a ridiculous dress make me amazing?"

"No, your heart makes you amazing," he said softly, and stroked her jaw. "You got all dressed up for Suzanne. You love her."

"I knew she'd have good food."

He shook his head. "Play tough if you need to, I see right through you."

Yeah. He did, he saw right through her.

Terrifying.

NICOLE'S PLAN WAS to stay busy at work. That way she didn't have to think about Ty. The way he'd looked so good at the engagement party she'd wanted to gobble him up whole. The way he'd whispered those hot, sexy words in her ear as he held her close, which was every moment. The way his intense eyes had promised her the world even as he let her go home—alone.

She managed to use work to keep her busy for small periods of time, but Ty was proving to be hard to forget. One day the following week she stood studying a patient's chart in the nearly deserted nurses' station, lost in her own world.

Until Dr. Watts came up behind her. "You smell good," he whispered, standing inappropriately close. So close in fact, that the front of his thighs brushed the backs of hers.

"Back up," she warned. He had her pinned between the counter and his body, but she was far more pissed than worried. She could drop him to the floor in an instant; she just didn't want the scene that would follow.

"Why do you resist me?" he asked, his fingers stroking her neck.

She slapped his hand away. "I'm going to tell you one more time. Keep your paws off me."

"Or what?"

"Or you'll be sorry. Now back off."

His soft laughter was her only answer; he still stood in her space. Then he brushed his hips to hers and she saw red.

"You feel good—" he started to say, but ended on a whoosh of a breath when she plowed her elbow into his belly and stomped on his foot hard enough to drop him to the floor like a log.

"Well, then."

With a sigh, she shoved her hair out of her eyes, turned around to face the new male voice, and came face-to-face with Dr. Luke Walker.

Medical chair. The man in charge of just about anything there was to be in charge of, including Dr. Lincoln Watts, writhing on the floor. "Problem, Dr. Mann?" he asked over Linc's body.

"Not any more."

He eyed the man on the floor, then looked her over carefully before he said quietly, "You should have come to me sooner, Nicole."

She let out a slow breath. "I'm fine."

"Good, then. Please, consider your shift over."

"But—"

"Not as a punishment." He stepped back as Dr. Watts struggled to his feet. "Consider it a small payment for your patience with the system. Dr. Watts, come with me, please."

Linc shot Nicole a look to kill, and she had to turn away to hide her grin. In fact, she grinned all the way to her car, then sang all the way home through South Village traffic, and actually got a great parking spot right out front before she remembered she didn't really want to go home.

She climbed the steps to the building thinking she

should have stopped for some takeout, but before she could let herself in, Suzanne was there, smiling at her.

Nicole scrunched her forehead, trying to remember. "Did I miss a wedding planning session?"

"Nope. I just wanted to say hello."

"Me, too, you twit." Taylor slung an arm around Suzanne's shoulders and looked at Nicole. "You ever heard of returning phone calls?"

She'd gotten their messages but hadn't had the time to get back to them. Now that she was looking into their relaxed, happy-to-see-her faces, guilt sank in. Why hadn't she made the time? "See, this is why I don't do the friendship thing." She unlocked her door and gestured them in. "I'm terrible at it."

"You're not, you're just busy."

"But you do have to remember we exist," Taylor told her. "That would be nice."

"I'm sorry. Work—"

"Yeah, yeah." Taylor put her hands on her hips and studied the ceiling she'd had patched. "I don't suppose you even noticed I had this fixed."

In truth, she hadn't. What did that say about her? Besides the fact she'd purposely been so busy she hadn't had time to breathe? "Um…"

"Rhetorical question," Taylor assured her. "Don't hurt yourself."

"Look, I have to—"

"You just got home from work, what could you possibly have to do?" Taylor sank into the futon couch in the living room and looked around. "You need furniture in a bad way."

"Yeah."

"That's a pretty noncommittal yeah. You planning on moving soon? Is that why you've never settled in here?"

"I've settled in. I have a bed."

"Uh-huh." Taylor lifted an eyebrow. "And half your kitchen is still in boxes on the floor."

"That's because Suzanne keeps bringing me food so I haven't had to cook." Nicole smiled at Suzanne. "Thanks, by the way."

Suzanne smiled back. "Should I stop? Would that make you stay? If you had to settle in here?"

"Stay? But..." She looked back and forth between them. "I'm not going anywhere."

"You sure about that?" Taylor stood, came closer. "Because I still have your rental app, which clearly states you haven't stayed in one place for longer than a few months. We're coming up on that mark now. Is it nearly time to move on? You've got a few people who care here, and I can tell it's unnerving you." She nodded as she studied Nicole far too closely. "Yeah," she murmured. "Nearly time to move on, isn't it?"

Nicole crossed her arms. "So I haven't lived in one spot for long, so what? Lots of people suffer from wanderlust and besides, I've had my job for a good long while, and that's not going to change. That's got to count as stability."

Suzanne's smile was sad. "I don't think it's really wanderlust affecting you, Nicole. I think it's fear of letting people close. I know, because before I met and fell in love with Ryan, I was the same way. Never really let people in."

Nicole turned to Taylor. "We have a vow of singlehood, have you forgotten? I'm pretty certain that means never letting people in."

"It means you don't put a diamond on the ring finger of your left hand. But you sure as hell can do just about everything else, and should." Taylor tipped her head to the side and studied Nicole until she squirmed. "You know we love you, right? And I think you feel something for us back."

"Well, mostly for Suzanne because she cooks for me," Nicole said, trying to tease past the sudden lump in her throat. She never quite knew what to do with emotion, with easy affection such as she was being offered.

"And I know you feel something for Ty——"

"Actually, what I feel mostly right now is irritation."

Taylor lifted a brow. "Are you saying you don't like him?"

"Well, I——"

"It was all over your face when he got hurt, Nicole."

"Because I'm a doctor! I hate to see *anyone* hurt, including a know-it-all Irishman."

"You were beside yourself because it *was* the know-it-all Irishman," Taylor pointed out. "So much so that you even forgot your training. That was huge, you panicking like that. Huge and very unlike you."

"You even took a day off," Suzanne so helpfully reminded her. "Remember?"

"How could she forget?" Taylor grinned. "She discovered soap operas and cheesy old classic reruns. And she allowed herself to feel, to care. Didn't you, Nicole?"

What Nicole remembered most was the simple pleasure of that day. Sitting, for a change. And yes, watching TV. But most of all, she remembered the sight of Ty in her bed. Remembered thinking she could get used to that.

"Or was it so good you scared yourself?" Suzanne asked quietly.

"You guys have far too much time to think, you know that?" Nicole hugged herself, feeling…naked. "Yes, I care. Okay? I care about a lot of stuff."

"How about Ty?"

"Yes, fine, Ty. Should I say it louder? *I care for Ty!* I

care for him a lot." She lowered her voice to a soft sigh. "So much that it terrifies me, and diving back into work was all I had. Happy now?"

Ty stood in the front doorway, eyes on Nicole, smile grim. "I'm a lot of things, actually."

Nicole nearly swallowed her tongue. When the hell had he shown up? "Ty, I—"

"I don't have much experience with happy," he continued. "But terrified?" He pondered that. "Definitely. I'm definitely terrified, Nicole."

Suzanne put her hand on his arm and gave him a gentle squeeze. "It gets easier."

"What does?"

"Why, love of course." She smiled into his shocked face and reached for Taylor. "We'll just leave the two of you alone—"

"No!" Nicole softened her voice with effort. Her heart was pounding. Her palms damp. She wanted to start running like hell and never stop. Love? Who'd said anything about love? For God's sake, couldn't one lust for someone without the L-word coming into play? "Taylor—"

Taylor just laughed at Nicole's face. "Oh, sweetie, if you could see your expression. Well, girlfriend, you've been too busy for too long, you never learned to slow down and take it all in. Now it's happened without your permission, hasn't it? And you haven't a clue what to do with it. Poor baby." She grabbed Nicole's face and gave her a smacking kiss. "Good news, Super Girl. You're smart, you'll figure it out."

Okay, maybe Nicole had only recently realized what she was missing in her life. Maybe she'd only recently understood that life wasn't all work and no play, but she still hadn't reconciled it all, she still didn't know how to get more for herself, or how to…

How to face Ty, the man she'd foolishly thought maybe, possibly, hopefully could be the one.

He *wasn't* the one. He wouldn't ever want to be the one.

And he'd heard her shout how she felt about him. God. Talk about humiliation. "Taylor—"

But they were gone. Leaving her alone with Ty, who was looking at her with an expression she supposed mirrored her own terror. "Well." She tried to smile. "My day is complete."

He blew out a breath and looked at her. Really looked at her. "Something else is wrong," he said.

"Besides you being here?"

"What is it?"

"Nothing," she muttered, a little cross that he could see through everything and find the lingering unease over the Dr. Watts scene. "It's just that work sucked and now—"

"Did that asshole try something again?"

She stared at him, a little shocked by his deep tone of instant rage. For her. "Everything is going to be fine in that department."

"Sure?"

His voice was every bit as low and gravely and sexy as she remembered, and she remembered plenty. "Very."

He drew another deep breath as if struggling for patience.

She knew the feeling. "So why are you here anyway?" she asked, more than a little defensively, crossing her arms.

"I have a job here."

"Oh, yeah." Now she felt just stupid. Of course he had a job here. What did she think, that he'd come to see her? How ridiculous that would be, how—

"I'll just get to it," he said, and turned to the door.

Only he slammed it shut while still on the inside, closing them inside the apartment together.

Alone.

CHAPTER ELEVEN

TY LOOKED AT NICOLE, who stood there seeming a little confused.

Good, that made two of them.

"What are you doing?" she asked warily when he came close. "I thought you were going to go do what you had to."

"I am." He wrapped his hands around her upper arms and hauled her up to her toes so he could get a good look into the face he couldn't seem to stop thinking about.

She gasped. "But...I thought you meant work. You had to get to work."

"Who said anything about work?"

"You— I—"

"There you go stuttering again." He set her down but didn't take his hands off her. "I'm beginning to think you only do that around me, and you know what? I like it. But let's stick to the subject. I want to set the record straight between us."

"Oh." Her face cleared of all expression. She was good at that, he'd noticed, but then again, so was he.

"I see," she said stiffly.

"I doubt it."

"No, I do. You regret what happened between us."

"Is that what you think?" He tipped up her face and saw that was exactly what she thought. "Is that why you left my bed?"

"Don't tell me you wanted to wake up with me." She pulled her chin free of his fingers. "I saw the look in your eyes before you fell asleep. Panic, pure and simple."

"What you saw was fleeting."

"Because you fell asleep." She closed her eyes. "And I didn't blame you for it, so don't worry. I'm not the kind of woman a man wants to wake up with."

He swore, then shoved his fingers through his hair and turned in a slow circle, trying to find the words. "Nicole, you're *exactly* the kind of woman a man wants to wake up with. You're smart, and sexy as hell. You're *amazing*. But I was lying there, holding you, still shaking like a leaf, damn it, from the most incredible…" He let out a disparaging sound, having no idea how to say it. "Look, what we shared was different. First of all, I've never come so hard in my life."

She blushed, her expression one of surprise.

"But it wasn't just sex," he said. "I know that sounds like a line, but it wasn't. What we shared was a connection, a real one, and yes, damn it, it scared the living daylights out of me."

She was very still. "Go on."

Go on. Hell. He licked his suddenly dry lips. "I felt closer to you than I have to anyone. Ever."

The fist around her heart, the one that had been there since she'd first set eyes on him, loosened slightly. "Really?"

"I felt like you knew me."

A warmth spread through her. "I did. I do. Ty, I do."

"No." Now he closed his eyes. "You don't understand." He turned away, his shoulders stiff. "I came from nothing, Nicole. I was nothing."

"No, never that." Her heart ached that he pictured himself that way.

"You have no idea some of the things I did to survive."

"No one would ever blame the child you were," she said fiercely. "No one. And you shouldn't either."

"I know." Misery radiated off him, so that she was propelled forward, propelled to put her hand on his back. His muscles leapt at her touch.

"But I'm still that boy deep inside," he admitted. "I'm still that wanderer. I still feel that need to keep moving. I…I started to feel that need again."

Now her heart all but stopped as he turned back to look at her.

"You…you're moving on?" she asked.

"I've thought about it. Then I heard from my sister and I *really* thought about it." There was nothing but truth in his eyes, the man who'd taught her the one thing no one else had ever managed, how to live outside the box. He was strong and smart and made her smile. He was passionate about work, about life, about everything in between. And unlike anyone before him, he made her feel the same way back.

"It'd be so easy," he said. "Easy to pick up and go start over." He lifted a shoulder. "New York sounded good."

"Yeah." She cleared her throat because it was so thick. He'd thought about leaving, walking away. "Ty…" *Don't. Don't go.*

Reaching out, he ran his fingers over her jaw. Slid them down her throat and cupped the back of her head, tugging her a step closer. Mouth close to hers, his turned down in a grim, unbearably sad smile, he said, "But then I met you."

He still looked so utterly intent on going that there was no logical reason why hope suddenly burned through her bright as the sun. "And…?"

"And…for the first time I wanted someone to know

about me, know my past. Accept it. We know we're different, Nicole. That I—"

She stopped him with her mouth on his. She knew his past shamed him. Just as she knew the man he really was, a man with a heart and soul dying for acceptance and love, just like anyone else. He could hold people off with his easy charm and laidback attitude, but he couldn't hold her off, not for another second.

He tried. Despite her mouth clinging to his, despite her arms wound around his neck, he hadn't touched her, not yet, so she pulled back and held his face in her hands. "Please want me, too, Ty, if only half as much as I want you."

"Half?" He let out a half growl, half laugh. "*Half.* Hell…"

"It's okay, I—"

"I want you more than my next breath, damn it." His arms came around her hard, lifting her up against him. "But you're supposed to know what's good for you. Nicole, you're supposed to send me away. You're supposed to stay away from me."

"I won't. I can't."

"Well, then God help the both of us." His mouth came down on hers again, but he shocked her with unexpected tenderness, with an irresistible gentleness, coaxing and nibbling her into a hunger only he could sate.

As if she needed coaxing. After a long, wet, hot kiss, he lifted his head and stared at her. The hunger must have been all over her face because he groaned, and then his mouth slashed across hers again, and this time when they tore apart for air, they stared wild and wide-eyed at each other.

"Not here," she said breathlessly, staggering when he pulled back. "My bed."

"Nicole—"

"My bed," she repeated, and grabbed his hand, tugging him toward her bedroom before he could come to his senses and say goodbye. She didn't want goodbyes, and she was banking on the hope he didn't really want them either.

It was late and the room was dark. She flipped on the light switch, then hesitated. Maybe she should leave them in the dark, give them some place to hide.

No. *No,* she thought, turning back to him as she pulled her shirt over her head and watched his gaze flare with unchecked desire. She wanted to see him want her. Wanted to capture that and save it. Store it in a part of her heart to pull out when she needed.

After he was gone.

"Nicole—"

She wanted to cry at the rough, low voice, tinged with regret. He wasn't going to change his mind, not now, he couldn't. She unbuttoned her jeans and he swallowed hard.

"Wait, I—" His words broke off into a rough groan when she shoved the jeans down her hips and kicked them free, leaving her in a siren-red lace bra and a sunshine-yellow silk thong. Laundry day, damn it. She never matched for him. But she couldn't worry about that now. To make sure he saw her, all of her, she turned in a slow circle, running her hands down her own body.

When she turned back to him, he was suddenly right there, so close she bumped into his chest. "Not fair," he whispered.

"What's not fair is that you haven't started." She tugged on his shirt. He raised his arms so that she could pull it off and toss it over her shoulder. The bruises on his ribs made her physically ache for him. "Are you okay?"

"Right now I am. I love your color choices today."

She grimaced. "One of these days I'll get it together and pay attention in the morning."

"No, I like it. Tough, cool tomboy on the outside, thoroughly unorganized siren on the inside." His palms slid up her sides to cup her breasts, while she combed her fingers through his hair, bringing his mouth back to hers for the hot, wet, deep kiss she'd been longing for.

"Nicole." His voice was hoarse, and he repeated her name as if he couldn't hear it enough. He kissed her jaw, beneath her ear, her throat, touching her everywhere his hands could reach. Then her bra fell to the floor, followed by her mismatched panties. "I don't want to hurt you," he said.

"Then don't." She opened his jeans and slid her hands inside, squeezing his very squeezable butt. Not enough, but she knew he couldn't easily bend so she dropped to her knees to work his jeans down. She tugged off his knit boxers, too, her mouth watering as his impressive erection sprang free.

"Nicole—"

She took him in her mouth and he staggered back a step, then swore reverently as his hands entangled in her hair. His head fell back. She ran her tongue up his length, and he shuddered, but then pulled away and hauled her up to her feet.

"Ty, I want to—"

"Bed. Now."

"But—"

"I'd play the hero and toss you on it," he said in a thrilling rough voice. "But—"

"Your ribs."

"My ribs," he agreed, following her down to the mattress. Lying at her side, he touched her feet, ran his hands up her calves, over her knees…then met her gaze as he wrapped his palm around her thigh.

"Careful of your ribs—" Her words ended abruptly when he splayed open her legs.

Staring down at her with such intense heat she felt herself go up in flames, he let out a slow breath. "I won't hurt myself, I won't have to. You're already killing me."

Very carefully, he shifted his weight. His intent became clear when she felt his warm breath high on her inner thigh. "Careful—"

"Shh." He kissed her quivering, slick flesh, and suddenly her skin felt tight, her chest too small to hold her heart. Then he kissed her again, and writhing on the sheets, she cried out.

"I want you." His gaze locked on her as he slid a finger into her body. Her moan of pleasure meshed with his. "I want you more than I've ever wanted anyone."

"I want you, too." She barely managed to put the words together, but sensed how much he needed to hear them to ground him here, to this place. To her. "I want you more than I've ever wanted anyone, Ty. Love me."

"Like this?" Sliding his hands beneath her, he put his mouth on her, and with one slow, sure, knowing stroke of his tongue he nearly drove her right out of her living mind. Then he sucked her into his mouth, and he *did* drive her right out of her living mind. While she was still trembling with the aftershocks, he came up to his knees, wrapped his hand around his erection and buried himself deep within her.

Then he went still as he uttered one concise and perfectly descriptive oath.

She was just about crazy with the need for him to move within her. *"What?"*

"Condom," he growled, and pulled out of her, his sex

glistening with her own wetness. She watched him grit his teeth as he got off the bed, searched out his wallet, opened a foil packet, and stroked a condom down the length of himself.

"Hurry," she said.

"This isn't the emergency room, Dr. Hot Pants. There's no hurry." And he proceeded to prove it to her by slowly, far too slowly, entering her again, watching her with hot, hot eyes as he did.

Oh, he destroyed her, completely destroyed her. Arching her hips, she tried to pull him in, faster, harder.

"Slow," he whispered, running hot, openmouthed kisses along her jaw, her throat, pulling a patch of her skin into his mouth to suck.

But she needed all of him and she needed it now. She needed that to ease her tight chest, to soothe her fear that she'd wake up and he'd be gone. "Ty—"

But he couldn't be rushed, so she slapped her hands to his tight butt and tugged. Still no go. He was a solid mass of muscle, with a mind of his own.

He held her like that, on the very edge. She would have been furious at the way he mastered her body if he hadn't been right there with her, head back, jaw clenched in a grimace of passion, just as on the edge as she. Then, when she was nearly sobbing in frustration, he thrust deep, stretching her, filling her. The penetration was so powerful and complete they both cried out, and then again when he withdrew only to plunge back in. His grip on her hips tightened as he stroked harder, deeper, his powerful body crushing her to the mattress.

Legs tightening around his waist, she moved with him, slowly at first, as he'd wanted, but the pressure built until her heart beat in her ears in tune to the thrust of his pumping hips.

Intense pleasure gripped her, shoved her over the edge as lights exploded behind her eyes and shudders rippled her body, robbing her of breath. Vaguely she felt him bury his face in her neck and groan out her name as he followed her over, but all she could do was cling to him, lost, as hot wave after hot wave continued to take her.

Ty collapsed to the side, hauling her with him. They lay still like that except for the sound of their racing hearts and uneven breathing.

Nicole concentrated on the physical, which was incredible, and refused to think of anything else. Then Ty kissed her shoulder and pulled back so he could look into her eyes. "Okay?"

"Definitely." She might have said fantastic. Euphoric. Better than she'd ever been. But he got out of the bed and disappeared into the bathroom.

She stared at the ceiling.

When he came back out, he stood by the bed, still naked, looking down at her with those depthless eyes. "Should I go?"

Go? The thought made her heart clench. No. No, he shouldn't go. To show him, she lifted the covers, held them open.

He flipped off the light, climbed in, and scooped her close. She put her face into the crook of his neck, loving the feel of his warm, strong arms around her, having his hard body cradling hers as if he never wanted to let her go.

She loved him.

She knew that now, even though she'd never felt such an overwhelming, terrifying emotion for a man before. It was a bitter pill to swallow that Taylor, smug Taylor, had been right. The Lword *was* involved.

Now what? Good God, now what? *Deep breath, Nicole.*

After all, she'd handled some pretty tough situations before, she could handle this.

They could handle this. Together.

That thought held her, made her smile in her sleep, made her smile as she woke up with the sun shining in her eyes.

She smiled all the way until she reached for Ty and found him gone.

CHAPTER TWELVE

HE COULDN'T REALLY be gone. Nicole cocked her head and listened, thinking he'd gotten in the shower, or was in the kitchen, though God knew, the fridge was so empty she couldn't imagine what was keeping him.

But, she heard nothing, and the truth hit her. Ty was gone and she was alone. No problem, really, as she was used to that, and she lay back in a relaxed pose to prove it.

But then she heard a sound in the hallway, and before she could think about it, she'd leapt from the bed so fast her head spun. Maybe he'd just gone for donuts and coffee.

If that was the case, she'd love him forever.

Hand on the front door, she realized she was still entirely naked so she went racing back into the bedroom, grabbed the blanket they'd tossed to the floor sometime in the deep, dark of the night when they hadn't needed anything but the heat they'd generated while making love.

Back at the front door, wrapped in the blanket now, she hauled the door open.

Nothing.

But since she still heard sounds, she tiptoed down a few stairs, thinking any moment now he'd pop into view with his grin, holding donuts and coffee, and she would offer to be his sex slave forever.

"Nicole? Is that you?"

Shit. Suzanne. Nicole whipped around and lifted a foot

to race back up the stairs, only she tripped on an edge of the blanket and ended up facedown on the stairs.

"Honey, you okay?" Suzanne came into view holding some sort of brass frame. At the sight of Nicole sprawled in her blanket, with her naked arms and shoulders peeking out, she stopped short.

"Don't ask." Nicole managed to sit up.

Holding the back end of the frame, Taylor came up behind Suzanne. "Rough night?"

Nicole tugged her blanket closer and remained silent.

"Hmm." From Taylor, that was a loaded *hmm*. "Tell you what, let's skip you for a moment and get right to me. I'm selling this antique brass quilt holder today, and I can't be here. Neither can Suzanne. I was hoping you'd be in bed with Ty all day and could handle the transaction for me."

"Ty is gone."

"He's gone out to get you caffeine?"

"He's gone out, all right. *Slunk* out." Nicole scrubbed her face with her hands. "Happy now?"

"Ah. We're back to this being about you."

Nicole dropped her hands and glowered at Taylor. "I'm the one sitting bareass naked here."

Taylor sat on the step next to her. "You and Ty do it last night?"

"What does that have to do with anything?"

"Did you?"

"Yes! Okay? Three times! *Now* is my humiliation complete?"

"Did you happen to mention you love him during any of those three times?" Suzanne asked.

Nicole resisted the urge to strangle her. "Why would I do that?"

"Because it's the truth."

Nicole glared at Suzanne, who continued just to look at her serenely. Confidently. Smugly.

"Did you?" Taylor pressed. "Did you tell him?"

"No." Nicole thought about how perfect the night had been, how many times they'd turned to one another, how she'd wondered how that much happiness could fit into her chest. "He didn't say it either."

"Maybe he's just as scared as you," Taylor said very gently, and put her arm around her shoulders. "Love is fairly terrifying."

Nicole looked deep into Taylor's eyes and saw a haunting pain. "You know this for a fact, don't you?"

"Oh, yes."

Suzanne sat on Nicole's other side. "Tell him. See what happens."

Nicole drew a deep breath, but never having been a coward, she stood up. "Yeah. Okay."

"Great, but…honey?" Taylor tugged a little on the blanket. "Much as I think Ty would appreciate what you're *not* wearing, I think you should get dressed first."

NICOLE DID GET dressed first, and then drove straight to Ty's house. There was a car parked next to his, and boxes in the driveway.

He was already leaving.

Well, she thought with a deep breath, he'd be taking her heart with him. Chin high, heart hammering, she knocked on his front door. *Tell him,* she coaxed herself. *Just tell him.*

The moment he opened it, she swallowed hard and said, "I love you."

For the longest heartbeat in history, he just stared at her. Then from behind him came a voice. "Ty?" A woman came up behind him, tall and beautiful, with bright blue eyes.

Since no big hole had opened up and swallowed her, Nicole took a step backwards. "I'm sorry."

"No," said the woman. "I'm sorry." She turned to Ty and smacked him on his arm. "You big lug, why didn't you tell me you had a girlfriend?"

That was it for Nicole, she whirled and ran toward her car, fumbled for her keys, and had just opened the driver's door when she was whipped around.

Ty stood there, his piercing blue eyes narrowed against the sun. He put his big hands on her arms and held her against the car, and when she would have wriggled free, he simply pressed his body in close.

As if he hadn't done the same thing all night long.

She closed her eyes and fought for control. "Please," she whispered, out of breath from the adrenaline and emotions running through her body. "It's been a long, humiliating morning. Just…just let me go."

He was out of breath, too. "Not until you repeat what you just said."

She opened her eyes, but kept her mouth stubbornly shut.

Ty sighed and gentled his hold, sliding his hands up to cup her jaw. "Nicole—"

"I'm late for work."

Still breathing unevenly, he put his forehead to hers. "I shouldn't have left this morning without a note. I realized that after I was halfway home. But I woke up early, and you looked so tired, and…and I needed to think. I went home and there was a message from my sister."

This made her open her eyes. "Did you find her?"

Just like that, Ty's heart tipped on its side. She was

shaking, visibly upset, and yet she could put it all away to ask about his sister.

Because she loved him.

It made *him* start shaking. "She found me, that's her in the house."

Nicole looked over at the young woman standing in his doorway with his own see-through blue eyes, his own dark, do-as-it-pleased hair, his own cool, easygoing smile that told the world she was tough-as-hell while on the inside she was terrified.

"Have you talked?" Nicole asked quietly.

"We've started."

"And I interrupted." She winced. "God. I'm sorry, I—"

"My sister and I will have our time." He cupped her face. "But right now it's *our* time. Nicole—"

"The boxes. I…thought you were leaving."

He gave her a half smile. "It sure as hell would be the easy way out, and I like that, believe me. Or I did, until last night."

"What happened last night?"

"I realized I was an idiot." He stroked his thumbs over her jaw. "An idiot who loves you right back, Nicole."

"You…" A half laugh, half sob escaped her. "Really?"

"Oh, darlin', if you only knew how much." He pulled her close. "I thought I enjoyed the wandering, you know?" He buried his face in her hair. "It kept my past off my heels. Moving around, I wasn't just a screw-up, a nobody from nowhere and no one. But then I ended up here, and suddenly there were these strings on my heart." Pulling back, he smiled. "California for one. God, I love it here." He ran a gentle finger down her earlobe. "And then I had a sister who wanted me in her life. That messed with my head for a while."

Nicole smiled. "She's stubborn. Like you."

"Yeah." He stroked a hand down her spine, keeping her tucked close because he couldn't get enough of her. That had given him some bad moments last night, not being able to get enough, which had led to him stupidly getting out of her bed before dawn. He'd convinced himself he shouldn't get used to having her around all the time, because she wouldn't want that. But now he wasn't ever letting go of her again. "And then there's you," he said, kissing her softly. "You, darlin', were the strongest string of all. I'm never cutting you loose. Say that's good for you."

"That's good for me. Really good."

"I want to marry you, Nicole. Have babies with you. I want to start a family and do it right."

She paled a bit, which made him laugh and hug her hard. God, he loved her. "We don't have to start right now. We could just…be. If that's what it takes to make you smile again. Just knowing you love me is good enough."

Her breath caught, and looking uncertain, she bit her lower lip. "What if I never want to get married? What if I never want children…what then?"

"I just want you, Nicole. That's all I need, the rest is a bonus, that's all."

Her smile was slow and brilliant and made his heart tip on its side. "You're my miracle, Ty. Knowing you love me that much."

"That I do, Nicole."

"It's…amazing."

"You don't think you're that lovable?"

"I know I'm not," she said with a laugh. "But I'm selfish enough to marry you anyway." She laughed again, as if shocked by the admission. "I even want to have a little boy who looks just like you."

"A little girl." Ty kissed her, not quite as softly this time. "With eyes just like yours, and a smile that melts me."

"We'll negotiate. How about saying 'I do' on a beach in Mexico? In our bathing suits?"

He tightened his hands on her and put his forehead to hers, overwhelmed and humbled by what she'd given him. "You just don't want to wear a dress."

She narrowed her eyes. "You have a problem with that?"

He grinned and kissed her again. "Nope. But Suzanne and Taylor will. Want to meet my sister? Again?"

"I'd love to meet your sister."

Ty had no more turned toward the front door and waved when Margaret Mary came bouncing out of the house with a hopeful smile on her face. "Is it okay? I didn't mean to upset anyone—"

"You didn't," Ty said, melting Nicole's heart when he reached out for his sister's hand and pulled her closer. "Margaret Mary, this is Nicole. My best friend, my soul mate, my future wife."

Margaret Mary's smile widened in surprise. "Oh my God, really? A sister-in-law? Ty, you're going to give me a sister?" Her eyes dampened and she gathered them both into a bear hug that threatened to choke the life right out of Nicole. "I've always wanted a brother and a sister," she whispered in a voice that brought a lump to Nicole's throat the size of a regulation football.

What could she do? She hugged her back. After a long moment, the three of them held hands and walked toward the house. "Ty?" Nicole asked, watching as he brought their joined hands to his mouth and kissed her fingers.

"We're not going to feel alone, ever again, are we?"

He smiled at her with so much love the lump doubled in size. "Never, darlin'. Never again."

EPILOGUE

Suzanne's Wedding

NICOLE STOOD AT THE TOP of the aisle listening to the wedding march begin on the piano. Good God, she was more nervous now than she'd been in her entire life. Her legs were sweating, as Taylor had forced her to put on a pair of pantyhose.

Bridesmaids wear nylons, Taylor'd said smugly.

Nicole had cheated with thigh-high stockings, and planned on getting mileage out of them later with Ty. In fact, she actually wore matching lingerie today, just for him.

Then Suzanne came into view at the back of the church, radiant and beautiful in a white satin wedding dress, her smile filled with warmth and love, directed right at her groom, who stood only a few feet from Nicole.

Ryan—tall, dark and stunning in a tux—had eyes only for Suzanne as well, eyes that looked suspiciously bright.

Nicole met Taylor's gaze. The church was full, but the music was loud enough that Taylor could whisper without being heard. "This will be you soon enough."

"We're eloping, remember?"

"Chicken."

"At least I can admit love is a good thing to have in my life," Nicole teased.

Taylor's eyes went dark. Haunted.

And Nicole's heart squeezed. Feeling like a jerk, she reached out for Taylor's hand. "Someday I want this to be you too," she whispered.

"Nope." Taylor shuddered. "Singlehood forever. I'll just go it alone."

Alone. Nicole had thought that was the way too, until she'd met Ty. She looked into the pews of the church, and found him.

He was looking right at her, his eyes filled with the heat, the affection, the love that never failed to steal her breath. "Taylor, trust me on this," she whispered. "Someday love is going to sideswipe you out of nowhere and knock you into next week."

"Sounds like a train wreck."

"Feels like one, too." Nicole grinned. "But somehow, it works for me." Ty shot her a slow smile that made her heart do a slow roll in her chest. "Yep, it really works for me."

* * * * *

WHATEVER REILLY WANTS...

Dear Reader,

I'm delighted to have one of my books included in the *Kiss Me, I'm Irish* collection.

No matter what a writer might claim, every one of us has a few favorites among their books. And *Whatever Reilly Wants...* is one of mine. So it's especially nice to see that Connor Reilly is being re-released.

I love writing about big families. About the relationships between brothers and sisters. About interfering moms and dads and mostly, about a family that stands together against all comers. That's the kind of family I grew up in and the kind of family everyone should have.

I'm Irish myself, so writing about Irish families is doubly fun for me. The Irish are loud and loyal. Funny and loving. They're stubborn and strong and they're always willing to take on anyone who threatens the ones they love.

This is the kind of family the Reillys are. Four brothers, a set of triplets and their older brother, a priest. They're all different. They're all Reillys, and they will all stand for each other.

In *Whatever Reilly Wants...* you'll meet Connor Reilly and his best friend, Emma Jacobsen. Connor's always been comfortable with Emma. She's "one of the guys." But Emma's had enough and she's ready to show Connor that best friends can also be the best lovers.

I hope you enjoy *Whatever Reilly Wants...!* I certainly had a great time writing it. Visit me at my website, www.maureenchild.com, and email me. Let me know what you think!

Happy reading,

Maureen Child

For Kate Carlisle. Thanks for being an emergency reader, for always being a friend and for never getting tired of meeting me for a latte to talk about writing!

CHAPTER ONE

"ONE DOWN, TWO TO GO." Father Liam Reilly grinned at his brother, sitting alongside him, then lifted a beer in salute to the two identical men sitting opposite him in the restaurant booth.

"Don't get your hopes up." Connor Reilly took a sip of his own beer and nodded toward his brother Brian, the third of the Reilly triplets, sitting beside Liam. "Just because Brian couldn't go the distance, doesn't mean we can't."

"Amen," Aidan said from beside him.

"Who said I *couldn't* go the distance?" Brian demanded, reaching for a handful of tortilla chips from the basket in the middle of the table. He grinned and sat back in the booth. "I just didn't *want* to go the distance. Not anymore." He held up his left hand, and the gold wedding band caught the light and winked at all of them.

"And I'm glad for you," Liam said, his black eyebrows lifting. "Plus, with you happily married, the odds of *my* winning this bet are better than ever."

"Not a chance, Liam." Aidan grabbed a handful of chips, too. "It's not that I begrudge you a roof for the church…but *I'm* the Reilly to watch in this bet, brother."

As his brothers talked, Connor just smiled and half listened. Once a week the Reilly brothers met for dinner at the Lighthouse Restaurant, a family place, dead center of the town of Baywater. They laughed, talked and, in general, enjoyed the camaraderie of being brothers.

But for the last month their conversations had pretty much centered around *The Bet*.

A great uncle, the last surviving member of a set of triplets, had left ten thousand dollars to Aidan, Brian and Connor. At first, the three of them had thought to divide the money, giving their older brother, Liam, an equal share. Then someone, and Connor was pretty sure it had been Liam, had come up with the idea of a bet—winner take all.

Since the Reilly triplets were, above all things, competitive, there'd never been any real doubt that they would accept the challenge. But Liam hadn't made it easy. He'd insisted that as a Catholic priest, his decision to give up sex for a lifetime was something not one of his brothers could match. He dared them to be celibate for ninety days—last man standing winning the ten thousand dollars. And if all three of the triplets failed, then Liam got the money for a new roof for his church.

Connor shot his older brother a suspicious look. He had a feeling that Liam was already getting estimates from local roofers. Scowling, he took another sip of his beer and let his gaze shift to Brian. A month ago the triplets had stood together in this bet, but now one had already fallen. Brian had reconciled with his ex-wife, Tina, and, now there was just Connor and Aidan to survive the bet.

"Don't know about you," Aidan said, jamming his elbow into Connor's rib cage, "but I'm avoiding all females for the duration."

"No self-control, huh?" Liam grinned and lifted his beer for another long drink.

"You're really enjoying this, aren't you?" Connor glared at him.

"Damn right I am," Liam said laughing. "Watching the three of you has always been entertaining. Just more so lately."

"Ah," Brian said, "the *two* of them. I'm out, remember?"

"Didn't even last a month," Aidan said with a slow, sad shake of his head.

Brian's self-satisfied smile spoke volumes. "Never been so glad about losing a bet in my life."

"Tina's a peach, no doubt about it," Connor said, just a little irritated by Brian's "happy man" attitude. "But there's still the matter of you in that ridiculous outfit to consider."

Not only did the losers lose the money in this bet, but they'd agreed to ride around in the back of a convertible, wearing coconut bras and hula skirts while being driven around the base on Battle Color day…the one day of the year when every dignitary imaginable would be on the Marine base.

Brian shuddered, then manfully sucked it up and squared his shoulders. "It'll still be worth it."

"He's got it bad," Aidan muttered, and held up both index fingers in an impromptu cross, as if trying to keep Brian at a distance.

"Laugh all you want," Brian said, leaning over the table to stare first at one brother, then the other. "But I'm the only one here having regular—and can I just add—*great,* sex."

"That was cold, man." Aidan groaned and scraped one hand over his face.

"Heartless," Connor agreed.

Liam laughed, clapped his hands together, then rubbed his palms briskly. Black eyebrows lifting, he looked at his brothers and asked, "Either of you care to back out now? Save time?"

"Not likely," Aidan muttered.

"That's for damn sure." Connor held out one hand to Aidan. "In this to the end?"

Aidan's grip was fierce. "Or until you cave. Whichever comes first."

"In your dreams." Connor'd never lost a bet yet and he wasn't about to start with this one. Of course, the stakes were higher and the bet more challenging than anything else he'd ever done, but that didn't matter. This was about *pride.* And he'd be damned if he'd let Aidan beat him. Besides, "No way am I gonna be riding in that convertible with Brian."

"I'll save you a seat," Brian said, grinning.

"Oh, man, I need another beer." Aidan lifted one hand to get the waitress's attention.

Another beer would be good. All he had to do was *not* look at the waitress. Connor's gaze snapped from Aidan to Brian and finally to Liam. "This game's far from over, you know."

"There's two, count 'em, *two* long, tempting months left," Liam reminded him.

"Yeah, well, don't be picking out roof shingles just yet, *Father.*"

Liam just smiled. "The samples are coming tomorrow."

THE NEXT MORNING Connor sat in the sunlight outside Jake's Garage and sighed heavily. South Carolina in July. Even the mornings were hot and steamy. The heat flattened a man until all he wanted to do was either escape to a beach and ocean breezes or find a nice shady tree and park himself beneath it.

Neither of which Connor was doing. He was on leave.

Two weeks off and nothing to do. Hell, he didn't even want to go anywhere. What would be the point? He couldn't date. Couldn't spend any time at all with a woman the way he was feeling. He was a man on the edge.

Two more months of this bet and he wasn't sure how he was going to survive. Connor *liked* women. He liked the way they smelled and the way they laughed and the way they moved. He liked dancing with 'em, walking with 'em and most especially, he liked making love to 'em.

So he'd never found the *one*.

Who said he was looking for her?

His mother, Maggie, had been telling her sons the story of her own whirlwind courtship and marriage to their father since they were kids. They'd all heard about the lightning bolt that had hit Maggie and Sean Reilly. About how they'd shared a dance at a town picnic, fallen desperately in love and within two weeks had been married. Nine months later, Liam had arrived and just two years later, the triplets.

Maggie had long been a big believer in love at first sight and had always insisted that when the time was right, each of her sons...well, except for Liam, would be hit by a thunderbolt.

Connor had made it a point to steer clear of storms.

"Boy, you look like you could chew glass." Emma Jacobsen, owner and manager of Jake's Garage, took a seat on the bench beside him.

Connor smiled. Here was the one woman he could trust himself with. The one woman he'd never thought of as, well...a *woman*.

She wore dark-blue coveralls and a white T-shirt beneath. Her long, blond hair was pulled back into a ponytail and braided, falling to the middle of her back. She had a smudge of grease across her nose, and the cap she wore shaded her blue eyes. She'd been his friend for two years, and he could honestly say he'd never once wondered what she looked like under those coveralls.

Emma was safety.

"It's this damn bet," Connor muttered, and leaned his elbows on the bench back behind him, stretching out his legs and crossing them at the ankles.

"So why'd you agree to it in the first place?"

He grinned. "Turn down a challenge?"

She laughed. "What was I thinking?"

"Exactly." He shook his head and sighed. "But it's harder than I thought it'd be. I'm telling you, Em, I spend most of my time avoiding women like the plague. Hell, I even crossed the street yesterday when I saw a gorgeous redhead coming my way."

"Poor baby."

"Sarcasm isn't pretty."

"Yeah, but so appropriate." She smiled and punched his shoulder. "So if you're avoiding women, what're you doing hanging around *my* place?"

Straightening up, Connor dropped one arm around her shoulder and gave her a quick, comradely squeeze. "That's the beauty of it, Em. I'm *safe* here."

"Huh?"

He looked at the confusion on her face and explained. "I can hang out with you and not worry. I've never *wanted* you. Not that way. So being here is like finding a demilitarized zone in the middle of a war."

"You've never wanted me."

"We're pals, Em." Connor gave her another squeeze just to prove how much he thought of her. "We can talk cars. You don't expect me to bring you flowers or open doors for you. You're not a *woman,* you're a *mechanic.*"

EMMA VIRGINIA JACOBSEN stared at the man sitting next to her and wondered why she wasn't shrieking. He'd never *wanted* her? She wasn't a *woman*?

For two years Connor Reilly had been coming to the shop she'd inherited from her father when he passed away five years ago. For two years she'd known Connor and listened to him talk about whatever female he might be chasing at the moment. She'd laughed with him, joked with him and had always thought he was different. She'd believed that he'd looked *beyond* her being female—that he'd seen her as a woman *and* as a friend.

Now she finds out he didn't even think of her as female *at all?*

Fury erupted inside her while she futilely tried to rein it in. Not once in the past two years had she even considered going after Connor Reilly herself. Not that he wasn't attractive or anything. While he continued to talk, she glanced at his profile.

His black hair was cut militarily short. His features were clean and sharp. High cheekbones, square jaw, clear, dark-blue eyes that sparkled when he laughed. He wore a dark-green USMC T-shirt that strained across his muscular chest and a pair of dark-green running shorts that showed off long, tanned, very hairy legs.

Okay, sure, he was gorgeous, but Emma had never thought of him as dating material because of their friendship. Now, she was glad she *hadn't* gone after him. He would have laughed in her face.

And that thought only tossed gasoline on the fires of anger burning inside her.

"So you can see," he was saying, "why it's so nice to have this place to hang out. If I want to win this bet—and I do—I've gotta be careful."

"Oh, yeah," she murmured, still watching him and wondering why he didn't notice the steam coming out of her ears. Of course, he hadn't noticed *her* in two years. Why should he start now? "Careful."

"Seriously, Em," he said, and stood up, turning to look down at her. "Without you to talk to about this, I'd probably lose my mind."

"What's left of it," she muttered darkly.

"What?"

"Nothing."

"Right." He grinned and hooked a thumb toward her office, located at the front of the garage. "I'm going for a soda. You want one?"

"No, but you go ahead."

He nodded, then loped off toward the shop. She watched him and, for the first time, *really* looked at him. Nice buns, she thought, startling herself. She'd never noticed Connor's behind before. Why now?

Because, she told herself, he'd just changed the rules between them. And the big dummy didn't even know it.

While the sun sizzled all around her and the damp, hot air choked in her lungs, Emma's mind raced. Oh, boy, she hadn't been this angry in years. But more than the righteous fury boiling in her blood, she was insulted...and hurt.

Just three years ago she'd allowed another man to slip beneath her radar and break her heart. Connor had, unknowingly, just joined the long list of men who had underestimated her in her life. And this time Emma wasn't going to let a guy get away with it. She was going to make him pay for this, she thought. For all the times she'd been overlooked or underappreciated. For all the men who'd considered her *less* than a woman. For all the times she'd doubted her own femininity...

Connor Reilly was going to pay.
Big-time.

A few hours later Emma was still furious, though much cooler. In her own house, she had the air conditioner set just a little above frigid, so a cup of hot tea was enjoyable at night. Usually she found a cup of tea soothing. Tonight she was afraid she'd need a lot more than tea.

Even after Connor left the garage that afternoon, she hadn't been able to stop thinking about him and about what he'd said. Anger had faded into insult and insult into bruised feelings, then circled back around to anger again.

There was only one person in the world who would understand what she was feeling. Alone at home, she set one of the last remaining two of her late mother's floral-patterned china cups on the table beside her, picked up the phone and hit the speed dial.

The phone only rang once when it was picked up and a familiar voice said "Hello."

"Mary Alice," Emma said quickly, her words tumbling over each other in her haste to be heard, "you're not going to believe this. Connor Reilly told me today that he doesn't think of me as a *woman*. I'm a 'pal,' A 'mechanic.' Remember I told you about that stupid bet he and his brothers concocted?" She didn't wait for confirmation. "Well, today he tells me that the reason he's hanging out at the garage is because he feels *safe* around me. He doesn't *want* me, so I'm neutral territory. Can you believe it? Can you actually believe he looked me dead in the eye and practically *told* me that I'm less than female?"

"Who is this?" An amused female voice interrupted her.

"Very funny." Emma smiled, in spite of her anger, then jumped up off the old, worn sofa in her family's living room and stalked to the mirror above the now-cold fireplace. "Weren't you listening to me?"

"You bet," Mary Alice said. "Heard every word. Want Tommy to call out the Recon guys, take this jerk out for you?"

Emma grinned at her own reflection. "No, but thanks." Mary Alice Flanagan, Emma's best friend since fifth grade, had married Tom Malone, a Marine, four years ago and was now currently stationed in California. It was only thanks to Mary Alice that Emma had ever discovered the mysteries of being female.

Emma's mother had died when she was an infant, and after that she'd been raised by her father. A terrific man, he'd loved his daughter to distraction, but had had no idea how to teach her to be a woman. Mary Alice's mother had filled the gap, and when they were grown, Mary Alice herself had given Emma the makeover that had helped her attract and then win the very man who'd left her heart battered and bleeding three years ago.

The two women stayed in constant touch by phone and email, but this was one night Emma wished her oldest and best friend was right here in town. She needed to sit and vent.

"Okay then, if you don't want him dead, what *do* you want?" Mary Alice asked.

Emma faced the mirror and watched her own features harden. "I want him to be sorry he said that. Sorry he ever took me for granted. Heck, sorry he ever *met* me."

"You sure you want to do this?" her friend asked, and the worry was clear in her voice. "I mean, look how the thing with Tony worked out."

Emma flinched at the memory. Tony DeMarco had done more than break her heart. He'd shattered her newfound confidence and cost her the ability to trust. But that was different and she said so now. "Not the same situation," she said firmly, not sure if she was trying to convince herself or her friend. "I *loved* Tony. I don't love Connor."

"You just want to make him miserable?"

"Damn skippy."

"And your plan is…?"

"I'm gonna drive him crazy," Emma said, and she smiled at the thought of Connor Reilly groveling at her feet, begging for just a *crumb* of her attentions.

"Uh-huh."

"I'm going to make him lose that bet."

"By sleeping with him?"

"Sleep's got nothing to do with my plan," Emma said softly, and ignored the flutter of something warm and liquid rustling to life inside her.

CHAPTER TWO

SAINT SEBASTIAN'S CATHOLIC CHURCH looked like a tiny castle plunked down in the middle of rural South Carolina. Made from weathered gray brick, the building's leaded windows sparkled in the morning sunlight. Huge terra-cotta pots on the front porch of the rectory, or priest's house, were filled with red, purple and blue petunias that splashed color in the dimness of the overhang. Ancient Magnolia trees stood in the yard of the church, draping the neatly clipped lawn with welcome patches of cool shade.

The church's double front doors stood open, welcoming anyone who might need to stop in and pray, but Emma drove past the church and pulled into the driveway behind the rectory.

She turned off the engine, then stepped out of the car and into the blanketing humidity of summer. The heat slapped at her, but Emma hardly noticed. She'd grown up in the South and she was used to the heat that regularly made short work of tourists.

Besides, if she was looking to avoid the heat, she could have stayed at the shop, in the air-conditioned splendor of her office, and had one of her mechanics drive Father Liam's aging sedan back to him. But she'd wanted the opportunity to talk to Connor's older brother.

Ever since her enlightening conversation with Connor the day before, Emma'd been fuming. And thinking. A combustible combination. She'd lain awake half the night, torn between insult and anger and even now, she wasn't sure which was the stronger emotion churning inside her.

She'd thought that maybe talking to Liam might help sort things out. Now that she was here, though, she didn't have a clue what to say to the man.

Muttering darkly, she headed past the small basketball court in front of the garage, down the rosebush-lined driveway and around to the front door.

She knocked, and almost instantly the door was opened by a tall, older woman with graying red hair and sharp green eyes. Her mouth was pinched into its perpetual frown. "Miss Jacobsen."

"Hi, Mrs. Hannigan," Emma said, ignoring the woman's usual lack of welcome. Practically a stereotypical housekeeper, she was straight out of an old Gothic novel. So, Emma never took her grim sense of disapproval personally. Mrs. Hannigan didn't like anybody.

Stepping into the house, she glanced around and smiled at the polished dark wood paneling, the faded but still colorful braided rugs and the tiny, diamond-shaped slices of sunlight on the gleaming wood floor. "I brought Father Liam's car back. Just want to give him the keys and the bill."

"He's in the library," the housekeeper said, already turning for the hall leading back down the house toward the kitchen. "You go in, I'll bring tea."

"That's okay—" Horrified, Emma spoke up quickly, trying to head the woman off. Everyone in Baywater knew enough to say no to Mrs. Hannigan's tea. But it was too late. The housekeeper ignored Emma's protest and strode down the hallway, filled with purpose, and Emma knew there would be no getting out of having to drink the world's worst tea just to be polite.

Grumbling to herself, she crossed the hall, opened the

door into the library and paused, waiting for the young priest to notice her. It didn't take long.

Father Liam Reilly set aside the book he was reading, stood up and smiled at her, and Emma had to remind herself that he was a dedicated priest. As she was sure *every* female was forced to do when face to face with Liam.

As tall as his brothers, he was every bit as gorgeous, too. His black hair, longer than the triplets' military cuts, was thick and wavy and his deep-blue eyes were fringed by long black lashes any woman would envy. His generous mouth was usually curved in a smile that set people immediately at ease, and today was no exception.

"Emma! I'm guessing your arrival means you were able to save my car again?" He crossed to her and dropped one arm around her shoulder, leading her to a pair of overstuffed chairs near a fireplace that held, instead of flaming logs, a copper bucket filled with summer roses.

"I brought it back from the brink again, Liam," she said, and handed him the bill she pulled out of her back pocket before taking the seat he offered. "But it's on life support. You're going to need a new one soon."

He grinned, then glanced at the bill and winced. "I know," he said, lifting his gaze to hers. "But there's always a more important use for the money. And Connor's promised to rebuild the engine when he gets a chance, so I'll wait him out."

Connor.

The very man she wanted to talk about. But now that she was here, she really didn't know what to say. How could she tell a *priest* that she wanted to kill his brother?

"Something wrong?" Liam asked, sitting down across from her and leaning forward, elbows braced on his knees. "What makes you ask that?"

He smiled. "Because the minute I said the name Connor, your face froze and your eyes caught fire."

"I guess poker's not my game, huh?"

"No." He shook his head, reached out, tapped the back of one of her hands and asked, "So, want to talk?"

Emma opened her mouth, but they were interrupted. She wasn't sure if that was a good thing or not.

"Tea, Father," Mrs. Hannigan announced as she bustled into the room carrying a wide tray loaded with a pitcher of a murky brown liquid, two tall glasses filled with ice and a plate of cookies.

"Oh," Liam said with heartfelt sincerity, "you really didn't have to do that, Mrs. Hannigan."

"No trouble." She set down the tray, dusted her palms together, then turned on her heel and marched out of the room with near military precision.

"We have to drink it," Liam said on a sigh as he reached for the pitcher.

"I know." Emma braced herself as she watched him pour what looked like mud into the glasses.

"She's a good woman," Liam said, lifting his own glass and eyeing it dubiously. "Though I can't imagine why the concept of tea escapes her."

Emma decided to get it over with and took a hearty swig. She gulped it down before it could stick in her throat, then set the glass back on the tray and coughed a little before speaking again. "So about Connor..."

"Right." Liam gagged a little at the tea, set the glass down and shuddered. "What'd he do?"

Intrigued, Emma asked, "How did you know he did anything?"

"Something put that flash of anger in your eyes, Emma."

"Okay, yeah. You're right." She jumped up from the

chair that was big enough and soft enough to swallow her whole and started walking. Nowhere in particular, she just felt as though she needed to move. "He did do something, well, *said* something and it made me so mad, Liam, I almost punched him and then I thought he wouldn't even understand why I was hitting him and then *that* made me even more mad, which even I could hardly believe, because honestly I was never so mad in my life and he didn't even have a clue. You know?"

She was walking in circles, and Liam kept his head swiveling, to keep up with her, following her progress around the room and trying to keep up with the rambling fury of her words.

"So, would you hate me, too, if I said I don't have the slightest idea what you're talking about?"

Emma blew out a breath and stopped in front of the wide windows overlooking the shady front lawn. The scent of the roses in the cold hearth mingled with the homey scent of lemon oil clinging to the gleaming woodwork. Outside, a slight wind tugged at the leaves of the magnolias and two kids, oblivious to the heat, raced past the church, baseball bats on their shoulders.

"He's an idiot." Emma turned and looked at him. "Connor, I mean."

"True," Liam admitted and gave her a smile that took the edge off her anger. "In fact, all of my brothers are idiots—" he caught himself and corrected "—maybe not Brian anymore since he wised up in time to keep Tina in his life. But Connor and Aidan?" He nodded. "Idiots. Still, in their defense, they're under a lot of...*pressure,* right now."

"You mean the bet?" Emma asked.

Liam blinked. "You know about it?"

"It's practically all Connor's talked about for the last month."

"Is that right?" Liam smiled again, wider this time. "Driving him crazy, is it?"

Emma grinned at him, despite the bubbles of anger still simmering inside her. "You're really enjoying this, aren't you?"

"I shouldn't be, should I?"

"I don't know," Emma said, her smile fading just a little, "okay, you're a priest, but you *are* still a Reilly."

"Guilty as charged," Liam admitted. "And this Reilly wants to know what Connor did that upset you so much."

"He dismissed me."

"Excuse me?"

Emma shrugged, as if she could shift what felt like a load off her shoulders, then shoved both hands into the pockets of her jeans. Blowing out a breath, she realized that it was just a little harder than she'd thought it would be to talk about this. Saying it all out loud only made it harsher and made her remember the stupid smile in Connor's eyes when he told her she was a "pal."

Gritting her teeth, Emma got a grip on her anger and muttered thickly, "He actually told me that he didn't want me, so I was safe to be around."

Liam groaned. "He really is an idiot."

"Yeah, well." Feeling the sting of Connor's words again, Emma turned her head and looked out the window, focusing on the gnarled trunk of the closest magnolia tree. She should just be mad, but there was an undeniable sting of hurt jabbing at her, too. And it was that niggling pain that bothered her the most. She hadn't let a man close enough to actually *hurt* her in three years. The fact that Connor could do it without even trying infuriated her.

"He's going to be sorry," she whispered, more as a solemn promise to herself than to Liam.

"Emma?"

She wouldn't look at him. How could she? She heard the concern in his voice, and though she appreciated it, she didn't need it. She'd be fine. Just as she'd always been. And once Connor had been taught a *very* costly lesson, things would go back to the way they should be. "I'm going to see to it he loses that bet, Liam."

He sighed and she heard him stand up and walk toward her. "Not that I wouldn't be pleased if the church got a new roof," Liam said when he stopped beside her. "But I feel I ought to caution you."

"About?" She slanted him a look.

Shaking his head, Liam said softly, "Sometimes the best-laid traps can backfire, Emma. They can spring shut on the one who set the trap in the first place."

Not if the trapper was careful.

"Don't worry about me, Liam," she said firmly. "I'll be fine."

"Uh-huh," he said, and reached out to turn her face toward him. "But you and Connor have been friends for a long time."

"So?" She didn't mean to sound so much like a cranky child. But she couldn't seem to help it. The fact that they *had* been friends was the very thing that had made this whole situation so infuriating.

"So," he said, "it's not that far a fall from friendship to love."

Emma laughed and shook her head. "Sorry for laughing, Liam. But trust me, there's no chance of that."

Number one, she wasn't interested in loving anybody. She'd tried that once and she still had the emotional bruises to prove it. And Connor wasn't looking for love either. Heck, if anything, he was trying to avoid women altogether. And clearly, she told herself, her spine straightening and her chin lifting, if he *were* to go looking for love… he wouldn't be looking at her. Nope. No danger here.

Still chuckling, she turned and headed for the door. "I've got to get back to the garage," she said. "And don't worry about giving me a ride back. It's only a few blocks. I could use the walk."

At the door, she stopped and turned back to look at him again. Father Liam was watching her with a concerned expression on his handsome face.

"Don't look so worried," she quipped. "I'm going to help you get that new roof."

"A new roof's not worth a broken heart, Emma."

If something inside her shivered, she ignored it. He meant well, but he didn't understand. This wasn't about making Connor love her. This was about making Connor want her, and then leaving him flat.

This was about payback.

"Hearts are *not* involved here, Liam."

Still worried, Liam watched her go. "For your sake, I hope you're right."

Two days later Connor couldn't stand his own company any longer.

He'd been avoiding his usual hangouts—except for Jacobsen's Garage—but Emma hadn't had much time to talk to him in the last couple of days. He might have thought that she was avoiding him, but that didn't make any sense at all.

To fill his time, he'd spent a few hours working in his mother's garden, played basketball with Liam and had even mooched a meal from Brian and Tina. But, Connor thought, as good a cook as his sister-in-law was, he just couldn't take another evening over there. Not with the way Brian and Tina were all over each other.

It was hell to be jealous of a married man.

But there it was.

"I think going without sex is killing off brain cells," he muttered, and shut off his car's engine. Instantly the air conditioner died and the temperature in the car started to climb.

Summer nights weren't much cooler than summer days and the humidity was enough to make a grown man weep. He stared through the windshield at the Off Duty Bar and told himself if he was smart, he'd fire up the engine, turn the car around and drive back to his empty apartment.

But damn it, temptation of women or not, Connor wanted a couple of hours of listening to music, drinking a beer and talking to his friends.

"I can do this," he assured himself as he opened the car door and stepped out into the sultry summer air. Music, loud but muffled, floated to him on the way-too-slight breeze and the scent of jasmine, coming from the bushes growing at the edge of the parking lot, was thick and sweet.

Connor slammed the car door, punched the alarm button until the car horn beeped, then headed for the front door. As he walked closer, a couple left the building, the man's arm wrapped tightly around his woman's shoulders as he dropped a kiss on her hair.

Connor groaned and seriously considered turning back while there was still time. But the lure of air-conditioning, cold beer and some conversation was just too strong. He grabbed the silver bar in the center of the door and gave it a yank. The door flew open, music slapped at him, and the scent of perfume, beer and cigarette smoke welcomed him.

He stepped into the dimly lit room and nodded greetings as he made his way to the bar. Signaling the bartender, Connor said, "Beer. Draft." He slapped a bill on the bar top and when his drink was ready, he lifted it and took a long pull.

The icy froth soothed him as it slid down his throat, and he shifted his gaze to take in the room. The bar itself was old. Probably fifty years at least. The walls were painted battleship gray and the furniture was scarred. From the open, beamed ceiling, hung memorabilia of the corps. Vintage helmets, bayonets in frayed scabbards, and even a ceremonial sword, belonging to the current owner, a retired Sergeant Major. The whole place was designed to make a military man feel welcome. A Marine, most of all.

There were pool tables at one end of the main room, and on the opposite end, a dozen round tables were lined up in a wide circle, so that the middle of the ring could be used for dancing. The jukebox, which looked older than Connor, blasted out current rock along with some of the classics.

Most of the regulars at the Off Duty were Marines. Winding down after a day of work or just stopping in for a cold one before going home. Of course, there were also a few civilians and more than a few women.

Not that Connor was noticing.

Then the crowd shifted. His hand tightened on the glass of beer. Through the gap in the people milling around the bar, he had an all-too-clear view of a tall blonde in a skirt short enough to be just barely legal.

She was bending over the pool table, lining up a shot.

Connor's mouth went dry.

Her long, blond hair hung in a honey-colored curtain down to the middle of her back. As she tipped her head to one side, that fall of hair shifted, off her shoulders and his gaze was caught by the way the overhead light picked out streaks of sun-kissed hair, brighter than the rest. She wore a pale-blue tank top that looked as if it had been glued onto her body, and the tiny denim skirt, just covering her behind, hitched even higher as she leaned farther over the pool table. Her shapely legs looked smooth and tanned and about three miles long. She wore black, sky-high heels on her small feet, and her ankles looked as fragile as her thighs looked sexy.

Sexy?

The woman *oozed* sex.

His fingers squeezed the glass of beer until he wouldn't have been surprised to feel it shatter like spun sugar in his grasp. Scraping one hand across his face, he inhaled sharply and watched, spellbound, as she lifted her right foot and rubbed it slowly against her left calf.

Need spiked.

His body went instantly hard.

His breath shuddered and his heartbeat staggered.

He watched one of the guys closest to her, lean in and whisper something, and Connor wanted to grab the guy and pitch him through a window.

Okay, *breathe.*

He sucked in air and told himself that he was only reacting like this because of his recent dry spell.

But it was more.

There was something about her.

Something that called to him from all the way across the room. Something that made a man want to toss her over his shoulder and carry her off to a cave where he could have her, over and over again. Where he could listen to her moan and taste her sighs.

He took another gulp of beer, hoping the icy drink

would put out some of the fire. But he knew better. Damn it, he never should have come in here.

The blonde straightened up slowly, then hitched one hip higher than the other as she laughed. That tight, short skirt of hers hugged her behind. She shook her long blond hair back from her face, and Connor was captivated, watching the thick, wavy fall of blond shift and dance around her.

He swallowed hard.

Then she tipped her head back and playfully patted the other guy's chest.

Connor dropped his beer.

The glass shattered at his feet, splashing ice cold beer on everyone close by.

He didn't notice.

He couldn't take his eyes off the blond with the body made for sex.

"Emma?"

CHAPTER THREE

EVEN OVER THE POUNDING rhythm of the jukebox, Emma heard the glass shatter.

But then, her ears were attuned to everything. She'd seen Connor walk into the bar—which was exactly why she'd maneuvered herself to the end of the pool table. She'd even opted to take a *lousy* shot, because she knew *exactly* what kind of picture she'd make, leaning over the pool table.

Nerves hit her hard and fast. Her stomach spun, and the edges of her vision got a little foggy, but she could deal with that. Had to deal with it. Too late now to change her plan.

Smiling up at the guy she'd just beaten at pool, she ignored the sensation of Connor's gaze boring into her back. "That's twenty bucks you owe me, Mike. Want to go double or nothing?"

The tall Marine smiled down at her as he handed over a twenty-dollar bill. "How about you let me buy you a drink instead?"

"How about you take off?" Connor's voice was nothing more than a low growl.

Emma shifted a look at him and had to force herself not to smile at the stunned-to-his-toes expression on his face. Good. She definitely had his attention.

"Connor," she said, in mock surprise. "I didn't see you come in."

Viciously he rubbed the back of his neck, then let his hand drop to his side. "Yeah, well. I sure as hell saw *you*."

"Friend of yours?"

Emma glanced back at the man she'd just beaten twice at pool. Tall and good-looking, any other night she just might be interested. Tonight, though, every thought was centered on Connor. But Mike didn't look too pleased at the idea of sharing.

They were attracting a small crowd, drawn no doubt by the bristling testosterone in the air. Emma wanted to shake her head at the ridiculousness of it, but there was a small part of her enjoying the whole show.

After all, she spent most of her time being just what Connor had called her. One of the guys. A pal. Well, she'd been underestimated most of her life. True, she'd probably played into it by never bothering to dress the part of "female." But she'd always figured she shouldn't have to. A woman who was a successful business owner should be accepted on her own terms without having to stand in killer high heels and skirts so short she felt a breeze *way* too high up.

"Emma," Mike said, bringing her up out of her thoughts with a jerk. "You know this guy?"

"Oh, yes," she said, sending another look to Connor and really enjoying seeing him watch the other guy through narrowed eyes. "Connor and I are old *friends*."

"And we need to talk," Connor said, not bothering to take the warning out of his voice as he faced the other Marine. "So why don't you get lost?"

"Yeah?" Mike snarled. "I don't remember inviting you over."

Connor's chin went up, Mike stiffened and curled his hands into fists, and Emma suddenly felt as though she were in the middle of a special on that cable channel about animals. The men were like two bull elephants about to butt heads.

And in spite of the anger she still felt toward Connor, a purely female spurt of delight shot through her—which she quickly shot down. Seriously, two men go caveman and woman reverts right along with them. Must be contagious.

Stepping in between them, Emma smiled up at Mike Whatever-his-last-name-was and said, "It's okay. I do need to talk to Connor so..." She let her sentence trail off and shrugged an apology.

He didn't like it, but he moved away, rejoining his friends at the bar. Connor glared after him, then shifted his gaze back to Emma.

With a calm she wasn't quite feeling, she folded the twenty-dollar bill she'd just won and tucked it into her bra—the push-up kind that gave her more cleavage than God had ever gifted her with. And she didn't miss Connor's gaze following the action.

A swirl of something hot and thick simmered within, and she told herself it was purely a female reaction to a male stare of appreciation. Although, she hadn't exactly been panting when Mike was giving her the once-over.

Doesn't matter.

All that mattered was that her plan was working.

She smiled to herself and rubbed the tip of her cue stick with a square of chalk. Then, setting it aside, she pursed her lips and blew gently on the tip. Connor swallowed hard.

This is just *fun,* Emma thought.

"So," she said, tipping her head to one side so that her hair fell around her like a gold curtain, "what'd you want to talk about?"

He snorted and swept his gaze up and down her. "You're kidding, right?"

She leaned one hip against the pool table, while she idly stroked her fingers up and down the cue stick. "Is there a problem?"

"A *problem?*" Connor's eyes bugged out and his mouth worked a time or two, as if he was trying to speak but just couldn't convince the words to cooperate. Finally he got a grip on himself, leaned in toward her and said in a strained hush, "Damn it, Emma, *look* at you. When you were bent over that pool table, I could see clear to—"

She raised one eyebrow and hid the delighted smile she felt inside. "Clear to *where,* Connor?"

He straightened up. "Doesn't matter." He inhaled sharply. "What *does* matter is that every guy in here is looking, too."

Okay, there was just a tiny stirring of uneasiness. She'd *wanted* Connor to get an eyeful, and she'd known going in that she might attract some attention from other guys. But the thought of a roomful of Marines scoping her out gave her a chill that wasn't quite the thrill she might have guessed. If anything, she felt a little…*outnumbered.*

But she wasn't going to let Connor know it.

"And how is this any of your business?" she asked.

"Well," he started, then stammered to a stop. He glanced around, giving the evil eye to one guy sidling a little too close for his comfort, then shifted a glare back at her. "We're *friends,* Em," he said. "I'm just trying to look out for you. That's all."

"That's the only reason you came over here, then?" She didn't believe him for a minute. There was a flash of something dark and dangerous in his eyes and it didn't have a thing to do with feelings for his *pal.*

"Why else?"

Okay, fine. They'd play this out. She could go along. In fact, this worked out better for her. The longer he tried to hold out against her, the harder she'd make it for him.

Pushing away from the pool table, she picked up her cue stick, then ran the tips of her fingers along the top edge of her tank top, as if she were hot. She didn't miss Connor's gaze snapping right to where she wanted him to be looking.

"Well, thanks, Connor," she said, licking her lips slowly, provocatively. "I appreciate the concern."

He gritted his teeth, and she watched a muscle in his jaw tick.

"No problem. In fact," he added, "if you're ready to leave, I'll just take you home. Make sure you're okay."

Emma smiled up at him despite the urge to smack him over the head with her cue stick. Instead she laid one hand on his chest and felt the drumbeat of his heart beneath her palm. "That's so sweet," she said softly. "But no, thanks, I'm not ready to leave yet."

"You're not—"

"Tell you what," she said, sliding past him in a move that put her between his rock-hard body and the edge of the pool table. As she moved, she heard him hiss in a breath. Good. "Now that you've scared off my playing partner, you ready to take me on instead?"

He scowled. "Take you on?"

She snapped her fingers in front of his glassy eyes. "Pool, Reilly. You want to play me a game of pool?"

"Right. Pool. Sure." He scrubbed both hands over his face, then looked at her again and blinked as if trying to clear blurry vision. "It'd be better if we just left and—"

"Oh, you go ahead," she said, letting her gaze slide around the room, as if she were considering picking a different challenger from the men in the bar. "I can find someone else to play."

"I'll bet," he muttered darkly. "Look, Emma, I just don't think you should be hanging out here—not tonight. Not the way you look—"

One blond eyebrow lifted again, and slowly she hitched one hip higher than the other and tapped the toe of her shoe against the floor. Around them, people laughed and talked and a handful of couples danced on a small square of unoccupied floor. She paid no attention to any of it.

"What?" she asked. "I look what, exactly? Good? Bad?"

He scowled at her. "Different."

She turned to hide her smile and offered herself a small internal *whoop* of congratulation. Mission accomplished. Connor Reilly had taken notice. In fact, if he'd noticed any harder, he'd be standing in a puddle of drool. A sense of power swept through her, and Emma hugged it close.

A heady sensation for a *pal*.

She picked up the triangle-shaped rack hanging on the side of the pool table, then set it down in position on the green felt. Not even looking at him, she said, "I wasn't born in coveralls, you know."

"Sure. I know that," he said, and reached into the corner pocket to pull out a handful of the striped and solid balls. "It's just…"

Emma sighed and muttered under her breath. Okay, she'd thought to surprise him, but this was ridiculous. It was as if he were staring at a dog who'd suddenly learned to talk. How was she going to seduce the man—make him lose that stupid bet—if she couldn't get him to move past *stunned* into *hunger?*

She straightened up and moved closer to him. His gaze went right to the top of her scoop-necked tank top and stayed there. Her breasts looked high and full, thanks to the "miracle" bra that was currently strangling her. And Connor was certainly appreciating the view.

And that's what she'd wanted, right?

"Look," she said, "I want to play pool. If you don't want to, I'll just ask Mike, or one of these other guys, if he wants to go another round and—"

"Leave him and anybody else out of this," Connor muttered thickly, lifting his gaze to hers. "I'll play."

Now, a girl could take that one of two ways. Play *what* exactly? Pool? Or something else, entirely? For the moment, she'd go with pool. "Twenty bucks a round. Eight ball."

"You're on."

"Then," she said, walking past him to circle the table and head for the opposite end, "as the challenger, you rack 'em."

"Yes, ma'am."

CONNOR COULDN'T TAKE his eyes off her.

Damn it, who would have guessed that little Emma Jacobsen was packing concealed weapons?

And man, she had weapons to spare.

The tops of her breasts pushed teasingly against the edge of her tiny tank top. Her hips swayed when she walked and the hem of that incredibly short skirt just barely managed to cover the gateway to paradise. And her legs. God, her legs.

He dropped one of the billiard balls and had to bend down to snatch it up off the floor. Which gave him much too good a view of those amazing legs as she walked away from him. And why had he never noticed the sweet curve of her behind?

How could he have missed it?

His whole body was stiff as a board. He felt hot and

eager and pushed to the very edge of self-control. Damn it, it had been a mistake to come here. He'd known it before and he was sure of it now. But if he hadn't, he might never have seen this side of Emma.

The very side that was making it an effort to walk. He suddenly wished that his jeans were a hell of a lot baggier.

And even as he thought it, he straightened up, his grip on the fallen billiard ball tight enough to crush it to dust. *This is Emma,* he reminded himself. *Good old Emma.*

Pal.

Buddy.

He shifted his gaze to her and felt his throat close up. Her blue eyes looked wider tonight. Her mouth looked edible. Her tanned, smooth skin was the color of warm honey and looked just as lickable.

Oh, man.

She was watching him with a curious expression on her face and he really couldn't blame her. Hell, they'd been hanging out together for a couple of years now and he'd never stuttered around her before. Just like he'd never taken the time to notice that her breasts were just the right size to fill a man's palm.

Damn it.

She held her cue stick in her left hand. Idly, she slid her fingers up and down the slim, polished wood, trailing her touch delicately enough to drive him insane by wondering how those fingers would feel on *him.*

"Man, get a grip, Reilly." His voice was thick and his muttered whisper was soft enough to be buried beneath the onslaught of rock music pouring into the room. At least, he hoped it had been.

He really didn't want Emma knowing that he was getting hard just watching her.

It's just the bet.

That's all it was.

He was hard up.

Frustrated.

Walking the fine edge of sanity.

But man, she looked good.

"How long's it take to rack some balls?" she asked.

Connor winced and shot her a quick look. "A little patience goes a long way."

She laughed and the deep, throaty, full sound of it, rippled over the conversations in the bar and danced to the rhythm of the music. It seemed to reach for him and grab him by the throat.

"You?" she asked. "Patient?"

Her fingers were still caressing the cue stick and he had to force himself to look away. But meeting her gaze wasn't much safer. Had her eyes always been that color of blue? Sort of summer skyish? He gritted his teeth.

"I can be patient when I have to be," he countered. Like now. It had been a long month. The stupid bet with his brothers was making him crazy. But he was patient— even if Emma didn't think so. And he'd make it through the next two months.

As long as she didn't bend over again.

"Yeah?" She tilted her head, and that fall of hair swung out past her shoulders. "How are you at pool?"

He lifted the rack off the triangle of balls, hung it on the hook at the end of the table and forced a nonchalant shrug. "Take your best shot and let's find out."

She nodded slowly. "Twenty bucks a game."

"High stakes."

"What's the matter?" she asked, a smile tugging at the corners of her mouth. "Scared?"

Well, that helped. His dignity won out over his hormones. "Hell, no. I can take you."

"Really?" she said softly. "And just *where* did you plan on taking me?"

She didn't wait for a reply. Instead, she bent over the table, lined up her cue stick and drew it back and forth between her fingers while she aimed her shot.

Unfortunately, this gave Connor *way* too much time to appreciate the view of her breasts, practically spilling out of her tank top.

His body went to DefCon 2.

And he suddenly knew *just* where he'd like to take her.

A back room.

A flat surface.

On the damn pool table.

Crap. He rubbed his face and damn near slapped himself. He wanted *Emma.* Now. More than he could ever remember wanting anything else in his life.

The only thing that stopped him was he was pretty sure it wouldn't have worked. Just because he was acting like a slobbering horn dog didn't mean she was feeling the same thing. And the only thing worse than falling off the wagon and losing the bet would be trying to lose the bet and having Emma tell him thanks but no thanks.

She took her shot, and the triangle of balls scattered across the green felt surface. She looked up at him and grinned, and Connor's breath caught in his throat.

"You sure you're willing to risk the twenty bucks?" she asked, her voice teasing.

"I'm not afraid of a challenge," he countered, leaning both hands on the cherry wood edge of the table. "How about you?"

"Oh, don't you worry about me, Connor. Trust me, I'm up to the challenge."

"Yeah?" he asked. "And after I've won your twenty bucks, then what'll we play for?"

Emma lined up her next shot, then paused to slant him a look. "Oh, I'm sure we'll think of something."

CHAPTER FOUR

EMMA JACOBSEN WAS DRIVING him over the edge and damned if she didn't seem to be enjoying the ride.

Connor lost two games of pool and couldn't even resent the laughter from the handful of people gathered around to watch the competition. How could he? Hell, if he'd been watching, he'd have been laughing his butt off at the poor guy getting worked by the petite woman in the tank top.

But damned if he could help himself.

How was a man supposed to concentrate on a game when he kept getting distracted by a woman's breasts? Or her legs? Or her laughter? Or the way she walked?

Damn it.

Emma crossed to the wall and set her cue stick into the rack before slowly maneuvering through the crowd to his side. Holding out her hand, she waited for him to hand over his last twenty.

"You were using secret weapons," he said and dropped the bill into her hand, too wary of actually *touching* her. Though the thought of his fingers brushing her palm sent a jolt of heat darting through him, he figured he shouldn't risk it. Hell, he wasn't sure he'd be able to *stop* touching her if he got started.

"Is that right?" she asked, and grinned up at him. Her smile packed a hell of a punch. Something else he'd never noticed. Emma had smiled at him maybe hundreds of times over the past couple of years. Why had it never hit him just what a great mouth she had? What...had he been going through his life blind or something?

"Oh, yeah." Connor forced the words past the hard knot in his throat. "Trust me when I say you weren't fighting fair."

Shaking her head, she laughed and said, "And here I thought I just played way better than you."

"Another match another time," he promised. As long as she was wrapped up in an Eskimo jacket.

"I'm always ready for a challenge." She smiled and tucked the twenty-dollar bill into the dip of her cleavage. He watched it disappear and his mouth went dry.

Behind them, a couple of guys moved in to take over the pool table. Emma stared up at him for a long minute or two, and Connor's brain tried to kick into gear. He had to say something. Something to convince—if not her, then at least himself—that he wasn't a slobbering moron.

But apparently his mind was taking the night off.

In those sky-high heels of hers, she was taller than usual. Her mouth was close enough to kiss and tempting enough to make him want to risk it. He could almost taste her and that thought splintered inside him until he had to curl his hands into fists to keep from reaching for her.

Damn it.

This was *Emma*.

Has to be the bet, he told himself.

Then she spoke and he listened up. Her voice was soft, so he had to strain to hear her over the clash of music and conversation. Not to mention the thunderous pounding of his own heart.

"You're staring at me."

"No, I'm not." Stupid.

"Okay," she allowed, a smirk curving her lips. "You're staring at the wall behind me and I'm just in the way?"

He scraped one hand over his face, hoping to stir himself out of the sexual coma he'd slipped into. Didn't help much. "Sorry. Thinking."

Yeah, thinking about tossing her onto the pool table and peeling her out of that tank top and skirt. Geez, he could almost feel her amazing legs wrapped around his hips.

DefCon 1.

He was definitely in too deep here.

"Uh-huh," Emma said, with a shake of her head that told him she wasn't buying the whole "lost in thought" excuse. Already turning, she said, "Well, it's been fun, Connor, but I've gotta be going."

She was leaving.

He should be grateful.

He wasn't.

"What's your hurry?" he asked, voice tight.

She stopped and looked up at him.

He mentally scrambled for something to say. Something that would convince her to stay for a while. He wasn't finished torturing himself. Wasn't finished being amazed by the surprise that was Emma.

Blowing out a breath, he said, "I'd offer to buy you a beer, but somebody just won all my cash."

A quicksilver grin flashed across her face and was gone again in an instant. "So if I was a good sport, I'd buy *you* a beer?"

"Something like that." Anything, he told himself. He just wasn't ready yet for this time with her to be over. Wasn't even sure why, but he knew he wanted to be with her. Even over all the other scents colliding in the air of the bar, he could almost taste the scent clinging to her alone. It was fresh and citrusy and reminded him of long summer nights under star-filled skies.

And he couldn't quite believe it was Emma Jacobsen

making him feel all these things. Maybe that was why he didn't want her to leave yet, he told himself, grasping for a reason, *any* reason. Maybe he had to prove to himself that it wasn't Emma herself affecting him. That it could have been any woman at this point in the bet. That he was just a hormone-plagued, needy Marine, and any good-looking woman could have been the last straw on this particular camel's back.

No doubt about it, either, she was real good-looking. Up, down or sideways, Emma had something that was making him reel.

"Sorry," she was saying. "Work tomorrow, so I'm heading out."

She turned and weaved through the crowd, moving for the front door. Guys she passed craned their necks for a better view. Connor was surprised there wasn't a river of drool running through the bar. As he watched them watch her, he felt the sudden, driving urge to slam all their heads together and let them fall.

Where the hell did they get off watching Emma?

A couple of long seconds ticked by before he reacted. But then he was moving fast, pushing past the people in his way, as if they were deliberately trying to separate him from Emma. He caught up with her just outside.

The scent of jasmine was thick and sweet in the hot summer air. The silence, after the door swung closed behind him, was almost startling after the prolonged exposure to blaring music. And in the relative quiet, he heard her steps, crunching in the gravel of the parking lot. Instinctively he followed.

She spun around, right hand raised and fisted, with keys jutting out from between her fingers.

"Whoa!" Connor held both hands up in mock surrender.

Emma sighed and let her hand fall. "Darn it, Connor, you *scared* me."

"Sorry, sorry." He hadn't thought about it. Hadn't considered the fact that she might get a little spooked having someone chase her into the parking lot.

In fact he'd *never* stopped to think about Emma that way and suddenly, he realized that she must cross lots of dark parking lots. What about at night, when she closed up her shop and she was alone? And he wondered why he suddenly felt as though he wanted to be the guy protecting her.

Oh, man.

This just kept getting worse and worse.

"What do you want, Connor?"

He lifted her right hand, ignoring the heat that spread from her hand to his and up his arm. Silently he examined the keys she held primed between her fingers. "You were ready for trouble, weren't you?"

"Uh, *yeah.*" She pulled her hand free and released her tight grip on the keys. "A smart woman pays attention and doesn't take chances. So, why'd you follow me out here, Connor? Forget to tell me something?"

"No," he blurted, and took her elbow in a firm grip. She felt warm and soft and, damn it, way too good. "I just thought I'd walk you to your car."

She glanced down at his hand on her arm and he wondered if she felt the same sweeping sensation of warmth that had jolted through him at first contact.

"That's not necessary," she assured him, pointing off to her left. "My car's right there."

He glanced in that direction and spotted her small, two-door, silver sedan about thirty feet away, parked directly beneath one of the light poles. Smart, he thought. Emma'd always been smart.

Then he shifted his gaze back to the sky-blue eyes still watching him. "Fine. You don't need me to do this. But it's necessary for me."

"I can take care of myself, Connor. I always have."

"I know." He'd never thought about it until tonight, but now he wondered why the hell he hadn't. Emma'd always been his friend. Someone he could shoot the breeze with as easily as he could one of the guys on base. He'd never really stopped to think of her as being female.

But looking at her tonight, he couldn't imagine thinking of her as anything else ever again.

"Humor me."

"Why should I?"

He smiled. This was the Emma he knew. Stubborn, ready to argue at the drop of a hat, unwilling to accept help if she figured she could handle something—and she *always* figured she could handle anything.

"Because," he said, smoothing his fingers over her elbow, enjoying the slide of skin to skin, "you just beat me into the ground in front of about a hundred witnesses. Every Marine I know is going to be giving me hell about losing a game of pool to you."

"*Three* games, but who's counting," she corrected.

"*Two,*" he said and leaned closer, "and *I'm* counting."

"Of course you are." Connor'd always been competitive. Which was why he'd gotten himself involved in that silly bet in the first place.

The bet.

The reason she was here, dressed like...well, she didn't really want to think about what she was dressed like. She'd spent most of the evening feeling *really* exposed. At least, until Connor had arrived. Then she'd pretty much just felt warm.

Emma inhaled slowly, deeply and told herself to get a grip. But it wasn't easy. The feel of Connor's hand at her elbow was swamping her brain with way too many emotions and too few clear thoughts.

She'd thought this was going to be easy.

Work him into a frenzy, seduce him, then tell him how she'd tricked him into losing the bet with his brothers.

She hadn't expected that *she* would be having trouble keeping focused.

But having his heated gaze locked on her body for the past two hours had churned her up so much that it was hard to remember to breathe. In fact, she hadn't taken an easy breath at all until the minute she'd stepped out of the bar and started across the parking lot.

Connor coming up behind her and scaring her out of five years of her life hadn't helped anything, either. But now he was here. So close. Close enough that she could look up into his eyes and see her own reflection staring back at her.

"So, are you going to let me play white knight?" he asked softly, "Or are you going to force me to follow you at a distance to make sure you're safe?"

Something inside her softened and then toughened up again. Sure, it was nice having someone care enough to make sure she got to her car safely. But if she'd wanted, or needed, an escort, one of the bouncers would have walked her out. The fact that Connor was all of a sudden acting like Sir Walter Raleigh or something was both flattering and infuriating.

She hadn't missed the fact that he'd only treated her like a girl when she was dressed as *he* thought a girl should be. If she was smart, she'd play along, keep reeling him in to the fact that for the night, she was a soft, helpless female type.

But she just couldn't do it.

"First tell me something."

"What?"

"How come you never offered to walk me to my car before tonight?"

"You know," he admitted, lifting one hand to brush the side of his head, "I was just asking myself the same thing."

She watched him, admiring the strain of his black USMC T-shirt across his broad, muscled chest. "And did you get an answer?"

He straightened up again, and looked down into her eyes, pinning her gaze with his until Emma saw that his deep, ocean-blue eyes were churning with emotions she'd never expected to see.

"Only one," he muttered, taking a firmer grip on her elbow and steering her across the dark lot. The lights rimming the lot shimmered in pools of brightness splashed across the shadows.

"Which was?" She hurried her steps to keep up with his much-longer legs.

He stopped and looked at her. "I'm an idiot."

She smiled. "I can accept that."

Standing in one of the pools of light thrown from overhead, Connor's face was in shadow, but she felt him watching her anyway.

"You surprised me tonight, Em," he said, and his voice sounded softer than the breeze that drifted past them.

Her stomach did a slow spin. "Why's that?"

He shrugged. "I just never thought of you as—"

If he came right out and said, "I never thought of you as a girl," again, Emma might just have to punch him.

"As what?"

He paused, then seemed to catch himself. He took a step back, shook his head and muttered, "A pool player."

Disappointment curled in the pit of her stomach. He could have said, sexy, or hot stuff or gorgeous. But, no. Apparently, the shock was still too much for him. Well, fine. So she wouldn't be seducing him on the first try. She had time. She'd get him into bed yet.

"Live and learn," she said, and stepped past him to open her car door. She slid inside, rolled down the window and looked up at him. "See you, Connor."

"Right. See you."

She put the car in Reverse and pulled out of her parking space. As she slipped the gear shift into Drive, she looked in the rearview mirror to see Connor, standing where she'd left him, still watching after her.

The fact that she really wanted to go back and kiss him meant absolutely nothing.

"It's *Emma*, for crying out loud." Connor snatched the basketball thrown at him, then dribbled it absentmindedly.

"You gonna play or what?" Aidan ran up to him, grabbed the ball away from him, turned and made a jump shot, sending the basketball through the hoop.

"Maybe he's got something else on his mind," Brian said, wiping sweat off his face with his forearm.

"What about Emma?" Liam asked, grabbing the ball in rebound and bouncing it back down the driveway behind the rectory.

Connor looked at his older brother and wondered how in the hell he could explain what had happened to him two nights ago. Hell, he still couldn't figure it out for himself.

But since the moment Emma'd hopped into her car and driven away, he hadn't been able to think of anything else but her. And that was just way too weird.

"I saw her the other night," he said, and instantly a vivid

image of Emma in that short, tight skirt leaped into his mind and hovered there to torment him.

"So?" Aidan moved in closer, taking the beer from Brian's hand and draining it.

"Hey!" Brian complained.

"Get another one, geez," Aidan sniped.

Sunshine poured down on the concrete driveway and bounced off the cement surface to surround the brothers in steamy summer heat. Hardly a breath moved through the trees and there wasn't a cloud in sight. But they'd made plans to play basketball today and come hell or dehydration, they were going to play.

Brian snapped the top on another beer and held it far away from Aidan's reach. Taking a drink, he glanced from Connor to Liam and winked. "Hey, looks like you've got another brother about to topple."

Connor straightened up and scowled at him. "No way. I can make it. Unlike *some* people."

Brian just laughed. "Hey, I don't get the money, but I *do* get laid. *Often.*"

"Bastard," Aidan muttered, then added, "can't understand why a woman as great as Tina would put up with you."

"She wanted the best," Brian assured him.

"Yeah, yeah." Aidan threw the ball at him, Brian caught it and sent it toward the hoop.

As they moved off, Liam stepped up to Connor and slapped him on the back. "So, anything you'd like to share with your friendly neighborhood brother slash priest?"

Connor shook his head. "You're in no position to give advice on women, Liam. I may be out of the game for two more months, but you're in it for life."

Liam shrugged, reached down into the open cooler beside him and pulled out two cans of beer. Tossing one to Connor, he opened one for himself and said, "I wasn't born into the priesthood, you know."

"Yeah, I remember."

"So? Feel like talking?"

"No." Connor took a long gulp of the beer and felt the icy froth race down his throat and send a welcome chill throughout his body. But it wouldn't help for long, he knew. Ever since seeing Emma at the Off Duty, he'd been hot and hadn't been able to cool off. Thoughts of her plagued him. Memories of the way she moved, the way she smiled, the way she smelled, were becoming a part of him.

Which was exactly why he'd stayed away from her garage the past couple of days. He needed space. Time. He needed to figure out just what the hell had happened to him the other night. And until he did, it wasn't safe for him to be around Emma.

Going into his second month of forced celibacy, Connor was balancing precariously on a razor's edge of control. One little push either way, and he was a goner.

And the way Emma had looked the other night, she was just the one to give him that push.

"That's it?" Liam asked. "Just *no?*"

"Liam, the day I need a priest's advice on women, is the day you can shave my head and send me to Okinawa."

"You're a Marine, moron," Liam reminded him, setting down his beer and moving back to the top of the basketball court, where Aidan and Brian were dueling it out. "Your head's already shaved and you've *been* to Okinawa."

Connor scowled at him.

Hell, maybe he *did* need advice from a priest.

CHAPTER FIVE

"HE HASN'T BEEN BACK, Mary Alice." Emma leaned back in the office chair that had once belonged to her father and was now all hers.

"You expected him to come running right over?"

"Well, *yeah*." She twirled the coiled telephone cord around her index finger so tightly her skin turned bluish purple. Quickly she unwound it again. "If you could have seen him drooling all over me, you would have thought so, too."

"Uh-huh," Mary Alice said, "and what were you doing while he was drooling?"

"You mean besides falling out of my top?"

"Yeah. Were you drooling back?"

"A little maybe." Okay, *a lot*. But she couldn't very well admit that to Mary Alice, could she? Not when her friend had warned her going in that this was a bad idea? Oh, maybe it *had* been a bad idea.

For two days now Emma'd been doing little else but think about Connor. Which was weird. He'd been a part of her life for two years, but until this week, she'd never once imagined him naked in bed with her. And, oh, boy, her imagination was *really* good.

"I knew it," the voice on the phone said, disgusted. "I knew you'd be setting yourself up again. Honestly, Em…"

"This is different," Emma protested, not sure if she was trying to reassure her friend or herself. Memories of three years ago and a broken engagement darted through her mind and were just as quickly extinguished. "I'm not looking for forever," she said. "Just a little right now."

"Uh-huh."

Emma scowled at the phone. "You don't have to sound so unconvinced."

"Please, Em. You are *so* not the one-night-stand kind of woman."

She stiffened. "I could be."

"Yeah, and I could be a runway model, if not for the extra twenty pounds."

"Funny."

"I'm not trying to be funny," Mary Alice said. "I'm *trying* to make you come to your senses before you get in so deep with this guy that your heart gets broken again."

"Wow. First Father Liam warns me about the dangers of seduction turning into love and now you." Emma blew out a breath. "My heart is perfectly safe. It's my hormones that are getting the workout."

Well, that set Mary Alice off. A floodgate of warnings poured from her, and she barely paused for breath.

While she listened to her friend's worries pouring through the receiver, Emma glanced around the tiny Jacobsen "empire."

The office was filled with potted plants, and flowering vines fell from baskets hanging in the corners of the room. The wide glass windows gleamed in the sunlight and gave Emma a bird's-eye view of the flower beds lining the front of the shop. Zinnias and petunias added color and scent to the shop and welcomed customers with unexpected beauty.

Her father had started the business more than thirty years ago and had never really concerned himself with making the place "pretty." He'd built a reputation based on honesty and fair prices and when he passed away five years before, he'd left that business in Emma's capable hands.

She knew her way around an engine—hard to grow up the only child of a mechanic and *not* learn—but as she'd helped the business grow, Emma had found herself spending more time lately on paperwork than on actual engines. Though there was still nothing she loved better than restoring classic cars.

The two mechanics she had working for her were good at their jobs and didn't have a problem taking orders from a woman—especially one who could do a tune-up in less than thirty minutes.

"Hello? Earth to Emma."

"Huh? What?" Emma shook her head, sighed deeply and said, "Sorry. Zoned out there for a minute."

"I'm giving you all this great advice and you're not listening?"

"I didn't say that. I heard you. I just think you're going a little overboard."

"No such thing. You're not experienced enough with guys to know how to protect yourself."

"Gee, *Mom,* thanks."

"You *did* call me to talk about this, remember?"

"Yeah," she paused and pushed a long strand of blond hair behind her ear. She'd given in to a weak moment and called her best friend in the world because Emma was getting a little nervous. This wasn't working out quite the way she'd planned it. She was supposed to be driving Connor insane with desire—not herself. "I remember."

"So, talk to me."

"I already told you about the other night at the bar."

"Yeah," Mary Alice said with a sigh. "Wish I could have seen you balancing on those heels while playing pool."

"Hey, I'm better at it than I used to be." She grinned, though, remembering how many times she'd fallen on her behind when Mary Alice had coached her through actually *walking* in high heels. That had only been four years ago. When she'd first decided to remake herself in the hopes of falling in love. Back before she realized that love only really mattered if the guy was in love with the *real* Emma.

"God, I should hope so," she chuckled, then continued, "so you said Connor was all droolly, right?"

"Like a starving man looking at a steak."

"This is a good thing."

"Yes, but I haven't seen him since." Damn it. Emma'd thought for sure that Connor would come by the garage the day after their pool match. The way he'd stared at her breasts and her legs, she'd have bet money on him being completely hooked.

She would have lost.

"Figure he's avoiding you on purpose?"

"Seems like that's the case."

"Then you must have worried him."

Emma smiled, dropped her feet from the desk and sat up. "Hey...I hadn't really thought about it like that."

"If he doesn't trust himself around you, I'd say you're close to getting him to lose the bet."

"Good point." She'd been so busy being annoyed that Connor was keeping his distance, Emma'd never really asked herself *why* he was suddenly so determined to avoid her. Maybe he wasn't thinking of her as a pal anymore, and that had him worried. Maybe her too-tight skirt and too-small shirt had done the deed after all.

But then why didn't he come over for another look, damn it?

She stood up and walked around the edge of the desk, stretching the coiled phone cord as far as it would go. Outside, the summer sun blasted down on the city streets, heat shimmering in the air, giving Baywater the wavering look of a mirage. On the main street traffic bumped along, and as she watched, a black SUV made the turn into the garage's driveway.

A chill swept instantly down her spine, and Emma tried to tell herself it was just the icy breeze from the air conditioner affecting her. But she knew better.

She licked suddenly dry lips. "He's here."

"What?"

"Connor," Emma said, her fingers tightening on the receiver. She watched him step out of his car and wince as the heat slapped at him. Oh, he looked way too good. Despite the summer heat, he wore faded jeans that clung to his long legs. His white T-shirt strained across his broad chest, and his jaw was tight and set as he stuffed his keys into his pocket and headed for the office—and her.

A jolt of pure anticipation lit up her insides and made her mouth water.

"What's he look like?" Mary Alice demanded.

"Dessert," Emma groaned. "Gotta go." She hung up while her friend was still talking, then eased one hip against the corner of her desk and tried to look nonchalant. Not at all easy when your stomach is spinning and your heartbeat is crashing in your ears.

Emma couldn't take her gaze off him, and she wondered just when this little game she'd started had turned on her. He was the one who was supposed to be going all gooey-eyed, not *her*. But here she stood, watching his long legs move across the parking lot and wishing he'd turn around so she could get a glimpse of his very nice behind.

Her stomach took another nosedive, and she slapped

one hand against it as he opened the door and stepped inside. Instantly her small office felt darn near claustrophobic.

Connor ground his back teeth together as he looked at her. Big mistake coming here. After leaving his brothers, he'd gone home to take a shower, but hadn't been able to sit still. Thoughts of Emma had plagued him as they had been for the past two days, and he'd finally decided there was only one thing to do about it.

If he hoped to keep his friendship with her, then he needed to stay the hell away from her for the duration of this stupid bet.

He wasn't about to risk his nice, easy relationship with Emma just because he was so damn horny he could hardly see straight. Emma was his *friend*. The bet was the only reason he was acting like a moron around her now. And damn it, he wouldn't give in to it. He was no teenager stuck on the first girl to smile at him.

He was a Marine.

He was tough.

He was hard.

And getting harder by the second.

His gaze swept over her quickly, thoroughly. She was wearing a pair of pale-green coverall shorts that displayed miles of smooth, tanned leg. And under the bibbed coverall, was a dark-pink tank top edged with lace. Her blond hair was pulled into a high ponytail and then braided into a thick rope that lay across her right shoulder. And his fingers itched to touch it. He wanted to undo the tight braid and rake his hands through the softness.

Whoa.

He stiffened slightly, instinctively shifting into a *braced for battle* position. Feet wide apart, arms crossed over his chest. Ordering himself to stand down, he knew, more than ever, that he'd done the right thing in coming here. He had to explain to her that he wouldn't be seeing her for the next couple of months. Had to tell her—what?

That he didn't trust himself around her?

That he all of a sudden was spending way too much time thinking about her trim little body?

That he wanted to sink his teeth into her shoulders and then lick his way down the length of her?

Oh, yeah. That'd be real smart.

"Emma, we have to talk." The words came out a little harder than he'd planned, but then, his jaw was clenched so tight every word was an effort of will.

"Really?" She smiled and edged off the corner of the desk.

Her sandals were white with little daisies on the top strap. Her toenails were painted the same dark shade of pink as her tank top, and she wore a gold toe ring that winked and sparkled in the sunlight. Damn it. Mechanics don't wear jewelry on their feet.

He frowned. "Since when do you wear a toe ring?"

She looked down, then up at him. "Since three years ago."

"Oh." He scraped one hand across his face. Something else he'd never noticed. Or if he had, it had been ignored, because Emma was his friend. His buddy. But that was then, and this was now. "Look, Emma, about the other night—"

"What about it?" She moved a little closer and he got a whiff of her perfume.

The soft, haunting scent reached for his throat and squeezed. This was risky. Being this close to her. He should have called her. Should have kept his distance. But he hadn't wanted to, and at least he could admit that much to himself.

Hell, he couldn't figure out why this was happening to him at all. He'd never spent much time fantasizing about one particular woman. To Connor, women were like candy. You never wanted to stick with one too long, because you'd just get tired of it. He was a big believer in the "variety is the spice of life" theory on romance.

But since seeing Emma at the bar the other night, she'd been right up at the forefront of his mind. He hadn't been able to shake her. Hell, he hadn't been able to make himself *try*.

"You surprised me," he said.

She stepped closer, and her scent moved in for the kill. Damn it, she was wrapped around him now and he couldn't breathe without taking a piece of her inside him.

"Yeah, you said that already."

"Right." He had said it. Outside in the parking lot. When he'd tried to convince her *and* himself that he'd been surprised by her pool-playing abilities. He frowned, shook his head and looked down at her. Her summer-sky eyes were wide and incredibly blue. A man could lose himself just staring into those depths. And he didn't want to be lost.

"Look," he blurted, taking a hasty step back, hopefully out of range of her force field. "You want to go get some lunch or something?"

Her blond eyebrows lifted high on her forehead. "You're asking me to lunch?"

"Something wrong with that?" he demanded, as he silently cursed himself. For God's sake, you don't get over a woman by asking her out to eat. "Can't two friends share a meal together without making a big deal out of it?"

Her lips twitched, then her mouth slowly curved and he felt a tug of reaction deep inside him.

"Who's making a big deal about anything?"

"Nobody," he said, nodding as if trying to convince himself. "Not a big deal. Just lunch." He frowned. "So? You interested?"

"Sure. Just let me tell the guys I'm leaving."

She walked through the connecting door to the garage bay and God help him, Connor watched her go. Man. Short coveralls had never looked so good. There was nothing "friendly" in the way his gaze locked onto her—and he knew he was digging himself an even deeper hole.

DELILAH'S DINER was relaxed and casual.

Tourists and locals mingled together and the low hum of activity echoed throughout the place. Booths lined one wall by the window overlooking Pine Avenue. A dozen or more round tables were dotted around the rest of the room, with a long lunch counter sweeping around the back. Waitresses moved through the crowd with dazzling speed and the "order ready" bell rang out with regularity.

Emma leaned back against the white Naugahyde booth seat and folded her arms on the scrubbed red vinyl tabletop. Connor hadn't spoken to her at all since leaving the shop, and now he looked as if he'd rather be anywhere but here.

How was a girl supposed to take that?

While they waited for their order, she reached for her glass of water and took a long sip before asking, "So are you going to be silent all through lunch?"

"Huh?"

"You said you wanted to talk, but you haven't even opened your mouth since we left the garage."

"Miss the sound of my voice?"

He grinned, and the quick smile jolted something deep inside her. Emma took a long drink of water in an attempt to drown it.

"What's going on, Connor?"

"Nothing, it's just that—"

Their waitress chose just that moment to arrive with their meals. She slid Emma's chef salad across the table then carefully placed Connor's hamburger and fries directly in front of him. Emma rolled her eyes and watched, half amused, half irritated as the woman did everything but coo and stroke Connor's chest.

"Thanks," he said, smiling up at the redhead.

"You bet," the woman said on a sigh, barely sparing a glance for Emma. "If there's anything else you need—" she paused meaningfully "—anything at all, you just call me. I'm Rebecca."

"Thanks, Rebecca," Emma spoke up, startling the waitress out of her flirtatious mood. "We'll call if we need you."

The woman flashed her a frown, then shot Connor another smile before reluctantly wandering off.

"Amazing," Emma said, shaking her head in disgust.

"What?"

"You didn't notice?"

He picked up his hamburger and took a bite. Shrugging, he chewed and repeated, "Notice what?"

"Unbelievable. But then why would you?" Emma asked, not really expecting an answer. "You've probably affected women like that your whole life."

"What the hell are you talking about?"

"The redheaded waitress?" Emma coaxed. "The one who wants to have your child—here on the table?"

He laughed and picked up a French fry. "Don't you think you're exaggerating a little?"

She stabbed a forkful of lettuce and chicken and really considered stabbing him in the hand just for the heck of it. No wonder he'd never paid attention to her. He had women crawling all over him all the time. The man was a babe magnet. Any female between the ages of fifteen and fifty would turn for another look at him. "No, I'm not."

Connor shrugged. "She probably thinks I'm Aidan. He eats in here a lot."

She just stared at him. She'd never had any trouble at all telling the triplets apart. Sure, they were identical, but there was a little something different about each of them that made all the difference. With Connor, it was the way the right corner of his mouth lifted when he didn't really want to smile but couldn't help himself.

"What was it like?" she asked. "Growing up with two other people who look just like you?"

His mouth curved, just the way she liked it.

"Fun. We had a great time, the three of us. And Liam, too, before he went into the seminary." He paused and looked at her. "I can't imagine growing up like you did. An only child."

She lifted one shoulder and took another bite of her salad. "It was okay. My dad and I got along fine, just the two of us."

"Yeah, I bet you did. But you didn't have somebody to trade places with at exam time."

"You didn't."

"Sure we did." Connor laughed and his eyes flashed with memories. "Aidan's the brain. So come chemistry finals—he took all of our tests."

Emma laughed and shook her head. "I can't believe you got away with that."

"We did. For the first two years of high school. After

that the teacher wised up. Noticed that all three of us answered every question the same way."

"What happened when you got caught?"

He winced, then winked at her. "Let's just say our
mother is more than a match for her sons. None of us saw
the outside world for a solid month."

"Even Liam?" Emma reached for her ice tea. "He was
innocent."

"Yeah, but he was the oldest. Mom figured he should
have kept us out of trouble."

While Connor talked about his brothers, Emma watched
him and tried to remember that she wasn't supposed to be
getting more deeply involved in his life. This was just a
seduction. Pure and simple. A plot to get him to lose a bet
and be sorry he'd ever dismissed her.

But he smiled and she forgot about her plan. He laughed
and she just enjoyed the loud, rolling sound of it pouring
over her. Beneath the table, his foot brushed her leg, and
she felt the punch of electrical awareness dance up her
calf, past her thigh to simmer in a spot that was already
too hot for comfort.

He felt it, too; she sensed it.

His gaze locked with hers across the table, and the
humor in his eyes faded slowly away to be replaced by a
slow burn of hunger that scorched her, even at a distance.
"What're we doing, Emma?"

"Having lunch?" she asked, swallowing hard and trying
to steady her breathing.

"What else?"

"Is there something else, Connor?"

"I didn't want there to be, but it's damn hard to ignore."

A spurt of disappointment shot through her but didn't
do a thing toward cooling the fires within. "Well, that was
flattering."

"Emma, we're friends." He leaned across the table and took her hand in his. His thumb scraped her palm until the tingles of sensation speared through her.

She blew out a breath, but didn't let go of his hand. She liked the feel of his fingers entwined with hers. Liked the heat she found pulsing in him and the flames awakening in herself. "And friends don't see each other naked?"

"Not usually," he admitted, through gritted teeth.

She nodded slowly and, just as slowly, reluctantly, pulled her hand free of his. "Then we'll just have to stop being friends, won't we, Connor?"

CHAPTER SIX

STOP BEING FRIENDS?

Emma's words hit Connor like a fist to the gut.

"That's exactly what I'm trying to avoid," he muttered, his hand tingling with emptiness now that she'd let go of him. He rubbed the tips of his fingers together, as if he could still feel the silky slide of her skin on his. Damn it. He didn't have so many close friends that he was willing to lose one. Especially *this* one. He and Emma always had a good time together. They could talk about anything. He could laugh with her. Tell her what he was thinking.

When the new recruits in his charge were starting to drive him up the wall with frustration, Connor knew he could go to Emma's and forget about the world for a while. When his brothers made him nuts, she laughed with him about it. When the rest of the world looked less than warm and welcoming, Emma's smile set it right.

And he wasn't ready or willing to give that up.

"You can't always get what you want," she said with a little shrug that nudged the strap of her coveralls down her left shoulder.

He scowled at her. What was *that* supposed to mean? Did she *want* to end their friendship and try something different? Or was she trying to tell him that she wasn't interested in sex with him?

Why couldn't women be as clear as men?

"Don't start quoting song lyrics at me."

"A little touchy, aren't we?" she asked.

"Not touchy, just surprised you're so damn willing to toss our friendship for a quick roll in the hay."

"I didn't say *that,* either."

He actually *felt* his scowl deepen. "Then just what the hell are you saying?"

"Not much," she said, and her voice was cool, amused, even. "Just that if you want to go to bed, we'll stop being friends. If you don't, we won't."

"Oh, so it's all up to me?" He didn't believe that for a damn minute. There wasn't a woman alive who wasn't completely at the wheel of any relationship. And all men knew it. They just pretended otherwise to hang on to their pride.

Which was *precisely* why he'd always avoided commitment like the plague. Once a woman got a good hold on you, things changed. Your life wasn't your own anymore. You were going to chick movies regularly and worrying about putting coasters under your bottle of beer.

Not worth the effort. Leave the married life for people like Brian. For Connor, it was love 'em and leave 'em— quick.

She shook her head, and he watched that thick, honey-gold braid swing from side to side like a pendulum. "Up entirely to you? Not a chance. Look, you just said yourself you didn't *want* there to be anything else between us."

"Yeah, but—" Not fair to use a man's own words against him.

"So, there's no problem, right?"

He scraped one hand over his face. Something was wrong. Somewhere or other he'd lost the thread of this conversation, and he wasn't sure any more which side he should be defending. Damn it, a man needed a battle plan to deal with a woman. Any woman.

Especially, it seemed, *this* woman.

Emma grinned, tilted her head to one side to stare at him, and her thick, blond braid swung over her right shoulder. He wanted to reach across the table, undo the rubber band at the end of it and comb her hair free, burying his fingers in it.

"Do I make you nervous, Connor?"

"No." The answer came sharp and swift, and he had to wonder if he was trying to convince Emma or himself. Dismissing the idea entirely, he picked up his hamburger, took a bite and chewed like a man on a mission. However he'd lost control of this conversation, he could still get it back.

After he swallowed, he said, "I'm not *nervous*."

"Then what's the problem?"

Problem? Where to start? How about sitting across from his friend in a lunch diner and knowing he'd need about twenty minutes before he could stand up and walk out of there without embarrassing himself? How about the fact that he could smell her perfume—something a little different today, flowers and…lemons, but just as intoxicating.

He couldn't tell her any of that. Just as he couldn't tell her that he'd been lying awake at nights imagining her *naked*. That would damage the very friendship he was fighting so hard not to lose.

This was all his brothers' faults. Every last one of 'em. Brian being so happily married now—and delighting in telling Connor and Aidan about all the sex he was currently enjoying. Aidan being so determined to being the last man standing. And even Liam, standing on the sidelines, laughing at all of them as they tried to do for three months what he'd committed to for a lifetime.

He never should have made the stupid bet.

It'd been a pain in the butt from the get-go.

And it was only getting worse.

"Damn it, Em," he muttered thickly, fighting past the knot of need lodged in his throat, "it's the bet. You know that's what's behind all of this."

"Uh-huh."

He frowned at her less-than-convinced reply. When she took another bite of salad, then delicately licked a drop of dressing off her bottom lip, every cell in Connor's body lit up like a fireworks show. Inwardly groaning, he squashed the lightninglike flash of need bursting to life inside him.

"Look," he said, leaning toward her and lowering his voice to be sure none of the other diners could overhear, "we both know this bet is making me nuts. We both know that we're *friends*, nothing more."

She nodded and smiled. "You bet."

He inhaled sharply, deeply. His stomach knotted and he glanced down at his hamburger in sudden distaste. He couldn't force a bite down his tight throat now if someone had a gun to his head. Pushing the plate aside, he leaned both forearms on the table and held her gaze with his own. "I *like* you, Emma."

"Thanks, Connor," she said, daintily picking a piece of chicken out of her salad and popping it into her mouth. "I like you, too."

"Exactly!" He slapped one hand against the tabletop with enough force to make the iced tea glasses jump and shudder.

Several people turned to look at him, and Emma laughed. He didn't care.

"That's my point." He glanced around warily, then lowered his voice again. He felt like a secret agent in a bad movie. "We *like* each other too much to climb into bed together."

"Okay."

He sat back, stunned. *"Okay?"*

She shrugged again and this time the tiny spaghetti strap of her little tank top slid off her shoulder to join the strap of her coveralls. Connor gritted his teeth.

"Sure," she was saying, and he blinked away the haze of pure, one-hundred-proof lust clouding his mind so he could listen. "I mean it's no biggie to me. If you'd rather not, then fine."

"Just like that."

She smiled. "Did you expect me to throw myself across the table and plead with you to *take me now, big boy?*"

Maybe a little, he admitted silently. He'd thought sure she was feeling what he was feeling. That she'd wanted him as much as he had her. But apparently not. And why didn't that make him feel better?

"Sorry to disappoint you, Connor," she said, and idly lifted both straps off her upper arm to slide them into place. "But I'll survive if we don't hit the sheets together."

"I know that," he said, and wondered how in the hell this had all turned around. When had he set himself up to be turned down? When had *she* become the one to say no?

"Good." She took another bite of her salad and if she hadn't just a second ago told him she wasn't disappointed by the thought of not going to bed with him—Connor would have thought she was licking her lip deliberately. She did it slowly—tantalizingly slowly—and his body, still at DefCon 1 lit up like a demilitarized zone during a night landing.

She picked up her iced tea, took a long drink, and Connor's gaze fixed on the line of her throat. His vision blurred.

Then she set her glass down, glanced at her watch and said, "Oops! Gotta run."

"Now? You're leaving now?"

"I really have to," she explained, gathering up her brown leather purse and slinging it over her left shoulder. "But you go ahead and stay. The shop's only a block away. I'll walk it."

When he didn't say anything, she stopped scooting toward the edge of the booth. "Connor? Was there something else you wanted to talk about?"

"No," he grumbled. "Nothing at all."

"Okay, good." She leaned toward him and smiled. "I've got a bad carburetor coming into the shop in twenty minutes, so I have to be there."

"Right." He grabbed his own iced tea glass and cradled it between his palms, letting the cold seep into his skin, his bones.

She stood up and flashed him another smile as he looked up at her. Then she dropped one hand onto his shoulder and he swore he could feel the warmth of her skin right through the fabric of his shirt.

"I'll see you later, okay? And thanks for lunch."

"Right. Later." He nodded and swallowed hard.

She walked away and he couldn't help himself. He turned on the booth seat to watch her go and groaned as his gaze locked onto the curve of her behind. Grumbling under his breath, he turned back around and squirmed uncomfortably on the bench seat.

Rebecca, the friendly waitress, hustled right over and asked, "Can I get you anything else?"

He didn't even meet her eyes this time. Instead he drained his iced tea, then handed her the empty glass. He wasn't going anywhere until his body cooled down. Shouldn't take more than an hour—and since he couldn't very well take a cold shower, he'd have to settle for cold drinks. And maybe he should just pour the next one in his lap where it would do the most good.

"Bring me another one of these, would you? And make it a large."

She frowned, but he didn't notice.

Or care.

LATER THAT EVENING Connor drove from his apartment to the base. Sick of his own company, he'd decided to check in with his assistant drill sergeant. Now, watching the young troops trying to settle into life as Marines, he at least had something else to think about besides himself.

And they *were* young.

Most of them still in their teens, they were driven to the recruit depot at Parris Island at night. Brought across the long road winding into the base past swamp water and marsh grasses in the dark. Deliberately. Not to disorient, but to have them connect to *this* world almost instantly. To remind them that they and their fellow recruits were now a team. A family. That they'd become a part of something much bigger than they'd ever known before, and that the life they left behind had no place here.

Standing in the corner of the barracks, Connor watched DI Jeff McDonald striding up and down the aisle separating two long rows of bunks. Each new recruit stood in front of their beds, heads newly shaved, narrow shoulders thrown back and chins jutted out.

"Boy," McDonald shouted, stopping in front of a tall, thin kid, "did I just see you *smile?*"

"Sir! No, sir!"

Connor smothered a grin and watched as McDonald feigned disgust.

"You think you're going to a party, recruit?"

"Sir! No, sir!"

McDonald leaned in closer, his nose just a hair's breadth from the kid's. He pointed to the chevrons on his sleeve. "Then you better stop smiling recruit, or I'm gonna think you think I'm funny lookin.'"

The kid looked horrified by the idea.

"Do you think I'm funny lookin,' recruit?"

"Sir! No, sir!"

Connor watched from the shadows and silently approved. McDonald was good at his job. He'd intimidate the recruits, teach them what they needed to know to survive, and in the end he'd have their respect. And he would have turned out a new company of Marines.

Smiling, Connor told himself the kid would learn. They all would. Or they wouldn't make the grade. But most of them would. They were here because they wanted something more and, generally, were willing to work for it.

Connor shook his head, shoved his hands into his pockets and slipped out the side door. The summer night was warm, the air felt thick with the scent of the South and the humidity that was such a part of life here.

He stopped and tilted his head back to stare up at the black, star-studded sky. Things were running as they should be here. He wasn't needed. McDonald didn't have time to talk, and he wasn't in the mood to hunt down any of his other friends.

He still had days to go on his leave time. Hell, he should be *itching* to get into town. To grab a beer. Play some pool at the Off Duty.

Connor winced. He had the distinct feeling he'd never again be able to stroll into that bar without his brain replaying the image of Emma bent over the pool table, taking a shot. He scrubbed both hands over his face and shook himself like a big dog climbing out of a lake.

They'd settled *nothing* at lunch.

If anything, he'd only walked away more confused than he had been before.

So the only way to get this clear in his mind was to go and see Emma. Talk to her. Figure out what the hell it was that was driving him and then find a way to end it.

And if a small, rational voice in the back of his mind was warning him to steer clear of Emma Jacobsen—he wasn't listening.

EMMA SAT ON her back porch, staring up at the sky.

Star Jasmine flavored the warm, moist air and stirred in the gentle breeze that swept through the yard, then disappeared again. Sighing, she leaned against a porch post and stretched her legs out, down the steps leading to the grassy yard. She reached for the frosty margarita sitting beside her and lifted it for a sip.

Ordinarily she didn't drink much.

But after her lunch with Connor, and a long, dreary day of rebuilding a carburetor and then the depressing conversation with Mrs. Harrison, she'd felt she'd earned a drink or two.

Mrs. Florence Harrison, a widow who lived just outside of town had been disappointing Emma for two years now. All because of a '58 Corvette currently rusting in Mrs. Harrison's barn. The car had once belonged to the woman's son, now dead forty years. Emma had lusted after the 'Vette ever since the moment she'd first seen it. She longed to bring it into the garage and restore it to its full glory.

But Mrs. Harrison flatly refused to part with her late son's "baby."

"Ah, well," Emma said, and took a long, deep drink of the frothy concoction in her glass. She let the icy stream wash down her throat and send chills to every corner of her body. "What's one more *no* in the grand scheme of things, anyway?"

Connor didn't want her enough to lose the bet, and Mrs. Harrison was clutching that Corvette to her bosom like a long-lost child.

Pushing off the top step, Emma stood up and walked down the stairs and across the lawn. The damp grass felt cool and lush beneath her bare feet as she wandered aimlessly through the shadows. From down the street, she heard snatches of sound, letting her know her neighbors were also enjoying the cool relief of the summer night. Children laughed, dogs barked and the faint sound of a radio playing caught the air and hung on it.

When the wind kicked up suddenly, it swept through her hair, lifting it off her neck into a wild, brief dance. At the side of the house, the wind chimes tinkled merrily, and she smiled at the sound, in spite of everything.

"What're you thinking?"

The deep, familiar voice came from somewhere close beside her, and Emma's stomach jumped as she turned to face Connor. "You scared me," she said, though that wasn't strictly true.

Startled, yes. But scared? Nope. Much closer to a rush of hunger than a rush of fear. Funny how she'd never noticed before now just what kind of effect his voice had on her. Just when exactly had *that* started happening?

"Sorry. Didn't mean to sneak up on you," he said, and took a step closer. "But you looked like you were thinking serious thoughts—then you smiled. Intrigued me."

Still in the USMC T-shirt and jeans he'd been wearing earlier, Connor looked good enough to fuel dozens of dreams. At the thought she clutched her margarita glass a little tighter and took a sip, even as she acknowledged that it was false courage. "I, um, just liked the sound of the wind chimes."

As if awaiting a cue, the wind breathed past them again, and the chimes sounded out like fairy bells.

"Pretty," he said.

"Yeah, they are."

"Not them," he said. *"You."*

Whoa.

Head rush.

It wasn't the margarita. She hadn't had enough of that to matter. It was Connor. Plain and simple. In the moonlit darkness, he looked impossibly handsome. His strong jaw worked as though his teeth were clenched. His eyes were as dark as sapphires, and the reflection of stars danced in them. His mouth was tightened into a grim slash that made him look as though he regretted saying those words.

Well, too bad if he did.

He *had* said them and there was no going back now.

"Thank you."

"Emma…"

"Connor," she interrupted him neatly and took another sip of her drink to stall for a precious second or two. "If you're here to tell me again what a great pal I am and how you don't want to lose me—" she stopped and took a breath. "You don't have to bother. I get it. Understood. Go. Be happy. Fly free."

He glanced around the empty yard, and she knew he wasn't noticing the lushly crowded flower beds or the sweet smelling jasmine vines clinging to the fence wrapping around her property. He was waiting, thinking, maybe having as difficult a time as she was with whatever it was that lay between them.

And for one brief moment Emma wondered if she'd

done the right thing in setting this ball in motion. But there was no turning back. No avoiding whatever was coming.

Finally he looked at her and she read a decision in his eyes. She lifted her chin and braced herself for whatever was coming next.

"This isn't about our friendship, Em," he said softly. "This is about what's making me crazy."

"And what's that?" Oh, man. She held her breath and felt the sense of waiting all through her body.

"If I don't kiss you in the next ten seconds, I think I'm gonna lose what's left of my mind."

All of the air left her body and fire replaced it. She felt tongues of flame working their way through her insides. Her body went hot and ready and eager. Her mind clicked off and her emotions charged to the surface. But her voice was steady as she smiled up at him. "Time's awastin' then."

He grabbed her.

She dropped the acrylic margarita glass to the ground, spilling the icy drink across the grass.

He pulled her hard against him, stared deeply into her eyes for one heart-stoppingly long moment.

And then he kissed her.

CHAPTER SEVEN

CONNOR HUNG ON TO Emma as if it meant his life.

And in that moment maybe it did.

For the past several days, she'd filled his mind. Every thought, every dream was stamped with her image.

She fit against him as if she was the missing piece to his puzzle. And though one corner of his brain clanged out a warning bell, he refused to listen.

His arms wrapped around her, pulling her close, closer. His hands swept up and down her back, aligning her body with his, until he felt every inch of her pressed to him tightly enough that he felt her heartbeat fluttering wildly. His mouth took hers, his tongue tangling with hers in an erotic dance that fired his system with a need unlike anything he'd ever known before.

She sighed into his mouth, and he swallowed her breath, taking it inside and holding it. Her arms linked at the back of his neck, and she pressed herself even more fully against him.

He felt the pressure of her pebbled nipples pressing into his chest, branding his skin with heat that seared him right down to his soul. Connor groaned, and his arms tightened around her, lifting her feet clean off the ground.

Again and again their tongues tangled in a dance as old as time and as new as sunrise. She tasted of her icy drink and tantalizing secrets. He couldn't get enough of her.

Somewhere in the back of his mind, a voice shouted, *This is Emma.* His pal.

His buddy.

And right now the only thing in his life he desperately wanted.

Tearing his mouth from hers, he gasped for air like a wild man. Blindly, Connor stared down at her and saw her familiar features through a bristling red haze of passion. Her mouth was swollen from his kiss. Her summer-blue eyes were glazed with the same desire blasting through him. Her breath labored in and out of her lungs, and he wondered if her heart was thundering in her chest—as his was.

"Wow." She blinked up at him and smiled with all the wonder of a kid at Christmas, unwrapping a gift she hadn't even been aware of wanting.

Connor knew just how she felt. "Yeah," he said, "I think that just about covers it."

"Who would have guessed?"

He set her back onto her feet and released his viselike hold on her. Still, though, he was reluctant to break all contact. He lifted one hand and stroked her cheek with his fingertips. Her skin was as warm as sunlight and as soft as velvet.

Emma turned her face into his touch and closed her eyes as he caressed her face. She sighed a little, opened her eyes again and said, "Why *did* you come here tonight, Connor?"

Good question. He wasn't entirely sure he had an answer for her. Shaking his head, he said simply, "I don't really know. I just drove here. Didn't actually stop and think about it. Didn't plan it. Just followed my instincts and they led me here."

"Instincts, huh?"

He nodded and shoved one hand along the side of his head. Hard to admit, even to himself, that it was pure gut reflex that had brought him to Emma's door. But there it was. As a Marine, he'd learned long ago to trust the impulses that drove him. He didn't question, didn't doubt. He just *did.* That confidence in his own subconscious had saved his butt more than once.

And tonight those instincts had brought him here.

To Emma.

"What are they telling you to do now?"

If he told her that, she'd probably run for the hills. Because it was taking all of his self-control to keep from tearing her clothes off and tossing her onto the cool, damp grass. He wanted her naked. He wanted her beneath him. Over him. Astride him. He wanted her in every possible way, and as they stood there in the starlit shadows, that want continued to pulse and grow. "You don't wanna know."

She stepped up close, close enough that he could feel the heat of her body radiating out around her. "Yes, I do."

Her scent lifted into the air and filled his mind. The taste of her still lingered on his tongue. His blood raced, his body tightened until the pain of waiting was almost as fierce as the desire gnawing at him.

He hadn't meant to start this. To light a match to the stick of dynamite lying between them. But now that the first, most difficult, step had been taken, now that the lit fuse was lying there sparking and sizzling, there was no going back. Though his brain shouted at him to think about what he was doing, what he was thinking, his body wasn't listening.

His mouth hungered for another taste. His hands burned to touch her, to sweep along her skin, define every inch of the compact, curvy body that had been plaguing him.

"If you don't want this to happen," he managed to grind out, "say so now."

She was breathing as heavily as he was. Even in the pearly moonlight, he saw the flush on her cheeks and the glitter in her eyes. And he prayed—desperately—that when she made her decision it would be one he could live with. One that wouldn't haunt them both. Even as he thought it, though, he realized that the hell of it was, no matter what she said, they would be haunted.

Because after *this* night, nothing between them would ever be the same—whatever happened.

"If I didn't want this," she pointed out, "you would have known about it when you kissed me."

"Be sure," he said, and wasn't entirely sure himself why he was giving her this out. Why he was practically daring her to call a halt to this. Because if she did say no—it was going to kill him.

"I'm sure, Connor. Are you?"

"Decision made, babe." He grabbed her again, filling his hands with the thin fabric of her tank top. He pulled her close again and dipped his head to take her mouth with his. To drown in the taste of her. She sighed into him, and Connor's blood raced through his veins, thick and hot. He groaned, broke the kiss and stared down at her for a long second, before picking her up and tossing her over his shoulder.

"Hey!" She braced her palms against his lower back, pushed herself up and shouted, "What the hell are you doing?"

"I'm through wasting time, Em." He slapped his palm against her butt, and when she yelped, he grinned.

"What are you, a caveman?"

"Caveman, Marine...you tell me."

"I will if you'll put me down."

"Not a chance." He marched across the moonlit back-yard, took the five steps to the back porch at a dead run, then yanked open the screen door and stepped into her kitchen.

He paid no attention to the homey room with its glass-fronted cabinets. He glanced at the blender full of margaritas, then kept walking, out of the kitchen to the bottom of the stairs. He'd been to her house before. He knew his way around the ground floor—but he'd never been upstairs. Never been into her bedroom. Never even considered it until tonight. But that was then—this was now.

"Damn it, Connor," she said, slamming her fist against his back, "I mean it. Put me down."

"As soon as I see a bed. Trust me. I'll put you down. Where'm I headed?"

She sighed, then laughed, and the magic of it floated in the air like soap bubbles on a summer wind. "Upstairs, you Neanderthal. First door on the left."

"Got it." He took the stairs two at a time, his long legs making short work of the trip. Emma's slight yet curvy body hooked over his shoulder didn't slow him down one bit. It did, though, fill him with a fierce and frantic need to reach her bed—hell, *any* bed.

The first door on the left stood open in invitation and he rushed through it. Connor hardly noticed the room itself. All he saw was the double bed with the wrought iron head and foot rails. A colorful, flower-splashed quilt was spread over the mattress and a half dozen throw pillows in different colors and shapes were piled against the bigger bed pillows.

Every cell in his body urged him to hurry. To grab her, take her, fill himself with the taste and touch of her. Giving in to that urge, Connor flipped Emma over his shoulder and onto the mattress. She bounced a couple times and laughed even harder than she had downstairs.

"You're crazy," she said, grinning up at him in the moonlight pouring through the bedroom window overlooking the backyard.

"Been said before," he agreed, planting one knee on the edge of the bed and leaning over her.

She reached up and caught his face between her palms. Her gaze locked with his, and he felt as if she were trying to see all the way through him, down to his soul. And a part of him wondered what she'd find there.

Then philosophical questions faded from his mind as he slid one hand beneath the soft fabric of her tank top. At the first touch of her skin against his, he swallowed hard, and she hissed in a breath and let her eyes slide closed.

"Have to have you, Emma," he murmured, and bent his head to take one kiss, then two.

"Have to have each other," she answered, and snatched a kiss for herself as his hand slid higher, up her rib cage to cup her breast.

"No bra." The words slipped from him on a grateful sigh. His thumb and forefinger tweaked her pebbled nipple, and she arched into his touch, her breath sliding in and out of her lungs in hungry gasps.

Her skin was magic.

Warm silk.

He moved to straddle her body, his knees at her hips. He stared down at her as he pushed her tank top up and over her head, tearing it off and tossing it over his shoulder to land on the floor. A spill of moonlight lay across the bed and bathed Emma in a wash of pale light that almost made her skin glow.

He looked his fill and knew it would never be enough. He cupped her breasts in his hands and felt a hum of appreciation rush through him. Her nipples hardened at his touch. She reached up and ran her palms up and down his forearms, and he felt every stroke of her fingers like a live match against his skin.

Bending low, Connor indulged himself with a taste of her. He took first one nipple, then the other into his mouth, his tongue and teeth nibbling, pulling, teasing at her flesh until Emma was twisting and writhing beneath him.

Every move she made inflamed him. Every sigh that escaped her fed the flames engulfing him. Every touch made him want more. His eyes blurred, his brain shut down and his body took over. All he could think about was burying himself deep inside her. Feeling her damp heat surround him. Feeling her body quiver in climax.

He growled against her flesh and suckled her deeply. Emma's back bowed and she groaned his name as she clutched at his shoulders. "Connor, Connor don't stop. Don't stop doing that."

"Not a problem," he mumbled, surrendering to the hunger clawing at his insides. His mouth drew at her nipples again and again, feeling her need build, feeling his own desire ratchet up past the boil-over point, and still he wanted more.

Sliding down her body, he unzipped her shorts and as he moved, he skimmed them and the white lace panties beneath them, down and off her legs. In the moonlight, he saw the tan lines marking her body and felt his heart jump at the narrow strips of pale flesh over her breasts and at the juncture of her thighs. Why the thought of her in a tiny bikini could inflame him even while he was staring at her nudity, he couldn't figure out and didn't much care.

Everything he wanted in the world was there, at his fingertips. And he meant to enjoy it.

Emma felt him watching her and thought she might

just burn to ashes under that heated gaze. But instead her body lit up like a fireworks display. His hands on her legs, as he caressed her from her ankles to her thighs and…oh, boy—even higher, felt hot, heavy, rough and so damn sensual, she couldn't imagine how she'd lived so long without having him touch her.

Her blood was bubbling inside. That had to be the reason why her whole body felt so twitchy. She wasn't a virgin. She'd had sex before.

But she'd never had sex like this before.

Not when she felt as though the top of her head was going to fly off into space—as though her insides were so jumbled with an intensifying need, that she might never feel normal again.

Connor's lips replaced his hands on her legs, and she felt the warmth of his breath dusting her skin as he moved to the insides of her thighs, kissing, nibbling, licking.

Her breath rushed in and out of her lungs. She heard herself panting. She felt herself writhing and couldn't stop. Didn't want to stop. All she wanted was more. More of *him.*

Then his mouth covered her center. "Connor!"

Thank heaven he didn't stop at her shout. She parted her thighs wider, inviting him closer. She planted her feet on the mattress and lifted her hips, rocking with the soul-shattering rhythm that he'd set with his lips and tongue. He tasted her intimately, sending showers of sparks throughout her body. Emma felt the world around her tremble as anticipation built within.

She opened her eyes and looked at him, watched him taste her, watched as he learned the secrets of her body, and she felt a rush of something hot and primal burst into life inside her.

His hands cupped her bottom and squeezed. She licked

dry lips and kept her gaze locked on him as her body strained toward the shattering point that was now so close she could feel it.

Reaching down, she cupped the back of his head and held him to her. Her fingers pushed through his silky black hair and she groaned as he nibbled at her. "Connor, I feel—I need—"

He growled.

No other word for it.

He seemed to know exactly what she needed. He growled against her body, lifted her hips in his strong hands, and as she dangled helplessly above the bed, he pushed her over the edge into a chasm so full of sparkling lights and colors, it nearly blinded her.

"Connor!" She shouted his name, heard the wildness in her own voice and reveled in it as she rode a climax unlike anything she'd ever known before.

As the last tremor rocked her body, he left her, and she wanted to weep for the loss. Her eyes closed to better savor the incredible wash of satisfaction sliding through her, she heard foil tearing and then he was there, somehow already gloriously naked, over her, filling her.

She arched her hips and took him inside. His body pushed into hers and the moment she felt his length within, she came again, trembling anew, riding fresh waves of pleasure that tore at her and left her gasping for air.

"Beautiful," he whispered, his voice a hush of sound in her ear. "So damn beautiful."

She *felt* beautiful. Emma grabbed him, holding him, her arms wrapped around him, her hands splayed against his back, pulling him tighter, closer. She lifted her legs and hooked them around his waist, tilting her hips to take him even deeper.

He groaned as his hips rocked against hers in an age-old rhythm that sent flutters of brand-new need pulsing at the core of her. She met him, stroke for stroke, and enjoyed the feel of his body covering hers. The solid, heavy weight of him, pushing her down into the mattress. The ripple of muscles straining across his back.

Again and again he withdrew, then pushed himself home. Sweet friction escalated inside her, and Emma ran with it, eager to reach that peak one more time. The heady sound of flesh on flesh filled the room and became an intimate symphony.

He lifted his head to look down at her, and she gasped at the hunger glittering in his eyes. He looked like a warrior. Like the caveman he had pretended to be. He was intent. On *her*. On the breathless craving that had them both wrapped in a tight fist.

In the moonlight his broad, tanned chest looked delectable. She swept her hands around from his back and caressed his skin with her fingertips. At his flat nipples, she flicked the pebbled surface with her nails and watched as his eyes narrowed and his mouth flattened into a harsh line.

He grabbed her right hand, linked his fingers with hers and braced them both on the mattress. Staring down at her, he muttered thickly, "Come again, Em. Come with me this time."

As if his words alone had been enough to ignite new flames, her body erupted, and bubbles of expectancy churned inside her. She moved with him again, feeling every sweep of his body against the so-tender flesh at the heart of her.

Again and again he staked his claim on her. Then he dipped his head and took her mouth with his. His tongue swept aside her defenses and claimed all that she was. His breath mingled with hers until she didn't know where she began and he ended and didn't care, either.

She tasted his need.

She shared his greed.

And this time when the world around them tottered and fell, they were together as they took the leap and together still when they fell.

CHAPTER EIGHT

CONNOR'S WEIGHT PRESSED Emma into the mattress, making each breath an adventure. But she didn't mind. In fact, she loved the feel of him lying atop her.

She loved the hum still vibrating inside her body. She loved how he made her feel when he touched her. She loved touching him and seeing his response flicker in his eyes.

And she was using the word love way too many times.

She put a mental stop to that real fast. Opening her eyes, Emma stared blindly up at the ceiling and tried to get a grip on the emotions churning through her. But it wasn't easy. Connor's breath labored in her ear and his heartbeat raced in tandem with her own. And she wondered if his stomach was suddenly doing a weird little pitch and roll.

Probably not.

Guys didn't spend a lot of time thinking about the repercussions of sex. Guys only thought about *getting* sex, and then once they'd had it, they worried about getting it *again*. Life was simpler for the Y chromosome set.

But as far as Emma was concerned, things had just gotten really complicated.

"I'm smashing you."

"Only a little." Stupid. She shouldn't have said that. Should have said, Yes, you are. Move over. But she hadn't wanted him to move and what did that say? Oh, God, she wasn't sure she wanted to know what that said.

Instantly the memory of Father Liam's warning came crashing back at her, echoing over and over again in her mind. Something about "being careful because sometimes even the best-laid traps snapped shut on the wrong target."

She squeezed her eyes shut and deliberately shut down the memory. Her trap had worked fine. Just as she'd planned. She'd gotten him into bed, hadn't she? She'd proven to Connor that she was as female as the next woman and she'd made sure he'd lost that stupid bet with his brothers.

No problem.

She squelched a groan. So if everything was so great, why wasn't she celebrating?

Connor lifted his head and, poised above her, he blocked her view of the ceiling and forced her to meet his gaze. She stared up at him and her heart gave a slow jolt that shuddered through her body like ripples on the surface of a pond.

Oh, boy.

"Damn, Emma..." His voice trailed off as he brushed a stray lock of blond hair off her forehead.

His features were stamped with an expression of stunned surprise, and Emma wasn't sure whether to be flattered or insulted. And did it really matter?

"That was—" he stopped and grinned "—amazing."

Oh, yeah, it had been, she thought, feeling the power of his smile slam into her. Amazing, earth-shattering, completely befuddling. Emma squelched a groan that was building deep inside her. She didn't want to put hearts and flowers on this night. That wasn't what this had been about.

She wasn't in love with Connor Reilly.

Didn't *want* to be in love with him.

That wasn't in the plan.

She'd set out to make him lose that bet for being so damn insulting, and she'd succeeded. That's all she had to remember here. That her scheme had worked. She'd brought him to his knees—figuratively speaking—and okay, she thought as she remembered him kneeling between her thighs, literally, too. But that was it. It was over.

And she'd be doing herself a huge favor to keep that in mind.

In an attempt to do just that, she forced a smile she didn't really feel and gave his back a friendly slap. "So, guess I'm not just 'one of the guys' after all, am I?"

He frowned down at her and levered himself up onto his elbows, taking most of his weight off her. Emma would rather have curled up and died than admit she missed the feel of his body pressed onto hers.

"One of the guys?" he echoed.

"You remember," she prodded, reminding herself as well as him. "A week or so ago we were talking about the bet and you said I was 'safe to hang out with'?"

"I did?" The frown on his face deepened and he shifted position slightly.

Emma swallowed another groan that erupted when his body, still locked within hers, stirred into life again.

Keep your mind on the conversation at hand, she warned herself. Keep remembering that, until about twenty minutes ago he hadn't really considered you a woman. "Yeah. You did."

He moved one hand to fiddle with the rubber band at the end of her braid. But she refused to be distracted.

"And," Emma said, her breath hitching as his hips rocked against her, "you actually said, 'you're not a woman, Em...you're a *mechanic.'"*

"Huh."

She reminded him of the most humiliating moment of her life and all he had to say was *"huh?"*

His fingers undid her long, blond braid, and a part of her brain focused on the soft tug as he freed her hair. But mostly she kept reminding herself that she'd won a victory here. A victory for every woman—heck, every *girl*—who was just a little bit different from the rest of the crowd.

"Don't you remember?" she demanded.

"Not really."

"But you said it," Emma insisted, determined now to ignore the stirring of her body as he shifted position over her again.

"If you say so."

"If *I* say so?" She blinked up at him and paid no attention when he pulled her now-loosened hair across her shoulders and dipped his head to bury his face in the thick mass. "Seriously, you don't remember saying that?"

"Vaguely," he said, and moved again, this time trailing warm, damp kisses along the line of her throat.

"Vaguely?"

"Do you really want to talk right now?" he mumbled, his words muffled against her neck.

No, she didn't want to talk. Didn't want to think. Didn't want to do anything except revel in the soft slide of his tongue along the length of her throat. She arched into him, despite her best efforts, and tilted her head to one side, giving him easier access. He smiled against her skin.

A sigh of a breeze drifted through the partially opened window and carried the scent of summer roses with it. The night was soft, quiet, as if she and Connor were the only two people in the world. It was as if they were wrapped together in a cocoon of sensation.

He was distracting her.

And doing a damn fine job of it, too. But they were

getting off subject. She was trying to tell him that she'd tricked him into losing his precious bet, and he was too busy stirring her body up again to listen.

Determined now, Emma put both hands on his shoulders and shoved. He lifted his head and looked down at her, one corner of his mouth tugging into a half smile that did some incredible things to her insides. But Emma fought that reaction down and met his gaze steadily.

"What's wrong now?" he asked, and his deep voice rolled through the room like summer thunder.

"Nothing's *wrong,*" she said tightly. "It's just—" How was she supposed to have a conversation with a man whose body was even now swelling to fill hers again? Concentrate, she thought. It was the only way. "Connor, I'm trying to tell you that I got you into bed deliberately. I *tricked* you."

"Yeah?" He smiled again and gave her a wink. "Then, thanks." Dipping his head, he took one of her nipples into his mouth and suckled it briefly.

She hissed in a breath as white-hot sensation shot through her bloodstream like skyrockets. Her vision blurred, her breath went soft and hazy, and she had to fight to come up for air again. When she did, she gave his broad, muscled shoulders another shove for good measure. "You're not listening to me."

"I'd rather kiss you," he admitted as he reluctantly lifted his head to stare down at her. "I'd rather taste you again. Why the sudden need for chitchat?"

His eyes seemed to glisten with a new urgency. And as he spoke, Emma felt her own heartbeat quicken in anticipation. But before they indulged themselves again, there were a few things that had to be said.

"Don't you get it, Connor?" she said, capturing his face

between her palms. "I deliberately trapped you. Set you up, then knocked you down."

A short, sharp laugh shot from his throat. "Am I supposed to be sorry?"

"You lost the bet," she reminded him.

He frowned. "Oh, yeah…"

"I *wanted* you to lose the bet."

"Why?"

"To teach you a lesson," she said, and slid her hands from his cheeks, to his neck, to his shoulders, skimming over the hard, warm muscles and loving the feel of his skin beneath her palms. "To show you that just because I'm a mechanic doesn't make me less of a female."

He stared at her for a long moment, then slowly, a deep throated chuckle rumbled from his throat. "Well, you sure as hell proved your point, Em. I'm convinced," he said, still smiling as he dipped his head for a quick, hard kiss.

"Aren't you mad?"

"Should I be?" In one smooth move, he flipped onto his back, bringing her with him as he rolled over the mattress.

"You lost the bet."

"Seems like."

"I tricked you."

"Did an excellent job of it, too."

Straddling him now, Emma felt the thick, solid length of him pulsing within her. Unconsciously she rocked her hips and smiled when he hissed in air through clenched teeth. Watching him, she looked for signs of anger in his expression, but there was nothing there. He wasn't angry about losing the bet. Wasn't mad about being tricked.

What he *was,* was insatiable.

Thank heaven.

"But the money, Connor," she persisted. "It was down to just you and Aidan."

He reached up and covered her breasts with his hands, squeezing, rubbing, tweaking at her sensitized nipples until Emma moaned and let her head fall back.

"You think I give a damn about the bet now?"

Breathing hard, she lifted her head again and looked at him. "You don't?"

Shaking his head, he said, "I never would've made it, Em." He grinned. "Not hanging around you, anyway. And hell, it's hard to mind losing a bet when losing's this much fun."

She shrugged, and her hair slid over her skin like golden silk. "There is that."

He lifted his hips and Emma gasped as she rose up high, like a bronc rider astride a wild mustang. Except this felt *much* better. Her brain went on automatic pilot, and every inch of her body was already alert and screaming for attention.

Still, though, she couldn't leave things as they were. She had to know one more thing.

"Connor, where do we go from here?"

He stopped moving beneath her and locked his gaze with hers. His hands dropped to her hips and held her tightly, every finger pressing into her skin as if somehow branding her—however temporarily.

"Why do we have to go anywhere?" His voice was low, soft and she had to strain to hear him over the thundering crash of her own heartbeat. "Why does this have to be more than one night of amazing sex?"

If there was a part of her that was disappointed in his reaction, she buried it. After all, she hadn't been looking for a commitment. She hadn't been looking for *love*. She'd already tried love once and that had turned into a disaster of near epic proportions.

She'd never planned on having more than this one night with him. Her imagination hadn't taken her quite so far as that.

So Emma told herself to be grateful that Connor was who he was. A friend. A friend who happened to have the ability to turn her blood into steam…but a friend, first and foremost.

"It doesn't," she said, and deliberately twisted her hips, grinding her center against him, taking his body deeper, higher within her own. Her whole system shivered and she shook with the force of it. When she could speak again, she said, "One night, right? We have this one night and then go back to the way we were?"

He sucked in a gulp of air, his eyes fired in the shadows and then he nodded. "We stay friends."

"Friends," she agreed, and went up on her knees, feeling his body slide free of hers before she sank on him again, enjoying the rich feel of his hard length invading her heat.

Connor watched her as she moved over him and lost himself in the glory of the moment. How the hell could he think about where they went from here? How could he possibly worry about losing that stupid bet when Emma was riding him in slow, sensuous movements?

Her hair, loose and free, streamed over her shoulders and across her breasts, her rigid nipples peeking through the golden strands to tempt him. She was more beautiful than he could have imagined. She was more *everything* than he had ever guessed.

Her body was hot and tight, surrounding his with a velvety grip that drove him to the edge of oblivion with every move she made. He bit back a groan and choked off the urge to surrender to the climax crashing within. He wanted this to last. Wanted to stretch out their time together, to make the most of every second he spent here in her room.

Tomorrow he'd confess to his brothers that he'd lost the bet. Tomorrow things would go back to the way they'd always been between him and Emma. They'd be friends, because her friendship was something he didn't want to lose. But tonight they were different. Tonight they were lovers, and he for damn sure meant to enjoy every minute of it.

She arched her back and moaned, a soft sigh of sound that shook him down to his bones. He tightened his grip on her hips and increased the rhythm sparking between them. Over and over again, she pulled free of his body only to capture him again with a nearly hypnotic effect.

Moonlight danced on her naked flesh and she let her head fall back again as she rode him. He felt his own release building and knew he wouldn't be able to hold out much longer. His breath staggered from heaving lungs. His brain was short-circuiting. His body felt electrified— surging with a power he'd never known before.

And Connor knew he wanted to take Emma with him when his body exploded. Dropping one hand to the spot where their bodies joined, he stroked her damp heat. Rubbed the one spot on her body that he knew would send her tumbling wildly over the edge.

"Connor..." She said his name on a throaty groan of need and passion.

He continued to stroke her, watching as her features shifted with the churning emotions slashing at her. She moved faster, rocking her hips with him in a timeless rhythm that swept both of them up in a frantic rush toward completion.

And when her body splintered, he caught her and held on as he let himself follow after.

"I'M OUT." Connor slid onto the bench seat at the Lighthouse Diner and shrugged when all three of his brothers just stared at him.

He hadn't been looking forward to this. Facing his brothers and admitting that he hadn't been able to last the full three months of their bet was humiliating. Even though, he thought, with a small inner smile, losing the bet had been the best time of his life.

When that thought crowded into his brain, Connor frowned and pushed it back out.

"You're kidding, right?" Aidan, sitting right beside him asked, with an elbow jab to his ribs.

"Ow." Connor looked from Aidan to Brian and finally to Liam. "Nope. Not kidding. I'm out. Fit me for the coconut bra."

"Woo-hoo!" Aidan hooted gleefully and signaled the waitress to bring another round of beers to the table. Shifting his gaze back to his brothers, he grinned and said, "This round's on me. In celebration."

"Hey," Connor reminded him, "just because I lost, doesn't mean *you* won."

"He's right," Brian chimed in. "We're out of the running, but you signed on for three whole months of no sex. You've still got another six weeks to go, man."

"Piece o' cake," Aidan said, reaching for the bowl of tortilla chips in the center of the table. "I'll show you guys how it's done."

"Right," Liam said, sarcasm dripping from his tone. "You're in complete control."

"Totally," Aidan boasted.

"Liar," Brian said, taking a sip of his beer.

"Hey," Aidan took exception. "Shouldn't you guys be ragging on Connor? *He's* the one who lost the bet, y'know."

"Thanks," Connor said, and absently smiled at the waitress as she brought them each a tall, frosty glass of beer. He took a long drink and let the icy, foamy drink slide through him, cooling him off.

It had been a long, hot day.

And every time his thoughts had returned to the night before, spent in Emma's arms, the temperature had only climbed.

"So," Liam asked in the sudden silence, "do we get to know who?"

Connor glanced up from his drink and found all three of his brothers watching him. Well, hell. Only a few weeks ago he'd sat in this very booth and laughed his tail off as Brian had confessed to dropping out of the bet. Funny, it had seemed hilarious at the time. Now...not so much.

"Emma," he said tightly.

"The mechanic?" Aidan's voice hitched in surprise.

A flicker of something hot and dangerous sparked into life inside Connor. He swiveled his head to stare at the brother sitting alongside him through narrowed eyes. "You've got a problem with Emma?" he asked tightly. "Something wrong with her?"

Aidan's eyes widened as he lifted both hands in mock surrender and shook his head. "Nope, not a thing. I was just surprised is all. Chill out, man."

"A little touchy aren't you?" Brian asked.

"And your point is..." Connor demanded, sparing the man opposite him a quelling look.

"No point, just an observation."

"Emma's a sweetheart," Liam's quiet voice spoke up,

and the three men looked at him. Liam shrugged. "Hey, she fixes my car and I think she's cute."

Brian lifted one eyebrow and chuckled. "You *are* a priest, remember?"

"I'm a priest, I'm not dead." Liam shook his head and then turned to focus on Connor. "So you and Emma are together now?"

Panic reared up inside Connor. He leaned back into the booth, as if to distance himself as much as possible from that question. "Together? No. We're not a couple or anything. We're just friends."

"*Naked* friends," Aidan said on a laugh.

"Best kind." Brian lifted his beer in salute.

"Friendships change," Liam mused quietly.

Connor slanted him a wary glance. It didn't help at all that he himself had been thinking the same damn thing all day. His friendship with Emma was important to him. They got along great, shared a love of cars and old movies and thunderstorms. They could talk about anything, and he trusted her as he trusted few other people in his life.

Connor's friends were important to him.

And Emma was a *friend.*

"Whatever you're thinking," he grumbled, "just forget about it. I'm not looking to get married like poor ol' Bri here."

"Hey," Brian objected. "It's not like I'm caught in a trap trying to chew my leg off to get free, you know."

"I didn't say that," Connor snapped. "I just said that it wasn't for me." Never had been, never would be. He didn't want to be married. Didn't want to have anyone depending on him. Didn't want to change who he was to accommodate someone else.

He liked his life just the way it was. Hot and cold running women streaming in and out of his life in a constantly shifting smorgasbord of femininity.

Emma was a great woman—but she wasn't going to be the *only* woman.

That's not what he was looking for.

Connor waved Brian off and concentrated on his brother the priest. "Don't start thinking that just because Emma and I heated up the sheets that it's going to be anything more than that, Liam."

"I don't know, bro," Aidan pointed out, helping himself to another chip, "you *did* give up a shot at ten thousand bucks for her."

Connor scraped one hand across his face and wished to hell he'd been born an only child. "It was just sex."

"You sure?" Liam asked quietly.

"Of course I'm sure." Connor picked up his beer and took a long swallow. As the conversation between his brothers went on without him, he fought down the stray thought niggling in the back of his mind.

The one that claimed he wasn't as sure as he was pretending to be.

CHAPTER NINE

"Mrs. Harrison," Emma said as she stalked around the confines of her small office, tethered by the coiled phone cord. "If you'd just reconsider, I could make you a very good offer for the car."

The woman on the other end of the phone line sighed, then said, in a soft, Southern drawl, "I know it seems silly to you, Emma dear, but I just can't bear to part with Sonny's car. He loved it so."

"But that's my point, Mrs. Harrison," Emma plunked down on the one uncluttered corner of her desk and stared off through the front windows at Main Street. "If Sonny loved the car so much, wouldn't he want to see it restored to all its former glory?"

"Well…"

While the older woman thought about that, Emma stared out at Baywater. Summer traffic was still as thick as the humid air. Even at sunset, tourists crowded the sidewalks and cars backed up at the streetlights. Horns blasted, people shouted, and kids, apparently immune to the heat, dashed along sidewalks on skateboards, dogs nipping and yelping at their sides.

A typical, ordinary, summer evening.

So why did everything feel so different?

Because *she* was different.

Emma sighed and told herself to get over it. To get past it. But how could she? For hours the night before, she and

Connor had made love. It was as if neither of them could bear to stop touching the other. He'd stayed with her until sunrise, leaving only when the first streaks of crimson splashed the horizon.

She'd walked him to the door and watched him stride to his car and then drive away and she hadn't once given in to the urge to call him back.

But it had been there.

A crouched, needy thing deep inside her. She'd fought it back and made herself remember the promise they'd made to each other after their first bout of soul-shattering sex.

Friends.

They'd vowed to remain friends and she wanted that. Absolutely. But she also wanted him in her bed. And just how was she supposed to get past that?

Oh, things were fast getting more complicated instead of easier.

"I don't know, dear," Mrs. Harrison said, dragging Emma gratefully away from her thoughts. "It just doesn't seem quite right to me somehow."

Emma sighed, but she wasn't really surprised. She spoke to Mrs. Harrison at least once a month, hoping to get the woman to part with that old Corvette. Sonny Harrison had been dead for forty years, but his mother still wasn't ready to let his car—all she had left of him—go. So Emma would give up today and try again in a month.

"I understand," she said, and a part of her really did. It had to be hard, losing the one last link to a past that felt more real than the present. It was pretty much how she'd felt the day she'd packed up all of her girly clothes after her ex-fiancé, Tony Demarco, had shown his true colors. But she'd gotten over the death of her dreams, and one of these days maybe Mrs. Harrison would, too. "I hope you don't mind if I keep trying to convince you, though."

"Not at all, honey. You call again real soon."

When they hung up, Emma smiled. She had a feeling that the elderly woman would never sell her that car—mainly because then she'd lose the fun of Emma's phone calls and visits.

The phone rang again almost instantly, and for one brief shining moment, Emma thought that maybe Mrs. Harrison had changed her mind. "Hello? Jacobsen's Garage."

"You haven't called me with an update."

"Mary Alice?"

"Who else?"

Emma smiled, walked around the edge of her desk and sat down in her chair. Kicking her feet up, she crossed her legs at the ankle on top of a stack of papers at the edge of the desk and said, "I've been meaning to call you."

"Uh-huh," her friend said, "and I've been meaning to go on a diet."

"Another one?" Emma grinned.

"Let's not get off track here," Mary Alice said quickly. "This isn't about *me.* I want details. When last I heard, Mr. Gorgeous Reilly was walking up to your office looking like dessert."

"Oh, wow…"

"I'm guessing that this is going to be a long story?"

"You have no idea." She'd meant to call Mary Alice. She really had. But she'd gotten so involved with her own plans and preparations for snapping a trap shut on Connor, that Emma'd completely forgotten about everything but the task at hand.

And after the night before, she thought, her insides curdling into a warm puddle of something sticky, she was lucky she could think at all.

"So talk."

"Where do you want me to start?" Emma asked, "With the first time or the last time?"

Mary Alice sucked in a breath that was audible even from three thousand miles away. "How many in between?"

"Three." Connor, Emma had learned during the long night, was a pretty amazing man. In stamina alone, the Marines were lucky to have him.

And so was she.

Whoops. A minor mental slip there.

She didn't actually *have* him, now did she?

"Oh, boy." A heavy sigh drifted through the phone line. "Hold on a sec."

A lot more than one second ticked past before Mary Alice spoke again. "Okay," she said. "I'm back. I needed a glass of wine for this. Start talking and remember to linger over the details."

Emma laughed and silently thanked her friend for calling when she most needed her. "God I love you."

"Ditto. Now spill your guts."

CONNOR'D HAD EVERY intention of staying away.

He'd reassured himself all day long that there'd be no problem in keeping his distance. It was for the best, anyway. For both of them. Last night had been amazing, but it was one night out of their lives.

Emma was his friend. That she was also the woman who'd nearly set his hair on fire the night before, wasn't important. The friendship *was.* So with that thought firmly in mind, he'd made a solemn vow to himself that he'd steer clear of her for at least the next few days.

Give them both a little breathing room.

Make the memory of last night a little dimmer before they spent time together again.

After dinner with his brothers, he'd even driven halfway home before he'd found himself turning around and heading back to Emma's house. The disappointment he'd felt at seeing the house dark and empty wasn't something he wanted to think about. And what he should have done was take her absence as a sign from above. Someone up there was looking out for him. Steering him away from Emma even when he was trying to hunt her down.

Instead though, he'd driven to the garage.

Over the past two years, there had been plenty of times when he'd worked late with her, helping her with a stubborn oil change or just sitting in the office talking. In fact, he hadn't really noticed—until he started trying to stay away from her—just how much time he actually spent with Emma.

Somehow or other, when he wasn't looking, she'd become an integral part of his day. She was usually the one he complained to about whichever new recruit was giving him fits. She was the one he laughed with over the stories Aidan told. She was the one who listened to him grouse about his dates, his job, his life.

Emma was more than a friend.

She was his *best* friend.

"And now you know what she looks like naked." He groaned tightly and told himself to shut that thought off fast. No way could he concentrate on driving if his brain was filled with images of Emma's smooth skin in the moonlight.

Beside him at the stoplight, a carload of teenagers were whooping and hollering. The girls looked shiny bright and the boys were busy trying to be cool. Music blasted through their open windows and into Connor's, shattering his thoughts. He smiled to himself as the light changed and the car sped off with a squeal of rubber on asphalt. He almost envied them.

Summer nights were made for long drives and laughter. For stolen kisses and slow walks. For sighs and whispers and the promise of more.

And damn it, he *wanted* more.

More of Emma.

"You're in bad shape," he muttered grimly as he steered the car toward the garage. His fingers clenched the steering wheel until his knuckles were white. His stomach jumped and his brain was shouting at him to stay the hell away from Emma.

But he wasn't listening.

He couldn't.

Besides, he thought, staying away from her was probably not the answer. *Not* seeing her only made him think about her more. Maybe *seeing* her would help him keep this whole business in perspective.

That thought made him feel a little better about the whole situation. Slapping the steering wheel with the flat of his hand, he nodded and said, "Exactly. She's your friend. So going to see her is just proving to both of you that you can deal."

If a small voice in the back of his mind whispered that he was just making excuses...he ignored it.

He pulled into the parking lot in front of Jacobsen's Garage and noticed that the office was dark but that lights were on in the garage bay. The oversize garage door was closed, but the half-moon-shaped windows above the door shone with soft lamplight.

Turning the engine off, he set the brake, clenched his jaw and realized that for the first time in his life, he felt like retreating.

That thought alone was enough to get him out of the car and moving toward the shop. The hot summer night closed in around him as he stalked across the parking lot like a man on a mission.

Emma'd always liked working late. She liked being here alone. Having time to think, she called it, and Connor wondered what she was thinking about tonight.

Opening the office door, which she should have had locked, damn it, Connor scowled and closed it behind him, turning the lock for good measure. What the hell was she thinking, working late and leaving the door open for just anybody to stroll inside? His stomach fisted as the thought of "what might have beens" rushed through his brain.

Idiotic, he knew. Baywater was a safe, tiny community and no doubt there was nothing to worry about. But he suddenly didn't like the idea of Emma working here late at night, all alone. He suddenly didn't like the idea of her *being* alone. And what the hell did *that* mean? It hadn't bothered him last week or last month or last year. Oh, man—

Shaking his head, Connor stepped into the air-conditioned office and headed for the connecting door to the garage. A wave of hot, steamy air rushed at him. The garage was not air-conditioned, since it would have been impractical, with the door wide open all day. There were fans whirring in every corner, but they didn't do much to reduce the ovenlike effect.

Connor didn't care, though. He stepped into the heat and closed the door to the office behind him. He heard the music first, and smiled in spite of the thoughts churning in his mind. Classic rock and roll, and if he knew Emma, she was singing along, safe in the knowledge that there was no one to hear her.

He paused in the shadows, giving himself time to simply admire the view.

She hadn't heard him come in—not surprising since

the radio volume was set at just under ear shattering. She wore coverall—standard, gray coverall that before wouldn't have given him a moment's pause. Today, though, he wasn't fooled. Today he knew what kind of weapons she was hiding beneath the too-baggy work uniform. And his body went hard just thinking about it.

She did a quick little sidestep, her hips swaying to the rhythm pounding out around her and her blond ponytail swung with her movements. She kept time with the rhythm even as her small, capable hands worked on the carburetor lying in pieces on the workbench.

He grinned when she picked up a wrench and, holding it as if it were a microphone, sang into it along with the voice pouring from the radio. Even though she had more enthusiasm than talent, Emma poured her heart into the song of love and loss, and something inside Connor twisted as he watched her.

Beautiful.

Even in the ugly gray coverall, she was beautiful.

Sure, he thought. *Friends*. No problem here.

Scraping one hand across his face, Connor breathed deeply, hoping to ease the instinct clamoring within. The one that was prompting him to march across the garage, grab her up and bury himself inside her as fast as he could. Every cell in his body was on high alert.

Coming here had been a lousy idea.

But he couldn't have left if it had meant his life.

When she lifted both arms high and did a spin to co-incide with the end of the song, she spotted him. Stopping dead, she squeaked out a half-choked-off scream and slapped one hand to her chest.

"Connor!" She took a deep, steadying breath, then blew it out in an exasperated rush. Reaching across the work-bench, she hit the volume button on the radio and cranked it down to background level. "Geez, you scared me half to death. Do you have to be all stealthy?"

Stealthy? Hell, he was surprised she hadn't heard his heart pounding over the blast of the radio. "Sorry. Didn't mean to surprise you."

"Next time say something."

"Like?"

"Like, hello?" Still agitated, she dropped the wrench onto the work surface, then rubbed her palms together. "How tough is that?"

Right now, he thought, pretty damn hard. Hard to talk at all past the knot of need lodged in his throat. But he forced a smile and said, "Fine. Hello, Emma."

She smiled, tipped her head to one side and studied him. "Something wrong?"

Hell, yes. He'd been thinking all day about getting his best friend naked again. That was wrong in so many ways.

But all he said was, "No."

"Didn't think I'd be seeing you today."

She wiped her hands on a clean rag, then tossed it onto the bench behind her. From the radio came a soft rush of guitars and drums, pulsing out around them.

"Yeah, me, neither."

She shoved her hands into the pockets of the coveralls. "So why are you here?"

Good question.

"Because we said we'd stay friends, Em. Because if I stay away from you because of last night, we'd lose that."

"True."

"And," he admitted, "I wanted to prove to myself that I could come here—see you—and not want to take you to bed again."

She frowned at him and he could have sworn the temperature in the garage dropped a few degrees. "Gee, that just makes me feel all warm and fuzzy."

"That probably came out wrong," he muttered.

"You think?"

"Damn it, Emma." He started across the garage toward her. He closed the distance between them with four long strides that took him around the front end of the sleek little convertible waiting to be serviced. When he was right on top of her, he stared down into her eyes. "This is new territory for me, ya know? I generally don't spend a lot of time thinking about getting my friends naked."

She grinned, and he felt the power of that smile reach in and grab his throat.

"Good to know."

"The point is," he said, letting his gaze slide across her features, from her tiny, straight nose to the curve of her mouth and back up to the depths of her eyes. He inhaled and blew the air out again in a rush. "The point is, I *am* thinking about getting you naked. And I'm thinking about it *way* too much."

She shivered and he fisted his hands at his sides to keep from reaching for her. If he touched her now, that would be it. No going back, no reining in, no turning away.

"So stop," she said, lifting her chin.

"Easier said than done."

"Yeah," she said on a sigh, "I know."

The tight, cold fist around his lungs eased back a little. "You, too?"

"Only every other minute or so." She backed up from him, as if just talking about this was getting a little too difficult. "But it'll pass. Right?"

"Shown no signs so far." He kept pace with her, taking one step forward for each of her backward steps.

"Only been a day."

"A *whole* day," he said.

"Right." She glanced around the shop as if looking for the nearest exit, then caught herself and stopped at the front end of the red sports car. "Twenty-four whole hours."

He nodded and moved in closer. "Thousands of minutes."

"Uh-huh." She licked her lips and stared up at him. "We're gonna do it again, aren't we?"

"Oh, yeah." He wanted her with everything in him. He'd never known such all-consuming hunger before, and a part of him wondered if it would always be this way. Was there no going back to the way things had been between him and Emma? Did he really *want* to go back?

Hell, no.

But at the same time Connor was forced to admit that if they couldn't go back, they'd have to go forward. There was no standing still.

Though maybe there *could* be. Just for tonight. Tomorrow was soon enough to think about the repercussions. Tonight all he wanted to do was recapture those hours he'd had with her the night before. Wanted to lose himself in the taste of her, surround himself with her heat and watch as her eyes glazed over with pleasure.

Everything else could just wait.

He bent, grabbed her up and kissed her, long and hard and deep. His tongue swept into her warmth and claimed another piece of her soul. Her breath mingled with his. Her tongue teased his. Her heartbeat shuddered in time with his own and when she arched into him, Connor's mind emptied of everything but the raging need pounding inside him.

Desperate to touch her, to have her, he reached for the zipper at the front of her coveralls and whispered, "I've gotta know what you're wearing under this thing."

Her eyes went wide. She grabbed his hands and held them still.

"What?" He met her gaze and saw embarrassment dart across the surface of her eyes. "What's wrong?"

"Nothing," she hedged, and lowered her gaze, still keeping a tight grip on his hands. "It's just…"

"Tell me."

She took a deep breath and forced herself to look up at him. "Fine. When I shut the garage bay doors, it was really hot in here and—well, I was all alone and—you know," she pointed out, "the shop was closed…"

"Will you just spit it out?"

Emma let go of his hands and huffed out a breath. "Fine. It's hot in here, so…"

"So?" Impatience clawed at him.

"So, I'm not wearing *anything* under it."

Connor's blood rushed through his veins. His body went hard and tight and eager. His breath staggered in his lungs. Looking down into her flushed face, he smiled and took hold of the zipper again. Giving it a tug, he stared at her lusciously delectable, completely naked body beneath those ugly gray coveralls and smiled as he whispered, "It's Christmas."

Emma laughed, but the sound ended abruptly as his hands covered her breasts. Thumbs and forefingers squeezed, tweaked and pulled at her nipples. She gasped and felt the drawing sensation right down to the soles of her feet.

From the corners of the room, fans pushed hot air at them, and still Emma felt as though she couldn't catch her breath. His hands. She'd been daydreaming about his hands all day and now suddenly, they were here, on her, driving her up that wild, slippery slope that led to an amazing reward.

"Gotta have you, Em," he murmured thickly as he leaned over her, pushing her back, back, until she lay atop the hood of the red convertible.

"Need you, Connor. Right now. Oh, please," she whispered as his mouth closed over one of her nipples, *"right now."*

His right hand dipped down her body, sliding across her abdomen, past the nest of tight curls at her center until he touched the heart of her. Light, skimming strokes pushed her higher, faster, than she'd ever been before. And still it wasn't enough.

"Now, Connor," she begged and even hearing the pleading in her own voice couldn't stop her from begging again. "I want you inside me. Now."

"Right now, baby." He lifted his head, pulled his hand free of her heat and reached for the shoulders of her coveralls. In one slick move, he'd scooped the fabric off her shoulders, down the length of her body and off. Then he was laying her back against the hood of the car and all she could think was, the metal still felt cool against her skin. Despite the hot air and the heat he created within her, the metal was cool and slick beneath her body.

Emma opened her eyes and watched him as he quickly undid his jeans and stepped out of them. Pulling his shirt off, he came to her, strong, muscular, tanned and ready. Emma's hands itched to touch him, to scrape her fingernails down his back and over the curve of his behind. She wanted to feel him atop her. Feel him fill her until all the lonely, empty spaces inside were quiet.

She licked her lips as if awaiting a treat, and he caught the motion and gave her a slow smile. Grabbing a condom from his wallet, he tore the paper open, smoothed the fragile rubber over himself and came to her. She lifted her legs, parting them wide in welcome and held her breath as he entered her on a sigh.

The radio played, a fast, pulsing tune that gave them the rhythm they both needed. Fast, hard, hungry. Again and again, they parted and rejoined as he plunged within her and each time was harder, stronger, more relentless than the last.

And as the end crashed down around them, Connor looked down into her eyes, and Emma lost herself in his dark-blue gaze. She cried out his name as the heat swallowed them and bound them even more tightly together.

CHAPTER TEN

"Okay," Emma said as soon as she was able to talk without her voice quavering, "this was a mistake."

"Hard to look at it like that when you're in my position," Connor quipped and grinned down at her.

That grin was such a potent weapon. And with his body still pressed to hers, still intimately invading hers, she could hardly argue the point. *However*, one of them had to make a stand—even if she was lying down when she did it.

"Get up, Connor."

"What's your hurry?" He nibbled at her throat, then deliberately ran his tongue across her skin.

Bubbles of fresh anticipation frothed to life inside her. She could almost hear her blood boiling. Every inch of her body felt alert, awake, *alive*—all because of him. How had they managed to know each other for two years and never discover the chemistry that lay sizzling between them? And how could they get back to where they'd been, now that they *had* discovered it?

Emma's stomach jittered at the thought that maybe they wouldn't be able to go back. Maybe by finding something special, they'd lost something equally important. She closed her eyes and bit back a groan. Then, gritting her teeth, she said, "I mean it, Connor," and slapped one hand against his back for emphasis. "Get up."

"Bossy little thing, aren't you?" he asked, lifting his

head to look down at her again. A self-satisfied half smile curved his mouth, and it was all she could do to keep from reaching up and defining that curve with her fingertips.

"How come I never noticed that about you before?"

"There are a lot of things you didn't notice."

"Yeah," he wiggled his eyebrows and leered at her. "But I'm catching on quick."

He rocked his hips against her, and her bones melted— along with what little resolve she'd been able to muster. Before she succumbed completely, though, she ordered, "Connor..."

"I'm moving, I'm moving."

He did. Slowly, tantalizingly. As if he were tormenting her for ending this little...*session.*

Emma stifled a groan and bit down on her bottom lip to keep from asking him to stay. To make love to her again. Oh, she had to be out of her mind. Here she had a gorgeous, talented lover at her disposal and she was telling him thanks but no thanks?

Her brain screamed at her to be rational, and her body was shouting just as loudly to stop thinking and just feel. She wasn't sure which of them was the stronger at the moment, so as soon as she could, Emma slid off the hood of the car and quickly grabbed up her coveralls. With clothing, might come clear thinking. Heaven knew it wasn't there when she was naked.

The fans blew a constant stream of heated air against her sweat-dampened skin, and chills rippled along her spine. She shivered and kept moving.

Stepping into her clothes again, Emma kept her back to Connor until she was dressed, with the zipper pulled up to her throat. Stupid, since he'd already seen her naked, but hey, she needed all the armor she could get at the moment. Shoving the oversize sleeves up to her elbows, she took a deep breath, ignored the hum still reverberating throughout her body and turned around to face him.

He had his jeans on, but he was still bare-chested, and a more tempting sight Emma couldn't imagine. Her mouth watered and she felt her resistance melting like ice in a warm drink. Oh, she'd really opened up a huge can of worms by starting all this. And if she could have figured out how to do it, she would have kicked her own behind.

They'd been happy. Fine. Good friends. Then she'd let herself get all huffy and offended, and now see where they'd landed. Up a creek without even a boat—let alone a paddle. And she had absolutely no idea how to undo it.

Or even if she wanted to.

And that one thought worried her.

Because she was slipping.

She could feel it.

Her heart ached, just looking at him. If the situation were different—if *she* were different, she might have allowed herself a little dreaming. Might have let what she already felt for him blossom. Might have indulged in the hopes and fantasies that she'd once believed in.

But fantasies were fragile, and dreams were tricks your mind played on you. She knew that. She'd learned her lesson the hard way. So she ached at the knowledge that nothing would ever be the same between Connor and her again.

Their easy friendship was gone, burned in a fire she hadn't expected to find.

"Whatever you're thinking," he said softly, "it looks serious."

"What?"

"Should I be worried?" He yanked his dark-red T-shirt over his head and shoved his arms through the sleeves.

"One of us should be," she murmured. Then louder she said, "We can't keep doing this."

He grinned again. "Give me five minutes, I think I could change your mind."

No doubt he could. But that wasn't the point. "Connor, I'm trying to do the right thing, here."

"Well, cut it out." Scowling, he reached over and flipped off the radio. With the music suddenly cut off, the whir of the fans was the only sound as they faced each other.

Emma could have sworn she could actually *see* electricity flashing back and forth between them. Heaven knew she felt the heat. But she closed her heart to it. Sighing, she said, "Last night was a bump in the road."

"More than one," he commented wryly.

She ignored it. "But tonight just proves that this is getting out of hand."

Scowling, he said, "Okay, I admit, things got a little out of hand tonight—"

"Yeah, just a little."

He shook his head and folded his arms over his chest. He braced his long legs in a wide apart, battle stance and Emma wondered idly who he was preparing to fight? Her? Or himself?

"You should know this isn't why I came here tonight."

Of course she knew that. After all, no one would *plan* to have sex on the hood of a car. She sighed again. "I know, it's just—"

"I came to talk since I couldn't find you at home," he continued, cutting her off neatly. "And, hey—" he broke off and glared down at her "—by the way, lock the damn door when you're here alone, Emma."

"Excuse me?"

"The door to the shop. It was unlocked. For God's sake, anybody could have come in."

"Anybody did," she said, stiffening in self-defense.

"Yeah, but you *know* me."

"I used to think so."

"What's *that* supposed to mean?" he demanded.

Temper flared into life inside her, and Emma clung to it desperately. Anger was easier to deal with than whatever it was she was feeling for Connor at the moment. "It means that whether or not I lock my doors is up to *me*."

"Who the hell said it wasn't?" He unfolded his arms and threw his hands high as if trying to catch the threads of the argument that were quickly spiraling out of his control.

"You did," she snapped, folding her own arms across her chest and glaring back at him. This was comfort. This was safety. An argument with Connor she could handle. Tenderness from him left her wary and unsure of herself. "I'm perfectly safe here."

He frowned at her, his dark-blue eyes getting nearly frosty. "Probably," he admitted. "But it's stupid to take chances, Emma."

"I'm not stupid, and I don't need you to tell me what to do."

He gaped at her. "I didn't say you were stupid."

"You did, too, just a minute ago."

"I said it was stupid not to lock the door."

"And since I didn't, I'm stupid."

"What the hell's going on with you, Emma?" His voice growled out with the strength and ferocity of a grizzly bear coming out of winter hibernation, looking for a meal.

She didn't *know*. God help her, she just didn't know. Thoughts, emotions, feelings, splintered inside her and the slippery shards were too fragile...too many to identify. All she knew for sure was that she needed to be alone. She needed to think. Desperately she fought to control the rising sense of panic clawing at her insides. "I don't like being ordered around."

He sucked in a huge gulp of air, swallowed it and paused, as if silently counting to ten. Or twenty. Emma could have told him it wouldn't help. She'd already tried it.

Finally he spoke again, keeping his voice low and even. "I'm not *telling* you what to do. I'm just saying I was worried when I saw you were vulnerable and—"

Oh, she was plenty vulnerable. But not in the way he meant. Everything inside her was a churning, dazzling swirl of need and fury. She wanted him and couldn't have him. Needed him and didn't want to. Loved him and—

Oh, God.

She staggered back a step.

Felt the blood drain from her head until the room tilted ominously.

She loved Connor Reilly.

Air rushed in and out of her lungs in short, sharp gasps. The edges of her vision sparkled with white and blue dots, and she wondered absently if this is what an out-of-body experience felt like. For a second or two she worried that she might faint. Then the thought of waking up and having to explain to Connor just what had prompted the faint quickly slapped her back into shape.

Heat pulsed inside her, then was rapidly replaced by an icy chill that made her shiver reflexively.

Love?

OhGodohGodohGod.

Trouble. Big trouble.

No way out.

She slapped one hand to her forehead and rubbed at

the sudden throbbing of a massive headache. But it wasn't going anywhere. Her brain felt as if it were about to explode. Her mouth was dry, it hurt to swallow and still she had to speak. Had to say something to keep him from noticing that she was currently in the middle of a minor nervous breakdown.

She pulled in a shaky breath and blew it out before trying to speak. "I'm not *yours* to worry about Connor."

How did the man go from smoldering lover to scolding big brother in ten seconds flat? And for pity's sake, how could she *love* him for it?

"I-didn't-say-that." Each word was bitten off as if it tasted bitter. "All I said was—"

She held up one hand and tried not to notice that it was shaking. Then, curling her fingers into her palm, she said, "I heard you the first time. But whether or not I lock the door is no concern of yours."

He was right, though, and that only made her madder. She never worked late without locking herself in the garage. Baywater was safe, she knew, but she didn't take foolish chances. And if she *had* locked the stupid door, then Connor couldn't have sneaked up on her, they wouldn't have made love again and *she* wouldn't have had to face the completely startling fact that she'd gone and fallen in love.

"Now I can't worry about you?"

She shot him a hard look, fired by the anger rippling through her at her own stupidity. "Did you worry *before* we went to bed together?"

He started to speak, then closed his mouth again. But then, she didn't need to hear his answer. She already knew what it was.

"No, you didn't," she said for him. Fury pulsed wildly inside her, like a living, breathing creature, completely separate from her. He was just like Tony, she thought frantically. This was déjà vu and she didn't want to go back there. Didn't want to remember the pain, the disappointment, the regret of having loved someone who couldn't or wouldn't understand her.

Like Tony, Connor wasn't seeing the *real* her.

"When we were just friends," she said hotly, "you assumed I could take care of myself. Now that we've been naked together, apparently I've lost a few brain cells."

"Damn it, Em," he took a step toward her, then stopped dead. "I didn't say that, either."

"You didn't have to," she snapped. "I can see it in your face. God, Connor, it's practically stamped on your forehead."

"What're you talking about?"

"You. Me. *This.*" She waved one hand at the car where they'd just made love and nearly shivered. But she stiffened her spine instead. "I've been down this road before, Connor. Trust me, I'm not going to do it again."

"What's that mean?"

"You're just like Tony."

He threw his hands high. "Who the hell's *Tony?*"

"I was engaged to him three years ago."

He blinked at her. His expression was thunderstruck. He looked like a man who'd just been pummeled with a two by four and wasn't sure whether to stagger or fall down.

"Engaged?" He repeated after a moment or two. "You were *engaged?* Why didn't I know about this?"

"You never asked."

He opened his mouth, then snapped it shut again.

She shook her head and stared up at him, too wound up to be quiet now, even if that might have been the better thing to do. "You're just like him, I swear. He never noticed me until I wore girly clothes. Just like you, Connor.

And when I was just *me,* he wasn't interested. He even wanted me to sell the garage. Become the perfect little wife who baked cookies and drove in car pools. Well, there's nothing wrong with that, but it's not *me.*"

"And I'm like that moron exactly *how?*"

"Oh, please," she said, on a roll now and unwilling to quit. "You never looked twice at me until that night at the bar."

"That doesn't—"

She cut him off, unwilling to listen to lame-ass excuses. "When I'm a woman, you want to protect me. When I'm *me,* that all changes. Well, guess what, Connor? I'm the same person. Whether I'm in a skirt or these coveralls."

"I know that—"

"I don't think you do. I think you're all hot and bothered over the girly Emma. Well, that's not who I am, Connor." She waved a hand at the grease-spattered coveralls. "*This* is me. The real me. And she's not someone you'd go for. Face it."

"So now you read minds?"

She choked out a laugh. "Yours isn't that hard to read."

Darn it, everything was falling apart. Just like she'd known it would. She never should have let this get started. Never should have tried to set him up, because in doing so, she'd knocked the earth out from under her own feet and now she was on shaky ground.

And the fact that a part of her almost wished she were the girly-girl type—the kind of woman that Connor would want—really irritated her.

"So you've got this all figured out," he said tightly.

"You bet."

"You get engaged to a jerk and then figure every other guy is just like him?"

"Not every guy."

"Just me."

She nodded, not trusting herself to speak.

"The man was an idiot."

"Yeah," Emma said, "but at least he was honest about what he wanted. You're not being honest, Connor. Not with me. Not with yourself."

"That's just perfect," he muttered, shoving both hands along the sides of his head as if trying to keep his skull from exploding.

Well, she knew just how he felt. Funny how the warm, delicious buzz she'd been feeling only a few moments ago had completely faded away. Now all that was left was a sense of loss.

And just a touch of mind-numbing panic.

"You should probably just go, Connor."

"Not till we talk about this."

She laughed and the sound of it was shrill, even to her. "We've been talking, Connor. And we're going in circles. What's left to talk about?"

"Us. What's going on. Where we go from here."

"We did that last night. We decided to remain *friends*—" God, that word sounded empty "—remember?"

"Yeah," he said with a glance at the car's hood, "that seems to be working real well."

"Well it would have if you hadn't come over," she snapped.

"Ah." Connor nodded slowly, his deep-blue eyes hazy with an emotion she couldn't quite read and wasn't sure she wanted to. "So the secret to us handling this is to stay the hell away from each other?"

"Apparently."

"And our friendship?"

Emma looked up at him and felt her defenses crumbling. If he stayed much longer, she just might do something totally idiotic, like throw herself into his arms and say to hell with doing the smart thing. But that wouldn't solve anything. It would only serve to make this harder eventually. Because she knew that Connor wasn't looking for love.

Heck, he never dated the same woman more than three times.

He wasn't a man to build fantasies around, even if she was still into daydreaming. Which she most certainly was *not*. She'd learned her lesson about love. And this time she'd take her lumps in private. Connor would never know that she was hurt. She wouldn't let him close enough to see that he had the power to crush her—whether he wanted it or not.

Tony Demarco's betrayal had hurt her.

When Connor did the same thing, it would kill her.

Nope.

She wouldn't let that happen.

"I'm not going to lose what we have," Connor said, when she didn't answer him. He stepped close enough to drop both hands onto her shoulders and squeeze. "Damn it, Emma, I *like* you. The *real* you. I like spending time with you and I don't want to lose that."

He *liked* her and she was in *love*. Oh, yeah. Fate had a twisted sense of humor.

"We've already lost it, Connor."

His hands tightened on her shoulders. "What's that supposed to mean?"

She swallowed hard, yanked free of his grip and turned her back on him, headed for the office. He caught up with her in a few long strides, grabbed her upper arm and turned her around to face him. His grip on her arm felt strong and warm. And the thought of never feeling his hands on her again made her want to whimper.

But because she was feeling just a little shaky, she straightened her spine, lifted her chin and met his gaze squarely. "You know just what it means. How are we supposed to pretend nothing's changed when everything has changed?"

"There's a way," he said.

"Well, when you find it, you let me know."

Connor's brain scrambled, trying to keep up with Emma. Wasn't easy, either. Not when his blood was still pumping and his body was still hot and eager.

But looking into her eyes now made Connor *want* to say the right thing. Somehow or other, he'd lost control of whatever it was between them. Not that he'd ever really had control.

Damn it, she'd been *engaged*. To some clown who'd hurt her. And now he was hurting her, too. The one thing he hadn't wanted to do, he'd ended up doing, just the same. Really pissed him off. And left him with a helpless feeling that he wasn't used to experiencing.

"I think you should just go, Connor."

Her voice, small and quiet, snapped him out of his thoughts and back to the moment.

Instinctively he reached for her again. She stepped back, avoiding his touch, and he felt the sting of it jab at him. His hand fisted on emptiness and dropped to his side. Something dark and cold settled in his gut, and Connor had the distinct impression that it was there to stay.

"Emma—"

"Just go. Please."

He blinked at her, too surprised to speak. Momentarily. "You're telling me to leave?"

She gave him a sad smile. "I'm *asking* you to leave."

He swallowed hard and battled a growing sense of desperation. In all the time they'd known each other, they'd never been so far apart. And even though she was just an arm's reach away, Connor had the feeling that with every passing second, she drifted even further from him.

She sighed and lifted one hand to rub at her forehead again. Guilt zapped him. Damn it, he hadn't meant to make her feel bad. Hadn't meant to start an argument that had no beginning and no end. Hadn't meant to *hurt* her.

Hadn't even meant to come here tonight.

Just like he didn't want to leave her now. Not when nothing had been settled. Not when she looked so damn… *sad.* But if he stayed, he'd only make this worse. She didn't want him here, fine.

He'd go.

For now.

Nodding, he choked back his own wants and said. "Okay, I'll go."

She gave him a smile that was so small, it was hardly worth the effort. But he appreciated it just the same.

"Thanks."

"This isn't over," he said before he stepped past her and opened the door. He stopped on the flower-bedecked porch and felt the warm summer air wrap itself around him. Looking back over his shoulder at her, he worked up a half-assed smile and said softly, "Please lock the door, Emma."

CHAPTER ELEVEN

EMMA BURIED HERSELF in work.

For the past three days, she'd done tune-ups and oil changes and rebuilt two carburetors. She gave her mechanics a few days off and handled everything herself to make sure she kept busy. For three days she concentrated solely on the garage, and when she ran out of cars to work on, she replanted the flower beds.

Anything to keep from thinking about Connor.

And still it didn't help.

Mary Alice had sympathized and even offered to send her husband out to beat up Connor. But Emma didn't want him bruised—she wanted him to love her. Which wasn't going to happen.

Standing in the garage bay, she glanced toward where the car they'd made love on had been parked. And though the car was gone now, the memories remained.

Every touch, every sigh, every whisper was as fresh and clear in her mind as if it had just happened. She remembered his smile, the shine in his eyes and the feel of his hands on her skin. Her body ached for him and her heart just plain *ached.*

"Oh, man…" She set the torque wrench down and rubbed her eyes with the tips of her fingers. She hadn't slept more than a few hours in the past three days. Up at dawn, she worked late at the shop, trying to avoid sleep because every time she closed her eyes, Connor appeared in living color.

She'd done this to herself, she knew. She'd walked into this with her eyes wide open—and her heart undefended. But she hadn't ever considered that it would be in danger. How could she have guessed that the love she used to dream about would be found in the arms of her best friend?

"And the worst part," she said, picking up the wrench again and squeezing it tightly, "is that I can't talk to my *best friend* about any of it. And darn it, Connor, I *miss* you."

THE SUN WAS BRIGHT, the sky clear and the ocean calm. In short, it was the perfect day for some saltwater fishing. A couple of times a season, Brian borrowed a little sport fisher boat from one of his pilot buddies, and the four Reilly brothers had a long day at sea—away from phones and work. Ordinarily Connor would have enjoyed the day out with his brothers.

Today he was forcing himself just to pay attention. Disgusted, Connor shifted his gaze from the frothing sea to the deck, where his brothers gathered around an open cooler.

"I'm telling you," Aidan said, pausing to take a sip of beer, "the wind was so high, the chopper was rocking back and forth like somebody was trying to shake us out. J.T. had hold of the stick with both hands, fighting to keep us steady. Right under us, the Sunday sailor's clinging to the upended bottom of his boat and he's holding on for dear life."

"Probably glad to see you then, huh?" Brian smiled and snapped his right wrist back, then forward, casting his line out into the ocean. Then he stuck the bottom of his rod into the pole holder on the side of the boat and set the bail on the reel. Leaning back, he watched Aidan and waited for the rest of the story.

"See that's the deal," Aidan went on, looking from one brother to the next with mock outrage. "There I am, jumping out of a chopper into storm surf—the waves were seven, maybe ten feet high—just to save this guy's ungrateful butt and does he thank me? Hell no, he takes a swing at me when I try to get him into the rescue basket."

"What?" Liam sounded incredulous, but Aidan's story didn't surprise Connor. People always reacted weird in a panic situation. Which is why Marines came in so handy during a disaster. Cool heads.

And God knew Aidan needed a cool head doing his job. Working on the USMC sea rescue team, they were the guys called out to help stranded boaters or pick up pilots after they'd ditched their planes in the sea. The job was hard, dangerous and right up his brother's alley.

Aidan laughed. "No shit. The guy's panicked. Won't let go of the hull of his boat. Water's slapping at him, wind's howling, and he won't let go of the damn boat. Finally, he pries one hand off to take that swing at me, tells me he's afraid of heights and he wants us to send a ship out for him."

"A ship?" Liam asked laughing. "You mean like the one that sunk out from under him?"

"Exactly." Aidan leaned back against the side of the boat and drew both knees up, resting his forearms atop them.

"So how'd you get him in the basket?" Connor asked, drawn into the story in spite of the turmoil racing in his mind.

Aidan laughed. "I climbed into the basket myself and said, 'see ya.' The guy was so stunned that I'd leave him out there, he let go of the hull and jumped at the basket. I got out, got him in and Monk hoisted him up." He shook his head and sighed fondly. "Hell of a ride."

"Yeah, yeah, Mr. Hero," Brian teased and walked toward the hatch leading to the galley below deck. "Come on, hero. Help me carry up that mountain of sandwiches Tina made for us."

"Tina made food?" Aidan asked, clearly worried. "Is it safe?"

"Hey," Brian complained as he started down the short flight of steps. "She's getting better."

Aidan groaned and muttered, "She couldn't get any worse without killing us."

"Yeah, well," Brian said, chuckling, "Tina's not real fond of you, so maybe you should watch what you eat."

"What d'you mean she's not fond of me?" Aidan's voice was outraged. "I'm the *fun* one!"

But he followed Brian out of the sunshine into the galley, leaving Liam and Connor alone on deck. The screech of the seagulls sounded weird and otherworldly in the silence. Off in the distance a sailboat caught the wind and flew across the ocean's surface, its red sails bellied, as it raced toward the horizon. Overhead, clouds scuttled across a deep-blue sky and briefly blotted out the sun's heat.

Connor sighed and focused his gaze on the distant spot where sky and sea met, blurring the lines of both. In the quiet, the gentle smack of the water against the hull was soothing, but didn't seem to help the thoughts churning in his mind.

He probably shouldn't have gone along with his brothers today. But if he'd tried to get out of it, he'd have had to come up with explanations he wasn't ready to make.

"Want to tell me what's going on?" Liam asked and

sat perched on the edge of the boat's stern. He braced his hands on his knees and waited.

Connor flicked him a glance, then shifted his gaze back to the horizon's edge. "Nope."

Liam nodded, reached out and fiddled with the reel on Connor's fishing rod.

"What're you doing?"

"The bail was locked. Anything nibbles at your line, you lose the rod."

Connor sighed. Hell, he hadn't made that mistake since he was a kid and their father had taken them all out on the half-day fishing boats. "Thanks."

"You're welcome."

Liam fell into silence, gaze fixed on Connor until he shifted uneasily under that steady stare. "What're you looking at?"

"A man with a problem."

Major understatement, Connor thought, but kept his mouth shut. He just wasn't the kind of guy who needed to "vent" his feelings. He'd never wanted to hug and cry and learn and grow. He didn't mind listening to his friends' problems when they needed someone to talk to. But his own problems remained just that. His own.

"Knock it off, Liam."

"Hey, just sitting here."

"Well, sit somewhere else."

"It's a small boat," his brother said, shrugging.

"Getting smaller every damn minute," Connor muttered. He lifted his right foot and braced it on the stern. "Don't you have a rosary to say or something?"

Liam grinned, unoffended. "I'm taking the day off."

"Lucky me."

"True."

"What?"

Liam smiled again. "You are lucky, Connor. You have a career you love, a family willing to put up with you and a beautiful day to do some fishing. So, you want to tell me why you look like a man who just lost his best friend?"

That last, stray statement hit a little close to home, and Connor winced. He stood up, walked to the edge of the boat and braced both hands on the gleaming wood railing. He shot Liam a quick look, then shifted his gaze back to the unending, rolling sea. "I think I *have* lost my best friend."

"Ahh…"

Connor snorted in disgust. "Don't give me Father Liam's patented, generic, sympathetic sigh."

"You want more specific sympathy, tell me what's going on."

"It's Emma."

"I figured that much out already." When Connor looked at him again, Liam shrugged. "Not that hard to work out, Connor. You lost the bet to her and now I'm thinking you lost something else to her as well."

"Like?"

"Your heart?"

Connor jerked up straight, as if he'd been shot. He viciously rubbed the back of his neck, then pushed that hand into the pocket of his jeans shorts. "Nobody said anything about love."

"Until now," Liam mused.

"You know," Connor pointed out with a sidelong glare, "you can be pretty damn annoying for a brother, *Father*."

"So I've heard." Liam stood up, too, and faced his younger brother. "Talk to me, Connor."

With a quick glance at the galley steps to make sure Brian and Aidan were still out of earshot, Connor blurted, "I think I'm losing my mind." Then he glared at his older brother. "And it's all your fault. The stupid bet. That's what started all this."

"Ahh..." Liam turned his face away to hide his smile. He wasn't entirely successful.

Connor muttered, "That's great. Laugh at your own brother's misery."

"What's a brother for?"

The boat rocked, sea spray drifted with the breeze and, overhead, seagulls kept watch, looking for supper.

"What's making you miserable?" Liam asked.

"Emma."

"This is getting better."

"Damn it, Liam." Connor stalked to the corner of the boat, then turned around and came back again. "Something's wrong."

Liam frowned. "With Emma? Is she okay?"

"*She's* okay. I'm the one in trouble."

"Oh."

Connor blew out a breath and viciously rubbed his face with both hands before dropping them to his sides. He couldn't believe this was happening. Not to him. Not to the man who'd firmly believed that the reason God had created so many beautiful women was to make love and marriage unnecessary.

All his life, one woman had been pretty much like the next. He'd figured if he lost one, there'd be another one right around the corner. Now? Now the only woman he wanted, didn't want *him.*

It had been three long days since the night he'd left Emma in her shop. Three days and three even-longer nights.

He'd tried everything he knew to keep his mind off her. He'd thought about asking some other woman out, but he just couldn't work up any interest in someone who wasn't

Emma. He'd gone to his favorite hangout, but every time he saw that pool table, he saw Emma, stretched across it, her perfect legs tormenting him. Hell, he couldn't even work on his car without thinking about her.

His dreams were full of her image and every waking thought eventually wandered back to her. His chest felt tight every time he realized that she just might not want to see him again. Unconsciously he rubbed his chest with one hand and looked at Liam. "She won't talk to me."

"Does she have a reason?"

"Maybe." Remembering the look on her face when she'd told him about the idiot Tony, Connor winced. He hadn't been looking for a relationship. Hadn't wanted one. Hadn't expected to find one.

He'd lived his life pretty much on his own terms and had never considered changing. So *why,* he wanted to know, did the fact that Emma wouldn't talk to him, hurt him badly enough to make his whole insides ache with it?

Love?

Inwardly he reared back from the thought. Love? *Him?* Panic chewed on him.

He didn't *do* love.

"Hell," Connor muttered, still trying to get over the shock of what he might be feeling, "I really don't know anything anymore."

"Never thought I'd hear *you* say something like that."

"What?" Connor asked wryly, "a priest doesn't believe in miracles?"

"Good point." Liam leaned against the stern, crossed his arms over his chest and stared at him. "What are you going to do about this, Connor?"

He shook his head. "I think I've done enough already." Hell, he'd made his best friend throw him out of her place.

He'd fixed it so she wouldn't talk to him. So she couldn't stand the sight of him. Oh, yeah. His work was done.

"So you're gonna quit? Walk away?"

Connor fixed him with an evil look. "You're manipulating me."

"No kidding."

"And who said anything about quitting?"

"Then, what's the plan?"

"If I knew that, would I be standing here being insulted by you?"

Liam grinned. "Okay, but aren't you the guy who said, and I think I'm quoting here, 'the day I need advice on women from a priest is the day they can shave my head and send me to Okinawa'?"

Man, the hits just kept on coming. Blowing out a breath, Connor grumbled, "Fine. I'm an idiot. I need advice."

Liam slapped one hand on his brother's shoulder. "Then here it is. You've already opened your eyes about Emma— maybe it's time you opened your heart."

"That's it?" he asked. "That's all you've got?"

Liam laughed. "Think about it, grasshopper. The answers will come."

"*Before* I'm old and gray?"

"Probably." Liam bent and opened the cooler. "Want a beer?"

"Open my heart." Connor snorted and stepped out of his car into the humid night air. Liam's words echoed in his mind as they had all day. He looked at the garage, the light gleaming behind the windows and knew Emma was in there. His stomach fisted like he was about to tiptoe through a minefield.

Love?

Was he in love with Emma? He still didn't know the answer to that one.

He *liked* her. More than he ever had anyone else. It bothered hell out of him that they weren't speaking. That she didn't want to see him. And it really bothered hell out of him that he couldn't think about anything *but* Emma.

"But that's all going to change now," he murmured. It had taken him most of the day to figure out what Liam's advice had meant. Then it had finally hit him.

Stop treating Emma like his *friend* and start treating her like a *woman*.

He smiled to himself as he reached into the car and pulled out the white-tissue-paper-wrapped bouquet of red roses. Their scent was heavy, cloying and just right. Still smiling, he held the flowers in his left hand and grabbed up the gold foil box of expensive chocolates.

Finally. He felt in control.

This he knew.

"*This* I'm good at." Hell, he could write a how-to book for guys on how to smooth talk a woman out of being mad. Flowers, chocolate and a few kisses had bailed him out of trouble with women more times than he could count.

All he had to do was show her that he appreciated her. Show her that what they'd found was more than a one-night—or two-night—stand. Then, once she was softened up, they could find a way to deal with the changes in their relationship.

He straightened up, kicked the car door closed and headed for the garage. Automatically he tried the door-knob and was pleased to find she'd locked it. "At least she listened about that."

Clutching the box of candy, he rapped the door with his knuckles and waited what felt like forever for her to answer. When she did, she opened the door only a few inches and peered out at him.

Through that narrow opening, he could see only one of her beautiful eyes and the tips of her fingers wrapped around the edge of the door. Partially hidden as if protecting herself, she was wearing the gray coveralls again, and a part of him wondered if she was naked beneath it. But then his body stirred and his mouth went dry, so he attempted to steer his brain away from the roller-coaster ride it was headed for.

"Connor. What're you doing here?"

"I needed to see you, Em," he said, and lifted the roses and candy, just in case she hadn't spotted them. "And I wanted to bring you these."

"Roses."

He smiled and took a step closer. "And candy."

She laughed shortly, a harsh, stiff sound that held no humor, and pushed the door a bit more closed. "You still don't get it."

Confused, he frowned and stared at her. "Get what? I'm just trying to be nice, here. What's going on, Emma?"

She looked at him for a long, silent minute. Connor could have sworn he could actually *hear* his own heartbeat in the deafening quiet. Then at last she opened the door wider and stepped out from behind it. Folding her arms across her chest, she shook her head and stared up at him.

Only then did he see the sheen of emotion glistening in her eyes. And he knew, instinctively, that he'd done something wrong. But for the life of him, he couldn't figure out *what*.

"You brought me roses."

"So?"

"I hate roses."

Something clicked in the back of his brain and he

wanted to kick himself. He'd *known* that, damn it. Known that Emma's favorite flowers were carnations. His left hand squeezed the bouquet tightly as if he were hoping he could just make the damn flowers disappear. But he couldn't, so he said, "You're right. I didn't think. I—"

Emma lifted her chin and stared into his eyes. To Connor's horror, those beautiful eyes of hers filled with tears, and he prayed like hell they wouldn't spill over.

"No, you didn't think," she said sadly. "Not about *me*. You bought me your traditional make-up present and figured that would do it."

"Emma..." This wasn't going the way he'd planned. Nothing was working out. He was getting in deeper and felt the quicksand beneath his feet sucking at him.

Desperation clawed at him as he realized that by trying to make things better between them, he'd only made them worse.

"I told you three days ago, Connor," she said, her voice still just a low, disappointed hush, "the foo-foo girl thing is *not* me. The me you were with before doesn't exist. Not really. And the me I really am, you don't want."

His insides trembled, and he scrambled to find the right words to say. But nothing was coming to him. The one time he needed the ability to smooth talk, he was coming up empty.

He'd hurt her again.

And that knowledge delivered a pain to his soul like nothing he'd ever known before.

Suddenly it was more important than it had been to get through to her. He felt as though he was sliding down a rocky cliff, trying to grab something to stop his fall. But there was nothing there. "Emma, I know I did this wrong..." He let his hands, still holding the offerings she hadn't wanted, fall to his sides. "I just wanted us to be friends again."

"I don't want to be your *friend,* Connor."

Her voice was too small, too hushed, too full of pain, and every word she spoke fell like a rock into the bottom of his heart. "Why the hell not?"

"Because I love you, Connor."

"Emma—"

"Don't say anything, okay?" She held one hand up for quiet. "Please." She choked out a laugh that sounded as though it had scraped her throat. "This is my fault and I'll get over it—*trust me.*" She inhaled sharply, deeply, then blew it all out again, lifting one hand to swipe at a single, stray tear glistening on her cheek.

Connor's chest tightened as though he were in a giant vise and some unseen hand was forcing it closed around him. He couldn't breathe. His heart hurt, his hands ached to hold her and he *knew,* without a doubt, that if he tried to reach for her, Emma would turn him away. And he didn't know if he could take that.

So instead he stood there like an idiot while the woman who meant so much to him battled silent tears.

"I can't be your lover anymore, Connor," she said and he swallowed hard at the calm steadiness in her eyes. "It would kill me to have you and yet never have you—you know? And I can't be your friend anymore, either—"

She gulped in air and kept talking, her words rushing from her in a flood of emotion that was thick enough to choke both of them.

"Emma—"

"No. I can't be your buddy and listen to you complain about the women in your life. I don't want to hear about the date of the week or the hot brunette who caught your eye."

Guilt raged inside him and battled with another, stronger feeling that was suddenly so real, so desperate, he trembled with the force of it.

For the first time in his life, Connor felt helpless.

And he didn't like it one damn bit.

"Go away, Connor," she said as another tear slid down her cheek. Stepping back from the doorway, she pushed the door closed. As she did, she said softly, "And do us both a favor, okay? This time when you go? Stay away."

Then the door closed, and Connor, the damn roses in one hand and a box of chocolates in the other, was left standing alone in the growing darkness.

Despite the hot summer night, he felt cold to the bone.

CHAPTER TWELVE

THE NEXT MORNING EMMA had a pickup truck that needed a new timing belt, an SUV with bad brakes and a headache that wouldn't quit.

Too many tears and not enough sleep.

And the way she was feeling, she didn't see things changing anytime soon.

For most of the night she'd agonized over blurting out her love to Connor. *Why* hadn't she just kept her big mouth shut? Bracing her elbows on her desktop, she cupped her face in her hands and tried desperately to forget the look on his face when she'd said the three little words designed to inspire panic in the hearts of men everywhere.

"Oh, God." She swallowed hard and took a deep breath. "Emma, you idiot. You never should have said it. Now he *knows.* Now he's probably feeling *sorry* for you. Oh, man..."

She jumped up from the desk, started for the door to the garage bay, then changed her mind and whipped around, walking toward the bank of windows instead. She couldn't go into the garage. She didn't want to talk to the guys. Didn't want them wondering why her eyes were all red. Didn't want anyone else knowing that she'd allowed her heart to be flattened by an emotional sledgehammer.

"Maybe I could sell the shop," she whispered. "Leave town—no, leave the state." Then she caught herself and muttered, "Great. Panic. Good move."

She wasn't going to leave. Wasn't going to hide.

What she *was* going to do, was live her life. Pretend everything was normal and good until eventually, it *would* be. Positive mental attitude. That was the key. She'd just keep her thoughts positive and her tears private.

Everything would work out.

Everything would be good again.

"God, I'm such a liar." Sighing, Emma thought about going home, but that wouldn't solve anything. At least here, in the shop, she had things to concentrate on. She could catch up on paperwork.

Of course, what she wanted to do was lie down somewhere in the dark and go to sleep. Then hopefully, when she woke up again, her heart would be healed and she'd be able to think of Connor without wanting to either hug him or slug him.

But it wouldn't be that easy, she knew.

She was going to have to deal with Connor—at least until he was transferred to another base or deployed overseas or something. She'd have to find a way to learn to live with what had happened between them. Learn to survive with her heart breaking.

Shouldn't take her more than ten or twenty years. "Piece of cake."

A florist's van pulled into the driveway off Main Street and Emma nearly groaned. Oh, God, more flowers. Last night he'd brought the "Gee, I'm sorry, please forgive me" bouquet. What was up today? she wondered. Maybe a little something from the "Too bad you're in love and I'm not" sympathy line?

"This just keeps getting more and more humiliating," she said as she hit the front door and marched across the parking lot to head off the delivery guy.

The sun was hot, the air was stifling, and even the asphalt beneath her feet felt as if it was on fire. All around her, Baywater was going about its business. Behind her in the garage bay, she heard the whir of the air compressor. Kids played, moms shopped, guys cruised in their cool cars, looking for a girl to spend some time with.

And here, in this one little corner of town, Emma prepared to take a stand. She didn't want Connor's pity bouquets. She didn't want his guilt.

All she wanted now was to speed up time so that this whole mess could be safely in her past.

"Emma Jacobsen?" The delivery driver shouted as he jumped down from the van, holding a long, white box, tied with a bright purple ribbon.

"Yes," she said, remembering that the flowers weren't *this* guy's fault. He was just doing his job. "But if those are for me, you can just take them right back."

"Huh?" He was just a kid. Couldn't have been more than eighteen. His almost-white blond hair stood up in spikes at the top of his head, and he pulled his sunglasses down to peer at her over the rim. "You don't *want* 'em?"

"No, I don't." Be strong, she told herself. Be firm. Be *positive.*

He laughed and shoved his glasses back up his nose. "He *said* you'd say that, but I didn't believe him. I never had anybody say no before."

"Happy to be your first," she snarled, really annoyed that Connor had *predicted* that she wouldn't want his latest attempt at reconciliation. Turning sharply, she headed back for the shop, but the kid's voice stopped her.

"Hey, wait a minute. He told me to tell you something if you said no."

She shouldn't care.

But damn it, she *did.*

"Fine." Emma squared her shoulders and turned back to glare at him. "What?"

"Sheesh, lady, don't shoot the messenger."

"Sorry." She inhaled sharply, then let the air slide from her lungs in an attempt to cool down. "What?"

"The guy said to say—" he screwed up his face trying to remember every word "—are you too chicken to even look?"

"Chicken?" she repeated, amazed. "He actually said *chicken*? What? Is he in fifth grade or something?" She frowned at the kid. "You're sure he said 'chicken'?"

"Yeah." The kid shrugged, still holding the long white box crooked easily in one arm. "So. Are you? Chicken, I mean? No offense."

"None taken," she said, then stomped toward him. "Fine. I'll take them." Even though she *knew* Connor was manipulating her into it. He'd known darn well that she'd respond to a dare. Her heart twisted a bit. How could he know her so well *and* so little?

"Sign here."

She did, then took the box, which was a lot heavier than she expected it to be. She shot the kid a quizzical look.

He shrugged. "You got me, lady. I just deliver 'em." Then with a wave he jumped back into the van and pulled out of the lot.

Emma carried the box back to the office and set it on top of the desk. Her fingers danced across the lid, as she decided whether or not to open it. The ribbon felt cool and slick and the gold seal beneath the ribbon read Scentsabilities, the exclusive flower and gift shop at the outskirts of town.

"Fine," she muttered, glaring at the box as if it were a personal challenge—which, she admitted, it *was*. "I'll look. That doesn't mean I'll *keep*."

She pulled the ribbon off, lifted the lid and then poked through several layers of pale-blue and green tissue paper. She stopped and stared. Her breath caught. Hot tears filled her eyes, and her lower lip trembled as she smiled and reached into the box.

A single white carnation lay atop a collection of brand-new, top-of-the-line, *socket wrenches.*

"Oh, Connor," she said, running her fingertips over the cool, stainless-steel tools. "You wonderful nut."

He'd touched her, damn it. He'd known just how to do it and he'd touched her heart again. Why? Why was he doing it? What did it mean? And how could she keep her heart from jumping to dangerous conclusions?

"What're you doing, Connor? And why're you doing it?" She dropped into her desk chair, holding the single carnation close to her heart—and tried desperately not to read too much into this.

CONNOR HAD A PLAN.

He'd spent most of the night coming up with it, and now all he had to do was wait and see if it would work.

Leaving Emma the night before had been the hardest thing he'd ever done. Forget boot camp. Forget active duty in a war zone. They were nothing.

Walking away from a woman you'd hurt was immeasurably worse. Especially when that woman meant more to you than you'd ever realized. Why is it that you never really knew how important someone was until you'd lost them?

He'd been up all night, figuring out what to do, figuring out just what he *wanted* to do.

At first, he hadn't been able to think beyond the memory of Emma's tear-stained face and heartbroken voice. He'd stalled and relived that moment over and over again before it had dawned on him what the answer was to the situation.

And once he'd faced the truth, the solution was blindingly simple.

The answer was *Emma*.

Always *Emma*.

He couldn't imagine his life without her in it.

For two years they'd laughed together and worked together and talked about anything and everything. She'd been the center of most of his days, and he'd never picked up on it. Then finally, because of that stupid bet... The nights he'd spent with her in his arms were the most perfect he'd ever experienced. He'd found magic with Emma. A magic that had slipped up on him. Magic he'd almost lost through his own stupidity.

Now all he had to do was convince Emma that he was smart enough to recognize the best thing that had ever happened to him.

BRIGHT AND EARLY the next morning, Emma stumbled into the dimly lit kitchen, looking for coffee. She pushed her hair out of her eyes and tossed a glance at the still-silent phone.

She'd expected Connor to call her last night.

Naturally, he hadn't.

"The man never does what you expect," she murmured and grabbed a blue ceramic coffee cup out of the cupboard and turned for the coffeepot. She poured herself a cupful, then headed to the back porch to drink it.

She stepped into the early-morning cool and sighed as a soft breeze caressed her bare legs. Soon enough, the summer heat would start simmering Baywater in its own juices. But now, in the minutes before dawn, the air was fresh and sweet and still-damp with dew.

Swinging her long hair back over her shoulders, she sat down on the top step and cradled her cup between her palms. The rich coffee scent stirred her mind and opened her eyes. She took a sip and felt the liquid caffeine hit her system like a blessing.

Thoughts of Connor had again kept her up most of the night, but this time there'd been fewer tears and more questions. The socket wrenches had been a balm to her bruised heart. He'd seen *her*. Paid attention to *her*.

"That's something, isn't it?" she wondered aloud.

"Talking to yourself's a bad sign."

She sucked in a breath and whipped her head around. "Connor? What're you doing here?"

"Wishing I had some of that coffee, for starters," he said, and walked through the garden gate off the driveway. He wore jeans and a dark-blue T-shirt that hugged every rippling muscle of his chest.

She watched him come closer and wished to high heaven she'd taken the time to at least brush her hair. Or get dressed. Good God, she was wearing her summer pj's—a pair of men's boxers and a dark-pink tank top with a teddy bear on the front. Curling up smaller on the step, she flashed Connor a frown. "You shouldn't be here."

"I had to be here," he said and reached out to grab her coffee cup. Taking a sip, he sighed, then smiled and handed it back. "You look beautiful."

"Oh, yeah. Right."

"I'm the one doing the looking, aren't I?"

His gaze drifted over her in a lazy perusal, and Emma felt her blood begin to boil. Her skin felt hot and tingly. Her breath was strangled in her throat, and her heart pounded like a bass drum in a Fourth of July parade.

She scooped her hair back from her face and blew out a fast breath. "Why are you here?"

"To show you something."

"More wrenches?"

He grinned and her heart sped up. "You liked 'em?"

"Yes," she said, lips twitching. "Thank you."

"You're welcome." He held out one hand toward her. "Now, come with me."

"Connor..." She lifted her gaze from his outstretched hand to his eyes. "You don't have to—"

He grabbed her hand and pulled her to her feet with such strength she flew at him, her chest slamming into his. He wrapped one arm around her waist, looked down into her eyes and said, "Just trust me, Em. This one time, will you just trust me?"

Emma would have agreed to anything while his body was pressed to hers. She felt his heartbeat thundering in time with hers, and shockwaves of sensation rocketed through her. Despite how good it felt to be close to him again though, Emma had to at least attempt to protect herself. Pulling back, she looked up at him and nodded. "Okay. Five minutes. Then I'm going inside and you're going home."

He smiled and lifted one hand, running the tips of his fingers along her jawline. "Five minutes, then."

He tightened his grip on her hand and dragged her behind him as he stalked across the yard toward the gate. A wooden lattice arch rose over the garden gate, and deep-blue morning glories spread their beauty and scent along the rungs. He drew her under the arch and through the gate, saying, "Close your eyes."

"Connor..."

"Five minutes, Em."

"Fine." She closed her eyes and stumbled barefoot behind him. The dewy grass became river stone pavers and then the already-warming asphalt of the driveway.

Emma held on to Connor's hand, and in a corner of her mind she told herself to enjoy this. The feel of his hand on hers. The joy of seeing him first thing in the morning. The sparkle in his eyes and the warmth of his smile.

Then he came to a stop and announced, "Open your eyes, Emma."

She did and immediately gasped aloud. Dropping her hold on his hand, she walked toward the banged-up, rusted, completely ruined hulk of a '58 Corvette. Its red paint had oxidized, the chrome bumpers were peeling and crumpled, the leather seats were cracked and springing out in tufts of cotton batting.

And it was the most beautiful thing she'd ever seen.

Whirling around to face him, she said, "How? How did you get Mrs. Harrison to part with Sonny's car?"

"You like it?"

"*Duh.*" She glanced over her shoulder at the car, as if to make sure it hadn't disappeared in the last moment or two. "But how? And how'd you get it here?"

He shoved his hands into his jeans pockets. "I went to see her yesterday," he said. "I convinced her that Sonny's car deserved to be everything it was *meant* to be."

"You did?"

"Yep." He smiled proudly and she couldn't blame him for it. "As to getting it here, Aidan has a friend with a tow truck. We unhooked it at the end of your street and pushed it up your driveway so we wouldn't wake you up." He rolled his eyes. "Surprised you didn't wake up, anyway, with all of Aidan's whining about it. Almost gagged him."

"I can't believe you did this," she whispered, looking from him, to the car and back again.

He shrugged and added, "I also promised Mrs. Harrison that once we'd restored the 'Vette to its former glory, that we'd come out and take her for the first ride."

"We?"

"Caught that, did you?" he smiled, and took a step toward her.

She took a deep, steadying breath. "Connor, no one's ever done anything like this for me before. I don't even know what to say."

"Good," he said quickly, stepping forward and grabbing her shoulders. "Speechless. That means I've got a shot to have my say."

"Now just a darn—"

"Too late," he said, talking over her, his drill sergeant's voice drowning her out with no problem at all. "My turn, Em." He slid his right hand from her shoulder to her neck and up, to cup her cheek. "I see *you*, Emma. The *real* you."

His thumb traced her cheekbone with long, gentle strokes, and he silently prayed that for once in his life, he'd find the right words. The words he needed to win this woman—because without her his life looked long and lonely.

"Last night, when you closed the door and sent me away," he said, shaking his head slowly, as if unable to bear the remembered pain of being shut out, "I finally *knew*."

"What?"

"I love you, Emma Jacobsen."

"Oh, Connor," she whispered, "no, you don't."

"Yeah. I do."

His voice was steely and every word stood on its own, loud and proud. Her eyes went wide and filled with tears, but she blinked them away, for which he was grateful.

"Hey, surprised me, too," he said, a strained, half laugh choking him. "I'd always thought that I didn't need love. That my life was fine, just the way it was. But the only reason it *was* fine, is because *you* were in it." He cupped her face between his palms and stared directly into her eyes. "When something good happens, *you're* the one I want to share it with. When I feel like hell and nothing's going right, I head right here—to talk to *you*."

She reached up and covered his hands with hers. "Connor, I..."

"Without you, Em, there's no laughter." He shook his head and smiled down at her. "There's no warmth. There's only emptiness. And I don't want to live like that. I want to live with *you*. I want to marry you. Have babies with you. Build a *future* with you."

"You what?" She dropped her coffee cup, and it landed with a solid crash on the asphalt, spilling hot coffee as it went.

Instantly Connor scooped her into his arms and held her cradled close to his chest. "You okay?" he asked. "Burned? Cut?"

"I'm fine," she said on a whisper, lifting one hand to stroke his face. "Unless of course, I'm dreaming, in which case I'm really going to be disappointed when I wake up."

He smiled down at her, then bent his head and stole a quick kiss. "Not dreaming. In fact, I feel like I'm just waking up."

"I do love you," she said softly.

"I love you, too, Em," Connor said, smile gone and gaze steady on hers. "I want us to be like that old car. I want us to be what we *deserve* to be. Together."

Her heart felt full enough to explode, and her eyes blurred with tears of happiness so thick she could hardly see. And yet there he was, in all his blurry glory. He'd been her friend, then her lover and now, finally and forever, he would be her husband.

Emma blinked away her tears, because she wanted this moment to be clear in her memory. "I'll marry you,

Connor. I'll have a family with you. And I promise I will love you forever."

"That's all I'll ever ask, Em," he said, and carried her beneath the arch of morning glories into the shade-dappled yard.

"That's all?" she teased.

"Well," he hedged, "that and a cup of coffee. I've been up all night, waiting for you to wake up."

"Then let's forget about the coffee," she said, reaching up to hook her arms around his neck, "and head right to bed."

Connor grinned. "You know, I think I'm gonna like being married."

Emma laughed aloud and hung on for dear life as she and her best friend started their new life together in the first sweet hush of dawn.

* * * * *

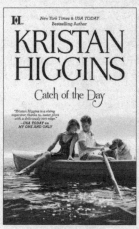

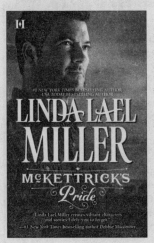

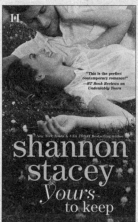

PRESENTING...

More Than Words

STORIES OF THE HEART

Three bestselling authors
Three real-life heroines

Even as you read these words, there are women just like you stepping up and making a difference in their communities, making our world a better place to live. Three such exceptional women have been selected as recipients of Harlequin's More Than Words award. To celebrate their accomplishments, three bestselling authors have written short stories inspired by these real-life heroines.

Proceeds from the sale of this book will be reinvested into the Harlequin More Than Words program to support causes that are of concern to women.

Visit

www.HarlequinMoreThanWords.com

to nominate a real-life heroine from your community.

REQUEST YOUR FREE BOOKS!

2 FREE NOVELS
FROM THE ROMANCE COLLECTION
PLUS 2 FREE GIFTS!

YES! Please send me 2 FREE novels from the Romance Collection and my 2 FREE gifts (gifts are worth about $10). After receiving them, if I don't wish to receive any more books, I can return the shipping statement marked "cancel." If I don't cancel, I will receive 4 brand-new novels every month and be billed just $5.99 per book in the U.S. or $6.49 per book in Canada. That's a saving of at least 25% off the cover price. It's quite a bargain! Shipping and handling is just 50¢ per book in the U.S. and 75¢ per book in Canada.* I understand that accepting the 2 free books and gifts places me under no obligation to buy anything. I can always return a shipment and cancel at any time. Even if I never buy another book, the two free books and gifts are mine to keep forever.

194/394 MDN FELQ

Name	(PLEASE PRINT)

Address	Apt. #

City	State/Prov.	Zip/Postal Code

Signature (if under 18, a parent or guardian must sign)

Mail to the **Reader Service:**
IN U.S.A.: P.O. Box 1867, Buffalo, NY 14240-1867
IN CANADA: P.O. Box 609, Fort Erie, Ontario L2A 5X3

Not valid for current subscribers to the Romance Collection
or the Romance/Suspense Collection.

Want to try two free books from another line?
Call 1-800-873-8635 or visit www.ReaderService.com.

* Terms and prices subject to change without notice. Prices do not include applicable taxes. Sales tax applicable in N.Y. Canadian residents will be charged applicable taxes. Offer not valid in Quebec. This offer is limited to one order per household. All orders subject to credit approval. Credit or debit balances in a customer's account(s) may be offset by any other outstanding balance owed by or to the customer. Please allow 4 to 6 weeks for delivery. Offer available while quantities last.

Your Privacy—The Reader Service is committed to protecting your privacy. Our Privacy Policy is available online at www.ReaderService.com or upon request from the Reader Service.

We make a portion of our mailing list available to reputable third parties that offer products we believe may interest you. If you prefer that we not exchange your name with third parties, or if you wish to clarify or modify your communication preferences, please visit us at www.ReaderService.com/consumerchoice or write to us at Reader Service Preference Service, P.O. Box 9062, Buffalo, NY 14269. Include your complete name and address.

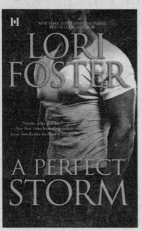